WHEN WITCHES CAN'T CAST

MATILDA LOCKWOOD

NIMBLE PIG PRESS

Copyright © 2025 by Matilda Lockwood

When Witches Can't Cast

Cover design by Angelina Sakhatska of GetCovers

Interior design and formatting by Atticus

First Edition

ISBN: 979-8-9892935-8-2

Printed in the United States of America

For more information, visit:

matildalockwoodwrites.com

CONTENTS

For the women who have been feared for their fire,
the witches who made magic from knowledge and survival,
and the quiet hearts who dared to stand beside them.
May you always find your circle, your garden, and your voice.

INTRODUCTION

This is a story about survival—and what it means to move beyond mere survival into something richer, deeper, and defiantly hopeful.

Set in 1758 England, When Witches Can't Cast follows women who have been accused, silenced, and threatened, yet who choose to root themselves in knowledge, community, and quiet acts of rebellion. There is no real magic in these pages—only the kind that's made from friendship, healing, longing, and fierce love. Still, the word "witch" lingers over every chapter, as both accusation and identity.

This book contains references to historical systems of violence against women, including false accusations, confinement, emotional abuse, and the lingering threat of religious or legal persecution. These themes are handled with care and do not appear graphically, but they are present—because they were real. And because they are still, in many ways, real.

But this is also a book about beauty. About joy. About women choosing each other, again and again, across bruised years and borrowed time. There is romance, there is firelight, there are hands brushing in libraries and gardens, and there is a place—Blythewood Hall—where women who were once cast out begin again.

I wrote this book for anyone who has ever been underestimated, misnamed, or misunderstood—and for those who dare to grow something green and wild in that place.

Welcome.

CHAPTER ONE

THE MOB AND THE MUD

*D**edham Vale, England, 1758*

The village square reeked of damp straw and stale sweat, and Gatty Carter sat in the center of it all.

The chair beneath her creaked ominously, its legs half-sunk in the churned mud, as if it too wanted to disappear. Around her, faces pressed close—a wall of sneers, furrowed brows, and whispering mouths, hungry for a spectacle. She recognized most of them: neighbors who once nodded to her in passing, now leaning in like wolves scenting blood. So many of them she'd helped—delivered elderflower when their fevers ran high, mixed horehound into syrup when the children couldn't breathe. It hadn't taken much, just a few herbs and a willingness to listen. But they didn't remember that now.

Edward Fenton stepped forward, raising a hand to quiet the crowd. "I have no joy in bringing this to you, neighbors," he began, his face set in a mask of heavy sorrow. "But my barn—my livelihood—was lost to flames just last night. And there are questions that demand answers."

A murmur rippled through the gathering, uncertainty spreading across the sea of faces like frost. It was always like this—first doubt, then fear, then fire.

Edward sighed, shaking his head slowly, like each word weighed more than the last. "Yes, I saw her," he continued, gesturing toward Gatty. "Gatty Carter. She was near my fields not an hour before the blaze. Her hands moved in strange gestures, and her lips…" He paused, letting the silence grow thick. "Her lips moved as if in prayer—but not to any God I know."

Gasps fluttered through the crowd. Gatty stiffened, pulse roaring in her ears, but forced herself to sit still. Her skin itched under their stares. They don't want truth. They want something to burn.

Behind Edward, his sister Daisy stood tight-lipped and grim. Gatty's gaze flicked to the far edge of the crowd, where Edward's eldest son lingered near the property line that edged up to her own. She knew exactly why Edward wanted her gone—he'd made her an offer for her land just last week. She'd turned him down. Politely, but firmly. Apparently, that was enough to be called a witch these days.

"I saw her too," piped William Harper, stepping forward eagerly as the crowd made room for him. His wiry frame twitched with the excitement of being noticed. "Coming back from the hedge path,

I did. Saw her waving her arms, like she was conjuring something. Thought it odd, but didn't think much—until I heard about the fire." He glanced around, his earlier grin replaced by a performative frown. "We all know what that means, don't we?"

The crowd's murmurs grew darker, rolling through the square. Gatty felt their eyes crawling over her skin—hot, greedy, itching to find something monstrous in her face.

She rose slowly, pushing herself upright despite the sinking legs of the chair. "This is madness," she said, her voice low but clear. "I was walking back from the miller's. Same as I do every week. I had a loaf of bread tucked under my arm. Ask Tom Miller's wife, she saw me go. I never went near that barn."

William let out a short bark of laughter. "Oh, but you'd say that, wouldn't you?" He leaned in, breath sour. "That's just what a devil's handmaiden would do—deny the truth."

Laughter flared—uneven, nervous. A woman in a threadbare shawl pulled her child behind her skirts. An old man spat near Gatty's feet.

Gatty's jaw locked. Her tongue felt like iron, her throat raw from holding back. They always punished her worst when she let her anger show. *Be quiet, be clever, be small.*

But she was tired and angry, and in that moment, she was done being small. "If the devil's handmaidens are real, William, then surely you'd know—you've spent enough time groveling for his favor." Her words cracked through the laughter like a whip. "You've always hated me, simply because I can read my own name. You're a pig, and you'll die rooting in your own filth."

A few in the crowd blinked, taken aback. Someone stifled a laugh. Others glanced uneasily toward William.

His face turned crimson. "Don't let her twist your thoughts!" he barked. "She's poisonous! Always has been. How dare you speak against your betters?"

"She cursed Tommy's stomach!" cried Daisy suddenly, her voice high and shrill. "He was fine 'til she glared at him. I saw it!"

Mary Tanner stepped forward, eyes wide. "My goat dropped dead the very morning she passed by the fence! Tell me that's not witchery!"

"She was at the apothecary, trading herbs for coin," someone hissed from the back. "Not ordinary ones either. The kind that don't grow this side of the forest. She deals in conjure."

A small, sick flicker of something burned in Gatty's chest—almost like laughter. Conjure? It was valerian, and hawthorn, and a bit of foxglove—not poison, not spells. *But once they name you, it doesn't matter what's in your basket.*

Edward raised his hands again, calling for silence. He turned back to the crowd, his expression carved from somber stone. "I take no joy in this," he said. "But we can't ignore the signs." He spread his hands like he was appealing to heaven. "The magistrate calls it superstition. The priest turned me away. But you—my neighbors, my kin—you know what you've seen."

Gatty's hands gripped the arms of the chair. Seen? They'd seen nothing. Not the truth. Only what Edward told them to look for. She wanted to scream it, to stand and shout them all down—but her throat tightened like a snare. *They don't want your voice. They want your silence.*

"God's teeth," she muttered, half to herself, as anger stirred behind her ribs. "If you'd just leave me be..."

But no one ever did. A woman alone was never just left to be. She was watched. Measured. Judged. Until she slipped, or spoke, or said no.

"She's no kin left to speak for her, poor dear," Mary Tanner said sharply, with no trace of pity in her voice. "Living alone on that patch of land, turning down Edward's proposal like she's better than the rest of us. No family. No husband. It's a tragedy, truly."

A tragedy, Gatty thought, *but one they'll gladly fix by tossing me in the river.*

"A tragedy's not the same as a crime," called a voice from the back.

Gatty turned toward it, heart lurching. It was Maud Hutchins—a widow with clouded eyes and trembling hands, but a spine that hadn't yet given in. She'd once traded eggs for Gatty's feverfew tincture, back when it was safe to do so. Gatty had shown her how to steep it with lemon balm to ease her cough. Not magic. Just plants. Just knowledge.

"It's no sin to refuse a marriage proposal," Maud added, louder now. "What matters is whether she set fire to that barn. Did anyone actually see her do it?"

A ripple of discomfort passed through the crowd, not conviction—giving Gatty hope.

"And what would you know of it, Maud?" snapped a man near the front—Daisy's jackanapes of a cousin, all fire in the belly and bluster, Gatty thought, though she'd never learned his name. "You taking her brews? Letting her mix you up something special in return for silence?"

The crowd pivoted, hungry for a new target. Gatty's stomach turned as Maud flinched, their stares crawling from her like parasites. Her hands tightened on her shawl until her knuckles shone white.

"I—I only ever asked for help with my cough," Maud stammered. "Not charms. Not magic." But the courage that had flared for one brief, shining moment was already draining from her voice. Fear did that. Gatty knew the taste.

Then Daisy's husband Nathaniel straightened, puffing up his chest like a rooster on a fencepost. "I saw it, too. Gatty Carter pointed at the barn, and flames shot up like a devil's matchstick." He crossed himself quickly, his fingers fumbling the gesture. "With my own eyes, I did."

Gatty's rage surged like a kicked hornet's nest. Her hands trembled with the need to strike the lies from his smug mouth. Her whole life she'd been told to hold her tongue, smooth her voice, keep her temper tucked away like a loose hem. But what good had it done?

"You liar," she spat. "You've lived three fields from me for years and never had the courage to look me in the eye before now. I turned Edward down last week, and now you all circle like dogs at the scent of blood."

"She speaks the truth," Maud said quietly, though her voice barely carried. "He's had his eye on her land since his wife died. Everyone knows it."

"She's making it up!" Edward bellowed, stepping back into the circle, his tone sharpening. "No one's talking about taking her land. This isn't about marriage. It's about danger." He turned slowly, sweeping the crowd with his gaze. "The magistrate would not hear me. The priest dismissed me. But you—you are the people who must live beside her. What if next time it's your barn? Your child?"

The words struck like sparks to dry hay. A low growl of dread passed through the crowd, growing teeth as it rolled forward. Gatty searched their faces—neighbors, former customers, people she'd once helped or fed or spoken kindly to. She searched for even a flicker of doubt. Just one. Please. Just one person to see the truth. "I beg of you to see through this madman's lies!"

"Sit her down!" William barked, puffed up with borrowed authority. Two men lunged forward, one on either side of her, making Gatty jump. She twisted, elbowing one in the ribs, but they caught her, their strong hands biting into her shoulders. One shoved her hard into the chair. She hit it awkwardly, her spine jarring, and for a moment, stars danced in her vision.

Then came the slap.

An open palm, swift and sharp. Her head snapped to the side. Pain flared, white-hot. The copper tang of blood filled her mouth. She spat into the dirt and raised her eyes, trying not to show her fear.

The man leaned close, his breath thick with beer and rot. "You're braver than you are smart," he muttered. His fingers coiled in her hair, yanking it back until her throat stretched bare. "And bravery won't count for much when you're burning."

A hush swept through the crowd as William stepped forward, brandishing a glass bottle like a trophy. The liquid inside sloshed, catching the early light.

"This'll settle it," he announced. "Holy water. From the church font itself."

Gatty narrowed her eyes. "Holy water?" she said, her voice cutting through the noise. "If it were truly holy, William, it'd already be burning holes through *your* filthy hands."

There was a pause—just a breath—then a flicker of nervous laughter, thin and hesitant. Someone gasped. A woman's hand flew to her mouth.

"She twists words," William shouted, too loud now. "Like a snake. Don't let her twist yours!"

Then from the back: "Dunk her in the river!" The cry was sharp and gleeful, and Gatty's eyes widened. "Dunk her!" someone echoed.

"Dunk her! Dunk her!" others shouted, the chant building with frightening speed. The frenzy rose like a tide, each voice feeding the next until it became one deafening roar. Gatty flinched, not from the sound, but from the knowing—it was over. No one would save her now.

William lifted his arm like a conductor drunk on his own music. "Let's see if she floats," he said, triumphant.

"No!" Gatty shouted, lurching against the chair. "Please don't—"

But her voice was swallowed whole by the chant. *They didn't want your words. They wanted your silence. Your confession.*

Hands clamped down on her shoulders again, tilting the chair back as if she weighed nothing at all. Gatty kicked and twisted, boots sliding in the mud.

"Get her down from there!" a woman's voice cried out—faint and distant, quickly drowned by the chant. Through the shifting bodies, Gatty caught a glimpse of a few women clutching children, being ushered away, heads bowed, faces pale. *Even they won't stay. Even they'll let it happen.*

The River Stour glistened beyond the green, dark and restless beneath the morning light. Its brown water coiled like rope, quickened by the spring rains, and here and there, white foam snagged on the rushes like teeth bared in a snarl. Her stomach turned to stone.

She couldn't swim. They were going to drown her. They were truly going to do it.

Survival on her mind, she thrashed, boots flailing wildly. Her heel connected with something solid—a man's nose. He howled, stumbling back. The chair wobbled dangerously in the confusion, one side momentarily unsupported. Gatty seized the moment. Twisting her body with everything she had, she flung herself sideways.

The chair toppled with a sickening crack, landing hard in the churned mud. Pain shot through her spine. Her hands splintered against the rough wood as she clawed her way free. She didn't think—thinking would stop her. Her body took over.

She rolled, gasping, skirts soaked and tangled. The world spun—shouts rising behind her—but she was already on her knees, mud to her elbows, her heart a war drum.

Gatty scrambled upright, skirts bunched in her fists, and ran.

"Get her!" Edward's voice cut through the uproar like a blade. But she was already gone.

She darted toward the trees at the edge of the square, branches like reaching fingers, shadows like cloaks. Her pulse thundered in her ears. The mob roared behind her—an unholy chorus of fury and fear, their boots churning the earth in pursuit.

Branches whipped her face. Thorns scored her arms. She barely felt it. Somewhere ahead, she heard the rush of water. The river.

She ran toward it blindly, lungs burning, mud sucking at her boots. The scent of wet bark and churned earth filled her lungs.

When she burst onto the riverbank, she skidded to a halt.

The river was swollen, churning with recent rain. It writhed like a living thing—black, merciless. The current snarled, hissing against stone and root. A bitter spray stung her cheeks.

She hesitated, chest heaving. There's nowhere to go.

"There she is!" a voice bellowed behind her. "Don't let her get away!"

Panic surged, white-hot and blinding. She ran further still away from the voice, then turned toward the water. It looked bottomless, eternal. A shadow bobbed in the current—driftwood and flotsam, she thought, until it turned, revealing what looked almost like an arm. A body. Her stomach twisted. The mob wanted her gone, and the river would oblige. No trial. No scream. Just a ripple, and then... nothing.

Her eyes scanned the shore, desperate.

There—a massive tree leaning over the bank, its roots like claws, grasping at the river's edge. A hollow gaped at its base, dark and damp and waiting.

It wasn't safety. But it was a choice.

Gatty dropped to her knees, fingers clawing at the earth as she dragged herself into the hollow. The bark scraped her arms. Cold and rot wrapped around her like a second skin. She shoved branches over herself, stuffing leaves into the gaps, forcing herself down into the dirt like a root. She gritted her teeth to silence her breath. *Still. Still. Don't move. Don't even be.*

"She's not here!" someone shouted, close now. A boot crunched above her head.

"She must've gone into the river," another voice said, loud and uncertain. "I don't see her. You?"

Gatty didn't blink. Her heartbeat thundered like hoofbeats in her ears. Her lungs burned, but she kept her mouth shut.

"Wait—what's that?" someone called sharply.

Her breath froze. Her stomach lurched.

"That's her!" another voice cried. "Down there! In the current—she's gone."

"Isn't that wood?" Edward asked skeptically.

"Wood the shape of a man, maybe," someone retorted.

Silence fell like a shroud. Even the mob seemed caught off guard by their own words.

"This has gone too far," William muttered. His voice, once bloated with pride, now cracked. "It was supposed to be sport, not... not this."

Sport. That's all she'd ever been to them. Not a neighbor. Not a healer. Not a woman. A game. A warning. A thing to throw into the fire to feel safe again.

"Sport?" Edward snapped. "You were the one waving holy water like a prize goose. What did you think would happen?"

"I thought she'd run," William said weakly. "Maybe scare her a bit, make her think twice."

Gatty lay still, their words settling on her chest like stones. Sport. That's all she'd ever been to them. Not a neighbor. Not a woman. Just a story to pass around, a scapegoat to toss in the fire when the shadows grew long. She'd given them balm for fevers, roots for coughs, lavender for grief. And now they called her a danger.

"Let's go," someone muttered. "If she's in the river, she's already dead. There's nothing to see."

"You're right," William agreed quickly. "Come on—before someone comes looking."

Their voices drifted away, muffled by distance and the roar of the river. Still, Gatty didn't move.

The cold crept deeper, turning muscle to stone, bone to ice. Her body screamed from the stillness, from the tight hollow, from the strain of holding herself small and unseen. But she stayed silent. Buried. Invisible.

She was supposed to be dead.

And for now—she would let them believe it.

Let them gather at the tavern and toast the cleansing of the valley. Let them whisper that the river had taken her. Let them pray over their breakfasts and feel safe again. She'd give them that comfort, if only to keep her name out of their mouths a little longer.

Hours passed. The stars shifted overhead, sharp and distant. The forest exhaled its mist into the cold. And at last, when the wind grew still and the world felt hollow with quiet, Gatty moved.

Her limbs screamed as she uncurled herself. With shaking arms, she pushed aside the damp branches and crawled from the hollow. Her body was stiff, her fingers raw and half-numb. Mud clung to her skin like a second, rotting hide. Her skirts were soaked and stiff, dragging at her legs with every movement. Her stomach growled low and bitter.

The square was quiet. The woods held only the hush of wind and river. No more shouts. No more boots. No more chanting.

The mob was gone.

The river surged beside her, black and wild in the moonlight—a beast that had nearly swallowed her whole. She stared at its surface, the water dancing silver around a half-submerged log, and thought: I could have vanished. I still might.

They think I'm dead.

The thought hit her like a slap. Equal parts relief and fury. It opened something inside her—a cold, hollow ache—and filled it with fire. *Let them think it. Let them whisper and clutch their crosses. I'm still here.*

And that, for now, would have to be enough.

She rose to her feet on trembling legs. The riverbank was slick and treacherous. The mud sucked at her boots like it meant to pull her down again. Every step hurt. The cold gnawed at her bones, and her breath fogged the air like smoke.

But she moved. Because if she didn't, she might never again.

Time blurred. The moon vanished behind clouds. A fox barked in the distance. Her hands throbbed, then numbed. Still, she walked.

Just before dawn, a sound broke the hush—the groan of wagon wheels and the soft clop of hooves on frozen earth.

Gatty froze. Her pulse jumped. *Someone's coming.*

She dropped low, slipping into a tangle of brambles. The earth sucked at her skirts again, but she didn't flinch. Through the thorns, she saw it: a farm cart, piled high with blocks of peat and heavy sacks of grain.

The driver was an older man she didn't know, wrapped in a thick coat with a wide-brimmed hat shadowing his face. He hummed a low, tuneless melody as the cart creaked past. It sounded so ordinary, so alive, that Gatty nearly wept at the absurdity of it.

Then he stopped. Another man emerged from the trees, and the two broke into argument.

"You told me the road was clear!" the driver barked, voice hoarse with cold. "If I'd known about the washout, I'd have taken the mill route."

"It's barely a washout," the other man grunted. "A bit of mud's nothing. You're just looking for an excuse to whinge."

"That's easy for you to say," the driver snapped. "You're not the one who'll be knee-deep in muck, dragging a cart free with a rope and prayer."

Their voices echoed faintly down the road. Neither of them noticed her. Not yet. The cart's back gaped open, its stack of peat shifting slightly beneath a wind-rustled tarp. Gatty's chance.

Her boots were silent on the soft earth. The smell of peat hit her like smoke and stone and warmth remembered. She gripped the wooden slats and hauled herself up, scraping knees and palms on rough timber. Her muscles screamed, but she didn't stop.

The blocks were cold, but not like the air. She burrowed in deep, letting them settle over her—hiding her scent, her shape, her past. She tugged the tarp down, inch by inch, sealing herself into the darkness.

The argument ended with a grunt. A stomp of boots. Then the groan of the driver climbing back into place.

The cart lurched. The horse snorted, hooves crunching frozen soil. The wheels turned.

Beneath the tarp, Gatty curled into herself. Every muscle throbbed. Her skin itched beneath layers of grime and cold. But the road moved beneath her.

She was going forward. And for now, forward was enough.

CHAPTER TWO

THE STRANGER'S PRICE

The cart jolted hard enough to rattle Gatty's teeth, wrenching her from a fitful sleep. She blinked into the gloom, every bone in her body aching, her limbs stiff and bruised from the night's escape. The scent of peat clung to her like smoke—earthy, bitter, and dense. She'd burrowed deep into the load for warmth, but it hadn't lasted. The cold had found its way in, settling in her joints, her spine, her heart.

Outside, the wheels groaned over frozen ground, the cart swaying with the uneven rhythm of the rutted road. Gatty kept her breathing shallow, listening through the steady clop of hooves. The driver muttered in clipped, irritated tones—curses strung together with the ease of habit. She caught fragments: cracked wheels, tight-chested mornings, his blasted luck.

Then came the coughing.

It tore out of him sharp and ragged—like barked orders turned inward. The cart slowed. The man fumbled with the reins, the horse snorting in protest.

Gatty's body went still, her muscles coiling. If she was going to run, this was the moment.

She shifted, inching toward the edge of the cart. Her fingers brushed the rough timber, splinters biting into her palms. The coughing masked the creak of her movement, but her heart pounded loud and erratic, like it might betray her out loud.

Another curse. Another heave of breath. The man coughed so violently, it sounded as though his lungs might tear loose.

Gatty gritted her teeth and swung her legs over the side. The cart dipped slightly as she dropped to the ground, knees bending hard to absorb the shock. Cold shot through her boots. She didn't stop. She darted into the roadside brush, crouching low beneath the bare branches, breath shallow, heart clawing at her ribs.

No shout followed.

The coughing faded, and the cart creaked forward, its load lighter now. The driver carried on. Only when the cart vanished over a distant rise did Gatty allow herself to fully exhale.

The road stretched ahead, barren and bone-pale, bordered by frost-bitten grass and skeletal trees clawing at a pewter sky. It was all foreign. Exposed. Wide in ways the village never had been—no hedges to hide behind, no tight corners to duck into. Just sky and mud and silence.

She wiped at her cheek, smearing away peat—and winced as the bruise flared under her fingers. It was nothing, really. Just a slap. But it throbbed like a warning bell. The deeper bruise sat lower, in the place where safety used to live.

"They think you're dead," she whispered aloud. The words felt strange in her mouth. Too final, but true.

And for now, truth was all she had. It was armor of a kind, brittle but better than nothing. If they believed her gone, they'd stop looking. They'd tell stories about her floating face-down in the current, and pray over their breakfasts, and get on with their lives. And she would keep moving forward.

A part of her wanted to curl up in the ditch, to fold inward and let the cold take her. Her name was gone. Her neighbors, her home. Her place in the world had been cut loose, severed like a thread from the loom. But she didn't curl. She set her eyes on the road. *One foot in front of the other. Forward.* Somewhere ahead, someone might take her in—or at least not ask too many questions.

The walking hurt. Every step jarred through sore legs and cold feet. Mud clung to her hems like dead hands. Her shawl caught the wind like a flag. The silence of the countryside wrapped around her, and though it wasn't friendly, it wasn't angry either. Not yet.

In time, the trees thinned. Through the branches, Gatty glimpsed rooftops—slate-gray and low, clustered tight in a shallow valley. Smoke curled from narrow chimneys. No bells, but signs of labor: the distant ring of a hammer, the bark of a dog.

A village.

Relief stirred in her belly—but it didn't warm her. She had no illusions left.

Gatty slowed near the tree line, breath puffing in faint clouds. The village wasn't large. A handful of cottages, a squat stone church, a muddy green. The buildings leaned into each other like old gossips, huddled against the wind.

It looked alive. But not kind.

She felt it already—that tightness in the air. The weight of eyes that hadn't even found her yet. The way strangers were always seen, but never truly welcomed. A place like this would spot her as out-of-place in a heartbeat. Still, she couldn't stay hidden forever. Her stomach ached. Her hands had gone numb again. And her lie—her careful, practiced lie—was ready.

Gatty pulled her shawl tighter, lifted her chin, and stepped onto the road.

The village was stirring, but not welcoming. Smoke curled from crooked chimneys, footsteps left shallow prints in the frost, and windows blinked open like wary eyes. The place had a rhythm—but she didn't belong to it. These were people who knew each other's habits, who traded bread and gossip in the same breath.

Straightening her spine, she stepped out of the brush and started down the path. Her boots sank into the thawing mud with every step, thick and sucking, as though the road itself resented her passage. A man unloading grain from a cart paused to squint at her. A woman carrying firewood clutched her bundle tighter and gave her a wide berth.

It wasn't the first time Gatty had been looked at like that, and it wouldn't be the last.

She paused beside a moss-streaked cottage where linens flapped weakly on a sagging line. A woman stood in the yard, sleeves pushed up, hands pinning cloth with the ease of habit. She looked up as Gatty approached—her gaze sharp and unreadable, her body still as a post.

"Morning to you," Gatty offered, keeping her voice even, respectful.

The woman's eyes flicked over her—the road-worn hem, the too-bright eyes of a girl trying to look older, the weight she carried like a second cloak. "Aye," the woman replied at last. Her tone wasn't unfriendly, but it wasn't warm, and she didn't offer her name. "What's your business?"

"I'm looking for work," Gatty said. She lowered her head just enough to suggest humility, but not desperation. "Cooking, cleaning—anything honest."

The woman didn't respond right away. Her fingers stilled at the edge of the cloth, and her gaze rested on Gatty. "You're not from here."

"No," Gatty replied. Her voice stayed quiet, firm. "From the north. Lost my family some time back. Been walking ever since."

"That so? What's brought you this far south?"

"Widow's life doesn't leave much to hold you still," Gatty answered. She'd practiced the words, but the grief in her voice wasn't a lie—it only came from a different wound. "Too many ghosts in one place can rot a person. I needed... a different road."

The woman watched her for a beat longer, then finally turned back to her washing. "Work's scarce, same as everywhere. But the tavern might take you on. The keeper's always cursing about needing help. Don't expect much more than a crust and a place to stand."

Gatty dipped her head. "Thank you. I'm grateful."

The woman gave her a small, tight smile, but she didn't turn away until Gatty had moved on.

The tavern crouched at the center of the village—broad and sagging, its sign swinging tiredly on rusted hinges. A rooster scratched at the frozen mud near the door, indifferent to the wind. Gatty hesitated, then reached for the door handle and stepped inside.

Heat hit her first—then the stink. Stale ale, damp wool, smoke, and too many unwashed bodies crowded into one low room. The fire snapped in the hearth, barely keeping up with the cold seeping through the walls.

A few men sat at rough-hewn tables, their eyes flicking to her with idle interest just as the older woman's had, then drifting away. She kept her gaze low, careful, and approached the bar.

Behind it stood the tavern keeper—a thick-necked man with a face like a thumbprint in dough, his thinning hair plastered back with effort but little effect. He looked up at her approach, his scowl already waiting. "Help you?" he said. His voice scraped like bark peeled from a tree.

"I'm looking for work," Gatty said, forcing calm into her voice even as her shoulders tightened. "I can clean, cook, or serve. Whatever you've need of."

He snorted, folding his arms across a broad chest. "You're not from here."

She had braced for it, but the words still felt like a slap. *You're not from here.* She imagined they'd follow her like a shadow. "No, sir," she replied. "I've come down from the north. Looking for honest labor. My hands are quick and willing."

He didn't answer right away. His eyes dragged over her—boots caked in mud, skirt patched at the seams, the tired way she held herself upright like it might be her last bit of pride. "The north, eh?" he said at last. "That's a long walk for a scrub bucket."

Gatty managed a thin smile. "Farther than I meant to go. But life doesn't always follow the path we draw, does it?"

He grunted. "Work's hard. Pay's worse. Folk here don't trust strangers."

"I'm not asking for trust," she said quickly. "Just a chance."

The tavern keeper studied her a moment longer, then jabbed a thick finger against the bar. "Ashes need clearing. Floor needs scrubbing. Do it quick, and maybe we'll talk again."

Relief sparked low in her chest. She nodded and ducked behind the bar, grabbing a bucket and a stiff brush. *No pay. No promises.* But she was inside—and for now, that was something.

The fire hissed as she knelt by the hearth, soot rising like smoke signals from another world. Gatty worked silently, letting the scratch of the brush anchor her. Her hands blackened quickly, the bristles biting into her raw fingers. Cold still stiffened her joints, and the ache in her arms deepened with every movement.

The scrape of the brush echoed too loudly in her skull. But she kept moving. She knew what it meant to be watched. She'd learned what came after.

Boots clomped across the threshold as the day crawled on—farmers, laborers, men with wind-chapped cheeks and thirsts bigger than their coin purses. Gatty didn't look up. She stayed low, her gaze on the floor, her hands steady even as her knees burned. No one said her name. No one called her witch. The silence was almost kind. Almost.

By the time she rinsed the bucket behind the tavern, her arms shook with weariness. Inside, the air had thickened with smoke and heat and voices. Ale sloshed in tankards. Laughter rolled off the rafters. The firelight burned brighter now, but not warmer.

When she stepped back in, she felt it before she saw it.

A gaze—slow, heavy, lingering longer than it should. Not cruel. Not yet. But curious. And that was worse.

She moved to pass unnoticed, hugging the edge of the room. But a knot of men blocked her way—clustered around a long, battered table, tankards in hand, their voices sticky with drink.

One of them was wiry, sharp-nosed, with a glint behind his eyes, like he thought pain made things more interesting. "Well, now," he purred. "What's this? A new bird in the nest?"

Gatty didn't answer. She kept her eyes on the hearth and angled her body to step around him.

The man grinned wider and elbowed the farmer beside him—broad, stooped, worn down by work. "Don't see her kind here often, do we?"

The farmer didn't meet her gaze. "Leave her be, Jory," he muttered, but it was the kind of protest born from routine, not conviction.

"Just being friendly," Jory said. His smile sharpened as he stood, his tankard sloshing carelessly. "Oi, miss. What's your name, then?"

Her pulse quickened. Her spine stiffened. But her voice stayed calm. "Name's none of your concern."

Jory laughed, the sound loud and eager, laced with something brittle. He turned back to the table with the swagger of a man who'd never been told no by someone he thought beneath him. "Did you hear that?" he called. "Sharp tongue on this one. I like that."

Gatty edged toward the bar, keeping her steps even. She put a table between them, but he followed unsteadily, ale on his breath, hunger in his eyes. Not lust, exactly—just the twisted curiosity of someone who wanted to see what happened when you poked a thing too many times. A man who liked reactions.

She was cornered before she'd realized it. And she was done pretending she didn't feel it.

"Come on now. No need to be shy," Jory coaxed. "You're not from here, are you? Bet you've got stories worth hearing."

"I've got work to do," Gatty snapped. Her voice was steel wrapped in smoke. "And you've had enough to drink."

The table barked with laughter—too loud, too sharp. Jory's grin faltered, pride bruised behind ale-flushed cheeks.

"Careful, girl," he said, voice lowering. "You don't want to start something you can't finish."

"Funny," Gatty said, lifting her chin. "I was about to say the same to you."

That did it.

The laughter died like a candle snuffed. Chairs stilled. The whole room leaned toward her, waiting. She could feel the tavern keeper's eyes boring into her back. But she didn't flinch. She was tired of shrinking.

Jory lunged, fingers aiming for her arm, but she moved first. The nearest tankard was in her hand before she thought about it—sour ale sloshed across his face with a hiss. He sputtered, blinking foam from his eyes, his mouth curling in disbelief.

For a second, the tavern went still.

Then it erupted.

Jory swung wide, but Gatty ducked, her instincts kicking in like a door forced open. Chairs scraped, men shouted, tankards flew like missiles. She backed toward the wall, every nerve alight.

"Enough!" the tavern keeper roared, but his voice drowned in the thud of fists and the crack of furniture.

A table went down. The fire spat embers like sparks from a forge, shadows dancing madly across the walls.

Gatty grabbed a stool, hefting it like a shield as Jory came at her again. She swung hard. Wood met ribs. He fell back with a groan, but someone else laughed—sharp, wild.

"Serves you right, you sod!" someone jeered.

The moment flickered—almost light—but then another man lunged. He grabbed her arm with rough fingers that bruised. Gatty twisted, slammed her heel down on his foot. He howled and let go. But more hands were coming.

The fight had spun loose, spilled far beyond her. Voices blurred. Tankards shattered. Someone crashed into the wall behind her. Gatty ducked and wove, breath burning in her chest, eyes darting for an exit.

But there was no forest this time. No dark path to vanish down. Just the walls closing in.

Then—the door slammed open. Cold air sliced through the smoke, and with it came the constable, flanked by two armed men.

"That's enough!" he barked. His voice cracked like thunder. "Break it up! Now!"

The room froze. Jory, dripping and furious, jabbed a finger toward her. "Her! She started it!"

"That's a lie!" Gatty shouted. Her voice was hoarse, her body trembling. "He grabbed me!"

The constable didn't blink. He gave a sharp nod. Two men surged forward, seized her arms, and hauled her from the floor.

"Let go of me!" she protested, but they didn't even glance at her. Their grip was like iron, and suddenly it was as if she was back in Dedham Vale, in front of the same mob who called her a witch.

The constable's men dragged her out the door, and the villagers streamed after them like crows scenting a feast. Murmurs turned into jeers. Their faces—some eager, others merely curious—blurred into a familiar wall of contempt.

And then—there they were. The stocks.

Worn wood gleamed dark with frost. Gatty stiffened, resisting the pull toward it, but they shoved her forward. The wood yawned open, the cold biting before it even touched her. Wrists. Neck. The world tilted. Locked.

She didn't cry out. Not when the clamp fell. Not when the jeers rose. Not even when a clump of frozen mud struck the ground beside her boot.

Her breath came sharp. Angry. Not fear now. *Fury.*

They thought they could humiliate her into silence. They thought they could break her just because she had nowhere else to go.

Let them think it. They'd see soon enough.

They would not break her.

Chapter Three

RELEASE AND RECKONING

The rough wood of the stocks pressed against Gatty's wrists and neck. It had been hours. Her fingers had gone numb from cold and pressure, but it wasn't the weather that left her trembling—it was rage. Humiliation pulsed in her veins like fever. This wasn't punishment. This was performance. A lesson. A spectacle.

The square had mostly cleared. Only a few onlookers lingered near the church steps, still casting furtive glances her way as if half hoping she might bare her teeth or sprout horns. Gatty kept her head low, jaw clenched tight, refusing to give them the satisfaction.

Then came the voice.

"Yes, yes, that's her." The words cut through the air like a knife through linen. "Constable, unbind this woman."

Heads turned. The black-cloaked figure who strode forward moved as if the very ground made way for her—tall, composed, her face obscured by a large fur-lined hood. Her cloak billowed behind her, as though summoned by some theatrical gust.

"Who are you to interfere?" a man flanking Gatty demanded.

The woman stopped a few feet from him and drew back her hood. Her face was twenty years older than Gatty's and striking—sharp cheekbones, dark curls, a mouth set somewhere between disdain and pity. "Lydia Eversley," she said in a crisp, smart tone. "I speak on behalf of the Hartford family of Blythewood Hall. And who is your captive, may I ask?"

Gatty blinked against the sunlight, her eyes adjusting to the silhouette now standing before her. *Lydia Eversley.* The name meant nothing to her—but the effect *Blythewood* clearly had on the villagers around her was immediate. A ripple of murmurs spread like a draft beneath a closed door.

"None knows her name." The constable puffed up. "But this woman was involved in a tavern brawl. The stocks are lenient. I've half a mind to—"

"She was provoked, says the tavern staff," Lydia said smoothly, her voice like the edge of polished steel. "I've just spoken with them. And it is not lost on me that none of the men involved found themselves displayed for public ridicule. Curious, that."

He flushed. "Be that as it may, this is not your—"

Another voice emerged, quieter but somehow more final. "Is it your decision to defy the Hartfords, then?"

A man stepped forward from behind Lydia, tall and still as shadow. He was perhaps ten years younger than his companion, and wore a travel-worn coat, a leather folio tucked under one arm, and an expression of measured silence. His hair was dark, tied neatly back, and his green eyes held the unnerving calm of someone used to being obeyed.

The constable faltered. "James Hartford," someone whispered. "When did he return?"

The name cut through the air. The crowd stilled.

James said nothing more. He didn't need to. His eyes flicked briefly to Lydia, a subtle nod exchanged between them—a wordless rhythm honed over long acquaintance. Not affection exactly, but familiarity, and something steadier beneath it: trust.

Lydia stepped closer to Gatty in the stock, her gaze narrowing as she studied her.

"You there," she said quietly. "Before we go to the trouble—just answer me three questions."

Gatty's brows furrowed. "Why?"

"Because I'm choosing who to trouble myself over," Lydia said, almost pleasantly. "And I prefer not to waste my time."

She knelt slightly, bringing herself level with Gatty's gaze. "First: If you saw a fire in a locked room and the only way in was through the window, would you break it?"

Gatty gave her an incredulous look, then decided she may as well humor the woman. "Is someone inside?"

Lydia's lips quirked faintly. "Yes."

"Then yes," Gatty said. "Break it."

"Second," Lydia said, tilting her head, "do you believe a knife is dangerous because it's sharp, or because it's wielded?"

"Because it's wielded," Gatty answered without hesitation. "The sharpness is just waiting."

James glanced at Lydia again, the corner of his mouth twitching slightly—an expression that might've meant approval or amusement. She didn't look at him, but something in her posture eased, as though she'd heard the unspoken.

"And last," Lydia said, lowering her voice so that only Gatty could hear, "what is stronger: fear of the truth, or fear of being believed?"

The question landed like a stone in a still pond. Gatty stared at her.

"...Being believed," she said quietly. "Fear of that will kill you quicker."

Lydia held her gaze for a long moment. Then she nodded once, as if closing a ledger.

"She'll do."

Only then did Lydia turn back to the constable. "Release her."

The constable hesitated, then sighed. "Who am I to defy James Hartford? The wench is your problem now." He fumbled with his keys and opened the stocks with a harsh click.

Gatty stumbled forward, arms aching as circulation returned. Her knees nearly buckled, but she forced herself upright. She eyed Lydia and James warily.

"Who are you?" she rasped, voice raw.

"The ones offering you a way out," Lydia said. "Food. Warmth. A roof. And no more stocks. You've no reason to trust us. But I'd wager you've even fewer reasons to stay."

James gestured toward the waiting carriage beyond the square. He didn't speak, but his gaze met hers briefly—steady and unreadable, with the weight of someone who'd seen enough to recognize someone standing on a precipice.

Gatty turned slowly, eyes sweeping the faces still watching her—half eager, half afraid, all judging. A woman who'd screamed for her punishment yesterday now clutched her child, averting her gaze.

She swallowed the burn in her throat. Then nodded once. "All right," she whispered. "I'll go."

Lydia smiled faintly, as if Gatty's answer had been inevitable. She turned on her heel, her cloak sweeping behind her like smoke, and walked toward the carriage. James fell into step beside her, saying nothing—but when Lydia's gloved hand brushed the folds of her skirt and nearly grazed his coat, he shifted just slightly, his stride slowing to match hers with unconscious precision. They moved like clockwork gears—not affectionate, but attuned.

Gatty cast one last look over her shoulder. No one met her eye. The square that had burned with accusation now ignored her as though she'd never existed. Jaw tight, she forced her legs forward, stumbling only once as she followed Lydia and James away from the stocks.

The carriage rocked gently as it rolled down the uneven road, its wheels groaning against packed earth and frostbitten ruts. Inside, the air was heavy with the faint smell of damp velvet and travel. Gatty pressed her back into the corner of the seat, wishing she could melt into the upholstery.

Lydia sat opposite her, spine straight and gloved hands folded neatly in her lap. Her gaze, sharp and unblinking, made Gatty feel like a specimen pinned for study. James sat beside Lydia, more relaxed in posture but no less alert. He watched the window, fingers tapping lightly on the side of his knee—a steady rhythm, thoughtful rather than impatient.

Gatty's hands, still stained with soot, rested in her lap. Her wrists ached from the stocks, and each jolt of the carriage sent aches through her limbs. But it wasn't the pain that unsettled her most—it was the silence, thick and expectant.

Lydia broke it at last. "You're quiet, Miss Carter."

Gatty's gaze flicked up, wary. "I'm tired."

Lydia tilted her head. "Silence is a tool," she said, as if offering a lesson. "Those who survive often know how to wield it."

James didn't look at Lydia, but the corner of his mouth lifted faintly. Lydia noticed and arched a brow. Nothing was said—but the flicker of shared amusement passed between them like smoke over kindling.

Gatty didn't respond. She wasn't sure if that was praise or warning.

"You seem the type who watches," Lydia went on, her voice light but not unkind. "What did you see, back in the tavern?"

Gatty hesitated, unsure whether this was small talk or a test. "Men who wanted to forget the cold and their worries. Some used laughter to do it. Others used anger."

"And Jory—the man I hear began the skirmish?"

Gatty's voice was dry. "He wanted to feel like a man others feared. It made him bold. Stupid."

Lydia gave a small, satisfied nod. "You're a woman who sees things clearly."

Gatty bristled. "I wager most do, but I'm one of the fools rare enough so speak it. My silence, as with many, is borne of necessity."

James turned his head slightly, his voice the first ripple of calm in the room. "And what do you need now?"

The question hung between them.

Gatty answered without flinching. "A place where no one knows my name."

James gave the barest hint of a nod and looked back to the window, his profile catching the last of the weak afternoon light.

The carriage jolted suddenly, and Gatty gripped the seat's edge to steady herself. Lydia leaned forward.

"Tell me something else, Miss Carter," she said, her voice softer now, yet still unnervingly precise. "Do you dream?"

Gatty blinked. "What?"

"Dreams," Lydia said. "Do you have them?"

Gatty frowned, unsure where this was going. "Sometimes."

"Do they speak to you? Not in words, necessarily. But in feelings. In warnings."

Gatty opened her mouth to scoff, then closed it again. The question wasn't entirely unfamiliar. "Sometimes I wake up and feel like something's changed. Or like I've just been somewhere I shouldn't have left."

Lydia smiled, and for a fleeting moment, her expression softened—not warm, but curious. Interested.

"And do those dreams ever return?"

Gatty hesitated. "Yes."

James stirred again, his tone low but without skepticism. "What kind of dreams?"

Gatty shifted. "There was one," she admitted, despite her reticence. She'd play this game and see where it led. "Where I was standing in a field, but the grass was silver. And every time I took a step forward, something behind me caught fire. But I couldn't turn around. I wasn't allowed."

Lydia sat back slowly, her gaze never leaving Gatty's face. Her expression was thoughtful—but not surprised.

Gatty shifted uncomfortably. "It's just a dream."

Lydia's voice was barely above a whisper. "Some dreams are maps."

Silence returned. Gatty glanced between the two of them, unsettled—and for the first time, unsure who was guiding whom.

Finally, James spoke again, his voice low and grounding. "Have you ever heard of Blythewood Hall?"

Gatty shook her head.

"It's an old place," he said. "Older than it looks. Built on older things still."

"Haunted?" Gatty asked, trying to keep her tone dry.

Lydia smiled again, though this time it didn't reach her eyes. "It depends on what you mean by haunted."

The carriage creaked as it turned, and Gatty felt the change in the air before she saw it: the landscape opening, the trees thinning, the faint scent of woodsmoke carried on a cold wind.

Lydia didn't speak again, but her gaze lingered on Gatty a moment longer before she leaned back. Across from her, James adjusted the cuff of his coat—his knuckles brushed Lydia's glove, and she moved her hand just slightly, not flinching, not pulling away. The moment was gone before Gatty could be sure it had even happened. *Are they...together?* She truly couldn't tell.

"What kind of stories?" she asked warily.

James shrugged, but it was Lydia who answered. "Ghost stories, mostly. Whispers of lost souls and restless spirits. The sort of tales that keep children awake at night."

Gatty hesitated. "Do *you* believe in ghosts?"

Lydia's smile was slow and unreadable. "I believe the world is full of things we don't understand. Some call them ghosts. Others call them shadows. Depends on who you ask."

The words left Gatty more unsettled than reassured. She turned her attention to the window just as the trees gave way to long, frostbitten fields bathed in twilight. The carriage slowed, wheels crunching over gravel, and a cold draft slipped in through the seams.

Then she saw it.

Blythewood Hall came into view like a fortress exhaled from the earth—immense and still, its red-brick walls touched by ivy and dusk. Towers loomed at either end, rooftops piercing the pale evening sky. The windows, tall and many-paned, reflected the last slant of light like watchful eyes, as if the house watched the world in quiet judgement.

A stone archway led into a wide courtyard flanked by weather-worn statues—knights or guardians, their visages eroded until they were nearly faceless. Time had smoothed their features, as though the house itself was slowly erasing its keepers.

"Impressive, isn't it?" Lydia said lightly, as though she'd long since stopped noticing the awe it inspired.

Gatty nodded slowly, her voice caught somewhere behind her ribs. The Hall didn't feel like a home, but like a monument. It felt almost... aware of her. "This belongs to your family?" she finally managed, her gaze tracing the stretch of stone and shadow.

James' smile was thin, unreadable. "By law, yes. The Hartfords have held it for generations. But between you and me..." His voice softened, almost conspiratorial. "No one ever truly owns Blythewood. Names are carved into deeds, but the house keeps its own counsel. We are only its stewards, for a time."

Gatty caught Lydia giving him a look of such beautification that she was now certain there was something between them, whether the man realized it or not.

The carriage rolled to a halt. A stable boy appeared from the mist to take the reins, his eyes respectfully lowered. James stepped out first and offered Lydia his hand. She accepted it with practiced grace, pausing only a breath before releasing it. Then she turned and waited for Gatty, holding out her own.

Gatty hesitated, then placed her palm in Lydia outstretched hand. Her grip was firm but not forceful, steadying her as her boots hit the gravel. The air smelled different here—wet stone, hearth smoke, and something older. Something buried.

She looked up at the Hall, scanning its many windows. And then she saw it.

A figure. Pale and still, framed in one of the upper panes. It didn't move. It didn't blink. But it watched.

"Do you see that?" she asked, her voice low.

Lydia followed her gaze, squinting. "The windows here like to play tricks. This time of day, the light bends in peculiar ways."

"It's not the light," Gatty murmured. The figure hadn't flickered. It hadn't shifted. It had simply... been.

James stepped beside her. He followed her line of sight, frowning faintly, though he said nothing.

Lydia's tone turned brisk. "It's nothing. The Hall holds old reflections, that's all. Come. The cold will freeze you solid if we linger."

But Gatty stepped forward again, boots crunching softly. The figure remained, unmoving.

"It's only a shadow," Lydia said more gently this time, placing a gloved hand on Gatty's arm. "Blythewood has many shadows. You'll learn which ones matter."

Reluctantly, Gatty let herself be guided up to the massive house. When the oak doors creaked open, lamplight and the scent of beeswax and kindling into the evening air. Lydia and James stepped forward first, their figures swallowed by the heavy archway.

Gatty's heart beat hard against her ribs. She drew a breath, tasting damp earth and woodsmoke. Whatever lay inside, there would be no turning back. She gathered her courage, squared her shoulders, and crossed the threshold.

The doors shut behind her with a quiet, inevitable thud.

Chapter Four

HOUSE OF SHADOWS

The heavy oak doors of Blythewood Hall groaned open, their hinges protesting like old bones. Inside, the air was colder than the wind outside—ancient and still, steeped in the damp hush of stone and polish and forgotten prayers. Sputtering candles clung to life in wrought-iron sconces, casting long, warped shadows that crawled across the flagstone floor.

Gatty stepped into the hall and felt it at once: not welcome, not sanctuary, but judgment. The kind of quiet that measured a person from the inside out.

Lydia entered ahead of her, each footfall crisp against the stone. Her black cloak dragged behind her. James followed with a soldier's step—no cloak, no fanfare, only the steady presence of someone who saw everything and spoke little. Gatty hovered near the threshold, every muscle taut with hesitation.

She should run. But the road behind her was cold and empty, and the door had already closed.

"This way," Lydia said, without turning.

Gatty obeyed. Her boots scraped softly across the floor as they moved deeper into the hall. Carved wood panels lined the walls—biblical scenes rendered in painstaking relief. Open palms. Lowered eyes. Women kneeling before men or angels, faces carved in expressions of sorrow and surrender. Above the hearth, a tapestry dominated the wall: Mary Magdalene at Christ's feet, her red robe spilling across the woven ground like blood. A sinner sanctified, but punished first.

They began to climb the staircase, its balustrade polished to a sheen. "This house has stood for nearly four hundred years," Lydia said smoothly. "Once it was a place of grandeur—banquets, hunting parties, invitations written in gold leaf. But those days faded, as all foolishness does." She glanced over her shoulder, the edge of a smile barely visible. "Now, a significant portion of Blythewood serves a higher calling."

Gatty's voice came out hoarse, her throat still raw from the stocks. "And what calling is that?"

"To redeem women who have lost their way," Lydia answered without pause. "We offer structure, purpose, and a chance at reformation through scripture and work."

She paused at the landing and turned to face Gatty, her eyes catching the candlelight. They were not cruel, exactly—but they were precise.

"Are you familiar with piety, Miss Carter?"

"Well..." Gatty's brow furrowed. "I know how to kneel in a pew."

Lydia's mouth twitched—somewhere between amusement and caution. "Then you'll learn the rest. Piety isn't a posture. It's the surrender of pride. Of chaos. It is obedience in the face of discomfort."

The words settled like dust.

Behind them, James remained quiet, but his gaze flicked briefly to Lydia at the word obedience. A subtle look passed between them—nothing showy, nothing indulgent—but Gatty caught it. He said nothing, but his presence filled the space between Lydia's words.

Before Gatty could respond, a high-pitched laugh pierced the corridor.

A blur of motion—small feet, brown curls, and a rag doll clutched tight. A small girl barreled into view, skidding to a halt at Lydia's skirts.

"Mama!"

Lydia crouched smoothly, catching a falling bonnet from the doll before it hit the floor. "Ivy. What have I said about running indoors?"

"But it's boring upstairs," Ivy pouted. "And James said you were back."

Lydia gently brushed a leaf from her daughter's curls and adjusted the fraying hem of her dress. "Miss Carter will be staying with us for a while," she said, casting a glance toward Gatty. "You'll treat her kindly."

Ivy turned her wide eyes on Gatty. "Are you a maid?"

Gatty blinked. "Not exactly."

"Well," Ivy said, appraising her plainly, "Begging your pardon, but you look like one. My mama will replace everything you're wearing if you let her." She dipped into a solemn little curtsy, then dashed back down the corridor, her laughter echoing against the stone.

Gatty stared after her. "She's spirited."

"She's five," Lydia replied, rising with grace. "The world hasn't bruised her yet. And she's not wrong about the clothes."

Staring down at her clothes, Gatty admitted, "It's been ages since I had something without holes. I'd appreciate warmer ones." She gave a hesitant smile.

Lydia nodded primly. "Then we'll fix that. Perhaps I should be grateful for my daughter's silliness, if she spotted something so quickly that could yield such a grin."

"She's as silly as her mother is serious." James stepped forward then, quiet until now.

Lydia glanced at him sideways. "I wish she had not picked up your disregard for silence."

His lips tilted—just barely. "You call it disregard. I call it clarity."

That flicker passed again between them: two people who knew each other's sharpest edges and had chosen not to dull them.

Gatty looked between them and said nothing. But a new question stirred at the back of her mind—one more pressing than tapestries or obedience or nettle tea.

What kind of house *was* this? And why did it feel, despite her reticence, like it had been waiting for her?

She watched Lydia glance again at James, and though he said nothing, the brief nod he gave her was almost imperceptible—habitual, practiced, the sort of silent conversation forged through trust rather than instruction.

Lydia turned back to Gatty with the cool curiosity of someone examining the sharp edge of a blade. "Miss Carter," she said, "may I ask you something unusual?"

Gatty shrugged, wary. "You've brought me to a strange house. I'd be more surprised if you didn't."

That earned the faintest ghost of a smile from Lydia. "Have you ever lowered a fever without a physician?"

The question filled her with pride, and began the wheels of her mind turning. "I have," Gatty said slowly. "Willow bark tea. And cloths soaked in vinegar and rose water. A midwife showed me. It works."

Lydia gave a small nod, as if confirming something she already suspected. "And when does nettle grow sharpest?"

"Early spring," Gatty said, her answer swift, unthinking. "When the frost is lifting but the ground's still angry."

There was a flicker of amusement in James's eyes. He said nothing, but Gatty caught the almost-smile he aimed—quietly—at Lydia.

"Young nettles are also the most nutritious." Lydia stepped closer. "Have you ever made fire without flint?"

Gatty hesitated, bracing for a trap. "Once," she admitted. "Caught it in a metal bowl, when the sun hit just right. Smoke came before flame. I nearly dropped it."

Her voice tensed when Lydia and James exchanged a look. "It's not sorcery. It's sunlight and a bit of luck."

"No," Lydia said, not unkindly. "It's skill."

The quiet that followed was thick, but not unfriendly. It hummed with decision.

"Excellent. You passed." Lydia suddenly turned without warning, her cloak flaring as she moved down the corridor. "This way."

James lingered behind her, his gaze following Lydia as Gatty followed her. *Passed what?* She didn't know why, but she was afraid to ask the question out loud.

They turned down a dim passage and entered a small chamber tucked between the chapel and the scullery. It was modest, spare—walls bare but for a cross above the hearth and a shelf buckling under the weight of Bibles, prayer books, and a few worm-riddled tomes without titles. The long oak table was scratched and scorched, a single candle burning low in its holder. The air smelled faintly of nettle and old ash.

"This is where you'll be instructed," Lydia said, her voice assuming the clipped rhythm of something well-practiced. "You'll read scripture daily, reflect in silence, and write your thoughts. You'll work in rotation—laundry, kitchens, cleaning, care of the ill. Here, labor is not punishment. It is remedy."

Gatty raised a brow, trying to hide her irritation and wondering how long she'd have to do this. "And if I'm already worn to the bone?"

Lydia didn't blink. "Then you'll learn how far the body can stretch after the spirit has snapped."

She opened her mouth to retort, then visions of accusatory mobs in both her old village and the new swam before her. Perhaps she would keep her head down until she could plan her next steps with a clear head. Wearily, she nodded her assent.

From the doorway, James leaned against the frame, arms folded. "Most adjust," he said. "The ones who don't usually leave before the second frost."

Gatty's eyes darted between them, trying to discern what they weren't saying. Lydia's gaze held hers a moment longer, searching, weighing. Then she turned to the doorway and snapped her fingers once.

A woman stepped out from the shadows. Hawk-nosed and severe, her gray apron starched within an inch of its life. Her expression was harder than stone, but not cruel—just watchful.

"This is Mrs. Havering," Lydia said. "She'll see to your... transition."

Mrs. Havering gave a single, stiff nod. "Come on, then. No use standing like a wet sheet."

Gatty left Lydia and James, and followed the woman down a series of narrowing corridors where the air grew colder, the stones rougher underfoot. They reached a squat washroom lined in cracked tile, a battered copper tub steaming faintly at the center. The scent of lavender mingled with something sharper—rosemary, perhaps, or lye. A coarse shift and a plain gown waited on a low stool.

"Don't dawdle," Mrs. Havering said. "Water cools quick. No second boil."

Gatty didn't argue. She stripped with her back to the wall, her fingers stiff from cold. When she stepped into the water, it seared her skin—a reminder of how numb she'd gone.

Mrs. Havering didn't leave. "You used to work?" the older woman asked, arms crossed. Her tone was not exactly curious, but it wasn't dismissive either. "You seem like the type who's too sharp for her own good."

"I worked," Gatty said, settling deeper into the warmth. "Scrubbed floors, plucked geese, helped a midwife now and then. Enough to stay fed."

"Good," Mrs. Havering said. "That'll keep you alive longer than cleverness will."

As Gatty reached for the soap, her fingers snagged something sharp beneath the surface. She jerked back, eyes narrowing, and pulled out a long straight pin. It gleamed in the steam-slick candlelight. She held it up. "Should I be worried this is part of the cleansing?"

Mrs. Havering's gaze flicked to the pin. Her face didn't change, not really. But her reply was a fraction too fast. "Must've come off a cuff. The linens aren't always sorted proper."

Gatty washed quickly, efficiently. When she stepped from the bath, flushed and raw, she dried off with the rough towel and slipped into the shift. Mrs. Havering waited with arms crossed, patient as a gargoyle. When she didn't ask for it back, Gatty tucked the pin into the side seam of her new gown.

Once Gatty was dressed, without a word, Mrs. Havering turned and led her down a corridor where cracked wainscoting bore the faded scent of beeswax, and the rushes underfoot gave off a sharp tang of vinegar and drying herbs. The torchlight licked the walls, casting soft-edged shadows that trembled as they walked.

This house had offered her food. Shelter. A way out. And yet, Gatty knew better than to believe anything came without a price. She took a deep breath as she prepared to see more of her new temporary home.

The dormitory opened before them, long and dim. Rows of narrow cots lined the walls, simple pallets stuffed with straw but neatly made, their linen covers freshly laundered and smelling faintly of lavender water. A few women lay already in the beds, faces turned toward the ceiling, hands folded atop their blankets as though in prayer or uneasy sleep.

"This is where you'll sleep," Mrs. Havering said, her voice low but not unkind. "No noise. No questions. Morning prayers ring at dawn."

Gatty paused in the doorway, her gaze sweeping the long chamber. Beneath the spare, washed surfaces, she caught traces of an older life in the house—carved beams high above, fine joinery, a wide hearth at the far end, though it held no fire tonight. Cold air curled through the space, but it was dry, and the stone beneath her bare feet had been scrubbed clean.

Gratefully, she crossed to an empty cot near the wall. As she lowered herself, the straw crinkled beneath the shift, rough but mercifully free of damp. Beneath her palm, the hidden pin pressed cool and familiar against her skin. She closed her fingers around it.

Her gaze lifted to the ceiling, where the old plaster bore the faint traces of a painted border, long faded but still there—like ghosts of ivy twining across the beams. Her heart steadied.

It wasn't home. Not yet. But it was shelter. It was warmth, and it was life.

What kind of place have I stepped into? she wondered. But tonight, she would let herself rest.

———

Morning came early, announced not by sunlight but by bells—thin and distant, echoing down the halls like a summons. Gatty's joints protested as she rose, stiff and aching, her breath visible in the cold. The others stirred like clockwork. No words passed between them as they slipped into plain gowns and cloaks and filed out, silent as ghosts.

The chapel was narrow and dim, its walls damp with age and sanctimony. Candlelight flickered along the stones, casting long shadows. A scent hung thick in the air—familiar, bitter. Not just beeswax and smoke, but something older. Herbal. Medicinal.

Gatty's breath caught. *Feverweed.*

The sharp, clinging smell of it drifted from a smoldering coil on the altar—burned now not to cure illness, but to sanctify silence. Her grandmother had boiled it into bitter brews when the fever came. Here, perhaps it was used to still the mind.

The women knelt on thin cushions in rows, heads bowed in practiced surrender. Gatty hesitated before sinking to her knees, wincing as they met the cold stone beneath the mat.

At the front of the chapel stood Lydia, robed in somber gray, her voice steady and low as she read from a weathered Bible marked with velvet ribbons.

"Blessed are the meek, for they shall inherit the earth.
Blessed are those who hunger and thirst for righteousness, for they shall be satisfied."

The incense curled around her, gilding her outline in soft gold. To Gatty, she looked like a saint carved into the side of an ancient cathedral—watchful, distant, unknowable.

Her eyes, however, were very much alive. And they found Gatty. "Piety begins with humility," Lydia said, closing the book. "You are not here to defend who you were. You are here to become someone better. Someone useful. Someone worthy." Her voice lingered in the hush that followed—not a blessing so much as a decree.

After prayers, the women were separated and assigned to their labors. Gatty was sent to the kitchens.

It was a cavernous, low-ceilinged chamber that pulsed with heat and urgency. The great hearth roared at one end, casting flickering orange light across soot-blackened beams and bringing a warm glow to her face. Copper pots bubbled above the flames. Steam and smoke rose in clouds. The air smelled of onions, turnips, and yeast—comforting scents, ruined by the edge of vinegar she could tell they used for cleaning.

Mrs. Havering reigned at the center, ladle in hand like a general preparing for battle. "Mind the bread, Sarah! Don't bruise the dough," she snapped. "And you, Miss Carter—scrub those potatoes like you're polishing your conscience. If I find a speck of earth, you'll eat it with your supper."

Gatty muttered under her breath and rolled up her sleeves. The water in the bucket was ice, each plunge of her hands stinging like nettles. She worked in silence, eyes flicking now and then to the others.

Most of the women moved with the same eerie rhythm—efficient, silent, unyielding.

But one stood out. Gatty watched out of the corner of her eye, as a woman with a hollow look to her stole a palmful of breadcrumbs from the chopping board and tucked them into her apron.

Mrs. Havering's voice cracked like a whip through the steam and clatter. "Ellen!"

The woman froze. Her hands stiffened mid-motion, a breadcrumb clinging to her fingers like evidence.

"Do you think God rewards thieves?" the matron demanded, stomping toward her with the weight of ceremony.

"I'm sorry," Ellen stammered. "I—I didn't mean—"

"No excuses." Mrs. Havering's eyes narrowed. But instead of striking her or dragging her from the room, she simply thrust the ladle toward the hearth. "One hour tending the fire tonight. No supper until the others have finished."

A hush fell. It was punishment, but not the kind that bled. Gatty straightened, her hands stinging from scrubbing. "And does God reward punishment, then?" she asked. Her voice wasn't loud, but it carried. "Why starve those you've saved?"

The silence that followed was brittle.

Ellen looked stricken. Others glanced down or away.

But Mrs. Havering only tilted her head, one brow rising. "God rewards discipline, Miss Carter. And as you'll learn, discipline comes in many forms."

She turned back to the hearth without waiting for agreement, leaving the room to crackle with unspoken questions.

The rest of the morning passed in wary silence, but Gatty noticed something shift.

Lydia appeared more than once in the doorway, her gaze skimming the kitchen like she was counting grains of salt. She exchanged a few murmured words with Mrs. Havering, who responded with a grunt and a sideways glance in Gatty's direction.

When Gatty was moved to kneading bread, Mrs. Havering hovered—closer than necessary, closer than comfortable. Gatty worked steadily, pressing her fists into the dough, folding and turning. The rhythm soothed her nerves—until something sharp bit into her palm.

She flinched and drew back. A sewing needle gleamed up from the dough, wicked and bright.

Mrs. Havering stepped forward and plucked it out, as casually as if she'd found a pebble.

"Careless of me," she said, not sounding sorry in the least. "Does your hand smart, Miss Carter?"

Gatty met her eyes, her own narrowed. "Not as much as my temper," she said. "Is this how you test bread—or patience?"

A pause. "Both, perhaps." She walked away.

"I'm keeping this one, too," Gatty called after her.

Later, during the midday meal, Lydia summoned Gatty to the front of the dining hall.

"A small welcome," she said, handing her a flint and gesturing to the long row of unlit candles. "Would you do the honors?"

Gatty hesitated, aware of the eyes watching. She struck the flint once, twice—nothing. The wick was damp. Murmurs rippled along the benches. She gritted her teeth and tried again, muttering under her breath.

Strike.
Strike.
Strike. Spark.

The flame caught, and Lydia clapped softly. "Well done, Miss Carter. Persistence suits you." It was said lightly, even kindly—but something else lingered in her tone. Not surprise. Not pride. Recognition.

Gatty sat down with her heart ticking faster. That had been another test. She just didn't know of what.

By late afternoon, the pace eased. The women were given heavy black cloaks, each fastened with a different bone clasp, and sent out to the courtyard, where frost still clung to the cobblestones and pale light cut long shadows through the branches overhead.

Gatty found herself on a bench, beside Ellen.

The woman wordlessly passed her a crust of bread. "I'm not a thief, I'll have you know," she said. "I save things out of habit. Hungry?"

"Always." Gatty took it. "You've been here long?"

"Not long enough to forget what hunger feels like." She gave a crooked smile. "Norwich baker's wife caught me pocketing a biscuit. Said I was trouble. This place is cheaper than the gallows, so... here I am."

A heavier-set woman joined them, her face red from the wind, her hands rough with work. She didn't sit—just stood with her back to the wall and her eyes on the windows.

"Don't get comfortable," she murmured. "They're always watching. Always testing. Don't let 'em see too much."

"Testing what?" Gatty asked.

The woman—Alice, someone had called her—didn't answer. Her gaze stayed fixed on the upper windows of the Hall, where nothing moved but the glass.

By nightfall, Gatty's arms ached, her cheeks were chapped, and her hair smelled of flour and ash. But the weight in her chest had lightened. Slightly.

The rules were harsh. The work was harder. And something about Blythewood Hall pulsed with secrets too large to name.

But no one had called her witch. No one had dragged her by the hair. She'd slept in a bed, eaten bread, stood upright. That counted for something.

She returned to the dormitory with the others. The same even rows of mattresses. The same breathless hush. She lay down, and the straw prickled.

They're wacky, all right, she thought, watching the cracked ceiling fade into dark. *But I'll bide my time. Let them 'test' all they like. I'll be gone before they learn anything worth knowing.*

A floorboard creaked just beyond the dormitory door.

She closed her eyes and pulled the blanket up to her chin. The shadows of Blythewood Hall curled close around her—curious, waiting, and watching.

CHAPTER FIVE

A TRIAL OF TEMPERS

The next morning dawned gray and cold, the light barely more than a watery smudge against the frost-rimed windows of the dormitory. Gatty sat on the edge of her straw mattress, pulling on the coarse stockings provided by the house. Her fingers moved stiffly, but her mind was sharp—turning over Lydia's lingering gaze from the day before, the quiet way she seemed to hover in doorways like a judge behind a veil. Watching. Waiting. Not for answers, but for confirmation of something she already suspected.

The chapel bell rang—low and mournful, more like a warning than a summons. Gatty exhaled sharply, her breath fogging in the frigid air, and rose to join the others.

The day's assignment sent her to the scullery, where the scent of damp wood, wet linen, and boiled lye clung to the stone walls like sweat. A pile of soiled cloth lay beside a steaming cauldron. The task was simple—soak, scrub, rinse, wring—but the chill of the floor gnawed through her thin shoes, and the soap stung the raw skin of her knuckles. Still, her movements were steady, measured. Her mind, like always, kept working.

She had barely wrung out a second cloth when she felt the air shift. Lydia stood in the doorway.

Even here, among the clatter of pots and the hiss of steam, her presence landed with the hush of a sermon. She said nothing at first, only watched Gatty for a beat longer than was polite. Not scrutinizing—assessing. Measuring something beyond posture or effort. Gatty didn't look away.

"Miss Carter," Lydia said at last, her voice cutting through the noise like a slip of paper turned blade. "I need a word."

Gatty glanced at the pile of linens, then at the matron who supervised them, who gave a tight nod of assent. She rinsed her hands and dried them on her apron before following Lydia down a narrow corridor and into the kitchens.

The hearth fire here burned hot and steady. It smelled of roasting onion, of fresh bread rising. The sudden warmth hit her face like a slap and a comfort all at once. Lydia poured a small cup of cider from the steaming pot and handed it to her before seating herself at the long, worn wooden table.

Gatty took the cup without comment, but her eyes never left Lydia's face.

"Your adjustment here has been... noted," Lydia said, her tone unreadable.

Gatty curled her fingers around the tin cup. "Noted how?"

"With interest," Lydia replied. "You're not like most who come through our doors. Your silences aren't passive. They're calculated. You observe before you act." She tilted her head slightly. "That is not despair, Miss Carter. That is discernment."

Gatty bristled at the compliment—if it was one. "If I'm so discerning, why the scullery?"

"Because humility tempers sharpness," Lydia said smoothly. "And humility is the foundation of redemption. Or have you already forgotten why you're here?"

Gatty didn't trust herself to answer without talking back. She took a sip of cider instead. It was laced with cloves and apple peel and warmth—sweetened just enough to taste like comfort, though she knew better than to be comforted.

Lydia watched her carefully. Her tone softened, but her eyes did not. "Tell me, Miss Carter. Do you believe in the power of objects?"

Gatty glanced up, suspicious. "Objects?"

"A ring. A token. A charm," Lydia said, folding her hands together on the table. "Do you believe they can carry meaning beyond their shape?"

"That depends on who's holding it," Gatty said after a pause. "Some people can find strength in an old button if it belonged to the right person."

Lydia's mouth curved—somewhere between a smile and a smirk. "A wise answer."

This house has secrets, Gatty thought later that night, staring up at the blackened ceiling. *And I think they want me to find them.*

The morning came sharp and colorless, the air inside the dormitory brittle with frost. Gatty stirred beneath her blanket, her limbs aching from tension and cold. The shadows of the night clung to her thoughts like a film she couldn't rub away.

Mrs. Havering's voice rang out like a trumpet. "Up and at it, girls! The Lord has no time for the lazy!"

Gatty dressed quickly, the rough wool scratching at her skin as she pulled the gown over her head. As she tied her apron, she caught a glimpse of Ellen scurrying past with a bundle of damp linens. Their eyes met briefly—Ellen's wide and wary—and then she was gone, swallowed by the dim hallway.

In the large workroom, Lydia's voice sliced through the morning hush, as sharp and certain as always. The women sat on narrow stools or stood beside worn benches, heads bowed in silent obedience. Gatty took a place near the back, hands folded—not out of deference, but calculation.

"Today's tasks are simple but vital," Lydia began, pacing like a magistrate rather than a matron. "There will be no complaints, no laziness, and no foolishness. You have been granted mercy here. It is not a gift to squander, but a responsibility to bear."

Her tone wasn't cruel—but it wasn't warm either. It rang with the kind of authority that didn't expect to be questioned.

The silence held. Then Lydia's gaze swept the room—and landed on Gatty. "Miss Carter," she said, her voice smoothing like silk pulled taut. "You'll be working in the still room today."

A few women glanced up. A ripple of curiosity passed through the ranks, and Gatty straightened. "What sort of work?"

"Sorting herbs," Lydia replied. "A task that requires discernment. Patience. Precision." Her eyes narrowed slightly. "You strike me as someone who might benefit from such focus."

Gatty didn't rise to the bait. "You seem determined to test me."

"It would be foolish not to." Lydia turned and strode toward the kitchens. Gatty followed her through the maze of stone and wood, each corridor colder than the last. Finally, Lydia stopped before a heavy oak door tucked near the hearth and opened it with a key from her belt.

The still room was smaller than Gatty had expected—low-ceilinged and windowless, with shelves that lined the walls like altar rails. Jars of dried herbs stood in careful rows, labeled in precise hand. Bundles dangled from the rafters like witches' charms. The scent of rosemary and mint hung thick in the air, but beneath it lay something sharper—tansy, or feverfew, or something else that bit the back of the throat.

A fire snapped low in the grate, half-hidden behind an old alembic, tarnished and quiet.

"These," Lydia said, placing a bundle on the worn table, "need to be separated. Rue, tansy, feverfew. You must keep them distinct. Even a careless pinch can turn a tonic to poison."

Gatty raised an eyebrow. "Then why let someone like me touch it?"

"Because we all begin ignorant," Lydia replied, her expression unreadable. "But not all choose to stay that way."

She turned to go—but stopped.

At the threshold stood Lydia's daughter Ivy.

Her curls glowed in the firelight, haloed like a child from an icon painting. She took a step into the room, eyes wide.

"What are you doing?" she asked.

"Sorting herbs," Gatty said, gentling her voice. "Nothing too thrilling."

Ivy frowned. "Mama says herbs can carry memories. That they can fix things even doctors can't."

Gatty blinked. "Does she?"

"She says they listen. If you know how to ask."

Lydia's face tightened. "Ivy. This is not the place for stories."

"But Mama—"

"I said enough." Lydia's voice stayed low but cut cleanly through the room. Ivy shrank back, biting her lip. Her fingers twisted around the ribbon at her waist as she cast one last look at Gatty—then turned and darted away.

Lydia stood very still. "She has an active imagination," she said at last, her tone clipped. "Children repeat things they don't understand. Don't let her distract you."

Gatty didn't respond. But her hands had slowed on the bundle of herbs, her fingers ghosting across the stems with new wariness.

She'd sorted plenty of herbs before. Her mother had taught her—quietly, matter-of-factly. Dandelion for bloating. Meadowsweet for pain. Mugwort for dreams. But this—this was something else.

The still room didn't feel like a place of chores. It felt like a place of waiting. And she wasn't sure who—or what—it was waiting for.

She was nearly finished when the door creaked open again.

This time, it was Alice. The older woman ducked inside, her arms dusted with flour and her brow already damp from the kitchens. Her scowl was customary, but her voice, when she spoke, held a note of unexpected gentleness.

"Still breathing in all that vinegar and weed stink, are you?" she muttered. "Lydia keeps you close."

"I've noticed," Gatty said, watching her warily.

Alice smirked. "Means she's trying to figure out what you are. Best be careful what you let her learn." She stepped forward and pressed a small, tightly bound bundle of papers into Gatty's hands—sealed with a wax stamp half-cracked down the middle. "Take these to the library upstairs, will you? Second door on the right past the long hall. And mind the floors—they creak like guilty men." She turned away before the request could meet with protest.

Gatty looked down at the bundle. The paper was worn at the corners, the string tied just tight enough to feel purposeful. She opened her mouth to ask what they were—or why her—but Alice was already halfway out the door, muttering something about "old ghosts and nosy men" as she vanished.

The still room fell silent again, but the scent of tansy seemed to sharpen in her nose. Gatty hesitated a beat, then tucked the papers close and stepped into the hall. The farther she walked from the warmth of the still room, the colder the corridors became. Drafts slipped across the flagstones like breath. Light slanted in narrow strips through the tall windows, catching the dust in midair like suspended as h.

This part of the house felt older—less a hallway than a spine. The walls pressed inward, full of memory and hush. She could almost believe the house itself was watching.

Gatty found the door Alice had described, its wood worn smooth at the edges, the latch cool beneath her fingers. After a quick breath, she knocked.

No answer.

She knocked again, louder. The door groaned open on its own—just a few inches—but enough to let her glimpse the shadowed space beyond.

The library.

Gatty stepped inside, the door easing closed behind her with a soft, decisive click.

The room was vast and vaulted, lined floor to ceiling with shelves. Ladders rested against the walls like slumbering sentinels. Stacks of books and parchment hunched in corners, lit by narrow shafts of dusty light. The air was warm, but dry—thick with parchment and old ink and something earthy beneath it, like sage long since burned.

At the far end of the room, a single candle glowed on a battered desk. Behind it sat a man, hunched over a folio, scribbling with furious intensity.

"Excuse me?" Gatty said.

The quill stopped mid-stroke. The man looked up—and rose, scrutinizing her with knitted brows.

He was lean and pale, with dark hair pulled back at the nape and a smudge of ink along his thumb. His sleeves were rolled to his forearms, and his waistcoat was half-buttoned, as if he'd either forgotten to finish dressing or hadn't bothered. He moved like someone who rarely stood but thought often. His eyes—dark, unreadable, intelligent—landed on her and held.

"You're not Alice," he said flatly. "What do you want?"

There was no impatience in his tone—just curiosity, thinly veiled. And something else. A flicker of something that lit when he really looked at her, as if he were weighing her, filing her under a category he hadn't quite named.

"She sent me with this." Gatty lifted the bundle of papers. "These message is unknown, but urgency was implied."

"That is because these are late." He stepped forward, took them from her hands, and flipped through the pages with practiced efficiency. His brow twitched. "For the third time."

Was that why Alice had passed off this errand? "The world's full of delays," Gatty said, sharper than she intended. "I'm sure you'll survive this one."

That made him pause. His eyes lifted. Narrowed. Then—so brief she almost missed it—his mouth ticked up, a corner twitch of amusement. Or approval.

"Fair enough." He turned and dropped the bundle on the desk, his long fingers lingering just a moment too long on the string before untying it.

Gatty didn't move to leave. Neither did he.

He cast a glance over his shoulder. "You're new."

"Just arrived."

He nodded once, already distracted again by the papers.

She tilted her head. "What is this place to you? The library, I mean. Are you a historian? A writer?"

The man's eyes sharpened. "I am a keeper of dangerous knowledge," he replied with no little amount of pride. "A collector of forbidden histories. I know the spells they swore were lost, the names they scratched from the records, the truths they fear will be remembered." He let the weight of his words settle, her curiosity snaring tighter. And then, with a rueful smile and a hint of self-mockery, he added, "I'm the librarian."

She grinned, and as their gaze held, her heart leapt foolishly at the question in his dark eyes. Then he looked down again and because writing, as if she'd never interrupted.

Gatty turned to go, part stung, part intrigued. At the door, she glanced back. "What's your name?"

He didn't look up. "Leander."

"Gatty." The name escaped before she could stop it. "Agatha. But I'm called Gatty."

Now he looked at her. His expression didn't soften, exactly—but it shifted. "I know."

Gatty walked the long corridor back to the still room with her thoughts sparking like flint. Shed only just met him, but even in their brief exchange, Leander Hawthorne didn't feel like the other men shed known back in Dedham Vale. He didn't smile at her bosom while he spoke, nor ask the kinds of questions that felt like traps. He didn't test her the way others had.

There had been something in the way he said her name. Quiet, certain. Like he'd known it longer than she'd told him. Like it meant something to him already.

Gatty stepped back into the still room, set the finished bundle of herbs aside, and crouched before the hearth to stir the coals. Ash curled into the air, gray and fine. The scent had shifted—lavender, sage, and something darker beneath.

She worked in silence, fingers steady now, the motion grounding. Yet every so often, her eyes flicked toward the door. Half expecting a summons. Half dreading what it might mean.

But no one came. And the silence held—dense as smoke, soft as a secret not yet spoken.

CHAPTER SIX

THE LADY OF THE HOUSE

*H*elena Hartford was coming.

The words were on everyone's lips. The low thrum of wheels over gravel warned them before the carriage even breached the fog.

Gatty stood at the edge of the great hall, her hands clasped, pulse steady but shallow, while Mrs. Havering hustled the women into two stiff rows like pew-bound penitents. The air was thick with waiting, the scent of stone, soot, and beeswax suddenly more intrusive than usual—like even the house was trying to make itself cleaner.

"She's not one for lateness or sloppiness," Havering muttered, yanking the shoulder of a girl's gown into place. "Eyes down. No twitching. And for God's sake, don't fidget."

The great hall's height seemed to rise with the tension, its vaulted beams and leaded windows stretching into shadow. Afternoon light filtered through stained glass in gray-gold slivers, making the ancestral portraits on the walls appear watchful, their gazes fixed just above the women's heads. Gatty had the strange sensation that even the dead were lining up to see what Helena would do.

Then the doors opened. A rush of cold air swept into the room, and with it—Helena Hartford.

She entered like a gust trimmed in velvet. Her plum-colored gown, woven with threads of gold, caught the light like embers banked beneath ash. A sable cloak peeled from her shoulders and fell into the waiting arms of a silent footman. Behind her, a maid carried a velvet hatbox with the reverence of someone guarding a relic—or a weapon.

Helena didn't stop. Her swift, sharp gaze sliced across the assembled women. When her eyes passed over Gatty, it felt like standing too near a lightning strike: she wasn't burned, but something in her bones remembered the charge.

"Well," Helena said, her voice cool. "The fires are lit. That's something. Though the draft is still as persistent as sin." She glanced at the windows, then fixed her gaze on Lydia.

Lydia, usually a portrait of composure, dipped her head with what looked very much like nervousness. "Lady Hartford. Welcome home."

Helena's mouth twitched. "We'll see." Her attention flicked back to the women. No one dared move.

It was the sort of silence that came before a judgment—or a reckoning. Gatty kept her breathing shallow, spine straight.

James entered then, his boots striking a softer note than usual. "Aunt Helena," he said, with measured courtesy. "Welcome home!"

"My dearest nephew." Helena embraced him with both arms, giving him a clap on the back before stepping away.

"I trust your journey from Marble Hill was—"

"I've endured rutted roads, sleet, and a bishop with breath like a dying ox. Compared to that, the drive was nearly divine." She turned her gaze back to the line of women. "I've heard much of our new arrival," she said, voice velvet-wrapped steel. "Miss Carter, is it?"

Gatty's mouth went dry. She wasn't expected the grand woman to take any notice of her. Still, she stepped forward, careful, balanced, the way one might approach the edge of a cliff. "Yes, ma'am."

Helena tilted her head, as if studying the angle of a rare, dangerous bloom. "Three days," she murmured, "and I feel your presence here. You may be surprised at how perceptive I can be of auras only just introduced to me. After all, I knew Lydia was someone special even before we met. My nephew James as well."

The way she said their names—soft, knowing—made Gatty feel as if she'd wandered into a game she hadn't agreed to play. She said nothing. A respectful nod would be safer than a defense.

Helena's eyes didn't leave hers. "Interesting," she said quietly, almost to herself. Then louder: "Prepare tea in the drawing room. Miss Carter will join me. I'd like a proper introduction."

Lydia bowed her head. "Of course, Lady Hartford."

Without another word, Helena swept toward the grand staircase, her footman and maid trailing behind like shadows. The doors groaned closed behind her, and the moment snapped—the room collectively exhaled.

"Miss Carter," Mrs. Havering barked, breaking the fragile hush, "don't stand there gawping. Clean yourself up. You've been summoned by the lady of the house, and you'll not make us look foolish."

The drawing room was another world entirely.

Warmth filled the space, thick and deliberate, pooling across the wine-colored carpet like spilled velvet. The hearth crackled beneath a marble mantel carved with cherubs and flames, and the windows—tall, arched, and spotless—overlooked hedges so precisely trimmed they seemed unnatural. A garden of illusions. A dream with sharp teeth.

The air smelled of spiced tea. But beneath it, faint and iron-sweet, was something older. Something watchful.

Gatty stepped inside slowly. Her boots sank into the rug, muffling her presence, but the hush in the room was absolute. Everything gleamed—gold thread, burnished wood, polished silver. Nothing here had been left untouched by Helena Hartford's hand. This wasn't a sitting room.

It was a throne room.

Helena sat as if born to command it. Draped in plum silk and lit by firelight, she looked sculpted rather than seated—every line of her posture honed, every ring on her fingers catching the light just so. Lydia stood behind her like a lieutenant at attention, composed and unreadable. A maid poured tea in silence.

"Sit, Miss Carter," Helena said, gesturing with a flick of her hand.

Gatty obeyed, folding herself into the chair across from her. It was too soft. Too deep. It made her feel swallowed whole. Helena's eyes never left her.

"You've been here how long, exactly?" she asked, voice pleasant as linen—but pressed so tight it might cut.

"Three days, ma'am."

Helena smiled faintly. "And in three days, you've managed something most of our women never manage at all."

Gatty blinked. "Ma'am?"

"You've piqued Lydia's interest," Helena said smoothly. "And James's. That's no small feat. They're both far more guarded than they pretend to be."

Gatty resisted the urge to shift in her chair. "I've only done what was asked of me."

"Yes. And yet…" Helena leaned slightly forward, her voice softening. "You carry yourself like someone who's still listening to another voice—one that hasn't yet been trained out of you." She paused, letting the words settle. "That intrigues me."

Gatty held her gaze. "Doesn't it worry you?"

Helena's smile grew. "No. Not yet." There was something bright in her eyes now—not amusement anymore.

"I've never been able to silence it. I've never been one to hold back, which has gotten me into more trouble than I'd like." Gatty sipped her tea. It was excellent, and for a moment she concentrated on only the warmth of it on her tongue. When she spoke again, her tongue felt looser "A stubborn will, my ma used to call it. But you can call it listening if you like."

"I see something in and around you." Helena reached for the teapot and poured a second cup, this one for Gatty, her movements fluid and precise. "Let's see if that listening extends beyond instinct. I wonder…" Her voice trailed as she placed the cup before Gatty. "Do you believe in symbols, Miss Carter? In signs?"

"I don't know," Gatty said carefully. "Maybe. Sometimes."

"That's an honest answer," Helena said. She poured her own cup. The tea was fragrant—bergamot and something darker, something green and wild beneath the floral notes.

Gatty caught the whisper of heather... and foxglove. She put her fingers to the delicate handle, then hesitated. This tea was the most expensive she'd ever seen, let alone drank, and she wanted to savor it.

"There's plenty." Helena nodded in appreciation. "Drink. But leave a little at the bottom. Then we'll see what the leaves wish to show us."

Gatty lifted the cup. The porcelain was delicate, warm. She drank slowly, the taste complex—sweetness at the edge of bitter, like something that had tried to flower in the dark. She set us down carefully.

Helena picked up the cup without hesitation. She turned it slowly in her hands, eyes scanning the interior like a scholar with a sacred text. Lydia leaned slightly forward behind her—not too much, but just enough to mark her interest. Gatty had almost forgotten she was there, so commanding was Helena's presence.

The air thickened.

"A bird," Helena murmured. "Restless. Wings half-open. That could be flight... or escape." She turned the cup again. "And here—crossed lines. Intersections. You'll meet more than one fate, Miss Carter. You'll disrupt more than one."

Gatty didn't flinch, but her palms grew damp. "Do these always come true?"

"And here…" Helena's voice lowered. "A key." She set the cup down.

Lydia's expression didn't change, but Gatty saw her jaw tighten. "What could a key mean?"

"A key is rarely simple," Helena said softly. "It may open something hidden. Or close it forever. But a key doesn't appear by accident. It means access."

"Access to what?" Gatty asked, before she could stop herself. She didn't mean to play along so readily with the game, but she was almost morbidly fascinated to see how far it could go.

Helena leaned back, eyes glittering. "That remains to be seen." There was a beat of silence. "Still," she added, more to herself than anyone else, "it's been a long time since I've seen a key in the first reading. And never in a girl who hasn't yet found the lock."

"Well…" Gatty's heart kicked against her ribs. She wasn't sure whether Helena was speaking in riddles or reading her thoughts aloud. "I'd let you know if I do, but I'm not sure I'll know myself."

Helena smoothed her hands over her lap, but her eyes still gleamed. "Curious," she murmured again, more to herself this time—like a woman who had just glimpsed a rare bloom pushing through snow.

She looked up, voice dropping into something softer. "A key can mean many things. Access. Revelation. Or control. Some use it to open doors. Others to guard what's inside."

Gatty swallowed, her voice quieter than she meant it to be. "And which am I meant to do?"

Helena set the cup down with a delicate clink. Her rings shimmered as she folded her hands. "That, Miss Carter, depends on whether the lock belongs to you—or someone else." The answer struck like a match. It was too vague to challenge, too sharp to ignore.

Gatty was still lost.

"Agatha," Lydia's voice cut in, even but edged. "Lady Hartford's time here is limited. I suggest you take her advice to heart."

Gatty turned slightly, catching the flicker in Lydia's gaze—wariness, maybe. Or something more fragile. Anticipation. As though even Lydia didn't quite know what Helena had seen... or was willing into being.

"Do you believe in signs, Miss Carter?" Helena asked, abruptly, the question clean and sudden as a bell.

Gatty blinked. "Signs?"

Helena leaned back just a hair, regal and still. "Little things. Coincidences. Patterns that repeat. A stranger's words. The shape of spilled ink. A whisper of wind at the exact wrong moment. Do you believe the world ever tries to tell us something?"

Gatty hesitated. "I don't know. I've never thought I was the kind of person it spoke to."

Helena's smile returned. "Belief is a powerful thing. It shapes not only how we see the world—but how the world sees us. And what it chooses to reveal. How long have you bargained with yourself to stay here, before you depart on the wings of chance?"

Gatty's throat tightened. "I don't know," she said. "How long would you have me stay, if it was your choice? How long do these other women stay?"

Helena's eyes were bright. "Two years. If you choose to stay. At the end of that time, we will see what kind of woman you've become, and we can discuss your chosen next steps, whether outside this house or in another capacity within."

The fire cracked softly in the hearth. The words settled like ash Choose. Not must. Not will. Choose. Despite the supreme oddity of the entire situation, Gatty was suddenly sorely tempted to take her up on it.

Behind her, Lydia shifted slightly. The candlelight caught a flicker in her expression—concern, or curiosity. Or both. Gatty's fingers curled around the arm of her chair. "Two years is a long time."

Helena nodded once. "To some. To others, it's only a beginning. Lydia has been here since Ivy was born."

"And at the end?" Gatty asked. "What happens then?"

Helena didn't blink. "Some women leave. Some stay. A rare few prove themselves... indispensable."

The word hung in the air like a thread waiting to be pulled. Gatty tilted her head. "And what exactly is *your* work here, Lady Hartford?"

Helena's smile was light but deliberate. "We offer mercy. A difficult thing to find in a world that punishes women for surviving." She let that sit a moment before adding, with more weight, "But mercy, Miss Carter, comes with its own trials. And not everyone sees the value in what they've been given until they're asked to earn it."

Gatty didn't respond right away. The words mercy and earn twisted in her mind like vines around each other—beautiful, maybe, but still choking. She thought of the road behind her. The mob. The cold. The ache of always looking over her shoulder. Here, at least, there was food. Warmth. A bed. The illusion of safety. "I'll stay," she said at last. The words dropped like stones. "For now."

Helena's eyes lit faintly. "A wise choice. Though I suspect, in time, it won't feel like a choice at all."

Gatty glanced at Lydia. Her face remained a mask, but her hands betrayed her—folded tightly now, the knuckles gone pale.

As Gatty rose, Helena spoke once more—softer, almost gently. "Miss Carter."

She paused at the edge of the carpet. "Yes, ma'am?"

Helena studied her like a portrait she'd only begun to sketch. "You are not the first woman to come here with ghosts on her back. But let me offer this—ghosts only haunt what refuses to grow. Don't spend your days feeding the past when you were meant to bloom."

Gatty held her gaze. Firelight danced in Helena's eyes, making her look ancient. Or new.

"I'll keep that in mind," she said. Then she turned and stepped out into the hall, where the air was colder—but not quite so still.

The hallway stretched before her like a throat. A single candle guttered in a wall sconce, its flame dancing wildly in the draft, casting long shadows that stretched and curled across the stone floor. Gatty walked quickly, her new boots tapping in rhythm with the hum of her thoughts—each step echoing the strange new weight she now carried.

The dormitory was dim and still when she returned. A few women lay curled beneath their blankets, their outlines soft in the flickering candlelight. Gatty climbed into her narrow bed, the mattress giving beneath her with a tired sigh. She pulled the scratchy wool to her chin and stared up at the plaster ceiling—familiar now, like an old secret too stubborn to fade.

She thought of the tea leaves. The bird. The key. The tangle of lines. It was nonsense—wasn't it? But nonsense had a way of sticking. Like mud in a hem. Like whispers you couldn't unhear.

The soft rustle of blankets broke the quiet. Ellen, from the neighboring bed, leaned toward her—eyes wide, her voice a ghost of itself. "Well?" she whispered. "What did she want?"

Gatty turned her head. "To invite me to stay," she whispered back. "For two years."

Ellen's brow furrowed. "And you said yes?"

"I did," Gatty murmured. "What choice do I have?"

Ellen didn't answer. She just rolled away and pulled her blanket tighter.

Gatty lay still. Helena had spoken of ghosts—but it wasn't just memories that haunted this place. It was something older. Bigger. Blythewood offered mercy, yes. But the kind that came wrapped in riddles and steeped in ritual.

The kind that asked something of you in return.

CHAPTER SEVEN

VIOLET

G atty was back in the library.

The hush struck her first—thick, expectant. As if the room itself were listening. She hesitated in the doorway, the bucket clinking softly at her side, feeling every inch the intruder in a space that did not welcome newcomers easily.

Books lined the towering shelves like old guards, their spines cracked with age and gold-pressed titles dulled to shadows. The scent of ink and parchment clung to the air, threading with something older—pressed herbs, beeswax, a whisper of lavender turned sharp with age. It reminded her faintly of the still room, but quieter. More sacred.

She stepped inside.

The floor creaked beneath her boots, the sound quickly swallowed by the velvet hush of the space. Sunlight slanted through the tall, leaded windows, catching dust motes in slow, spell-like spirals.

"Oh! You're here."

The voice came from deeper within the stacks, quick and bright as flint. A girl popped into view—young, wild-haired, ink-smudged, and smiling like she knew something Gatty didn't.

"You must be Miss Carter," the girl said, hands on her hips as she gave Gatty a once-over. "Took them long enough to send someone."

"I wasn't told anything," Gatty replied, wary. "Just that I should be useful."

"Well, good," the girl said, already turning on her heel. "I'm Violet. I'm the reason this place doesn't collapse under the weight of all that 'precious knowledge.' Not that Leander would admit it."

"Leander?" Gatty echoed. "The librarian?"

"Yes," Violet said, with an exaggerated grimace. "Tall. Brooding. Prone to dramatic sighs when someone misplaces a folio by half an inch. You'll meet him soon enough."

Before Gatty could respond that she had already, Violet shoved a stack of books into her arms with practiced ease. "These go over there—top shelf, far wall. Don't drop them unless you want to get cursed."

Gatty adjusted the pile, the weight of the volumes surprisingly solid against her chest. "They're valuable, then?"

"Very," Violet said, brushing dust from her apron. "But knowledge isn't meant to rot behind locked doors. That's what Leander says. Right before muttering something in Latin and vanishing again."

Gatty followed her through the maze of shelves, the place strangely alive with silence. As they walked, Violet pointed out corners and curiosities like a tour guide in a temple.

"This is the local history section. Very dusty. Over there's theology—less dusty, but not half as interesting. That alcove with the carved chair? That's where Leander sulks when he's in a mood."

"Does he do anything besides sulk and hoard books?" Gatty asked, setting her stack gently on a side table.

"Oh, he's brilliant," Violet said with a shrug. "But he'd rather eat his own ink stained fingers than admit he likes people."

Before Gatty could reply, a soft cough broke the stillness.

From the far end of the room, a tall figure stepped into view—Leander. His coat swept the edge of a shelf as he moved, his dark hair tied neatly at the nape of his neck. He looked as if he'd been carved from shadow and sharp angles, with the sort of face that rarely smiled and eyes that flicked over her like a ledger he'd already begun.

"Miss Carter," he said, his voice low and clipped. "I trust you'll treat this space with more care than you would the scullery."

"Of course." Gatty straightened, bristling. "I'm here to help, not wreck your precious books."

His brow arched slightly at her tone, but he didn't rise to it. "See that you don't." Leander turned to Violet. "You've explained the rules?"

"Of course," Violet said with forced cheer. The look she shot Gatty said: *I definitely have not.*

Leander gave a single, curt nod. But his almost appraising gaze rested on Gatty a moment longer than necessary. As if he were trying to place her inside a story only he knew the ending to. Then, just like that, he turned and disappeared behind a curtain of shelves.

Violet waited until his footsteps faded before letting out a sigh. "See? Wet cat. But sharper than he looks."

Gatty wasn't sure what unsettled her more: his disapproval—or the way her heart had jolted under his gaze. She picked up the next stack of books, her hands steady even as her thoughts churned.

As the hours passed, the work found its rhythm. Gatty moved between the shelves, arms aching from the steady labor of shelving volumes and brushing dust from long-forgotten spines. Her fingertips grew gray with soot and old ink. Every now and then, she caught herself glancing toward the shadowed end of the library, where Leander loomed like a storm cloud on the horizon.

He had a way of appearing whenever she got too close to his corner—emerging from some hidden study or alcove with an arched brow and a silent scowl, like a cat convinced you were tampering with its territory. Then, just as quickly, he'd vanish again, always with the faint swish of his coat like punctuation.

Violet, by contrast, was a whirlwind. Her chatter filled the space between bookshelves with warmth and irreverence, her jokes keeping the silence from becoming too heavy. She moved like she belonged here—like the library was an extension of her own bones.

But Gatty's unease clung, quiet and stubborn. When Leander finally disappeared into what Violet called his "brooding hour"—a back room with a thick curtain and no explanation—Gatty saw her chance. She set down the book in her hands and turned to Violet, her voice low and sharp. "Why did they bring me here?"

Violet froze mid-reach for a pile of papers. Her smile faltered. "What?"

"You know what I mean," Gatty said, stepping closer. "Lydia, Helena. What do they see that I don't?"

Violet's expression shifted. The easy mischief in her face dimmed. "Keep your voice down," she murmured, glancing toward the curtained room. She gestured for Gatty to follow her, and they ducked into a dim aisle of theology texts, the high shelves muffling the rest of the world.

"I wasn't supposed to tell you," Violet said, folding her arms. "They usually wait until you've settled in, until you're so tired or grateful you don't ask too many questions."

"Well, I'm not grateful," Gatty snapped. "I'm still breathing, but that doesn't mean I owe them my silence. Why me? Why this house?"

Violet exhaled slowly. "Blythewood isn't just a Magdalene house. It never has been. It's more like... a sanctuary. But not for the reasons people think."

Gatty narrowed her eyes. "Go on."

"It's a place for women who've been cast out," Violet said. "But not just the usual kind. Helena has a way of seeing people, and Lydia hopes to be where she is someday. They finds the ones who are... different. Unsettling. The ones accused of things that frighten others."

Gatty's chest tightened. "Accused of what?"

Violet didn't flinch. "Witchcraft, of course."

The word hung in the air between them, heavy and absurd.

Gatty stared at her. "That's ridiculous."

"Is it?" Violet asked quietly. "They tried to drown you in your village, didn't they?"

"Sort of. How did you know? That doesn't mean I'm a—" Her voice faltered. "They were frightened. Stupid. They didn't understand."

"I'm not saying you're a witch, Gatty," Violet said. "But when Leander got word of what happened to you—how you vanished, presumed dead—he brought your name to Lydia. They didn't just come to find you. They came to save you."

Gatty's breath caught. "He brought my name?"

Violet nodded. "It's part of what he does. Keeps records. Patterns. Notices when women go missing in ways that... don't make sense. Especially the ones accused of being something other than what they are. Your reported death caught his attention. He thought you might be... one of us."

"There is no us," Gatty said bitterly. "I don't have visions or powers or—whatever they think witches are supposed to have."

"Neither do I," Violet said gently. "But that's not the point."

Gatty frowned. "Then what is?"

"You lived," Violet said simply. "When you weren't supposed to. You climbed out of a river and disappeared into the trees. Someone saw you, and told one of Leander's contacts. Lydia and James picked you up. And now you're here."

The words landed like stones in Gatty's gut. She opened her mouth to protest, but couldn't find the ground to stand on.

Violet leaned in, her voice soft but sure. "They didn't drag you into a scheme, Gatty. They offered you a thread when the world cut the rope. No one's saying you owe them. But you might want to ask yourself why people keep surviving things they shouldn't—and ending up here."

Gatty stood in silence, her hands curled around the edge of the shelf, the dust clinging to her skin.

She didn't believe in witches. She didn't believe in fate. But she was starting to believe in patterns—and something about this one made her feel both seen and cornered.

Violet stepped closer, her voice gentler now. "I know it feels like they've taken something from you. The choice, maybe. The truth. But this place... it's not just shadows and secrets. It's also safety. And safety's not something women like us get handed often."

Gatty's eyes narrowed. "Safety always comes with a price."

"They'll want to see what you're made of," Violet admitted. "That's the cost, I suppose. You prove yourself useful—or at least willing. Some come and leave in a week. Others..." She glanced down the aisle toward the curtained room. "Others stay. They learn things. About herbs. History. Themselves."

"Learn what?" Gatty asked, her arms folding tight across her chest.

Violet's lips twitched in a small, knowing grin. "That depends on you. But I'll help you figure it out."

The offer lingered in the air between them, too warm and too kind for how heavy Gatty's chest felt. She paced a few steps, boots scuffing against the worn floorboards. The towering bookshelves closed in like trees in a forest—quiet, patient, and full of things that watched.

"So, that's it?" she asked sharply. "They find women like me—accused of things we didn't do—and tuck us away in this drafty old house? Watch to see if we burn or bloom?"

"Not exactly," Violet said, leaning her shoulder against the nearest shelf. "It's not a school for witches, if that's what you're picturing. No spellbooks. No secret pacts. Most of us don't believe in any of that. But don't tell Helena. If you know what's good for you, let her think you're swimming in magic."

Gatty raised a brow. "Then what do you believe?"

Violet tilted her head, considering. "I believe women are powerful. That people fear what they don't understand. And Helena—well, she believes something extra. Something about women like you."

"Like me?" Gatty echoed, the words colder than she expected.

"She thinks you're rare," Violet said plainly. "That you've got something in you—potential, instinct, maybe magic. She won't say it outright, not yet. But the way she looked at you? The way she didn't tell you everything? That's her way of watching closely."

Gatty turned her face away, remembering the flicker in Helena's eyes, the deliberate softness that felt like testing more than care. "It feels like a trap," she said.

"Yeah," Violet agreed. "It did to me too. But it's not forever. You're not a prisoner. You can leave when you want."

"Can I?" Gatty asked bitterly. "Or do they just make it feel like leaving would be a mistake?"

Violet's expression sobered. "I won't lie—it's hard. Once you're safe, it's easy to confuse safety for kindness. Or freedom. But Helena doesn't lock the doors. She waits. Gives you space to figure out if you want to stay."

Gatty snorted. "Generous of her."

"More than most," Violet said. "You think someone with Helena's money and power usually spends her days worrying about girls who nearly drowned in rivers?"

The mention of Helena again sent a ripple of something—chill or curiosity—down Gatty's spine. "Why does she care?"

"Honestly?" Violet shrugged. "Because once, no one cared about her. And now she makes sure no one else slips through the cracks she crawled out of."

That struck something in Gatty she didn't want to name. She didn't trust Helena, but she couldn't quite dismiss her, either. Her jaw tightened. "And Leander? Where does he fit into all of this?"

Violet gave a low chuckle. "Leander's his own species. He's brilliant—won't admit it—but he's more comfortable with ink than people. Helena trusts him with the records, the archives, and the search for women like us. He sees patterns in stories most folks would overlook."

Gatty frowned. "So I'm just a pattern in his ledger?"

"For now," Violet said, though her tone wasn't unkind. "But you've already made it farther than most. He doesn't come out of hiding just to scowl at anyone. He's not going to kick you out of the library for working in the still room, if that's what worries you."

"It doesn't." Despite herself, Gatty felt one corner of her mouth twitch. "Some comfort all this is."

"Look," Violet said, brushing her hands on her apron, "I'm not saying you have to trust anyone here. But you've got a warm bed, food that doesn't bite back, and people who aren't trying to drown you. That's not nothing."

Gatty met her eyes, searching for any trace of mockery or condescension—but all she saw was something steady. Not pity. Just experience. A woman who had stood where she stood now. "Why are you helping me?" Gatty asked. "You didn't have to answer my questions."

Violet tilted her head. "Because I remember what it felt like to be angry and wild and ready to bite anyone who got too close. And because it's nice to talk to someone who doesn't already know which creaking stair means Leander's coming."

The honesty in her voice surprised Gatty. It warmed something sharp inside her that she hadn't meant to let thaw. She gave a small nod. "All right," she said. "I'll stay. For now."

Violet grinned, her familiar spark returning. "Good. Because I've got loads more to show you. And if we're lucky, we might even survive a week without getting exiled for dog-earing a manuscript."

Before Gatty could reply, the measured sound of footsteps echoed through the stacks. Leander emerged from the dimness like a ghost called back too soon, eyes sharp and posture stiff. His gaze landed on them like a blade. "Are you finished whispering?" he asked, his tone clipped. "Or shall I assume the theological texts are organizing themselves?"

"We were discussing classification systems," Violet said breezily. "To ensure maximum reverence."

Leander arched a brow. "If you're so reverent, I'd suggest you start by respecting deadlines."

"Of course, sir," Violet replied, sketching a dramatic bow before whisking away with a stack of papers. She tossed Gatty a wink over her shoulder.

Leander turned his attention fully to Gatty. He studied her for a long moment—too long—before saying, "Miss Carter, if you intend to be of use in this library, you'd best learn quickly. This isn't a place for idle minds or wandering hands."

"I'll keep that in mind," she said coolly, meeting his gaze.

His expression didn't change, but she noticed a flicker—barely there—in the way his eyes lingered just a beat too long. Then he turned and vanished into the deeper shelves without another word.

Gatty exhaled, and let her shoulders relax. She turned back to the books, dusting and stacking with a new, quiet purpose. Violet's words stayed with her, circling in her mind like cautious birds. The anger wasn't gone. But something else had taken root alongside it.

Not trust. Not yet.

But the beginning of something that might grow.

CHAPTER EIGHT

THE POISON GARDEN

The frost held stubbornly that morning, clinging to the windows of Blythewood Hall like a pale ghost refusing to let go. Gatty rubbed her hands together as she walked the corridor, her thin shawl useless against the creeping chill. The summons had come before breakfast—Helena wanted to see her. And when Lady Hartford summoned, there was no room for dawdling, as Mrs. Havering often sought to remind her.

The still room creaked open beneath her hand, releasing the familiar scent of dried herbs and smoke. Shelves crowded with glass jars lined the walls—row upon row of lavender, wormwood, rose hips, and root bundles. The scent was oddly comforting, like something halfway between a memory and a warning.

Helena stood near the hearth, where a kettle murmured quietly over the flames. The light cast her plum gown in shadowed ripples, her profile regal and sharp. She didn't look up right away—just plucked a single leaf from a bundle hanging by the chimney and rubbed it between her fingers. "Miss Carter," she said at last, turning with the grace of someone who expected obedience. "Punctual. Good. Come in."

Gatty stepped inside, the door clicking shut behind her like the closing of a vault. "You sent for me, ma'am."

"I did." Helena gestured to a small table at the center of the room. Laid out upon it were shears, gloves, and a bundle of dark, wiry herbs tied with twine. "I've been considering where your talents might best serve us. I believe I've found an answer."

Gatty's stomach tightened. Her hands itched to twist the edge of her shawl, but she kept them still. "And that is?"

"The poison garden," Helena said simply.

Gatty blinked. The words hit her like a gust of cold air. Of all the places within these walls, that one had always stood apart—rumored, watched, whispered about. Even among women with bruised pasts and quiet secrets, the poison garden had its own shadow.

"The garden?" she echoed. "With respect, ma'am... why me?"

Helena turned her full gaze on her, cool and appraising. "Why not you?"

Gatty said nothing, but Helena didn't wait for permission to continue.

"You've sharp eyes and a steady hand. You're cautious, but not afraid to speak your mind. The work requires care, discipline, and a willingness to understand what most people fear. You don't flinch easily, Miss Carter."

Gatty hesitated. That wasn't how she would've described herself—but something about it rang true. "And if I mishandle one of them?"

"Then you'll suffer the consequences. And you'll learn." Helena didn't blink. "Fear is not your enemy. Complacency is."

A beat passed. The silence crackled like kindling.

"But I don't believe you'll falter," Helena added. Her tone softened, barely—but enough to make Gatty's throat tighten unexpectedly. "Do you?"

Gatty straightened her spine, forcing her fear down. "No, ma'am."

Helena nodded once, then swept toward the door. "Follow me."

They crossed the grounds in silence, the morning air biting at Gatty's cheeks. The eastern edge of the estate was more overgrown than she expected, its hedgerows tall and unruly. As they neared the garden's entrance, she saw the wrought-iron gate tucked into the hedge like a secret.

Helena produced a key, its intricate shape catching the light. But before turning it, she glanced sidelong at Gatty.

"You've an unusual look about you," she said quietly. "Like a bird freed from its cage—still deciding whether to fly, or peck out someone's eyes."

Gatty wasn't sure whether to take offense or feel seen. "I've no quarrel with the work," she said carefully. "It just seems... a strange choice."

"I thought you might enjoy it," Helena said, inserting the key with a soft click. "You strike me as someone who sees what others miss. Finds value in what's overlooked."

The gate creaked open. Even in winter, the garden was striking—coiled vines, glass cloches rimed with frost, rows of dormant plants hunched beneath faded labels. It was quiet in a way that felt unnatural, as though the space itself were holding its breath.

"It's not a place for the faint of heart," Helena continued. "But then, I suspect you are not faint-hearted."

Gatty looked past her at the twisted beauty within the gate. Something stirred beneath her ribs—fear, yes, but something else, too. Recognition.

A flash of memory: her mother's voice murmuring the names of herbs while grinding them into pastes; the scent of sage and vinegar;

the way her hands moved swiftly and surely, even when Gatty asked a dozen questions she didn't always understand. Her mother had known things. Useful things. Powerful things.

Gatty swallowed hard. "If it's what's needed, ma'am, I'll do it."

Helena's smile curved like the edge of a knife as she gave Gatty her instructions. "Very well. The gloves are on the bench. Use them—always. Begin with the nightshade. Separate the roots and leaves. I'll return later to check your progress."

She left without another word, the iron gate clanging shut behind her like the start of a trial.

Left alone in the garden, Gatty stood still for a moment, listening. No voices. No footsteps. Only the wind combing through brittle branches and the distant creak of the manor's bones. Before her, the plants waited—rows of twisted stems and frost-dusted leaves, as still and silent as gravestones.

She stepped forward, slipping on the thick gloves Helena had provided. Their leather was stiff, lined with wool that scratched her wrists, but she welcomed the discomfort. It kept her sharp.

Names came to her in fragments, half-remembered whispers: belladonna, aconite, foxglove. She crouched beside the bed of nightshade, its dark, glossy leaves glinting like oil in the winter light. The frost had edged their margins in silver, a beauty both delicate and brutal.

She hesitated. Her gloved fingers hovered over the plant, uncertain. The garden felt sentient—watchful. As if it could sense her ignorance.

"Nightshade," she murmured, testing the name on her tongue. "Belladonna. Deadly... but useful."

She retrieved the shears from the bench and made the first cut. The stem gave with a soft snap, clean and final. The leaves shivered slightly in the breeze, and Gatty nearly imagined the plant recoiling. She shook the thought away.

The air was sharp with the scent of damp earth and old secrets. As she dug, the roots came free with a satisfying crunch, pale and coiled like veins. She separated them into baskets—roots in one, leaves in another—her movements growing steadier with each motion. It wasn't grace. It was control. And control, she realized, had become rare and precious.

She was so focused she didn't hear the creak of the gate behind her.

"You'll poison yourself if you're not careful," said a small voice.

Gatty startled, the shears clattering from her grip. She spun around to find Ivy standing just inside the garden, curls wild beneath a bonnet too large for her head, arms full of leaves she had no business picking.

"What are you doing here?" Gatty snapped, too sharply. "This is no place for children."

Ivy only shrugged. "I saw you from the window. Mama says you're working in the garden now." She narrowed her eyes in theatrical suspicion. "Does that mean you're a witch?"

Gatty blinked. "No. It does not."

Ivy padded forward, peering into Gatty's baskets. "Mama says witches know about plants. That they can make potions. Some for healing, some for hurting." She looked up. "Do you know how to do that?"

"I've only just started," Gatty said, warily. "And this garden is not for games. You need to go."

Ivy crouched beside her anyway, examining a cluster of leaves with curious reverence. "This one's pretty," she said, pointing. "But it's the kind that kills you, isn't it?"

"Yes," Gatty said quietly. "Even a little of it could."

Ivy's eyes widened, but rather than fear, there was fascination. "Like a secret weapon."

"It's not a toy," Gatty replied, gentler this time. "You shouldn't be here."

Ivy frowned, brushing at her skirts. "I wasn't going to touch anything." Her voice lowered. "You don't have to sound so cross."

Gatty sighed, the fight draining from her. "You shouldn't be in here. Not because I'm cross. Because you don't know what you're near."

Ivy tilted her head, studying her. "Do you like it?"

"Like what?"

"The garden," Ivy said plainly. "Mama said she thought you would."

Gatty froze. "Your mother said that?"

Ivy nodded. "She said you've got sharp eyes. And that you'd like having something to care for."

Gatty glanced down at her gloves, at the faint green smudges and dirt ground into the seams. The garden was exacting. Dangerous. A place where life and death nestled against one another in the same soil.

She didn't want to admit it—but yes. It called to her.

"It's fine," she said stiffly.

Ivy gave her a small, knowing smile. "You're not as scary as you pretend to be," she said, and turned back toward the gate.

Gatty watched her go. Then she bent back to the nightshade, though her hands moved slower now. Her thoughts lingered.

Lydia had sent her here. Or Helena. Maybe both. Maybe this wasn't punishment at all. Maybe it was something else.

The frost had begun to melt, the earth softening beneath her gloves. As she worked, she uncovered a thick root—coiled like a question mark. She brushed the dirt away slowly, the scent of it rising to meet her like breath.

Was this garden a challenge?

Or a gift?

The sun had sunk low by the time Gatty trudged through the hall's stone corridors, her skirts heavy with mud and her hands aching despite the gloves. The garden clung to her—its scent in her hair, its chill in her bones, its strange hush still echoing in her thoughts.

Mrs. Havering caught sight of her and immediately clucked her tongue. "You'll track half the grounds through the hall, girl." She thrust a damp rag at her with a grimace. "Clean up before you breathe on the linens."

Gatty scrubbed her face at the cold basin, the water biting into her wind-chapped skin. Her fingers were raw and red by the time she straightened, and she was halfway back to the dormitory when a low voice stopped her.

"Miss Carter."

She turned. Leander stood just beyond the threshold of the library, his silhouette framed by the warm spill of candlelight. His shirt sleeves were rolled to the elbow, and a pair of spectacles perched low on his nose, giving him the look of someone caught between thoughts too large for company.

"Sir?" she asked cautiously, already knowing it wasn't a question. She felt foolish, but she wished he'd ask her to come closer.

"Come in," he said, already turning back inside.

Gatty hesitated a beat before following. Her heart leapt foolishly, even as she'd sought to quell its ascent. She'd seen the library in daylight—dusty, imposing, still.

But now, under flickering candlelight, it felt alive. Stacks of books sat like half-built forts on every table, pages yellowed and edges curling, as though mid-thought. Ink bottles, dried leaves, scraps of ribbon and wax seals crowded the corners of the room like old confidences.

Leander moved through it with unconscious ease, his hand steadying a leaning pile here, brushing a page flat there. Finally, he stopped at a broad oak table where an open book lay beside a leather-bound journal marked in fine, neat script. "You've been in the garden," he said, not looking up.

"I have." Gatty frowned, unsure if it was a judgment or just fact. "Does my aroma suggest it?"

"No." He turned the book toward her, tapping the page. "Do you know what this is?"

She stepped closer, eyes catching on the intricate ink drawing—long spiked leaves, bell-shaped blooms. "Foxglove," she said slowly. "We harvested some today."

"Digitalis," he replied, his tone even. "Used properly, it strengthens the heart. Used improperly—" He glanced up, meeting her gaze. "It stops it."

She didn't look away. "Is that a warning, sir?"

"A lesson," he said. "Most are learned too late." His voice lacked its usual chill, and there was something behind his eyes—weariness, maybe. Or memory.

"I'll remember it," Gatty said softly.

Leander nodded and pushed the book toward her. "Take it. It's not superstition—it's science. But the line between the two is thinner than you might think."

She hesitated, the leather cover smooth beneath her fingertips. "And what am I to do with it?"

"Read it." He removed his spectacles and folded them with care. "Or don't. But if you plan to keep your hands in that soil, you should know what grows beneath."

There was something unsettling about his concern—because it wasn't disdainful. It felt real. "Why give it to me?" she asked.

"I understand that Helena expects you to know how the plants work with no training." Leander paused. "You don't strike me as the sort who tolerates ignorance."

Gatty held his gaze, something steady rising in her chest. "I don't."

"Then we understand each other." He turned back to his notes, already half-absorbed, but she saw it—the twitch of amusement, a softness that flickered like a match in the wind.

Gatty pressed the book to her chest. "Thank you," she said, more quietly this time.

Leander didn't answer. But she didn't need him to.

She lingered a moment longer, just long enough to watch the way the candlelight clung to the edges of his work. There was something steadying in the way he moved—like a man who knew how to survive the storm by studying its patterns.

Then she turned, her steps light as she slipped from the room. The book was heavy in her arms, but the weight didn't burden her.

It grounded her.

As Gatty returned to the dormitory, she couldn't stop the small smile tugging at the corner of her mouth.

The room was still, hushed and dark. The other women lay tucked beneath their blankets, their breathing slow and steady in the quiet. Gatty closed the door softly behind her, the book clutched to her chest as if it might vanish if she let go.

The fire in the hearth had dwindled to faint coals, pulsing like the last heartbeat of something dying slowly. She sat on the edge of her straw mattress and placed the book in her lap. Its worn leather was cool beneath her fingers, the gold-embossed title glinting faintly in the firelight: *A Practical Compendium of Botanical Science.* The words were measured. Unyielding. Like they had all the answers if you only knew how to ask.

A soft creak broke the quiet. Gatty looked up to find Violet watching her from two beds over, her chin propped on her hand, hair mussed with sleep.

"Still up?" Violet whispered. "Or has Leander turned you into one of his little scholars already?"

Gatty grinned and gestured to the tome in her lap. "You'll have to wait until morning to find out."

Violet's gaze flicked to the book in her lap. Her voice remained playful, but her eyes sharpened. "One of his treasures! He must like you."

"Oh..." Gatty flushed but kept her tone even. "He barely tolerates me."

Violet stifled a laugh. "That might be his version of affection." She hesitated. "What's the book for?"

"The garden," Gatty said, running her thumb along the edge of the cover. "He said I should know what I'm handling."

At that, Violet's smile faded a fraction. Something unreadable flickered behind her eyes—worry, maybe. Or memory.

"He's not wrong," she said softly. "That garden's taken its toll on women with gentler hands than yours."

Gatty looked up. "What do you mean?"

Violet's eyes shifted toward the dark window. "Some plants kill slow. Others fast. Some just trick you into thinking you're dying—which might be worse. Knowledge can save you, Gatty... but it can unravel you just as fast. Watch yourself."

Gatty nodded, the warning sinking deep. "I will."

"Good." Violet flopped onto her back with a groan. "Now go to sleep before you start muttering Latin in your dreams."

Gatty chuckled under her breath, but the quiet settled around her again as she looked down at the book. She flipped it open. The pages were thick and dry, the illustrations meticulous—belladonna, yew, hemlock. Each plant drawn with care, with reverence, as if the ink itself knew the stakes. She was delighted to see that notes lined the margins: *fever... hallucinations... paralysis... heart failure.*

Her mother's hands surfaced in her mind—bruised fingers grinding herbs into paste, murmuring their names like incantations. For fever. For pain. For sleep.

Gatty closed the book, her throat tight. She couldn't think about her mother. Not here. Not now. Not in a place where nothing felt soft or familiar. She slid the book beneath her pillow, its leather pressing cold and steady against her temple. It felt like a stone at first—strange and weighty—but also like something anchoring her to the moment. To the truth that, for better or worse, she was still here.

As the room settled into silence, Gatty let her thoughts drift to the garden. The scent of damp earth. The gleam of black leaves. The quiet thrill of danger curled in the roots.

It was a place of power. And maybe—if she was careful—it could become a place to grow.

She closed her eyes. This time, sleep came without the river. Without the mob. She dreamed instead of leaves dark as ink and roots that reached deeper than fear, curling through the earth like secrets waiting to be named.

CHAPTER NINE

PLAYING THEIR GAME

The frost hadn't yet lifted from the grass when Gatty stepped into the garden. Her breath curled white in the morning air, and the silence pressed close—thick and watchful, broken only by the slow groan of the iron gate as Helena opened it. The garden lay still beneath its winter veil, branches skeletal, soil silvered with rime. It looked like a cursed painting: quiet, cold, and waiting.

"This way, Miss Carter." Helena's voice was calm, clipped, and unmistakably in command.

Gatty followed, the hem of her gown dragging over frozen ground. She had yet to grow entirely comfortable in the poison garden's company—it felt like stepping into the pages of a forgotten spellbook, each plant a whispered warning. Even dormant, they seemed to lean toward her, as though recognizing something in her she hadn't yet claimed.

Helena stopped beside a narrow bench, where a neat row of glass jars gleamed beside a pair of ivory-handled shears and a mortar and pestle. Bundles of herbs—lavender, chamomile, and a darker, earthier root she couldn't yet name—were tied with twine and waiting like offerings.

"You've a steady hand," Helena said, examining the jars without looking at Gatty. "Today, you will test it."

Gatty stepped closer, frowning. "Ma'am?"

Helena lifted the smallest bundle, letting the scent unfurl between them. "These herbs are to be prepared for Lady Elspeth. She has difficulty sleeping. You will make an infusion to quiet the nerves. You know lavender?"

"Aye," Gatty said carefully.

"Chamomile, too," Helena continued, setting each bundle down in turn. "And this—valerian root. A pinch, no more. Too much, and it dulls the mind. Too little, and it does nothing at all."

Gatty eyed the valerian. Its scent was sharper than the others, bitter beneath the earthiness, and something about its twisted root shape reminded her of bones. "And if I misjudge?"

Helena's brows rose faintly. "Then you will begin again. Failure from caution is forgivable. Failure from carelessness is not."

A cold thread of dread twisted in Gatty's gut, but she said nothing. Her gloved fingers reached for the shears, and she steadied her breath.

Helena stood behind her like a sentry, hands folded neatly, watching. "Better to be slow and precise than hasty and dead wrong," she said, and the words fell like a blade wrapped in velvet.

Gatty bit back a retort and bent to her task.

The lavender was first, its familiar scent rising as she trimmed each stem cleanly. The chamomile came next—delicate, airy petals that disintegrated at the lightest pressure. The valerian root, knotted and stubborn, took more effort. Its earthy tang clung to her gloves, refusing to be forgotten.

Helena's voice came quiet behind her. "Do you know what valerian was used for in ancient times?"

Gatty didn't look up. "No, ma'am."

"They said it could calm the fiercest tempers. Soothe kings. Yet in the wrong hands, it has laid many in the ground."

Gatty paused, the pestle heavy in her grip. "Why tell me that?"

"Because knowledge is power," Helena said. "And power, Miss Carter, is the only thing that keeps a woman from being forgotten."

The cold had long since bitten through her shoes, but it was Helena's words that chilled her now. Gatty ground the valerian root slowly, deliberately, letting the sound of stone against stone settle her. She added the lavender, then the chamomile, watching the blend soften and turn familiar. It looked harmless. It wasn't.

When she finished, she stepped back. Helena moved forward without comment, lifting the mortar to study its contents with the same intensity one might use on a coded letter. Finally, she nodded. "Well done."

Gatty exhaled, only now aware she'd been holding her breath. "Thank you, ma'am."

Helena set the mortar back down and met her eyes. "It seems your hands are good for far more than scrubbing floors."

Gatty's jaw tightened, but her voice remained level. "You've a strange way of offering praise, ma'am."

Helena allowed a ghost of a smile. "Praise is cheap when it's given freely. You're earning yours."

She turned, her dark skirts brushing the frost behind her. Just before the gate closed, she glanced back. "See to it you learn the garden well. It may yet reward you."

And then she was gone.

Gatty stood alone in the winter light, her hands faintly stained green and her heart thudding hard. Around her, the poison garden stretched in eerie stillness, plants arching toward the weak sun like curious shadows.

"Reward me," Gatty muttered. "Or bury me."

She looked down at the completed infusion, its scent subtle, soothing—masking the potential inside. Helena's voice echoed like a riddle: knowledge is power. Gatty lifted the mortar carefully and began the slow walk back toward the Hall, each step measured. If Blythewood Hall intended to test her, it was only fair she start keeping score.

The still room was tucked into a quiet crook of the Hall, near the kitchens where the scent of woodsmoke and rising bread softened the edges of the cold. Gatty followed Violet down the narrow corridor, clutching the mortar of herbs Helena had bid her prepare. Her footsteps echoed off the stone, each one reverberating just a little too long—like the Hall was listening.

"Mind your head," Violet chirped, ducking beneath a crooked beam. Gatty jerked back just in time to avoid a bruised forehead, muttering under her breath.

The room beyond was warm and dim, almost womb-like in its hush. Shelves climbed the walls in uneven tiers, packed with jars labeled in neat, precise script: Lavandula. Salvia. Digitalis. Ruta graveolens. Bundles of dried herbs hung like votives from the rafters, and copper stills sat like strange relics on the countertops, their curves catching the candlelight. Rosemary and thyme mingled in the air with something darker—something medicinal and sharp enough to sting the back of the throat.

"Set it there," Violet said, waving to a table already cluttered with jars, bits of parchment, and wayward stems. "Spill it, and Helena'll have us scrubbing walls with toothpicks."

"I've been told I'm good with my hands," Gatty said dryly, placing the mortar down with exaggerated care.

Violet flopped into a chair with the grace of a collapsing marionette. "And look at you, already wriggling into Helena's good graces. That's practically witchcraft."

Gatty arched a brow. "Depending on who you ask."

"Depends how you use it," Violet said, tossing her a grin as she grabbed a bundle of lavender. "Now help me with these—leaves, stems, petals, all separate. If you mix even a whisper of the wrong bit, Helena'll have a vision and strike us down with lightning."

Gatty rolled up her sleeves and pulled a second chair forward. "She does give off a divine wrath sort of air," she muttered, though a smile tugged faintly at her lips.

For a few minutes, they worked in rhythm, the rustle of dried herbs and the soft clink of glass filling the quiet. Gatty let her hands fall into the motion—snip, sort, drop. The lavender calmed her, its clean, sleepy scent rising like memory. For a little while, she could almost forget why she was here.

But Violet wasn't built for silence. "So," she said, casually slicing another stem. "How'd you land here? I know some of it, but..."

Gatty's hands slowed. "Not by choice."

"None of us were," Violet said with a shrug. "But there's always a tale behind it. Mine involves a promise-breaking bastard and a magistrate who didn't blink."

Gatty gave her a sidelong glance. "And you stayed?"

"What else was there?" Violet's tone was airy, but something sharp glinted beneath it. "Helena calls it a house for wayward women. I figured, fine—let me be the best kind of wayward."

Gatty snorted. Then her expression sobered. "They accused me of witchcraft. Said I called fire to burn a barn. There were 'witnesses.' I never touched a match."

Violet's fingers paused mid-sort, her expression unreadable. "Of course there were so-called witnesses," she said softly. "Men who benefited from your downfall?"

Gatty exhaled through her nose. "Edward—the man who pointed the finger—owed half the village money. The barn was filled with wool he hadn't paid for. Third failed harvest in a row. People needed someone to blame." She hesitated, then added, "I only escaped because I knew where to crawl. Hollow tree by the riverbank." She shivered at the memory. "I stayed there all night."

For a moment, Violet said nothing. The warmth of the still room closed in around them, thick with rosemary and quiet grief. "And now?" her new friend asked at last, her voice low. "What are you looking for?"

Gatty stared at the petals in her hand, their soft purple folds bruised by the pressure of her thumb. "A place to breathe. Maybe a way to fight back, when the time comes."

Violet leaned in, her voice dropping to a whisper. "Then you've come to the right place. Helena may speak in pious riddles, but this house—it's always been more than it claims. There's potential here."

Gatty's brow furrowed. "What do you mean?"

But Violet hesitated, her fingers suddenly busy. "You're still new," she said finally. "Best you see it for yourself."

Gatty opened her mouth to press, but the muffled tread of footsteps echoed down the corridor. Violet straightened in an instant, slipping the last of the lavender into its jar.

"Helena doesn't care for gossip," she said under her breath, just as the door creaked open.

Mrs. Havering entered, squinting at them with all the suspicion of a warden inspecting cells. "Still at it, are you? Don't forget, chapel before supper."

"Yes, ma'am," Violet said sweetly, her tone just this side of insolent.

Gatty rose, wiping purple-streaked fingers on her apron. As they left the still room, the warmth of it clung to her skin, but her thoughts were elsewhere.

Later, she knocked softly against the library door, her knuckles grazing the wood. It was thick and unyielding, like so much of Blythewood Hall—resisting, as though it resented interruption. When no answer came, she pushed it open a crack and peered inside.

The room breathed in shadows. Towering shelves stretched toward the rafters, draped in dust and gloom. The faintest glow pooled in one corner where Leander sat hunched over a table, the tip of his quill scratching steadily against a narrow ledger. Candles guttered at his elbows, throwing long silhouettes across the desk.

Gatty cleared her throat tentatively, the jar of lavender clinking softly in her hands.

Leander didn't look up. "If it's tea, leave it and go."

"It's not tea," she said, stepping into the hush, her boots muffled by the worn rug underfoot.

Leander paused, lifting his gaze over the rim of his spectacles. "Miss Carter." His eyes flicked to the jar she carried, and he set his pen aside with deliberate calm. "So you're Helena's errand girl now?"

"Why not? You're the Hall's resident hermit," she shot back before she could think better of it.

To her surprise, Leander grinned. Then, a faint puff of laughter escaped him, soft and grudging. "A hermit would've found somewhere warmer."

Gatty bit back a smile and approached the table. She set the jar of dried lavender beside an open folio, careful not to disturb the neatly arranged piles of parchment and pressed leaves. "Violet said to bring this here. For your records."

Leander leaned forward, inspecting the jar. "Good color," he murmured. "Drying was clean. No clumping. Mold would've ruined the potency."

Gatty shrugged, though his quiet approval sent a spark of satisfaction through her. "I've a careful hand."

"So I'm told." His eyes met hers briefly before returning to the page, his pen resuming its restless scratch—like beetle legs on stone.

A comfortable silence settled. Gatty's gaze drifted to the books spread across the table. They were heavy things, cracked and worn at the corners, some held together with ribbons or thin leather cords. Botanical drawings spilled across the pages—carefully inked leaves and curling roots, labeled in tight, neat script. She recognized some of the names now. Others made her pulse flicker with unease.

"You spend all your time in here," she said, her tone more curious than accusing. "Why?"

Leander didn't look up. "Because books don't lie."

The certainty in his voice caught her off guard. "People do, though?"

He glanced up then, and his expression was strangely bare. "Constantly. Books hold truths. If you know how to read them."

Gatty studied him for a beat, unsure if he was talking about paper and ink or something else entirely. Her gaze dropped to the folio again, where a sprawling drawing of belladonna took up the whole page.

"Deadly nightshade," Leander said, his voice lower now. "Toxic. But in controlled doses? It eases pain. Slows the heart. One plant—two futures."

Gatty tilted her head. "Dangerous books and dangerous plants. You've an appetite for risk, sir."

Leander offered a smile, dry as ash. "Only fools fear knowledge."

She frowned, sensing an edge beneath the words. "And what about those who chase it?"

He met her eyes, and this time, it felt like a blade slipping between her ribs—not cruel, but clean. "That depends what they're hoping to find."

The air seemed to still. Gatty felt suddenly exposed, though she didn't know why. She dropped her gaze, the lavender now seeming far too fragile for the room. "The poison garden has much to teach," she said, quietly.

Leander's brow twitched, something unreadable passing through his expression. "It does," he murmured. "And it doesn't care who it devours."

She looked up sharply. "The book has been most helpful. Helena's teaching me to work with poisons."

"I think Helena is teaching you a great deal more than that." His voice was mild, but his meaning landed like a stone. "What you choose to learn is yours to carry."

"I'm not a fool," she snapped before she could stop herself. "There's no need to speak to me in riddles."

"I didn't say you were." Leander picked up his pen again, though he didn't immediately use it. "But fools aren't always born. Sometimes, they're made."

The words struck like a slap—not cruel, but coolly matter-of-fact. Gatty's spine straightened, her jaw tight. "Well, I won't be one," she said, her voice low and clipped. She turned for the door.

"Good day, Miss Carter," Leander called after her, and this time, the edge in his voice was gentler. Almost regretful.

She paused for a moment outside the library, the old wood shutting softly behind her. Her hands were fists. Her mind, a coil of tension. *Fools aren't always born. Sometimes, they're made.*

She began walking again, the long corridors of Blythewood stretching ahead, cool and cavernous. Somewhere above, wind moaned through the eaves, and behind the stone walls, the garden waited—still, cold, and full of secrets.

The jar of lavender still warmed her palm. So did the quiet knowledge that she was no longer afraid.

The afternoon light was already thinning when Gatty stepped back into the dormitory. The corridors had grown colder. Her fingers, still faintly lavender-stained from the still room, tingled with memory. She shut the door softly behind her.

The room was empty, quiet as held breath. Somewhere beyond the walls, the other women were scrubbing or stitching, kneeling stiff-backed in chapel under Mrs. Havering's hawk-eyed watch. For the moment, Gatty had solitude—and she welcomed it like warmth after cold.

She sank onto her straw mattress and glanced toward the pillow where the slim leather-bound book waited. Knowledge is power, Helena had said. What you choose to learn—that's up to you, Leander had echoed. Their words hovered in her mind like ash above a dying flame. Gatty looked upward at the ceiling beams, where ancient cracks veined outward like roots twisting through packed earth. The whole house felt like that—old, secretive, grown over with things best left buried.

The door creaked. Gatty sat up too quickly, her heart stammering against her ribs.

Violet strolled in, a half-eaten apple in one hand and her eyes glinting with mischief. "You've the look of a hare about to bolt."

"Maybe I am," Gatty muttered, sweeping her hair back from her face as Violet plopped onto the mattress beside hers.

Violet took a bite, chewing lazily. "I can't help but notice, every time you come back from the library, you look like you've walked through a thundercloud."

Gatty made a noise that was almost a laugh. Then, quieter: "Leander said something today. About fools. That they're made, not born."

Violet arched a brow. "And did he call you one?"

"Not directly." Gatty hesitated. "But he might have meant it."

"He means everything and nothing, all at once," Violet said with a wave of her apple. "Don't waste time trying to read between Leander's lines. He's half ink and half storm."

Gatty gave a small, grudging nod. "Still... I saw something strange in the garden today. Helena had me make an infusion for Lady Elspeth.

Lavender, chamomile, valerian. She said one wrong measure could sedate—or kill."

Violet's chewing slowed. "Sounds like Helena."

"But why trust me with it?" Gatty asked. "Why put that kind of choice in my hands?"

Violet tilted her head. "Maybe because you don't flinch."

Gatty blinked. "Is that... good?"

"Here?" Violet stood and brushed crumbs from her skirts. "It's necessary."

Gatty watched her move toward the door, a flicker of unease prickling beneath her skin.

Violet paused in the doorway, her voice suddenly low. "Whatever game Helena's playing, or Leander for that matter... you're smart to play along. Just don't forget who's really dealing the cards."

Then she was gone.

The door clicked softly shut. The dormitory felt colder, though Gatty hadn't moved.

She pulled the book from beneath her pillow, its leather cover worn smooth at the corners. She flipped it open. Foxglove. Hemlock. Belladonna. Their names stared back at her, etched in looping, patient ink. Dangerous things Deadly things.

Her mother's voice stirred in her mind, faint as a ghost: A careful hand can turn poison to cure. But the careless? They bring ruin.

Helena had called her steady. Leander, sharp. Violet, clever. Perhaps they were right. Perhaps that would be enough.

She closed the book gently and slid it back beneath her pillow, the weight of it grounding her like a stone in her ribs. Outside, wind rose against the Hall, its whistle like a warning curled against the eaves.

They might think they had her pinned—kept quiet through kindness, or caged by fear.

But Gatty Carter had learned to sharpen her edges.

She would learn what they meant her to learn. And when the time came—she'd decide what to do with it.

Play their game, she thought, eyes fixed on the cracked ceiling. But don't let them win.

Chapter Ten

A Ghost from the Past

The still room was steeped in the scent of rosemary and lavender, their sharp edges softened by the warmth of the fire and the gentle clink of glass jars. Gatty sat at the long wooden table, her hands moving steadily as she stripped rosemary from its stalks, forming neat little piles like she was trying to impose order on a world that had none.

Violet sat opposite her, humming a tune that had no beginning or end, only rhythm—a melody passed down from women who'd had to keep their voices quiet but their minds sharp.

"Watch the stems," Violet said absently, without looking up. "Helena says it's a waste to jar anything but the leaves. She'll tan your hide for bruising the lavender."

Gatty arched a brow. "I've survived worse than a scolding."

Violet smirked. "That's what Alice thought. Last week she swapped tansy for parsley. The stable boy's bowels haven't forgiven her."

Gatty snorted, biting back a laugh. "And yet they trust us with foxglove and belladonna."

"Trust?" Violet scoffed, rolling a stem between her fingers. "That's not the word I'd use."

The conversation settled into a quiet rhythm, like the careful sorting of herb from stem. Gatty found she liked this part—the calm repetition, the soft rustle of dried bundles, the sense that her hands could still do something useful. The garden had taught her that. Or maybe her mother had, long before.

"You're quick at it," Violet said after a while, her tone more curious than complimentary.

"It's in the fingers," Gatty replied, her voice quieter now. "My mother kept a garden. Not for poisons—kitchen herbs mostly. But she taught me how to tell what was safe, what wasn't. How to look closely."

Violet glanced at her, something flickering in her eyes. "You miss her."

Gatty's hands slowed. "She was the only person who ever taught me anything that mattered."

Violet's expression softened. "You were lucky. My mother wouldn't have known valerian from ragweed."

"She'd know it if it killed someone," Gatty muttered.

That got a real laugh from Violet, low and warm. "You're dark, Carter."

"You've no idea."

They lapsed into silence again, companionable but fragile, like something they might not be able to name just yet. Then the door creaked open.

Leander stepped inside without preamble, journal in hand, coat dusted with frost. His presence was like the cold itself—sharp, composed, and impossible to ignore. He nodded once, barely glancing their way.

"Miss Violet. Miss Carter."

"Afternoon, sir," Violet said with mock sweetness.

He didn't rise to it. "Inventory," he murmured, moving toward the wall of jars.

Violet gave Gatty a look and mouthed *hermit*.

Gatty almost smiled, but turned her attention back to her work. The last time she'd gotten caught in a back-and-forth with Leander, it had ended with her cheeks hot and her pride pricked.

He moved with quiet precision, fingers tracing labels, checking notes in his neat script. Gatty couldn't help watching him in the edge of her vision. There was a kind of reverence to his movements, like each jar held more than just dried leaves—like it held truth.

"Careful," Leander said suddenly, his voice slicing through the room.

Gatty looked down. Her fingers had begun to stray, almost mixing the rosemary with a bundle of feverfew.

"I'm not an idiot," she said, her tone sharper than she meant it to be.

"Then keep your herbs where they belong," he replied, not unkindly. "You've a good hand. Use it properly."

Gatty flushed, bristling with the sting of being corrected and the confusion of being seen. "I've yet to poison anyone."

"Yet," Leander said, lips twitching slightly. "Let's keep it that way."

Violet stifled a giggle, and Gatty shot her a glare.

Leander closed his journal with a soft snap. "Valerian and feverfew don't mix," he said over his shoulder, pausing at the door. "You'll find Helena less forgiving than I am."

And then he was gone, his footsteps retreating into the corridor like the echo of a closed book.

Violet waited a beat, then burst into a grin. "Why...he *likes* you."

"No." Gatty rolled her eyes. "He likes alphabetical order." Her fingers moved faster now, as though motion might distract her from the strange warmth blooming under her skin.

Later, Gatty stepped out past the gates of Blythewood Hall, bracing herself against the wind that cut down from the moors like a blade. The parcel in her hands—a neat bundle of herbs wrapped in muslin and tied with twine—felt heavier than it should. A simple errand, Mrs. Havering had said that morning, thrusting the bundle into her arms with all the gentleness of a butcher. "Deliver this to the woman on the edge of the village. Don't dawdle. Don't speak unless spoken to."

The path unspooled ahead of her like a thread drawn taut through frostbitten earth. Gatty kept her head down, her breath fogging before her face, and let her thoughts dissolve into the rhythm of her steps. It was strange, this sudden return to the outside world—the gray sky stretching wide above her, the brittle hush of fields lying fallow for winter. She felt exposed, like the air itself might name her.

The village emerged slowly over the rise, its squat stone cottages hunched close like gossiping old women, smoke curling from chimneys in wisps that smelled of peat and ash. Gatty's steps slowed as she neared the first houses, a familiar ache that was either apprehension or just plain fear tightening around her ribs.

Women looked up from their washing as she passed, hands still dripping suds, eyes sharp and searching. A boy paused mid-swing, his stick frozen in the air. Gatty turned her face away and walked faster, her borrowed gray dress doing little to disguise her.

The cottage she was meant to find stood at the village's edge, crouched beneath the shadow of a twisted yew tree. Ivy crept up its cracked walls, and its window had been patched with oiled paper that fluttered faintly in the wind. Gatty knocked once, her knuckles stiff from the cold.

The woman who answered had red, chapped hands and a face lined with years of biting wind and harder winters. Her eyes scanned Gatty with the flat suspicion of someone who'd learned long ago not to trust what the world offered. "Yes?"

"Herbs," Gatty said, her voice taut. "I have herbs here from…"

"I know where they're from." The woman snatched the parcel with a grunt. "Thanks."

Gatty nodded, already turning to leave. But the moment her boot met the road again, a voice cut through the air behind her like the crack of a whip.

"Carter?"

The name struck her spine like lightning. She froze mid-step. Slowly, she turned toward the sound.

Edward Fenton stood outside the smithy, a leather apron slung over soot-darkened clothes, his hands still stained from the forge. His eyes were as she remembered—cold, calculating—but now wide with something closer to shock than malice.

"You're dead," he said, stepping forward. "You're supposed to be dead. Everyone said you drowned."

Gatty's mouth went dry. Her fingers clenched around her skirts. Behind her, she could feel the village stir—the prickling hush of attention, as if every eye had suddenly turned her way.

"I don't know you," she said, her voice sharp enough to cut. "Leave me be."

But Edward wasn't deterred. "Don't lie to me, girl. I saw it. The river took you. And now you're standing here, bold as you please, delivering potions like nothing happened?" He advanced another step.

Heart in her throat, Gatty stood her ground, but only just. "Then maybe I'm a ghost," she said, her voice low. "And maybe you ought to ask yourself what brought me back."

For a moment, Edward faltered, just the briefest flicker of doubt in his eyes. But then he sneered, masking it with something uglier. "Ghost or not, you're still a witch. And witches should burn."

Something inside Gatty snapped. "Is that what you want, then? A second try?"

A hush fell across the square. Even the crows seemed to pause. Edward's lip curled, but he didn't answer. The fear was there—just beneath the surface, a glint in his eye that hadn't been there the last time. This time, she hadn't run. Not yet.

She turned from him, her hands trembling, and forced herself to walk—not to flee, though her legs itched to. Whispers rose in her wake. She could feel them latching on, crawling across her skin like smoke from a smothered fire.

It wasn't until the last cottage had passed behind her that she broke into a run.

The wind clawed at her cloak as she bolted down the road, lungs burning, feet pounding against the frozen ground. Her heart beat like it was trying to climb out of her chest.

Gatty didn't stop until Blythewood's gate loomed before her once more, and even then she didn't pause to catch her breath. She pushed through, wild and breathless, the quiet cold of the Hall closing around her like a cloak.

"You look like you've seen a ghost," came Violet's voice, sharp and real, cutting through the blur in Gatty's mind like a lifeline.

Gatty turned instinctively, breath catching. Violet stood in the shadow of a side door, sleeves rolled up, an apple core in one hand, concern etched across her usually bright face.

"What happened?" she asked, stepping closer.

Gatty opened her mouth, but no sound came. She pressed a trembling hand to her forehead, brushing away a curl damp with sweat. "It's nothing," she managed.

"Don't insult me," Violet said, her tone low but urgent. "You're white as linen, and your hands are shaking. What was it?"

For a breath, Gatty hesitated. Then the words tumbled out before she could stop them. "I saw someone. From before."

Violet's posture stiffened. Her teasing nature vanished like a snuffed flame. "From your old village?"

Gatty nodded, her throat tight. "Edward Fenton. He saw me. Called me by name. Said I'd drowned."

Violet swore under her breath, her eyes flicking to the empty path beyond the gate. "He's sure?"

"He called me Carter. And witch." The name felt like ash in Gatty's mouth. "Loud enough for half the square to hear."

Violet didn't waste another word. She grabbed Gatty's arm and steered her toward the kitchen entrance, moving fast and low. "Come on."

"I can't stay here," Gatty whispered, the panic blooming in her chest like wildfire. "If he tells someone—if he comes back—"

"He won't," Violet cut in, her grip tightening. "You're not on a village green anymore. You're at Blythewood. And no one gets through those gates without Helena's say."

The kitchen door creaked open, releasing a wash of warmth and the scent of yeast and smoke. Gatty stumbled inside, the heat colliding with her icy skin in a way that made her knees weak.

Violet pulled the door shut behind them, then turned, her voice lower now but fierce. "Listen to me. Helena's not some simpering lady of the house. If Edward Fenton comes sniffing around, she'll know before his boot hits the first step."

Gatty stared at her, unsure whether to laugh or cry.

"And the rest of us?" Violet continued, softer now. "We may not look it, but we stand together when it matters. You're one of us, Gatty. You're not alone in this."

The words settled over her slowly, like a blanket she hadn't realized she needed. Gatty couldn't quite believe them yet—not all the way—but the cold inside her chest loosened a little. She gave a small nod.

"Good," Violet said, her voice losing some of its edge. "Now sit. Breathe."

And just like that, the world felt a little less sharp around the edges.

—

The library was dim and cool, a welcome retreat from the warmth and noise of the kitchens. Gatty slipped inside and shut the door behind her with a quiet thud, the sound muffled by the thick stone walls. The scent of parchment and leather greeted her like a familiar voice, steadying the chaos still churning in her chest.

Leander sat at his usual table, sleeves rolled to the elbow, a book open before him. His fingers twirled a quill with idle precision, though his eyes flicked up the moment she entered—sharp, green, and unexpectedly alert.

"You again," he greeted. "I've half a mind to start charging you for the privilege of disturbing me."

"Then you'll have to take it out of my wages," Gatty replied, though the words came out flat. "Should I leave?"

"No." Leander said too quickly. "You're pale."

"I'm always pale."

"Not like this." He closed his book with a quiet snap. The scrape of his chair followed, and then his steps—unhurried, deliberate—as he crossed toward her. Gatty turned away, pretending to study the rows of spines that towered above.

"Why does something always have to have happened?" she muttered.

"Because," he said gently, "when someone looks like they've seen a ghost, it's usually because they have. Or worse."

Gatty's fingers rested on the edge of a dusty shelf, her knuckles white. "I don't want to talk about it."

"Then don't."

She turned. He stood just a few feet away, not looming, not demanding—simply present. His expression wasn't pitying, and it wasn't cold. Just watchful. Patient.

The silence stretched between them, soft and deep, broken only by the creak of the old beams and the scratch of a draft against the windows. Gatty let out a breath. "I saw someone," she said at last. "From before. From the village."

His face didn't change, but she saw something flicker in his eyes—understanding, maybe. Recognition. "And now you're afraid they'll follow you here."

She nodded once. "He said my name. Called me a ghost."

"You've been called worse, I imagine."

That earned a small, startled laugh from her. "More times than I can count."

Leander leaned back against the table, arms loosely crossed, still watching her. "Did you run?"

"Of course I ran." She bristled. "Would you have stood there smiling?"

"No," he said after a beat. "Running was wise."

She blinked. "You don't sound surprised."

"I'm not." His voice was low. "Books aren't the only things that hide in quiet places, Miss Carter."

That stopped her. She studied him, really studied him—the shadows under his eyes, the tightness in his shoulders, the way his hands always seemed to want something to do. He didn't just live in the library. He hid in it.

"I don't intend to live in the shadows forever," she said.

His gaze sharpened. "No?"

"No," Gatty said again, firmer this time.

Leander nodded once, slowly. "Then you'll need to be careful. And clever."

"I am both."

"I believe it."

It wasn't a compliment, not exactly. But something in the way he said it—quiet, certain—slipped under her guard. She looked down at her ink-stained fingers, unsure what to do with the sudden warmth in her chest.

Leander returned to his table without ceremony. "If you've nothing better to do, you might as well make yourself useful. I've herbs to catalog and no assistant worth the name."

Gatty raised a brow. "I'm no one's assistant."

"You are," he said dryly, "until the stack is sorted."

She considered arguing. But the room felt calm, and safe in a way she hadn't known she needed. With a small sigh, she crossed to the table and picked up a book.

They worked in quiet rhythm, the crackle of pages and scratch of quills filling the space. Every so often, Leander muttered to himself, and Gatty would glance at him—at the way he frowned in thought or tapped the end of his pen against his lip. She didn't interrupt. She just kept working.

Time passed. The candle burned low, and her shoulders ached with stillness. She set down her pen and leaned back with a groan.

"You've done well," Leander said, not looking up.

"You sound surprised."

"I'm rarely surprised," he replied. "But it's pleasant when it happens."

She rolled her eyes but couldn't quite suppress her smile. "Goodnight, Mr. Hawthorne."

"Goodnight, Miss Carter." There was a softness to it this time. Not warm, not gentle, but something quieter.

Gatty stepped out into the hall, the cool air brushing her cheeks. Edward Fenton's voice still echoed faintly in her mind, but it no longer rang so loud. The weight of it, for now, had been dulled—smoothed over by books, and ink, and the surprising steadiness of a man who rarely said what he meant, but meant it all the same.

I'll not have my life taken from me, she thought again, walking into the dark. *Not by him. Not by anyone.*

Chapter Eleven

KNOWLEDGE IS POWER

The morning air bit through Gatty's borrowed shawl like sharpened teeth. She stood at the threshold of the poison garden, her breath curling white against the stillness. The space beyond the stone archway was cloistered and cold, the walls high and moss-laced, as though trying to keep the world out—or keep something in. The plants huddled in crooked rows, their blackened leaves rimed with frost. This wasn't a garden so much as a warning.

Helena Hartford waited in the archway like an omen in human form, her dark cloak lifting in the breeze.

"You'll tend to the plants today, Miss Carter," she said, her voice quiet but unmistakably final. "They must be trimmed before rot takes hold. Leave nothing to waste."

Gatty's fingers flexed inside her gloves. "And if one of them poisons me?"

Helena's mouth twitched—not quite a smile. "Then you'll have learned a lesson the hard way. The garden has no mercy for the careless. Do be mindful, Miss Carter. The plants may not speak, but they remember." Without waiting for a reply, Helena turned and disappeared into the Hall, her silhouette swallowed by the heavy doors that shut behind her with a sound like judgment.

Left alone, Gatty turned back to the garden. The smell met her first—earthy, acrid, with a bitter edge like torn green stems steeped in something older than decay. Each row was marked by wooden placards carved with curling Latin. The letters meant little to her, but the plants didn't need translation.

To her right, henbane—its hollowed stalks rattling in the wind like windchimes made of bone. To her left, foxglove—its shriveled bells still clinging to the stems like ghosts refusing to go. Even in death, the poison clung to them.

Her mother's voice rose in her memory, calm and firm: *A careful hand, Gatty. Poison's only poison if you forget to show it respect.*

She crossed to the workbench, picked up the iron shears—blades honed thin and gleaming as razors—and tucked the leather satchel under her arm. The metal burned cold through her gloves.

Monkshood stood waiting along the far wall like a sentry line, its once-deep blooms now frost-blackened and curling inward. Aconite.

Wolf's bane. Her mother had spoken those names in a whisper, the way priests speak of sin.

Gatty crouched, the chill soaking through her skirts as she pressed the shears to a brittle stalk. "What did you do," she murmured, "to earn such a name?"

The shears snapped. The sound echoed through the walled garden like a crack of judgment. Gatty felt it in her bones—how the silence shifted, the way the plants seemed to lean closer. Not alive, not watching—but somehow aware. The wind stilled. Her breath caught.

As the minutes dragged, her unease grew—not from the cold, but from the weight of something old that hung in the air like damp wool. This place was no longer just a garden. It was a graveyard of knowledge that had once bloomed bright, then curdled in silence.

Near the final row, something odd caught her eye—a wooden marker half-swallowed by soil and time. Its edges were jagged, weathered, as if teeth had gnawed them. Gatty brushed away the dirt with trembling fingers. Beneath the moss, carved in cramped and careful hand, were the words:

Beware what takes root.

A chill coiled at the base of her spine. Someone else had worked this garden. Someone who'd known enough to leave a warning behind.

The groan of the iron gate snapped through the stillness like a warning bell. Gatty jolted upright, the shears slipping slightly in her gloved hand. She turned fast, heart hammering, but it was only Violet, framed in the arched doorway, her arms crossed against the cold.

"Blazing hells, you look like you've been hexed," Violet said with a grin, stepping forward. Her red hair burned bright against the winter-grey light, a spark in the shadows. "Did the flowers start whispering sweet nothings?"

"If they did," Gatty muttered, scowling, "they've no business knowing my secrets."

Violet laughed, but her eyes swept the garden with less amusement. Her gaze snagged on the row of monkshood, and something in her expression tightened—subtle, but there. "Helena's got you trimming the worst of the lot," she said, her tone lighter than her posture. "She must think you've got surgeon's hands."

"Or she wants to see if I'll poison myself," Gatty muttered. She hesitated, then nodded toward the half-buried marker. "Someone's been here before. Left a warning."

Violet followed her gaze. Her expression stilled—just for a beat—before she said, too evenly, "Plenty have."

The breeze stirred between them, lifting the edge of Violet's cloak.

"This garden's older than the Hall itself," she added. "It doesn't forget the women who've passed through it."

"What's that supposed to mean?"

Violet tilted her head, her grin returning, though this one was knife-edged. "It means Helena doesn't waste her time on girls who bore her. If you're out here, she's waiting to see what sort of root you'll grow."

Gatty's grip tightened on the shears. The iron weight in her hand grounded her—cold, solid, unforgiving. "Hopefully I'll give her something worth remembering."

Violet studied her, the sharpness fading from her grin. "Careful," she said softly. "Ambition can be a poison too. Tastes sweet going down. Turns sour when you least expect." She turned and strolled toward the gate, her boots crunching over frostbitten gravel. "Finish up before the cold finishes you. I'll fetch you when dinner's up—if you're not part of the compost heap by then."

The gate groaned closed behind her, and Gatty was alone again—just her, the frost, and the garden that never forgot.

She looked down at the marker once more, the carved warning stark in the dirt.

Beware what takes root.

The rest of the trimming passed in silence. Gatty worked until her fingers were numb and her back throbbed from bending. Her boots squelched in damp soil, her gloves damp with sap and something colder. The monkshood no longer looked half-dead—it looked sharpened, watchful. She couldn't shake the sense that something beneath the earth had stirred.

She placed the final stalk in the satchel and hefted it. It weighed no more than a loaf of bread—but it felt heavier. Heavy with knowledge. Heavy with threat.

"Full of death," she murmured, "and light as a feather."

She pulled the satchel strap over her shoulder and stood, squinting toward the sky as if it might answer the question pulsing at the back of her mind: Who left that warning? And what exactly had they survived—or not?

She turned toward the gate, the words echoing in her mind like a spell.

Beware what takes root.

From beyond the iron gate, the gravel whispered underfoot—slow, deliberate. Gatty turned, expecting Violet again.

But it was him.

Leander moved like a shadow stitched from ink, his long wool coat flaring behind him as he stepped into the garden. In one hand he carried a leather-bound book, its spine weathered, its corners softened by years of use.

Gatty straightened. She had seen Leander in many moods—irritated, unreadable, smug—but never out of place. And here, beneath the bare-limbed trees and watching plants in the clear light of day, he looked utterly foreign. Like something summoned.

"Well," he said, his gaze sweeping the rows she'd trimmed and the satchel at her feet. "You didn't perish."

"Not for lack of trying," Gatty replied, brushing the damp earth from her skirts. "Did Helena send you to see if I'd collapsed mid-task?"

Leander arched a brow. "Helena doesn't send me anywhere. I'm not one of her hounds." His eyes drifted to the satchel again. "You finished the work. That puts you ahead of most."

Gatty narrowed her eyes. "If you've come to gloat or scold, you're wasting your breath. I'm not one of your books to annotate."

To her surprise, a flicker of amusement crossed his face. "No," he said, coolly. "But you do look like a particularly smudged page." He gestured vaguely toward her dirt-streaked face, the dried sap on her gloves. "What did the garden do to you?"

"It's not the garden," Gatty snapped. "It's the woman who sent me into it."

Leander's expression sobered. He studied her with the kind of attention that made her spine stiffen—not cruel, but curious. "You think Helena meant to punish you?"

"I think she's trying to wear me down," Gatty muttered. "Like she's done with others."

Leander was quiet. Then, almost too softly, he asked, "And has she?"

The question caught her off guard. Gatty looked up, pulse tightening. He stood still, the frost-paled garden casting long shadows around him like warning lines.

"Not yet," she said.

Something shifted in his expression—too brief to name, but it landed like a thread of approval.

"Then perhaps," Leander said, "you're stronger than you believe."

Gatty blinked. The words—unexpected, undemanding—lodged somewhere deep. Before she could reply, Leander knelt beside her and placed the book gently on the old bench.

"Come," he said, nodding toward the satchel. "You've done the trimming. Let's see if you can read what it means."

"A map?" Gatty asked, dubious.

He opened the book, revealing pages of detailed diagrams: rows marked with Latin names, roots sketched in delicate ink, blooms rendered in careful strokes. Margins bore tiny notes in curling script. She spotted the monkshood instantly, the drawing too precise to mistake—its warnings penned in red.

"You should study this one as well," Leander said, voice quiet now, almost coaxing. "Knowledge is power, Miss Carter. If you're sharp enough to use it."

Gatty stared. The page felt alive beneath her eyes, heavy with risk and promise. Her mother's words rose again, whispering through her memory: *A careful hand, a keen mind. Know the earth, and it will serve you.*

She glanced up. "Why show me this?" she asked. "I thought you preferred I kept out of your way."

"I dislike waste," Leander replied, tone clipped. "You're not a waste. You're—stubborn. But useful."

Gatty opened her mouth to argue, but shut it again. She traced the jagged edge of a henbane leaf inked in the margin. "And if Helena's testing me?"

"Then don't fail."

He stood again. Gatty looked up at him, torn between suspicion and something perilously close to gratitude.

Before she could speak, he turned toward the gate, coat snapping in the wind. "Learn well, Miss Carter," he called over his shoulder. "You'll need it."

The gate groaned as it closed behind him, its hinges shrieking like a closing chapter.

———

After scrubbing the sap from her hands and changing into a warmer shawl, Gatty found herself at the library door before she'd quite made the decision to go. The heavy oak opened with a familiar creak, and the scent of lamp oil, ink, and dust wrapped around her like a second cloak.

The fire was low in the grate, casting long shadows against the tall windows and gilded shelves. Leander stood at his usual table, bent over a spread of papers, his coat draped across the back of a nearby chair.

He glanced up when the door clicked shut behind her. "You came," he said simply. There was no sarcasm in his tone—only acknowledgment. "I was hoping you would."

Gatty hesitated at the threshold, the second leather-bound book clutched tightly to her chest. "You said I should learn."

Leander nodded once, then gestured to the chair across from him. "Then let's begin."

She crossed the room, moving more slowly than usual, and set the book down. The fire's warmth touched her back as she took her seat. Leander slid his notes aside to make room for the volume between them.

"I thought librarians were supposed to be possessive of their books," Gatty said, tracing the cover with one finger. "You gave me both freely."

"I did." His mouth lifted into a quiet, reluctant smile. "But neither is just a book. It's a conversation. And I'd rather not speak alone."

Gatty blinked. "Is that how you see reading?"

"Often," Leander replied. "Especially when the book has something to say."

He opened it to a familiar page and tapped a sketch of henbane with his fingertip. "Let's begin here. What do you know of this one?"

She frowned. "Henbane. My mother used to say it could make you mad. But also that it dulled pain. It was one of the ones she warned me not to touch."

"She was right," Leander said. "Hyoscyamus niger. It was used as an anesthetic by some surgeons a hundred years ago—if they could get the dose right. Too little and the patient woke screaming. Too much, and they never woke at all."

He sat back, studying her expression. "It's a delicate plant. Like most things worth understanding."

Gatty folded her arms, leaning slightly over the page. "You know a lot about things that kill."

"I know a lot about things that can also heal," he said. "The line between them is often intention. Or error."

Gatty was quiet for a moment, eyes moving over the illustration. "Did you draw this?"

He nodded. "Most of them, yes."

"They're careful. Clean." She glanced at him. "A bit like you."

He looked genuinely surprised by that, though not displeased. "I'll take that as a compliment. Though I'm sure there are worse things to be called in this Hall."

Gatty looked down at the notes scribbled in the margin of one page. "Do you write in all your books?"

"Only the ones worth arguing with."

Her brow lifted. "You argue with plants?"

"Sometimes. But more often with the people who believe they understand them."

That made her smile. She turned another page—foxglove this time, drawn with its bell-like flowers and a long note about dosage. "It's strange, isn't it?" she said. "That men like you write about these things in books, but women like me are called witches for knowing them."

Leander was still for a moment, then closed his hands lightly around the edge of the table. "It's not right. But it's not new. Men are rewarded for what women are punished for."

"Especially when it comes to knowledge," Gatty said softly.

He met her eyes. "Especially then."

The fire cracked, filling the space between them with warmth and quiet tension. Leander glanced back down at the page.

"There's a passage in one of the older texts," he said. "Written by a monk who catalogued healing plants. He claimed women should never be taught to read because 'they would misuse the words, the way they misuse herbs—overmuch and without restraint.'"

Gatty snorted. "And what, men always get the dose right?"

"From my own experience..." Leander gave a quiet laugh, genuine and low. "Rarely."

Their eyes met again, and Gatty felt the flutter of something unexpected—not sharp or startling, but warm and slow and curious. She looked away, pretending to study the next page. "I've been thinking," she said. "If I learn all this... if I remember every name and every warning—"

"Then it's yours," Leander said gently. "No one can take it from you. Not even Helena."

Gatty swallowed hard. "It doesn't make me a witch, does it?"

"No," he said. "It makes you dangerous. In the best way."

She looked back at him, startled by the quiet certainty in his tone. "You're not afraid of that?"

"I think I am, a bit." His expression turned more serious. And yet he was still here, seated across from her in the firelight, turning pages.

"Will you keep teaching me?" she asked.

"As long as you keep asking questions," he said. Then, after a pause, he added, "And maybe, now and then, you'll let me ask one too."

Gatty tilted her head. "Such as?"

Leander leaned forward slightly, his voice barely above a whisper. "What made you so determined not to be broken by this harsh world?"

The question caught her off guard, but she didn't answer. Not yet. Instead, she looked down at the page between them. "Henbane," she said again. "Madness in the wrong hands."

Leander's voice was quiet, steady. "Wisdom in the right ones."

And for the first time since the garden, Gatty felt something bloom—not fear, not anger, but the sense that someone had seen her and not looked away.

Leander rested his elbows lightly on the table's edge. "The line between poison and remedy is thin," he said, not with warning, but with quiet awe. "Most of the plants in Helena's garden walk it better than we do."

Gatty looked down at the inked page. Her finger hovered just above the sketch of henbane. "And she wants me to walk that line, too?"

"She does," he said.

"Why?" Her tone sharpened despite her best effort. "What is she testing for?"

He leaned back, folding his arms. For a moment, the firelight danced in his eyes, and he seemed older, more worn—like someone who'd read too many truths and still hadn't found a comforting lie. "Helena tests for many things," he said at last. "Strength. Obedience. Cleverness. But mostly—endurance. She wants to know who will bend, and who will break."

Gatty's breath caught. Endure. The word clanged hollow in her chest, bringing with it too many memories of what it had cost her already. She looked back at the drawings—clean, careful, neat. Labeled with warnings. As though knowledge alone could prevent what the world might do to you.

"And you?" she asked, voice low. "What are you testing for?"

That question made him still. His gaze didn't harden—didn't flash—but turned inward, as though she'd reached deeper than she meant to. "I don't test people, Miss Carter," he said, and there was something steady and clear in the way he said it. "I observe. I record. There's a difference."

"But you notice things," she pressed. "You see what Helena does. What she wants."

His eyes flicked to hers, watchful and unreadable. "I see what I'm allowed to."

That didn't sound like obedience. It sounded like restraint. Gatty held his gaze a moment longer. "Do you ever wonder why she wants us here at all?"

That cracked something. Not much, but enough. A flicker passed through his expression—a door just barely opening, only to be shut again before she could see inside. "You ask a great many questions, Miss Carter."

"Better than asking none at all," she replied, and for once, there was no bite behind it.

Leander looked at her then, really looked. Not with suspicion or irritation, but with the strange reverence of someone seeing something they hadn't expected. Slowly, he nodded. "Perhaps."

The silence that followed was warm, not heavy. Gatty let out a breath she hadn't known she was holding and turned back to the book. Her fingers drifted to the margin, where the handwriting changed—messier, urgent. "Who wrote this?" she asked, tilting the book toward him.

Leander leaned closer, scanning the cramped script. "That's not mine," he said, almost to himself. "It's older. Could've belonged to one of Helena's... students. Or patients. Or projects, as she once called them."

"Projects?" Gatty's voice caught on the word.

Leander's eyes met hers again. "You're not the first woman to be brought to Blythewood Hall, Miss Carter." He didn't say it coldly—just plainly, as though it was a truth he didn't want to shield her from. "And you won't be the last."

The words struck like a stone dropped in deep water. She stared down at the page again, her thoughts pulled tight with questions she couldn't yet name.

Leander rose, the chair scraping softly against the stone. He adjusted the cuffs of his shirt, then looked down at her—his expression unreadable, but not unkind. "Keep studying," he said. "Knowledge is the only weapon you're allowed to carry here."

As his figure disappeared into the dim corridors beyond the shelves, Gatty was left alone in the firelight. The book lay open before her, its illustrations as fine and ordered as the world refused to be.

Knowledge is power, she thought again. But power—she was beginning to see—was never freely given. Her gaze returned to the scribbled notes, the frantic edge in the ink that betrayed their author's fear or desperation.

"Test the dose... weaker than expected..."
"Leaves respond well to frost—curious..."
"She could not endure. Burned the root."

Gatty sat motionless. These weren't idle notations. They were evidence. Traces of someone who had walked the same line Helena now asked her to toe—and had failed.

The fire snapped behind her, but she barely noticed. Her hand hovered over the page, and her pulse thudded like a drum beneath her skin.

She would not burn the root. She would learn it—its uses, its lies, its power—and then decide how to wield it.

The faint creak of a door pulled Gatty's attention up. She sat back as Violet slipped into the library, her red hair catching the firelight and throwing copper sparks through the dimness. She carried a basket filled with parchment scraps and splintered quills, muttering under her breath like someone waging war against paper.

"Tell me you're not still buried under that old muck," Violet said, setting the basket down with theatrical flair. "The dust alone will choke you before the monkshood gets a chance."

Gatty offered a tired smile. "I thought you were the one who called me a smudged page."

"And look at you—still smudged." Violet plopped into the chair opposite her and leaned forward to peer at the book. Her brows lifted. "Ah. The poison primer. Leander's favorite bedtime story."

"You've read it?"

"Bits. Enough to know he guards it like it's scripture." She tugged a broken quill from the basket and twirled it idly between her fingers. "Leander spends half his hours in here muttering over margins like they'll speak back. Not that he's ever thanked me for keeping the ink in stock."

Gatty frowned, her gaze drifting back to the open page. "He doesn't seem... feral."

Violet laughed, quiet and genuine. "You didn't see him when he arrived. Helena brought him back from somewhere—never said where—and for months, he barely spoke. Just scribbled and sulked and refused to make eye contact with anyone under the age of fifty." She smirked. "Honestly, we were all a little afraid of him."

"And now?"

"Now he's still odd," Violet said cheerfully. "But useful. Quiet men make better listeners. And better librarians, I suppose."

Gatty traced her thumb along the edge of the page, where ink faded into rough paper. "Why are you telling me this?"

Violet shrugged, her grin tilting sideways. "Because it helps to know the shape of a person before you decide whether to trust them." She stood, brushing dust from her skirts. "And because I think...I *know* he likes you, in the way one heart finds another kindred spirit."

Gatty looked up sharply.

Violet's eyes gleamed with mischief. "He gave you that," she said, nodding to the book. "Is that the second book? He doesn't lend those out lightly."

Gatty felt the weight of it again—the leather-bound tome filled with knowledge, warnings, margins scribbled by lost hands. It had been placed in hers deliberately. Not as a trap. As a key.

Violet nudged her shoulder gently. "Come on. Let's leave his dusty kingdom before he reappears and starts quoting Latin at us. You'll need a clear head to make sense of all this."

Gatty didn't move right away. But then she closed the book with care, pressing the cover down until it whispered shut. The sound felt final and promising all at once.

She rose and followed Violet out, their footsteps soft on the stone floor. The library exhaled behind them—quiet, watchful, waiting.

Knowledge is power, Gatty thought again. And now, she wasn't so afraid of what she might do with it.

Chapter Twelve

QUESTIONS AND ANSWERS

The parlor at Blythewood Hall was as cold and somber as its mistress that morning. Gatty knelt near the hearth, a rag clutched in her hand as she scrubbed at the soot-streaked tiles. The fire crackled halfheartedly, as though it too were reluctant to warm the vast, shadowed room. From her position, Gatty could feel the weight of the silence—thick, humming, and heavy as damp wool—and she dared not make a sound.

Lydia Eversley stood by the frost-clouded window, one gloved hand resting on the thick velvet curtain. Her posture was stiff, her gaze pinned to the distant trees, as though she could will away whatever storm was gathering beyond the glass. Behind her, James Hartford leaned against the fireplace mantel, one boot crossed over the other, turning a silver coin idly between his fingers. The coin caught the firelight in rhythmic flickers, casting brief glints along the walls.

Gatty worked quietly, her hands steady but her ears sharp. She'd been sent to clean the hearth—one of Lydia's favored punishments, she suspected, for having the gall to smirk when Violet had whispered something unkind under her breath. Now, she was a shadow in the room, beneath notice, which suited her fine—especially given the tension vibrating between the other two occupants.

"They're driving me to madness," Lydia said suddenly, her voice cutting through the stillness like glass underfoot. "Do you know what I caught two of them doing yesterday? Fighting over a crust of bread in the courtyard like stray dogs. Is this what Helena expects me to manage? A squawking flock of hens with their feathers half-plucked?"

Gatty kept her head down, scrubbing in slow, even circles. The rasp of the brush against stone barely registered over Lydia's sharp tone.

"They're frightened," James said quietly. "Fear makes fools of us all."

"Fear is not an excuse for chaos," Lydia snapped, whirling from the window. Her skirts swished as she crossed the room, stopping near the fire. "Helena expects results. Clean lines. Control. Instead, I have unruly girls and a household held together with string."

She stood just beside the hearth now, her presence looming. For a moment, Gatty thought Lydia might glance down and notice her kneeling there, hands raw from lye and heat—but her eyes remained fixed on James.

"And you," Lydia continued, her voice dropping low. "You stand there as if it has nothing to do with you. But it will. When the magistrate comes sniffing around, when some wandering curate gets wind of our... arrangements, what will you say then? That it's all just whispers? Is that enough?"

The coin stilled between James's fingers. "There's no proof," he said softly. But his voice held no comfort. It was the sound of someone bracing for winter.

"Proof?" Lydia let out a dry, brittle laugh. "Men like the magistrate don't need proof. They need only to catch the scent of something unseemly—and we both know they'll find it. We've given them enough shadows to follow."

Gatty's hand paused on the hearthstone. She glanced up, her gaze flicking between them. They stood like two statues in a tomb—cold, carved from the same marble, and caught mid-reckoning.

Then came a knock, light as a bird tapping on the glass. The parlor door creaked open, and in slipped Charlotte, her curls bouncing, her cheeks flushed. Her doll dangled from one hand like a tired companion.

"Mama," she chirped, blithely unaware of the room's temperature. Her eyes found James and brightened. "Uncle James! Mama says you look like a thundercloud when you frown."

Gatty saw it happen—the tension drop from James's shoulders, the subtle shift in his face. His smile, when it came, was small but true.

"Does she now?" he asked, crouching to the girl's level. "I'll have to smile more often. Can't have the horses bolting."

Charlotte giggled, a bright sound that cracked through the gloom like sunlight through stormclouds. Gatty, still kneeling, watched from her corner—this strange domestic tableau unfolding. Lydia's sharpness dulled by her daughter's presence, James's coolness warmed by something almost paternal. Almost.

"Charlotte," Lydia said, her voice taut, though not as severe as before, "what have I told you about knocking?"

The girl ducked her head, chastened. "Sorry, Mama."

"She's only curious," James offered gently, rising to his feet again.

Lydia's gaze cut to him, unreadable. "Curiosity is a luxury."

"Sometimes," James said, his tone even. "Sometimes it's the only thing left worth keeping."

For a beat, silence held. Then Charlotte tugged at James's sleeve and whispered something in his ear—words Gatty didn't catch. James gave her a quiet nod and tapped his finger to his lips, solemn as a vow.

"Off with you, little mouse," he murmured.

Charlotte scampered off, the doll trailing behind like a second shadow. The door clicked shut behind her, and Lydia's expression sealed over again like wax.

"You indulge her," she said, though the words came without venom.

"And you don't," James replied, not looking at her.

There was something else there now, something layered beneath the sparring—an understanding sharpened by history. Gatty couldn't name it, but she could feel it. It pressed into the room's edges, thick as the smoke curling from the hearth. It wasn't romance writ bold—but something older, wearier, and deeply kept.

"She'll have no place in this world if she grows up soft," Lydia said quietly, turning her face toward the window again.

James didn't answer.

Then Lydia's gaze shifted—and landed squarely on Gatty.

"Are you still here?"

Gatty started, knocking her brush against the hearth. "You told me to clean the tiles, ma'am."

Lydia studied her with the kind of scrutiny that could peel paint from plaster. "Then finish quickly and go to the library. Leander will put you to better use."

"Yes, ma'am," Gatty murmured, rising stiffly.

She gathered her pail and rag, her heart thudding as she crossed the parlor's threshold. But just before she passed into the hall, James's voice stopped her.

"Miss Carter."

She turned, glancing back.

James's expression was unreadable. "Be careful where you dig. The roots here run deep."

The fire popped behind him. Gatty nodded once, then slipped away.

She didn't look back—but she didn't forget.

The library felt different after what Gatty had overheard in the parlor. Her pulse still thudded faintly in her ears as she stepped into the cavernous room. It was colder than she remembered, the tall windows frosting at their edges like pale lacework. Shadows stretched long between the towering bookshelves, and the scent of old paper, beeswax polish, and leather mingled with the sharp bite of winter air.

"You move like a ghost."

Leander's voice came from the far end of the room. Gatty turned, startled, to find him behind the large oak desk, surrounded by a thicket of parchment and ledgers. His spectacles were pushed up onto his forehead, and his dark coat hung over the back of the chair. A book lay open in front of him, but he didn't seem to be reading it anymore.

"I was told to help," Gatty said, her tone guarded but polite as she stepped fully into the room. "If you've too many ledgers, I've two hands going to waste."

He leaned back slightly, the faintest suggestion of a smile tugging at his mouth. "Then it seems you've come just in time. I was starting to think the ink might stage a rebellion."

She arched a brow. "Does it often?"

"Only when provoked."

There was a beat of quiet. The library seemed to settle around them, as though listening.

He gestured toward a nearby table stacked high with cracked, aging volumes. "You'd be doing me a kindness to sort those. Alphabetically, if it pleases you. Or by size, if alphabet's had its day."

Gatty crossed to the table and eyed the heap. "If I touch them, will they fall apart?"

"Not if you're gentle." His tone was mild, not teasing, and when she glanced over, his eyes met hers without flinching. "Most things respond well to care, Miss Carter. Even books."

She let out a slow breath and reached for the first volume. Its spine was worn, the lettering half-gone, but her hands were steady. "Seems a great many books for one house."

"Seems a great many secrets for one house," Leander said quietly.

Gatty looked up, but he was already turning back to his desk, dipping his quill again in ink. The scratch of it filled the silence.

After a moment, she asked, "Do you read them all?"

His answer came without pause. "Not all. But enough."

"What do you find in them?"

"Sometimes history. Sometimes warnings. Sometimes women."

That last word made her glance up again, but Leander didn't clarify. He didn't need to. She thought of the margins in the garden manual, of the way Blythewood gathered stories like pressed flowers between its walls. Not all of them survived.

"I like women who read," he added, almost as an afterthought. "It's rarer than it should be."

Gatty's fingers paused on a book's spine. "I wasn't supposed to. In my village, I mean. My mother taught me when no one was looking."

Leander looked up at that, his expression softening. "A wise mother."

"She died before she could show me much else," Gatty said, more quietly than she meant to.

Leander nodded once, solemn. "Then the rest is yours to uncover."

They lapsed into silence again, the hush companionable this time. Gatty eased into the rhythm of sorting. The air smelled of dust and something faintly herbal—lavender, perhaps, from the sachets Helena insisted on keeping between the shelves. A kind of calm crept over her, fragile but welcome.

Until she opened the heavy cover of a ledger and something slipped out.

It was a slip of parchment—newer than the book it had been tucked inside. Folded crisply. Her fingers hesitated, then carefully opened it.

A list.

Names. Some crossed out. Others underlined. A sharp stroke of ink bisected the top corner.

Her heart gave a jolt.

"Don't meddle."

Gatty jumped, dropping the paper. It fluttered to the floor like a fallen feather. She spun around to find Leander standing only a few paces away. He hadn't raised his voice, but it echoed in the space between them.

"I wasn't meddling," she said quickly, though her voice caught. "It was just... there."

Leander didn't step closer. He stooped and retrieved the parchment, folding it without looking at it, and slipped it into his coat pocket. His expression wasn't angry—but it was unreadable, like a sealed page she wasn't yet allowed to open.

"Some things in this house are meant to stay where they've been hidden," he said. "That list among them."

Gatty's throat tightened. "Are they names of the women who came before?"

A pause. Then: "Yes."

She swallowed. "Why are some of them crossed out?"

Leander studied her. For a moment, she thought he might lie. But he didn't.

"Because some left. And some didn't."

His voice wasn't cruel, only honest.

"I don't scare easily," she said.

He held her gaze. "I believe you."

The words weren't flattery, and they weren't pity. They were something else—acknowledgment, maybe. A quiet offering of trust.

Leander stepped back toward the desk, the firelight flickering against his ink-smudged sleeve.

"You're not the only one trying to understand this place," he said as he sat. "But be careful where you look, Miss Carter. Even books have teeth."

She returned to the stack of volumes, her pulse still steady but her mind racing. She didn't ask any more questions—not yet.

But she would.

As she returned to sorting the books, her hands trembled faintly, but not from fear. Something was happening at Blythewood Hall—something larger than tricks and whispers—and she couldn't shake the feeling that she was already in far deeper than she'd meant to be.

By the time Gatty finished, the light filtering through the tall library windows had faded to a pale gray, clinging stubbornly to the edges of the room. She straightened her back, wincing as her muscles protested, and wiped her dust-smudged hands on her apron.

At the far end of the room, the steady scratch of Leander's quill continued like a clock's ticking. He hadn't spoken since retrieving the folded parchment, but the weight of his silence felt less like dismissal and more like shared contemplation.

"Is there anything else you'd have me do?" Gatty asked, her voice cutting gently through the quiet.

Leander didn't look up at once. When he did, his gaze was thoughtful, not critical. "You're not one of the maids, Miss Carter. You don't need to ask permission to rest."

She lifted a brow. "I'm not very good at resting."

He hummed faintly, as though unsurprised, then reached for a ledger—thick, leather-bound, and worn at the corners. He slid it toward her across the polished desk. "If you're truly set on usefulness, this one needs delivering to Helena."

Gatty approached, laying her hand on the book. Its weight was oddly alive, like it knew what it carried.

"Afraid of a few pages?" Leander asked, but there was no jest in his tone—only a quiet kind of curiosity.

"Not the pages," she said softly. "Just the woman who reads them."

He regarded her in silence for a breath, then said, with the faintest dip of his head, "She isn't as impervious as she seems. But she sees more than most."

"That's what worries me."

At that, something flickered behind Leander's eyes—not quite amusement, not quite concern. "Then go steady," he murmured. "And don't let her make you smaller than you are."

Gatty tightened her grip on the ledger, tucking it against her chest as though it might shield her. "Thank you," she said, without quite meaning to.

"You're welcome," Leander replied, and this time, he did look up—just long enough for their eyes to meet.

She turned from the desk, her skirts whispering across the stone floor, and stepped into the hall beyond.

The sconces lining the corridor guttered with weak, amber light, casting flickering shadows that clung to the walls like ivy. Gatty's footsteps echoed softly as she passed closed doors and dim recesses, each one steeped in the quiet menace Blythewood wore so easily.

The ledger was heavy in her arms. Heavier still were the thoughts pressing at her temples—Helena's warnings, the list of names, the ghost of Leander's voice: Even books have teeth.

Helena's study waited at the far end of the corridor like a sealed casket. The door was closed, the air just outside it colder than the rest of the house—as if the room within exhaled frost.

Before Gatty could knock, a voice—clear, composed—called, "Come in."

She hesitated, then pushed open the door.

The room was smaller than she expected, but no less imposing. A large oak desk occupied the center, scattered with neat stacks of parchment and bone-white porcelain teacups. A fire smoldered in the hearth, giving off more glow than heat. Helena Hartford sat behind the desk, upright, unmoving—like a figure awaiting confession.

"You're late," she said, though her tone was more observation than accusation.

Gatty blinked. "I didn't know I was expected, ma'am."

"Perhaps you should start expecting everything," Helena replied, her lips curving faintly—not in kindness, but in something colder and more precise.

Gatty stepped forward and placed the ledger on the desk, aligning its spine with the edge. Helena's eyes flicked to it, then back to her.

"Do you know what this is?"

"A ledger," Gatty answered. "It holds accounts."

"Correct," Helena murmured. She tapped one finger against the cover. "And do you know why we keep accounts, Miss Carter?"

Gatty hesitated. "To know what we have," she said slowly. "And what we've lost."

Helena's smile sharpened. "Very nearly. We keep accounts because they show patterns. Dependencies. Weaknesses. They tell us who is owed... and who is expendable."

A pause stretched between them.

"What do you think you bring to this house?" Helena asked quietly.

Gatty blinked. "Nothing, ma'am. I—I was brought here. I didn't ask to come."

Helena tilted her head, as if examining her more closely. "That may be. But you're still here. And I assure you, I rarely keep what is useless."

The flicker of firelight made Helena's eyes seem darker than they were. Gatty said nothing, her pulse quickening in her throat.

"We all have something to offer," Helena said, rising from her chair with the slow grace of a figure in a painting. She moved to stand by the hearth, her silhouette cast long across the floor. "Whether we see it or not."

She turned to face Gatty, her voice low and sure. "And I am very, very good at seeing what others cannot."

Gatty clenched her hands behind her back, resisting the urge to step away. "I'll keep that in mind."

Helena's smile returned, faint and unreadable. "See that you do."

Gatty turned to leave. As the door clicked shut behind her, she let out a breath she hadn't realized she was holding. The hallway pressed in around her once more, its quiet no longer neutral but expectant.

What had Helena meant by all that?

And worse—what if she was right?

Her thoughts spun as she passed the library again, where the faint glow of candlelight spilled beneath the door. She paused, one hand resting on the wood, debating whether to step back inside—whether she could stomach more guardedness after the cold scrutiny of Helena Hartford.

But the library called to her all the same.

Instead of opening the door, she turned away, descending the stairwell toward the garden. Outside, the air was bracing and honest. The twisted outlines of the poison beds glinted with frost beneath the waning light. She didn't enter—just stood still, breathing in the cold. Her fingers curled and uncurled against her skirts.

"We all have something to offer," Helena had said, her voice still echoing like a draft in the corridors of Gatty's mind.

Gatty scowled and kicked a loose stone across the path. "Maybe," she muttered. "But I'll decide what that is."

Eventually, she made her way back toward the library. The house creaked and shifted around her like it was listening. The sconces along the corridor flickered unevenly, casting long, shivering shadows. Blythewood Hall was its own kind of ledger, she thought—each woman within it another entry. Another debt. Another risk.

She slipped into the library again, letting the hush settle around her like a second shawl. The warmth struck her first, then the quiet. Leander was still at his desk, the tip of his quill scratching rhythmically over parchment. He didn't look up.

"Back so soon?" he asked, his tone even, without irony.

"I thought you'd still be hiding in here," Gatty replied, closing the door behind her. "But if you mean to barricade yourself all day, might I suggest lighting the fire properly? It's colder than a grave out there."

Leander's hand stilled. He glanced toward the hearth as if seeing it for the first time, then rose silently. He stoked the fire with a few practiced motions, sending sparks spiraling upward. The room brightened.

"There," he said, settling back into his chair. "No use haunting me if you're frozen through."

Gatty let out the faintest breath of amusement and crossed to the table where she'd sorted books earlier. She let her fingers skim the spines, grounding herself.

"So," she said after a moment. "Were you sent to keep an eye on me, or shall we pretend you're just exceptionally interested in my filing skills?"

He looked up at that, eyes glinting in the candlelight. "I'm interested in what people do when they think no one's watching."

"And what did I do?" she asked.

"You didn't steal the book," Leander said simply. "That counts for something."

Gatty tilted her head. "You sound disappointed."

"Hardly." He set down his quill. "Helena has eyes in many places. But not all of them are hers."

The cryptic remark lodged in Gatty's mind like a stone in a shoe. "And yours?" she asked, watching him. "Whose eyes do you serve?"

Leander didn't answer at first. Then he said, softly, "Mine serve the truth. And they're still learning how to see."

The answer surprised her. Not for its mystery—but for its honesty.

She turned back to the table and let her hand rest on a large, unmarked volume. Its leather cover was worn smooth, the faint outline of pressed vines barely visible in the flickering light.

"What's this one?"

"Physica Curiosa," Leander replied, rising and crossing the room with measured steps. "A botanical treatise. Few bother with it anymore."

"Botanical?"

"Plants," he clarified. "Their uses. Their dangers. The things people used to believe about them. Some true. Some... not."

He stopped beside her and opened the book. The pages were thick and vellum-soft, covered with finely inked drawings—roots and stems, medicinal diagrams, cryptic marginalia in Latin.

He flipped to a particular page. "Digitalis purpurea. Foxglove."

Gatty leaned in. The delicate rendering of the flower seemed to hum with quiet danger.

"And if used well?" she asked.

Leander nodded. "It can strengthen the heart. But the dose must be exact."

"So it's neither good nor bad," Gatty murmured. "Just what someone makes of it."

He looked at her then—not at the book, but directly at her. His voice, when he spoke, was quiet. "Exactly."

The fire popped behind them. She glanced up, surprised to find his expression open, unguarded.

"Why show me this?" she asked.

"Because you're curious," Leander said. "And because people have tried to cure curiosity out of you. That would be a shame."

Gatty felt something tighten in her throat. She didn't respond—she didn't have to.

The door opened behind them with a familiar creak, and Violet stepped into the room, cheeks flushed, skirts swishing around her ankles.

"There you are," she huffed, eyeing them both. "Lydia's been asking after you."

Gatty stepped back, blinking as though waking from a spell. "Has she now?"

Leander closed the book carefully, returning it to its place on the table with reverence. "Duty calls," he murmured, his expression neutral again—but Gatty caught the flicker of something quieter in his eyes. Not possession. Not demand. Just... interest.

"Always does," she replied, squaring her shoulders.

As Violet led her into the hall, she cast one last glance over her shoulder. Leander had resumed his seat but wasn't writing. He stared into the fire, his profile outlined by its flickering light.

When the library door clicked shut behind them, Violet bumped her gently with one elbow.

"Well," she said with a sly grin, "that was very nearly cozy."

Gatty snorted. "We were looking at foxglove."

"Exactly," Violet teased. "The plant that kills you or saves you depending on how you handle it. Seems appropriate."

Gatty tried to scowl, but her lips twitched despite herself.

Violet glanced sideways at her, more thoughtful now. "He doesn't look at anyone else like that, you know."

"Like what?"

"Like he's watching the stars move behind your eyes," Violet said, then shrugged as though it didn't matter. "It's not a bad thing."

Gatty didn't answer. But as they walked on through the dim corridor, something warm curled low in her chest—small and unwelcome and unshakably real.

Chapter Thirteen

A Stolen Moment

The magistrate arrived at Blythewood Hall beneath a sky the color of pewter, the clouds pressing low enough to feel like a threat. The air was thick with the scent of damp leaves and woodsmoke, heavy with the hush of a day holding its breath. Gatty knelt among the rows of frostbitten tansy, her hands buried in the earth, when the sound of hooves on gravel reached her ears. She stilled.

The rhythm was slow, deliberate—like judgment in motion.

From her vantage by the garden wall, she watched the carriage roll into the courtyard. It was unmarked but unmistakably official: sleek and dark as ink, with wheels that moved too quietly for comfort. The magistrate stepped out with military precision, his cloak settling around his boots like a dropped curtain. His face was lean, his expression honed to a practiced neutrality that felt more threatening than open anger. Behind him came two assistants, each armed with a leather-bound ledger and eyes that didn't bother to look at the women gathered near the kitchen door.

Gatty rose to her feet and brushed the dirt from her skirts, her heart drumming a wary rhythm. She heard murmurs ripple through the women—snatches of names and accusations, the rustle of worry passing hand to hand like contraband—but every whisper circled back to the same word: Helena.

Inside the Hall, the stillness pressed closer. Even the floorboards seemed to hush their creaking. When Gatty stepped into the great hall, she found Helena already waiting by the hearth, upright and composed, as though she'd been carved from ashwood and crowned with flame. Her posture held no apology. She was, Gatty realized, prepared for war—but dressed it in civility.

"Helena Hartford," the magistrate intoned as he entered, his voice cold and efficient. "I trust you were expecting me."

"I was informed of your arrival," Helena replied, her tone smooth as still water. "Though I admit, it seems a long road to travel for the governance of a humble Magdalene house."

The magistrate's lips barely moved. He had the look of a man used to quiet power, used to making others speak first. "This house has drawn attention," he said. "There are whispers of impropriety—of deviation from acceptable instruction. I'm here to see whether there's substance to those rumors."

Helena's smile didn't reach her eyes. "Impropriety, Magistrate? We offer repentance, routine, and scripture. Surely those are not offenses."

"And yet," he said, stepping forward, "your house draws a particular kind of woman. Women with pasts. Women accused—not convicted, perhaps—but named. Women touched by suspicion."

The fire crackled faintly behind Helena, but the temperature in the room dropped. Gatty lingered near the doorway, half-shadowed by a tapestry. She should have fled back to the kitchens, but something rooted her in place—something that felt like dread and defiance mingled.

"Accusation is a game of men's tongues," Helena said, not blinking. "I cannot unmake the stories the world tells about these women. I offer them work. I offer them peace."

"And in doing so," the magistrate said, "you may be offering shelter to witches."

The word landed hard, though it was spoken softly. Gatty felt it ripple through the room like a stone breaking the surface of a still pond.

Helena's expression didn't change, but her silence deepened. When she finally spoke, her voice was clipped. "Witchcraft is a relic of fear. A convenience for men who cannot understand women who won't kneel."

The magistrate tilted his head. "You dismiss it entirely?"

"I dismiss rumor. I dismiss superstition. I do not dismiss the harm they cause."

They stared at one another across the room, still as portraits. Then the magistrate turned to his assistants and gave a curt nod.

"My men will walk the house," he said. "You will permit them access."

"I have nothing to hide," Helena replied.

As the assistants were led away by a waiting maid, Helena's gaze flicked—brief, sharp—to where Gatty stood. Their eyes met, and Gatty flinched as though the weight of Helena's gaze could scorch her.

"Miss Carter," Helena said, her voice low but slicing. "Return to your duties. It would be... unwise to be seen loitering."

Gatty dipped her head and fled the hall, the beat of her pulse loud in her ears.

She didn't think—her feet moved of their own accord, carrying her toward the one place in the house where silence was a choice, not a punishment. The library.

She wasn't even sure if she meant to speak to Leander, or simply exist near him in the hush of paper and ink. All she knew was that outside the safety of walls lined with books, suspicion had entered the house like smoke—and she couldn't hold her breath forever.

As she pushed open the heavy library door, she was greeted by the familiar scent of leather and ink. Leander looked up from his desk, his expression sharpening as he noticed the tension in her face.

"The magistrate," she said breathlessly. "He's here."

Leander frowned, setting his quill aside with careful precision. "Helena warned us this might happen. What did he say?"

Gatty shook her head. "Enough to put everyone on edge. He's looking for something—or someone."

Leander's jaw tightened, his green eyes darkening, not with panic, but with focus. "Then we'd best be prepared."

The library was quiet, save for the faint scratch of Leander's quill on parchment. Gatty lingered near the door, unsure if she should speak. She'd sought refuge here instinctively, but now that she was standing in the shadow of towering shelves, the words she wanted to say felt heavy on her tongue.

Leander glanced up again, his brow lifting just slightly. "If you're planning to hover, Miss Carter, you might as well shut the door. That draft will do the ink no favors."

Gatty huffed, stepping inside and pushing the door closed with more force than necessary. "I just thought you might like to know the magistrate is nosing about the place," she said, folding her arms across her chest.

"I gathered as much," he replied, leaning back in his chair and watching her with the kind of calm that bordered on unnerving. "Helena wouldn't have allowed him through the gate unless she had no choice. The question is, what exactly is he looking for?"

Gatty moved closer to his desk, her boots whispering against the worn carpet. "Helena's playing it calm, but I could tell she's worried. He kept asking about witches and unnatural practices."

Leander's expression darkened. He tapped his fingers against the edge of the desk, then stood, the movement sudden but not abrupt. "The man's fishing—hoping to find cracks. It's the same trick every magistrate uses when they think they've caught the scent of something they can't name."

"And what happens if he finds those cracks?" Gatty asked, her voice quieter now.

Leander crossed to one of the shelves and selected a leather-bound volume with practiced ease. "Then he'll pry them open until the whole house splinters. Fear is a tool, and he knows how to wield it. The trick is not to give him anything solid to grip."

He returned to the desk and opened the book. The pages, aged and inked with precise illustrations, caught the lamplight as he turned them. Gatty watched the way his fingers moved—measured, careful, like someone used to protecting fragile things.

"Keep your head down, do your work, and let Helena steer him. She's weathered worse than this," he added, though his tone held more hope than certainty.

Gatty frowned, the heaviness in her chest settling deeper. She had spent so long trying to outrun suspicion, trying to survive its weight. Now, in the place that was meant to be her refuge, the same fear had returned like a second skin.

"Easy for you to say," she muttered. "You're not the one they'll point fingers at first."

Leander paused, one hand resting lightly on the edge of a page. He turned to face her fully, his expression unreadable, but not cold. "Do you think they'd spare me because I'm a man?" he asked quietly. "They'd call me a heretic. A corrupter. Or worse. There's no real safety here, Miss Carter—not for any of us. But knowledge..." He tapped the open page gently. "Knowledge is a weapon they can't burn."

Her eyes followed his hand as he gestured to the illustrations—roots, stems, blossoms drawn with reverent detail.

"If you want to survive," he continued, "you need to know how to protect yourself. That doesn't mean brute force. It means understanding what they fear—and how to make that fear work in your favor."

Gatty spent the next hour wandering through the library, her fingers brushing the spines of countless books. The air smelled of old paper and beeswax polish, a comforting contrast to the tension outside the library walls. Leander had returned to his work, seated at the heavy oak desk near the window, scribbling notes in his precise hand.

She wasn't sure why she stayed. Maybe it was the safety of the quiet space, or maybe it was the way Leander had spoken earlier—his quiet conviction that knowledge could be a shield. Either way, the library felt like a refuge, and Gatty allowed herself to breathe.

Her fingers paused on a thin, leather-bound book. The title, written in faded gold lettering, read *A Treatise on the Uses of Common Plants*. She pulled it from the shelf and opened it, scanning the pages. The language was dense, but the illustrations caught her eye—detailed sketches of roots and flowers, each labeled with notes on their properties.

"Good choice," Leander's voice broke the silence, startling her. She turned to see him standing a few feet away, his hands clasped behind his back. "It's not the most exciting read, but it's practical. That one belonged to a local apothecary who donated his collection to the Hall years ago."

Gatty tilted the book slightly, showing him the page she'd stopped on—a drawing of a nettle plant, its jagged leaves inked with a precision that made them look almost alive. "This says it's good for poultices and teas," she said. "But also... stinging people?"

Leander's mouth twitched, though the amusement in his expression was more thoughtful than teasing. "That's accurate. Nettles can leave quite a sting. Harmless, mostly—but memorable. It's their way of reminding the world they're not to be brushed aside."

She looked down at the page again. "So something that seems ordinary can still have power."

"Especially if it knows when to use it," Leander said. He stepped a little closer, not intruding but present, watching her take in the page. "Most people see weeds. But those who know better... see the medicine. The warning. The lesson."

Gatty closed the book slowly, her thumb brushing the soft edge of the page. "You think the women here are like that. Ordinary to some. Dangerous to others."

Leander nodded once. "It's all a matter of who's doing the looking—and what they're afraid of."

Gatty closed the book and hugged it to her chest, the smooth leather warm against her arms. "Why do you know all this? About herbs and the law and... everything?"

Leander's gaze dipped, his usual composure shifting—not gone, but momentarily less rigid. "Let's just say I've spent enough time around injustice to recognize it. I don't intend to sit idle while it spreads."

She studied him then, really studied him. The crisp lines of his coat, the ink smudge on his cuff, the way his shoulders sat slightly too still—like someone bracing for a blow that never came. He always seemed composed, deliberate. But now she could see the quiet toll that carried—the weight of watching too much and being able to stop too little.

"You're not as calm as you pretend to be," Gatty said softly, her voice teasing at the edges, though something gentler lay beneath.

Leander blinked, his green eyes rising to meet hers. The look he gave her wasn't amused or defensive—it was searching, as though he hadn't decided whether she was seeing too much or just enough.

"Maybe not," he said after a beat, his voice lower than before.

The words hung between them, fragile and electric. Gatty stepped forward, not consciously, just enough to close the space that had stretched like a wire between them. Her heart thudded hard, but she didn't look away. And Leander—Leander didn't move, didn't retreat, though his expression shifted, subtle and sharp, as though he'd caught the scent of danger and didn't yet know if he welcomed it.

"I don't think you're as calm as you think, either," he said, the corner of his mouth tugging upward—but this time, not with irony. With something like admiration.

The teasing note in his voice sent a flicker of annoyance through her, sharp enough to cover the warmth pooling in her chest. Without thinking, she shot back, "You talk too much."

Leander's brow lifted in quiet amusement, but he didn't answer. The space between them suddenly felt charged—no longer the polite, distant air of two people orbiting each other, but something taut, like a thread stretched tight and waiting to snap.

Gatty stepped forward, just slightly. Leander didn't move. If anything, he stilled completely, watching her with that quiet intensity he always wore, but now it was turned fully on her.

She opened her mouth—she didn't know to say what—but her words vanished when his hand rose, slow and unsure, to brush a curl from her cheek. His fingers barely grazed her skin, yet it sent a shiver down her spine.

"You don't have to pretend you're not afraid," he said quietly.

"I'm not afraid," she murmured. "Not of you."

The air between them seemed to pulse.

She wasn't sure who moved first—whether it was her, drawn forward like a moth to a candle, or him, tilting his head as though giving in to something he'd been resisting for far too long—but the distance dissolved in a breath.

His lips met hers, tentative at first, like a thought half-spoken. It wasn't rushed, wasn't clumsy—it was gentle, deliberate, and searching. Her eyes fluttered shut. She still held the book pressed between them like a barrier neither of them had quite decided to lower, but the kiss deepened slightly, slow and steady, as though both were learning a language they hadn't known they spoke.

Leander's hand found her waist—not possessive, not claiming her, just... anchoring her there. Present. Real. His mouth was warm and patient against hers, and Gatty leaned in just a little more, dizzy with the quiet want of it.

When they finally broke apart, it felt like surf pulling back from shore, reluctant and inevitable.

Leander's expression was unreadable, but his gaze lingered, softer than she'd ever seen it. He looked at her like he didn't know whether he was about to apologize or do it again.

"That..." he began, his voice rougher than before. He cleared his throat and stepped back, putting a breath of space between them. "That was probably unwise."

Gatty's cheeks burned, but she didn't look away. "Probably," she said, though her voice held the smallest smile.

They stood in silence for a long beat. Then, without another word, Leander turned back to his desk, the scratch of his quill resuming like nothing had happened. But his posture was different—tense in the shoulders, his writing more careful than before.

Gatty lingered near the shelves, the book still clutched to her chest, her heart drumming hard beneath her apron. The kiss had been quiet, but not forgettable. Not even close. It had pulled something to the surface—something fierce and trembling and alive. She wasn't sure what to name it. But she knew she wanted more.

When Violet appeared at the library door, calling her name, Gatty nearly jumped.

"Helena's asking for you," Violet said, her tone clipped but her eyes flicking curiously toward Leander. "She says it's urgent."

Gatty nodded, her heart still galloping, her thoughts an unspooled ribbon. She cast one last glance at Leander, who was back at his desk, head bent low over the page, scribbling with what looked like great focus—but the rhythm of his pen was erratic, the line of his shoulders drawn too tight. Pretending nothing had happened.

But something had.

As Gatty stepped out of the library, the corner of her mouth lifted against her will.

Later that night, the dormitory was cloaked in silence. The hush was broken only by the soft breaths of sleeping women and the creak of beams settling overhead like old bones. Gatty lay still on her narrow cot, eyes wide open, staring at the fractured ceiling above. The blanket was tucked close, but it couldn't warm the restless hum under her skin.

The magistrate's heavy footfalls, his ledger-bound certainty—it had all cast a chill over Blythewood Hall that not even Helena's composure could fully dispel. His gaze hadn't landed on her directly, not yet. But it would.

Still, that wasn't what kept her awake.

Her fingers drifted to her lips, brushing the place where his mouth had touched hers.

The kiss had been hesitant, a question wrapped in silence. And yet it had stirred something in her, as if his steadiness—his restraint—had passed into her through that quiet touch. He hadn't taken, hadn't demanded. He had simply offered. And maybe that was why she couldn't stop thinking about it.

He'd pulled away, of course. Snapped back into himself like a snapped shut book. But she'd seen the way he'd looked at her before he did—the war behind his eyes, the edge of something that felt far from casual.

It hadn't been a mistake. She knew that now. It had been the beginning of something neither of them quite knew how to name.

Gatty rolled onto her side and stared into the dark, the edges of her resolve slowly sharpening.

There was no room for softness, not right now—not with the magistrate in the house and danger pressing at the windows like fog. But the kiss had reminded her what it felt like to want something more than survival. It was foolish, maybe, but it gave her a thread of warmth to hold onto.

And Helena's words echoed back: *Every skill you learn here is another tool to protect yourself.*

Even if Gatty didn't trust Helena's intentions entirely, the sentiment rang true. The books, the garden, the whispered lessons tucked in every corner of the Hall—these weren't just tasks. They were weapons. They were freedom. And she wasn't going to waste them.

Her mind turned to the others. Violet, fierce and stubborn beneath her easy grin. Ellen, silent but steady. Even Helena, with her sharp tongue and her ceaseless tests, bore the weight of protection like armor. They had all been branded. Shunned. Punished.

Witches, Gatty thought. The word sat bitter and brilliant on her tongue.

It wasn't a curse. Not anymore. It was a warning.
Not to fear them—but to respect them.

The magistrate wouldn't see that. He'd see weakness where there was resolve, threat where there was only strength. He'd see women like her and flinch—not because they were dangerous, but because they could be.

And that was the point.

Gatty's jaw tightened as she curled deeper into her blanket. Blythewood had taken her in when no one else would. She'd nearly drowned—body and spirit—and here, she'd been pulled from the wreckage. She wouldn't let them burn this place down. Not for superstition. Not for fear.

She thought of the still room, of the belladonna and nettles. She thought of Leander's voice in the quiet, telling her that knowledge was a weapon no one could take from her.

For the first time, she believed him.

She would learn. For herself. For the women here. And maybe, if she ever made it out of this place, for others like her too—others who had been hunted, hounded, and hidden.

As sleep finally tugged at her, Gatty felt it—not peace, not safety, but something close to power. Fragile, flickering, and hers.

If they wanted to call her a witch, so be it.

Let them see what a witch really was.

Chapter Fourteen

CLOSE CALLS

The sharp cry of a street vendor hawking ribbons jolted Gatty from her thoughts as she made her way through the crowded market square of Harleston. It was the largest town she had ever set foot in—larger even than she imagined Blythewood to be in its heyday. The noise and energy of the place pressed in on her from all sides, like a tide rising too fast to outrun. Horses clopped over cobblestones slick with mud and refuse, their riders shouting at passersby to clear the way. The mingling smells of fresh bread, dung, tallow, and sweat coiled in her nostrils and made her stomach churn.

She kept her head low, the bonnet Lydia had lent her casting a protective shadow over her face. Even so, she felt every passing glance like the scrape of a blade across her skin. Lydia's instructions echoed in her mind: "Make no eye contact. Speak only when spoken to. Return quickly." A simple errand, just a quiet walk to fetch camomile, valerian, and dried pennyroyal from the apothecary. But the weight of what could go wrong hung over her like storm clouds, thick and close. Every raised voice made her flinch. Every man who looked too long made her pulse stutter.

Leander, striding beside her, looked as though he'd rather be anywhere else. He wasn't exactly an imposing escort; his tall, wiry frame was better suited to libraries than the bustle of an open market. Still, his presence steadied her, if only because he looked more alert than she felt. He scanned the crowd with darting eyes, his shoulders stiff beneath his coat.

"I suppose it's safer this way," he muttered, breaking the tense silence. "Helena wanted Violet to come, but I told her Violet in a market would be... disastrous."

"Would it?" Gatty asked absently, her gaze fixed on a butcher sharpening his cleaver with unsettling precision. The sound of metal rasping against stone set her teeth on edge.

"She'd spend all our coin on pastries and books, then convince some poor fool she's the Queen of Sheba," Leander replied. His tone was dry, but the corners of his mouth twitched as though suppressing a smile. "We'd have to carry her home in disgrace."

Despite herself, Gatty huffed a soft laugh. The sound felt strange in her throat—fragile, foreign. "And instead, I've got you," she said, raising an eyebrow. "A man who looks like he hasn't stepped outside in a decade."

He glanced sideways at her, feigning offense. "I'll have you know, I once spent an entire summer cataloging a garden's worth of botanical specimens. Outdoors. In full sunlight."

"I stand corrected," Gatty replied wryly. "A man of the wild."

Before he could retort, the apothecary's wooden sign creaked in the wind, and Gatty exhaled in relief. Her fingers were aching from how tightly she gripped the basket. She ducked inside, grateful to be out of the din of the square. The shop smelled of dried herbs and resin, its shelves crowded with glass jars labeled in Latin. The walls were crowded with shadows and rows of jars—each one a tiny world of crushed roots, curled leaves, or preserved things better left unnamed.

The apothecary, a stooped man with ink-stained fingers, barely glanced at them as they entered. While he gathered her requested items, Gatty moved slowly down the aisle, her hand trailing lightly over the nearest jars. The glass was cool beneath her fingertips, and the etched words felt familiar in a way that made her throat tighten.

Artemisia absinthium. Salix alba. She murmured the names in her mind like a prayer. The scents of lavender, dried citrus, and musty valerian root grounded her. Blythewood's garden lived in these jars—calmer days, measured tasks, quiet purpose. If she closed her eyes, she could almost pretend she was still there.

The door creaked open behind her.

Gatty didn't turn. She didn't breathe. She didn't know why, but she felt danger in the air.

The apothecary glanced up. "Ah. Good day, madam."

Then came the voice. Clear. Sharp. Too loud. "Good day, Master Groves. I've a prescription from my husband."

The voice sliced through Gatty like a blade. Her chest tightened. No—no, it couldn't be. She knew that voice. Her hand, still hovering near a jar of dried nettle, trembled.

"Is there something else, miss?" the unsuspecting apothecary asked Gatty politely.

Gatty couldn't answer. Her breath lodged in her throat. The woman behind her kept speaking, her tone friendly but commanding—the kind of voice that filled a room without raising its volume. A voice that drew attention. A voice meant to be heard. "Gatty Carter, is that you?"

The name struck like a thunderclap. Her pulse roared in her ears. Slowly, mechanically, she turned. Her vision tunneled.

There, framed in the doorway, stood Mrs. Harper—William Harper's wife.

Her bonnet was different. Her hair a little greyer. But her eyes, sharp and hard as flint, hadn't changed. "It is you," Mrs. Harper said, stepping forward. Her expression shifted from pleasant surprise to something far darker. "I'd know that face anywhere."

Gatty couldn't move. Her body remembered the village square before her mind did—the mob, the shouting, the chill of water filling her lungs. The world tilted.

Leander stepped closer, his hand brushing against hers in what might have been a steadying gesture or an accident. She glanced at him. He gave her the faintest nod, eyes on Mrs. Harper, jaw clenched like he was biting back fury.

"You must be mistaken," Gatty said, and the calm in her voice surprised even her. "I don't know you."

Mrs. Harper's lip curled. "Oh, I know you well enough. My William said you were dead, but it seems the devil keeps his own. I'm visiting relations nearby." She turned to the apothecary, her voice sharp and triumphant. "Do you know who this is? A witch, plain as day."

The apothecary froze mid-motion, a jar of dried hawthorn halfway to the counter. His expression turned wary. Around them, the shop fell deathly silent.

"Leander," Gatty whispered, her voice barely audible. "We need to leave."

But Mrs. Harper was already closing in, her presence as suffocating as the smoke of a snuffed candle. "What wickedness have you brought here, eh? Cursing good folk, burning barns—"

"That's enough." Leander's voice cut through the rising panic like a blade through silk—calm, but cold enough to freeze the air. He stepped forward, his body shifting just slightly to place himself be-

tween Gatty and the woman. "This woman is no witch. She's under
the protection of the Hartfords."

Mrs. Harper faltered, blinking at him. But the hesitation lasted
only a breath. Her eyes narrowed as they sized him up, searching for
weakness. "Hartfords or no, she's trouble."

"Trouble," Leander repeated, his voice like a blade sliding back
into its sheath, "is a woman throwing baseless accusations in public. I
suggest you stop before you embarrass yourself further."

Mrs. Harper's mouth twisted. She drew in a sharp breath, preparing to argue—but Leander didn't give her the chance. He took Gatty's
arm, gently but firmly, and turned her toward the door. "We're done
here," he said coolly to the apothecary over his shoulder. "Please forward the bill to Blythewood."

The bell above the door jingled as they stepped into the daylight.
Gatty wrenched her arm from his grasp the moment they were outside. "She recognized me," she hissed, the tremble in her voice barely
disguised by her fury. "She'll tell everyone."

Leander's face remained composed, but his voice dropped low, the
sharpness of it barely veiled. "Not if we move quickly. Come on."

The tension between them crackled, as charged as the air before a
storm. They wove through the crowded market, the chaos pressing
in from all sides. Gatty's hands trembled. Every shout, every sudden
movement made her flinch. Her eyes kept darting over her shoulder,

her mouth dry. She could still feel Mrs. Harper's stare burning into her back.

"Here," Leander said sharply, pulling her into a narrow alley that smelled of old fish and damp straw. The shadows here were deeper. The noise of the square dulled, replaced by the dripping of water from a broken gutter. "Wait."

"What are you doing?" Gatty demanded, panic pitching her voice too high.

"Creating a distraction." Leander knelt and pulled a small linen pouch from his coat pocket. He tore it open and scattered the contents across the stones—a pale, glinting powder that shimmered like frost in the sun. Then, with a flick of his fingers, he struck a match and dropped it.

The powder ignited in a sudden bloom of pale smoke and sparks. A sharp, herbal scent—burnt rosemary and something vaguely metallic—filled the air. People near the square turned at once, craning their necks toward the plume.

"Where did you—?"

"Library trick," Leander muttered. "Go."

They slipped from the alley into the churn of the crowd. The smoke curled behind them, the noise of confused onlookers rising as the diversion took hold. Gatty's heart pounded in her throat, her every step laced with dread. The further they moved, the more her sens-

es blurred—smells, colors, sounds all blending into one disorienting h
um.

The sharp tang of smoke still lingered in her nostrils as she followed
Leander down a narrow, twisting street, the chaos of the market fading
behind soot-streaked walls. The alleys twisted like a maze. The air felt
heavier here, close and damp. Gatty clutched her basket to her chest,
her fingers aching from how tightly she gripped the handle. Her eyes
scanned every shadow. "Is she following us?" Gatty whispered, her
voice trembling. Her legs ached with the need to run.

"No," Leander said. His voice was steady, but the tautness in his
jaw betrayed him. He glanced back more than once, his long strides
slowing just slightly to match hers.

"She could be. She might—"

"She isn't." He cut her off gently but firmly. He paused at a narrow
crossing, scanning both directions. "I've seen that woman before. Mrs.
Harper's more bark than bite. She won't follow us into the alleys—not
when there's a crowd to impress back in the square."

His confidence grated against her panic. "You don't understand,"
she said, her voice cracking. "People like her—they don't let things go.
She'll tell them I'm alive. That she saw me. And they'll believe her."

Leander turned to her sharply. "And panicking will help, will it?"
He stopped just short of snapping, then softened as his gaze met hers.
"We're safe for now, Gatty. Just keep moving."

But she didn't feel safe. She couldn't. Her mind reeled with images: the flash of a torch, the rope on her wrists, cold water swallowing her lungs. Her stomach twisted, and her vision swam.

They emerged onto a quieter lane lined with uneven brick façades. The wind stirred old leaves into spirals at their feet. Leander's voice dropped again.

"This way," he murmured, nodding toward a low archway between two buildings.

Gatty hesitated at the mouth of the passage, her pulse skittering like a frightened bird. "What if someone else recognizes me?" she asked, her voice hoarse.

Leander turned back, his green eyes narrowed beneath his brow. "Then you let me do the talking." He stepped closer. "I'm good at that when I need to be."

She bit her lip. "Good at talking or good at lying?"

Leander's lips twitched into something between a grin and a grimace. "They're too often the same thing," he said, but his tone had lost its edge. It sounded tired, like someone who'd learned that truth the hard way.

The passage opened onto a quieter courtyard, tucked behind the main street like a forgotten pocket of the town. The cobblestones were uneven and damp with moss, the kind that curled between cracks like creeping fingers. A single gnarled oak tree stood in the center, its leafless branches clawing at the overcast sky as though it, too, were trying to hold back a storm.

Gatty stopped beneath the tree. Her breath came fast and shallow, catching in her throat. She gripped the handles of her basket with both hands, white-knuckled, as though it might anchor her to the earth.

"She'll tell everyone I survived," she whispered, her voice breaking around the words. "They'll come looking for me. They'll..."

Leander let out a slow breath and ran a hand through his hair, his fingers catching in the tangles before falling heavily to his side. For a heartbeat, he looked as though he wanted to say something sharp. Instead, he stepped closer, close enough that the scent of parchment and rosemary clung faintly to the cold air between them.

"No one's coming," he said, softer now. "Listen to me, Gatty. People like Mrs. Harper—people who thrive on gossip—they don't follow their rumors, they nest in them. They'll talk. They'll whisper. But they won't leave their comforts behind to chase a ghost through the woods."

His voice was careful, deliberate—but underneath it, Gatty could hear what he wasn't saying: I'm worried too. That thin thread of tension ran beneath every word.

She shook her head. "You don't know that. You didn't see them. The way they looked at me—like I was already dead. Like I deserved it." Her voice cracked again, and she pulled in a shaky breath. "They didn't see a person. Just a thing they could burn if they shouted loudly enough about it."

Leander's expression changed—something sharp giving way to something quiet and raw. He hesitated, then reached out, not in haste but with steady intention, and laid his hand gently on her arm.

"I don't know what they did to you," he said. "Not fully. But I've seen what fear does to people. I've seen it twist them until there's nothing left but hate. And I know what it's like to be on the wrong end of that."

His fingers were warm even through the fabric of her sleeve. His touch wasn't possessive or presumptive—it was grounding, as if to say, You're still here. You're still real.

"You're not alone," he said. "And you're not going to be dragged back into that."

Gatty didn't answer. She stared at him, the air thick with silence. Her pulse pounded at her temples, and her thoughts were still spiraling, but the feel of his hand—steady, human, real—cut through the noise like light beneath a locked door.

She swallowed. "Why are you helping me?" The question slipped out before she could stop it, her voice hoarse. "Really."

Leander blinked, as if the question startled him more than it should have. "Because..." He paused, glancing away. His jaw worked, and when he looked back, something in his expression had softened. "Because you're worth helping." He said it plainly, without flourish or persuasion, as though it was just a truth he'd accepted.

The words landed with more force than she expected. Her grip on the basket loosened. Something uncoiled in her chest—something small, but defiant.

"Come on," Leander said after a moment, stepping back. His hand fell away. "We shouldn't linger here. Helena will be waiting."

Gatty nodded, her eyes blinking rapidly as she focused on the bare branches above them, the way they swayed like fingers reaching. Together, the unlikely pair stepped out of the courtyard, the quiet giving way to the muffled sounds of town life beyond.

But even as they walked, Gatty couldn't shake the feeling that Mrs. Harper's words were still behind her—insidious, persistent, and unwilling to die.

The alleys spilled them out into another street, wider than the last but quieter than the bustling market. Gatty's breaths came fast and shallow, each footstep loud in her ears. Leander walked just ahead, tall and purposeful, his frame angled like a shield between her and the world. His coat caught the wind as he scanned the street with sharp, restless eyes.

"Where are we going?" she whispered, her voice tight with panic.

Leander didn't look back. "Somewhere she won't follow. Keep your head down."

They turned the corner into a row of shuttered shops. A faded baker's sign groaned in the wind, and the musty scent of old flour lingered in the air. The street felt abandoned except for a stray dog sniffing at a crust of bread. Quiet, yes—but still exposed.

"What if she told someone already?" Gatty pressed. "What if she—"

"She didn't," Leander said, cutting in. He stopped and turned to face her fully, his face composed but edged with tension. "She was too stunned. Women like her... they like to gather a crowd before they strike. She'll want witnesses. A performance."

Gatty blinked, caught between her own spiraling dread and the uncomfortable truth of his words. "You don't know that."

"No," he admitted, voice low. "But I know the type. And I've seen what panic does to people. If we stay smart, we stay ahead."

She glanced behind her, the cobblestones stretching like a path back into a nightmare. "She'll tell them I didn't drown," she said, barely audible. "She'll say I ran. And they'll believe her."

Leander's expression darkened. He stepped closer, enough that she could see the faint pull in his jaw, the effort it took to remain calm. "Then we'll be ready. But right now, you need to trust me." His voice gentled, almost cautious. "I meant it when I said you're not alone anymore, Gatty. Not just at Blythewood...but with me."

The words landed hard, more than she expected. She looked away before he could see her eyes sting. "Fine," she muttered. "What's the plan, then?"

Leander's mouth curved into the faintest smile, dry but warm. "Plan? Survive the walk back without collecting another furious villager. I didn't exactly bring disguises."

Before she could reply, a voice shattered the quiet.

"Oi, you there! Girl!"

Gatty's blood ran cold. She didn't need to look—she knew that voice. Sharp. Triumphant. Mrs. Harper.

Leander reacted before Gatty could move, his hand closing around her arm as he pulled her toward the nearest doorway. "In here," he muttered.

The door belonged to an old apothecary, paint curling at the corners, the windows fogged with grime. Leander rattled the handle—it was locked. He hissed something under his breath, jaw clenched.

"Stay close," he said, already moving.

They ducked into the narrow gap between the apothecary and the butcher's shop, the air damp and metallic. Their backs pressed into the cold stone as Gatty tried to become smaller, to vanish into the shadow.

Footsteps rang out on the cobblestones. Mrs. Harper's boots struck like hammer blows, deliberate and menacing.

"Don't think I didn't see you!" she called, her voice thick with righteous glee. "Show yourself, you little liar!"

Gatty's heart slammed against her ribs. Her fingers bit into the wicker of her basket. The vision came unbidden—the village square, the river, the hands pulling her under.

Beside her, Leander shifted. He looked tense, yes—but not frantic. His eyes flicked between the alley and the street beyond, calculating.

"She'll look in here," Gatty whispered, the words trembling on her lips. "She won't stop."

"Not if we give her something better to chase," Leander murmured.

He reached into his coat, calm despite the tightness around his eyes, and pulled out a small, battered notebook. Its corners were dog-eared, its spine held together with care and habit.

"What are you—" Gatty began, but he raised a finger to his lips.

Then he crouched low and tossed the notebook out into the street. It skidded across the stones and came to rest in plain view, not far from the shop's door.

He reached for Gatty's wrist, not rough but firm, steady. His hand was warm, anchoring.

"When she goes for it," he whispered, eyes locked on the figure now closing in, "we move. Quietly. Understand?"

Gatty nodded, though every part of her was shaking. She didn't fully understand how he could stay so calm—how he could think like this when she could barely breathe.

But right now, she'd follow his lead.

Her pulse roared in her ears as Mrs. Harper's footsteps grew louder, her shadow stretching long into the alley.

"There you are," Mrs. Harper hissed, spotting the notebook. "Trying to leave your rubbish behind, are you?" She bent stiffly to pick it up, her attention locked on the object, muttering as she turned it over in her hands.

"Now," Leander breathed, tugging Gatty forward.

They slipped from the shadows, staying low as they darted past the apothecary and into a side street. Gatty's lungs burned, her skirts tangling around her legs as they rounded the corner. She braced herself for a shout, a chase—but it didn't come. Mrs. Harper was still crouched by the notebook, flipping through the pages, too consumed by her imagined discovery to look up.

Leander didn't slow until they were several streets away. The tight web of alleys gave way to a quieter stretch, the distant noise of the market a fading hum behind them. Only then did he release her wrist, his shoulders loosening slightly beneath his coat.

Gatty leaned against the cold stone of a wall, struggling to catch her breath. "What—what was that?" she managed, still breathless. "What was in the notebook?"

Leander glanced at her, a flicker of tired amusement playing at the corners of his mouth. "Nothing important. Crop yields. A few notes on seed storage. Possibly a crude drawing of a duck."

Gatty stared at him, still too shaken to laugh, though a startled huff escaped her lips. "You're absurd."

"Absurdity is sometimes underrated," he replied, his smirk sharpening just a little. "Especially when it keeps us from being dragged into a public stoning."

Gatty shook her head, half in disbelief, half in reluctant admiration. "You really thought she'd fall for that?"

"She needed to feel like she'd caught something," he said simply. "People like her don't want truth—they want confirmation of what they already believe. I gave her enough to gnaw on."

The weight of his words settled over her. She was quiet for a moment, then said, "Thank you. For what you did."

Leander studied her, his gaze serious now, the edge of playfulness receding. "You would've done the same for me," he said, as though it were obvious. And then, more gently, "Are you all right?"

She opened her mouth, then closed it again. "No," she admitted. "But I will be."

Leander nodded once, then turned, his coat catching the wind as he began walking again. "We've tempted fate enough for one day. Let's get back before Helena decides to send someone less subtle next time."

Gatty fell into step beside him, the space between them no longer taut with panic, but something quieter. She glanced at him out of the corner of her eye. There was steadiness in his gait, in the set of his shoulders—even if his hands were still curled slightly, as though the adrenaline hadn't quite faded.

The silence that stretched between them wasn't heavy now. It felt earned.

The road out of town unfolded like a ribbon, the wind sharper here, threading through the trees that lined the path. Gatty pulled her cloak tighter, the fabric rustling with every step. Leander walked a few paces ahead, his hand tucked inside his coat, head bowed against the cold.

Behind them, the sounds of Harleston faded, but the memory of Mrs. Harper's voice lingered—echoing in Gatty's mind like a splinter she couldn't pull free.

"You're awfully quiet," Leander said after a while. His tone was gentle, almost cautious. He glanced over his shoulder, his green eyes steady.

"What's there to say?" Gatty replied, hugging her basket to her chest.

He slowed until they were side by side. "That woman," he said. "Who was she to you?"

Gatty's steps faltered. The truth rose in her throat like bile. "She's from my old village," she said, her voice rough. "The one that tried to drown me."

Leander's face darkened. "She was part of it?"

"She didn't push me in," Gatty said bitterly. "But she didn't stop them either. She watched they chase me away. Her husband was part of the mob. And she believed every word they whispered about me. Still does."

Silence settled between them again, broken only by the crunch of frost underfoot.

"She won't come near Blythewood," Leander said at last. "Helena won't let her. Neither will I."

"You can't know that," Gatty snapped, her voice cracking. "People like her don't just vanish. They talk. They spread rot. And once it starts, it never stops."

Leander stopped walking. "And you think that giving her your fear will stop her?"

Gatty turned sharply to face him. "Easy for you to say! You weren't dragged to a river with a noose of accusations around your neck. You didn't hear them cheering when they thought you were dead."

The wind whipped around them. Leander didn't speak. Not right away. But his silence didn't feel like retreat. It felt like restraint.

And when he did speak again, it was quiet and unflinching. "No," he said. "I wasn't. But I've seen fear turn neighbors into executioners. I've watched it silence the good and arm the cruel."

His voice didn't rise. It didn't need to.

"You're right," he continued. "I didn't live what you lived. But don't mistake my calm for ignorance, Gatty. I know what hate looks like. And I know what it costs."

Gatty swallowed hard, the wind stinging her eyes. His words struck something deep—true in a way that made her chest ache. She couldn't bring herself to meet his gaze. "Let's keep moving," she muttered, brushing past him.

Leander didn't press. He only watched her for a beat, something unreadable flickering in his expression, before following. His footsteps on the frosted path were quieter now, deliberately so—as if not to crowd her.

They walked in silence the rest of the way, the landscape stretching out on either side like a gray, wind-swept sea. The chill clung to them, the kind that didn't fade even with movement. Gatty kept her eyes on the road ahead, her thoughts tangled, the weight of the encounter lingering like smoke.

When Blythewood Hall finally came into view, its familiar red-brick silhouette rising against the bleak sky, Gatty felt the first flicker of relief. The iron gates groaned open on weather-stiffened hinges, and the air smelled faintly of woodsmoke and damp earth.

Within the grounds, life moved on. Two women passed them carrying split logs for the hearth, their conversation hushed against the wind. Ivy scampered across the lawn after a fleeing chicken, her high laughter catching in the breeze like a bell.

"Safe and sound," Leander murmured, stepping ahead to pull open the main door. His tone was quiet, but there was something reassuring in it—as though he was saying it for her sake, not his own.

The moment Gatty crossed the threshold, warmth enveloped her. The scent of baking bread mingled with the familiar, loamy scent of herbs steeped in the walls of the old house.

She didn't speak. Her fingers trembled as she set the basket down on a side table, the day's weight pressing down on her all at once.

"Gatty?" Leander asked, his voice softer now, tentative.

She shook her head quickly, not trusting her throat to form words.

He hesitated, visibly debating whether to speak again. Then he said, almost lightly, "The library's warmer than this hall. And quieter."

Gatty looked up, startled. "Why would I—"

"It's where I go," he said, cutting her off gently. "When my thoughts won't settle." There was no invitation in his voice. Just the truth, offered plainly.

She wavered, her defenses still taut, but there was something unguarded in his face—something quieter than pity, deeper than politeness. She gave a single nod. "Lead the way."

He turned, not waiting for thanks, just moving as if it had always been part of the plan. Gatty followed, each step toward the library easing the tight coil in her chest.

The library welcomed them with firelight and silence. Shadows danced across rows of worn spines and old velvet drapes, and the air held that quiet, waxy scent of parchment and polish that always seemed to settle her.

Leander gestured toward a small alcove by the hearth, where two weathered armchairs sat angled toward the flames. "Sit," he said simply, and vanished briefly into the stacks.

Gatty sank into the chair, her bones aching, the fire licking gently at her boots. She didn't realize how cold she'd been until the warmth began to thaw her fingers.

Leander returned a moment later with a thick book and a steaming cup, which he placed beside her without comment. His sleeves were slightly pushed back, ink smudged faintly at the wrist. "You'll find more answers in here than out there," he said, nodding toward the book.

Gatty picked it up, running her hand along the cracked leather spine. "What is it?"

"Accounts from women accused of witchcraft," Leander said. "Their testimonies. How they endured. How they were failed."

Her throat tightened as she opened the book. The pages were filled with looping script and faded ink, stories that felt painfully close to her own.

She looked up suddenly. "Why do you risk yourself for me?"

Leander didn't speak right away. His gaze drifted toward the fire, the light casting gold across his cheekbone. "Because you don't give up," he said at last. "Even when everything in the world tells you to. You're an example of the kind of person I want there to be more of, in this world and the next."

Gatty looked down again, her fingers tightening slightly on the edges of the book. "Thank you," she said softly.

Leander said nothing. But when she glanced sideways, she saw him smile.

They read in silence, the kind that filled the room like breath. The fire crackled and hissed gently, the world outside shrinking until it was just this: two chairs, two minds still humming from danger, and a slow, flickering peace settling between them.

Gatty knew it couldn't last. But in the hush between words, in the space where thought met feeling, she found a kind of closeness with him no storm could steal.

Chapter Fifteen

GATTY'S RESOLVE

A week later, the first light of dawn crept through the frost-lined windows, spilling pale gold onto the stone walls of the dormitory. Gatty stirred, the coarse wool of her blanket scratching against her skin. She sat up, her breath fogging in the chilly air, and stared at the ceiling's worn timbers. It had been another restless night. Memories still tangled in her mind like smoke from a dying fire—the magistrate's visit, the sharp clang of panic in her chest when Mrs. Harper's voice rang out in the market, and Leander's voice in the library, steady and low, as though spoken not just to guide her hands but to anchor her

.

But something else flickered within her, too. Not hope—not quite—but resolve. Something stubborn inside her had lit and refused to die down. Gatty swung her legs over the side of her narrow bed, the stone floor biting at her bare feet. She didn't flinch. She'd lived through worse cold. If she had learned anything since arriving at Blythewood

Hall, it was that fear could be weathered—and sometimes even repurposed.

The garden. The library. The women. None of them had offered safety in the way she first expected, but each had offered something else: a place to grow. To reckon. To begin again.

She crossed the room, careful not to wake the others, and pushed open the heavy shutters. Below, the grounds lay cloaked in frost. The poison garden looked brittle and asleep, but she knew better now. The roots were still alive, still dangerous. Still full of potential.

Helena had given her a task. A patch of earth and warning looks, as if to say: earn your keep. And Gatty—tired, bruised, furious—had every intention of doing just that. "If they want a witch," she murmured to the pale morning light, "then I'll give them one worth watching."

The frost crunched beneath her shoes as she made her way down to the garden before the house was fully awake. The air stung in her lungs, sharp with the scent of dying herbs, but there was something steadying about it. She drew her shawl tighter and knelt beside the rows of sleeping plants Helena had assigned to her care.

Her fingers brushed dried hellebore, then foxglove—cautionary names now spoken with respect. She let her hand rest briefly on the soil, feeling for some trace of warmth beneath the surface.

She'd spent hours in the library studying Leander's texts, poring over pages filled with illustrations and precise instructions. His voice echoed in her memory—not just what he'd said, but how he'd said it: patient, exacting, and, when he wasn't watching himself, unexpectedly kind. Yesterday he had even once shown her how to grind herbs properly, steadying her hand with his own. She'd meant to learn about plants that day, but had left with her pulse a little unsteady and a warmth she couldn't shake. He'd smelled faintly of parchment and cedar and something else she hadn't placed, and she could just...

But it wasn't just the knowledge that mattered here. It was how that knowledge was worn, spoken, wrapped in mystery. Helena believed in fear as a tool, in power as performance. And Gatty—Gatty knew how to perform when survival called for it. She straightened, brushing dirt from her hands. She wasn't a witch. But she could become something close enough to pass.

The clatter and warmth of the kitchen grounded her later that morning. Her hands moved with careful precision as she selected the herbs for Helena's poultice: comfrey, ginger, willow bark. A simple request, but Gatty treated it with the gravity of something far more sacred.

Her thoughts wandered as she worked, back to the garden texts and the way Leander's hand had brushed hers when he'd shown her how to adjust the pressure. He had spoken in a low voice that made her lean closer without meaning to. And when she had glanced up, she'd caught him watching her—not the way men in taverns watched, but like he was reading a passage he hadn't expected to find in a book.

Gatty shook the thought off, biting the inside of her cheek as she crushed the ginger root. She didn't have time to be distracted.

The paste was nearly finished when she hesitated. Her fingers hovered over the saffron tin—its delicate threads the color of firelight. It was too dear for a morning ache. Too precious. But Helena didn't just want relief. She wanted presence. Drama.

With a breath, Gatty added a small pinch. The paste shimmered gold. Striking, strange. The sort of thing a witch might make, if one believed in such things.

She wrapped the mixture in clean cloth and tied it off with twine, cradling the bundle in her hands like a secret. It wasn't magic. But it looked close enough. And sometimes, looking the part was enough to survive.

The late morning sun hung low in the sky as Gatty carried the finished poultice through the hallways of Blythewood. Though small, the bundle felt heavier with each step—not from its weight, but from the questions twisting in her chest. Would Helena find it clever? Or presumptuous? Gatty knew the woman wasn't easily impressed, and this task felt less like an invitation and more like a crucible.

She paused outside the oak door to Helena's private sitting room. A faint scent of lavender and beeswax polish drifted through the crack, as did the low hush of someone setting down a teacup. Gatty closed her eyes for one breath—just one—then knocked lightly.

"Enter," came Helena's voice, velvet and steel all at once.

Gatty stepped inside, immediately struck—as always—by the room's precise luxury. Polished wood, porcelain cups, a fire that crackled just enough to sound elegant. Helena sat near the hearth, her spine as straight as ever, though a flicker of discomfort passed over her face when she shifted in her chair.

"I trust you've brought what I asked for," she said without preamble, gesturing with one hand.

"Yes, ma'am," Gatty replied, her voice as steady as she could make it. She stepped forward, fingers tight around the bundle, and offered it up like something sacred.

Helena took it and untied the twine with deft, practiced hands. The saffron-tinted poultice gleamed in the firelight, golden and unexpected. Helena's brows lifted—just slightly.

"Striking," she murmured, brushing her fingertips over the cloth. "What have you used?"

"Comfrey, ginger, and willow bark," Gatty answered. Then, after the briefest hesitation, "And saffron—for warmth. And... presence."

That word hung in the air. For a breath, Helena said nothing. Then, she smiled, and it was as if the warmth of the saffron spread across her face. "Presence," she echoed. "Indeed. Clever." The compliment was quiet, but it landed like a match struck in the dark. Gatty's heart gave a small jolt of pride as she watched Helena apply the poultice to her hand. Her sharp expression softened just a fraction as the warmth soaked in.

"Well done," Helena said after a pause. "It seems you've absorbed more than I expected in such a short time." She leaned back in her chair, her gaze assessing. "Tell me, Miss Carter—do you enjoy the work?"

The question caught Gatty off guard. She blinked. "It's... satisfying, ma'am," she answered carefully.

Helena's brow arched. "Satisfying? A dreary word. You work with plants as though they're old friends. As though they speak to you. Are you truly so unmoved by them?"

Gatty hesitated. Joy wasn't a word she used often. It felt exposed, as if admitting to it might invite someone to take it away. She tugged lightly at the hem of her sleeve. "I suppose it reminds me of things I used to do with my mother. Before..." Her voice trailed off, unwilling to step back into that shadowed place.

Helena regarded her for a long moment, then nodded. "The past shapes us, Miss Carter. But it is not owed our loyalty."

The fire crackled. A gust of wind whispered at the windows, but inside, the silence between them was heavy and intimate.

Finally, Helena shifted the poultice on her hand. "You have potential," she said. "So I'm assigning two of the other women—Alice and Margery—to work under you in the garden. Teach them what you've learned. Show me that you can lead."

Gatty blinked. "Lead, ma'am?"

"Yes. Lead." Helena's tone brooked no confusion. "This garden is more than a corner of soil. It is a refuge, a resource, and—when used correctly—a kind of weapon. I want to see what you can make of it."

The words settled over Gatty like a mantle. Responsibility. Expectation. Trust. They pressed against her chest, but they didn't suffocate. Not this time. "Yes, ma'am," she said, her voice clear.

Helena nodded once, satisfied. "Good. You may go."

As Gatty turned to leave, she caught her own reflection faintly in the polished glass of a cabinet door—her shoulders square, her face flushed with something that almost resembled purpose.

The corridor outside was cold, but her thoughts were burning. Not with fear. With possibility.

Helena trusted her. The garden was an opportunity, rather than the test she'd imagined. And for the first time, Gatty felt like she had something more than survival to hold on to.

The late afternoon air stung her cheeks as she stepped into the poison garden, the hem of her skirts soaking through with dew from the frostbitten grass. The garden sat in a quiet crook of the estate grounds, half-hidden from view, ringed in wrought iron and mystery. Twisted vines curled along the fence like old secrets. In the slanted winter light, the rows of labeled plants seemed caught mid-breath—foxglove bowing gently in the wind, nightshade leaves glistening with cold.

Alice and Margery waited near the gate, arms wrapped around themselves against the chill. Alice's eyes flitted between the shadows with quick, darting alertness, while Margery stood firm and skeptical, her jaw set like she'd been ordered into a punishment post.

"So," Gatty began, keeping her voice steady, "you've been assigned to the garden."

Alice tilted her head. "We were told it's full of poisons."

"It is," Gatty said evenly, her gaze sweeping over the rows. "But poison, in the right hands, can heal as well as harm. The difference is in knowing how."

Margery crossed her arms, unimpressed. "And you know all that already, do you?"

The jab prickled, but Gatty didn't rise to it. "I'm still learning. We all are. But I've spent time in this soil and with the books. Helena wants this place to be useful, not ornamental. So we make it useful."

"Useful for what?" Alice asked, her voice edged with doubt.

Gatty looked at her. "For the hall. For each other. For survival—if it comes to that."

Alice's expression shifted, her suspicion cooling to something more thoughtful. She gave a small nod. Margery remained stone-faced, but her eyes flicked to the garden.

Gatty crouched beside a tangle of dried foxglove stalks. The brittle stems rattled in the breeze, pale and paper-thin.

"This is foxglove," she said, brushing a fingertip across a seed pod. "Used carelessly, it'll kill you in a blink. But with care, it can slow the heart just enough to save a life."

Alice dropped into a crouch beside her, watching intently. "And how do you know when it's enough?"

"Practice," Gatty said, the ghost of a smile tugging at her mouth. "Dry it. Grind it. Measure carefully. There's a line between medicine and poison—and it's thin."

Margery hovered nearby, silent but no longer detached. Her arms were still crossed, but her eyes were drawn to the plant as if it might speak its secrets aloud.

Gatty rose and dusted her hands off on her skirts. "We'll begin with something safer." She pointed toward a low row of lavender, its silvery stems still fragrant despite the cold. "It's gentle. Soothes burns. Calms nerves. It's also hard to ruin, which makes it a good start."

Alice moved forward first, fingertips brushing the stalks like she was greeting an old friend. "So we're making remedies?"

"Among other things," Gatty said. She hesitated, then added, "Sometimes it's not just what you make, but how you make others see it. Helena appreciates a little... drama."

Margery snorted. "Figures. Half the women here think they're witches because someone mistook a toothache for a hex."

Gatty's jaw tightened, but her voice remained calm. "And yet you're here too."

Margery flinched, just barely. She said nothing.

"Look," Gatty continued, her tone softening. "I don't care what brought any of us here. Well, I care, but...oh, you know what I mean. I care what we do now. This garden can be more than a corner to hide in. We can make things that help. That matter."

"Right." Alice looked to Margery, then back to Gatty. "What do we do first?"

Gatty exhaled, a small knot in her chest loosening. "Start with the lavender. Cut low and clean—don't crush the stems. We'll hang them in the still room to dry."

As the two women got to work, Gatty turned back to the foxglove. Her fingers hovered over the seed pods, not plucking them just yet.

She thought of Leander—his ink-stained fingers guiding hers, his voice quiet and precise, speaking of plants the way some spoke of prayers. Knowledge is a weapon, he'd said. But so was resolve. And so was performance.

The garden was full of weapons. And this time, they were in her hands.

Later that evening, the soft glow of candlelight spilled out of the library's arched doorway, casting long shadows across the dim hallway. Gatty paused just outside, one hand resting on the worn stone frame. Inside, the scent of parchment and leather mingled with the crackle of a low-burning fire. Leander sat alone at his usual table, hunched slightly over a book, the lamplight painting soft gold across his tousled hair. One hand rubbed absently at his temple, the other curled loosely around a glass of claret he hadn't touched.

She hesitated, suddenly unsure of herself. But the moment stretched—and then she stepped through.

The old floorboards creaked beneath her boots. Leander's head lifted immediately. His green eyes, wary for a blink of a moment, softened when they found hers.

"Miss Carter," he said, his voice a low, familiar murmur. "To what do I owe the honor?"

Gatty smoothed her skirts, painfully aware of the way his gaze lingered, steady and attentive. "I thought you might still be here," she said, attempting nonchalance. "I was hoping to find something about... lavender."

One of his brows arched, curious. "Lavender?"

"I've started teaching Alice and Margery in the garden," she explained. "They'll need something simple to begin with, and I want to be sure I give them the right start."

Leander closed the book in front of him and stood, his movements unhurried but purposeful. "A commendable beginning," he said, his voice warm. "This way."

He led her toward the far end of the shelves, his shadow long in the firelight. Gatty followed, each step muffled by the thick rug beneath her feet. As they moved, she caught the faint scent of cedar and bergamot trailing behind him—familiar now, and disarming in ways she hadn't expected.

He reached for a high shelf, fingers skimming lightly over the spines. "This one," he murmured, selecting a worn leather-bound volume with care. He turned and offered it to her.

Their fingers brushed.

The contact was brief, but it lingered—his hand warm, her pulse quickening. For a heartbeat, neither of them moved.

"It's thorough," he said, a little quieter. "A bit dense. But worth the effort."

Gatty nodded, holding the book against her chest as if it might steady the flutter in her ribs. "Thank you."

His gaze didn't leave her. "You've taken to the garden," he said after a pause. "It suits you."

"It feels... different from anything I've known," she admitted. "Useful. Like I'm finally doing something that means something."

"That's rare," Leander said, his voice softening. "Rarer still to recognize it when it happens."

She glanced up at him, surprised by the sincerity in his tone—and by how clearly he seemed to understand.

"And you?" she asked. "Do you feel useful here?"

He was quiet for a moment. His fingers drifted to the edge of a shelf, tracing the grain absently. "Most days, the library feels like a refuge," he said. "A place apart from the world. But now and then, it feels like a cage."

Her brow furrowed. "A cage?"

He nodded. "Knowledge is power. That's what they say. But what good is power if it just sits on a shelf?"

Gatty's heart tightened. She understood that too well—the ache of having something to give and no place to give it.

"Maybe," she said gently, "you were just waiting for the right storm."

Leander's eyes snapped to hers. The intensity in them startled her—not just for its sharpness, but for the sudden, disarming vulnerability behind it. The air between them seemed to still.

"Perhaps," he said, and the word hung between them like the echo of a promise.

Gatty shifted, clutching the book tighter. "I should let you get back to your work."

But Leander stepped forward, his hand reaching out to gently touch her elbow. His voice dropped to a near whisper.

"Wait."

She stilled.

"There's something I want to show you."

His hand dropped away, but not before she felt the heat of it through the fabric of her sleeve. He turned and walked toward the long worktable near the hearth, and she followed, her breath tight in her throat.

Leander unfolded a piece of parchment, its edges curled and stained with time. A botanical sketch spread across its surface—foxglove, rendered in fine, delicate lines. Roots, leaves, blossoms—all labeled in Latin.

"This," he said, tracing the ink with a fingertip, "is one of the oldest illustrations in the collection. It details the proper dosages, the symptoms of overdose... and the antidotes."

Gatty leaned in, her shoulder brushing his. The warmth of him seeped through her bodice, and she found herself leaning ever so slightly closer.

"It's beautiful," she murmured, half-distracted by the brush of his breath near her cheek.

Leander didn't look away from the page. "Dangerous things often are." The words were quiet. But when she turned to him, he was already looking at her—and his expression said everything his voice did not.

She swallowed. "It's useful," she said, breaking the silence.

He nodded, but didn't move away.

"Very," he murmured.

And for a long moment, neither of them moved.

Leander crossed the library and returned with a thin stack of parchment, a tin of graphite sticks, and a folded botanical study already half-complete. "Have you ever tried to sketch the plants you work with?" he asked, setting the materials down on the long table beside her.

Gatty raised a brow. "Sketch them? I usually just... remember what they look like."

"Memory fades," he said softly. "Ink doesn't."

He slid the parchment toward her. The image on the page was a partially drawn foxglove, its bell-shaped flowers captured with precise strokes and faint notes written in Latin curling beneath each leaf. "If you want to teach Alice and Margery, you'll need more than instinct. A sketch helps you think differently. See differently."

Gatty hesitated, then sat, her fingers brushing the tin of graphite. "You drew this? It's even better than the one you showed me before."

He nodded once. "My handwriting's dreadful, but I've a steady hand when it counts."

There was a glint in his eye, the barest hint of a smile, and she found herself smiling back—small, surprised. "All right then," she murmured, picking up a fresh sheet.

Leander pulled his chair beside hers—not across the table, but beside, close enough that she could feel the brush of his coat sleeve against her arm. He reached toward the tin and selected a graphite stick, offering it to her. His fingers grazed hers as he placed it gently in her hand, and the touch lingered a breath too long to be entirely accidental.

"Start with the stem," he said, his voice lower now. "Trace its movement, the way it leans. Plants grow toward the light—you'll see it in their curve."

Gatty focused, letting her eyes trace the gentle bend of the stalk in his drawing. Her first lines were hesitant, but not clumsy.

"Good," Leander murmured. "Now the leaves. They're not symmetrical, but they have rhythm—like a melody written in green."

She glanced at him, her lips quirking. "Did you just compare botany to music?"

His expression remained calm, but his mouth curved at the corner. "I've always thought the two had more in common than most scholars admit. Both are patterns. Both are made for beauty and survival."

Gatty turned back to the page, her pencil gliding more confidently now. The quiet around them seemed to stretch and settle, filled only with the scratch of graphite and the soft pop of the fire.

She could feel him beside her—not just his presence, but his attention. He was watching her draw, not to judge, but to witness. To notice.

Her breath caught slightly as he leaned closer, their shoulders brushing. "Here," he said, his voice a low murmur. He reached over and adjusted her hand with a gentle touch, his fingers resting lightly on her wrist to guide her curve of a petal.

The contact was feather-light, but it lit something in her—like a spark caught in tinder. Her heart fluttered, sudden and real.

When she glanced up, he was already watching her. The flicker of the firelight caught the green in his eyes. Neither of them looked away.

"I didn't expect you to be so good at this," he said quietly.

"At drawing?"

"At letting someone in."

Her cheeks warmed. The graphite in her hand paused mid-stroke. "Neither did I," she admitted.

Leander slowly pulled back, his hand lingering for just a moment longer on the table between them. "You've a natural eye," he said, his tone gentler than before. "But that doesn't surprise me."

She looked down at the sketch. It wasn't perfect, but it was alive. Honest. "Thank you," she said softly.

When she stood to leave, she hesitated, then carefully tore the drawing from the parchment stack. She pressed it to his chest, just above his heart. "For your collection," she murmured.

His fingers closed around it with quiet reverence. "I'll keep it safe."

And as she slipped from the library, the warmth of his nearness still clinging to her skin, Gatty felt it clearly—whatever had started between them was no longer only curiosity. It was something blooming, quiet and slow as a bud in frost, but unmistakable.

The next morning, the poison garden shimmered under a fine layer of frost, the pale sunlight casting silvery halos around the ivy-draped walls. Gatty stood at its edge, a basket of tools in hand, her breath blooming in the crisp air. Her new mentees, Alice and Margery, waited nearby, stiff with nervous energy.

Alice, younger and slight, clutched a notebook to her chest, the edges of her fingers stained with ink and resolve. Margery, broader in frame and sharper in eye, stood with her arms crossed, her brow furrowed as if expecting something to go wrong.

"Right, then," Gatty began, forcing her voice to find the kind of calm she'd only recently begun to feel. "We'll start with lavender and feverfew. Simple, but useful. Follow me."

They trailed behind as she led them through the winding paths, frost crunching beneath their boots. The garden smelled of win-ter-dulled herbs and earth still holding the ghosts of warmth. Gatty moved with quiet confidence, the knowledge she'd earned—through Helena's trials, through Leander's sketches and half-smiles—settling into her like a second skin.

"Lavender's calming," she said, kneeling to gather a sprig, her gloved fingers careful. "It eases headaches, helps restlessness. Feverfew is for fevers and pain, but you don't use it if you're carrying."

Alice scribbled, her head bobbing as she wrote. Margery watched, arms still folded but eyes following every movement.

They set up near a flat stone warmed faintly by the rising sun, and Gatty demonstrated how to prepare a salve, stirring beeswax and herbs over a small brazier. The scent of lavender and honey wafted upward, catching in the air like a blessing.

"Why the beeswax?" Alice asked, leaning closer.

"It thickens it," Gatty explained, stirring steadily. "Makes it last longer, makes it easier to use. Nothing fancy—just care and precision."

Margery shifted closer, her stance relaxing. "You've a knack for it," she said, her voice still skeptical but edged with something softer. "Someone teach you?"

The question brushed old nerves, but Gatty didn't flinch. "My mother," she said, her voice gentler now. "She believed every plant had its place. That they were gifts. Not miracles—just tools, if you knew how to listen."

Alice looked up from her notes, her face open and earnest. "She taught you all this?"

"Not all," Gatty said, glancing toward the high windows of the Hall, where somewhere inside, Leander would be bent over his books. "Some of it I've learned here. From people who believe knowledge is something you pass on—not something you hoard."

The women exchanged a glance. Some of their initial hesitation began to thaw, as if her honesty had shifted the tone of the garden itself.

By the time the salve was poured into small tins and the brazier had cooled, the frost was lifting from the grass. Gatty handed each woman a tin, the beeswax still warm. The gesture felt symbolic, though she couldn't have said why.

"Take these," she said. "And remember—what we do here is for more than just survival. It's for strength. For choice."

Margery nodded, her grip tightening around the tin. Alice beamed, then slipped back into her usual shy smile. "Thank you."

A voice rang out behind them—sharp as flint. "Miss Carter."

Gatty turned to see Helena standing at the garden's edge, her gloved hands folded in front of her, framed by ivy and frost. Her eyes swept the scene—the brazier, the herbs, the tins in the women's hands—and came to rest on Gatty.

"An impressive start," Helena said, her tone measured but not cold.

"Thank you," Gatty replied, dipping her head.

Helena stepped into the garden, her boots crunching over gravel. "The garden is not merely a patch of soil, Miss Carter. It's history. It's reputation. It is a legacy. If you mean to take it on, you must do more than tend it. You must make others believe in it. In you."

The words struck something deep—part warning, part challenge. Gatty met Helena's gaze squarely. "I'll do my best."

Helena studied her a beat longer, then gave a faint nod. "I believe you will."

As she turned to leave, the frost crunching softly beneath her steps, Gatty looked back at the garden—the lavender and feverfew, the curled stalks of foxglove, the frost melting in delicate beads across each leaf. It felt different now. Not just a place for plants, but a place for possibility.

And somewhere behind her, in the still-warm library, she knew there was someone who had helped her see that.

She wasn't surviving anymore. She was becoming.

That evening, Gatty found herself alone in the poison garden, the air cool and damp as twilight draped the landscape in soft shades of gray. She sat on the low stone bench near the brazier, her fingers absently tracing the edge of the small tin of lavender salve she had kept for herself. Crickets chirped somewhere in the ivy, and the garden rustled like it was breathing—quiet and watchful.

The day's events looped through her thoughts: Alice's determined scribbles, Margery's grudging nod, Helena's gaze as sharp as it was approving. A legacy, she'd said—and for once, the word hadn't landed like a threat. It had felt... possible.

For so long, survival had been Gatty's only measure of success. Don't be noticed. Don't be caught. Don't speak too loud or step too far. But now, in this strange corner of Norfolk with its iron gates and whispered rumors, she felt something else building inside her. Not hope, exactly. Not yet. But maybe a shape that hope could take.

Her fingers tightened around the tin. The women of Blythewood weren't witches—at least, not in the way the world had tried to brand them. They were clever and bruised and hungry to be more than forgotten. Gatty thought of Alice's spark, of Margery's reluctant curiosity. Of herself, kneeling in the frost with foxglove at her fingertips. They had all been called dangerous for daring to understand things too well.

If this place could be more than a hiding place, she thought, *if it could be a forge—then maybe I can help make that happen.*

Her gaze lifted toward the garden gate. The windows of the Hall glowed faintly, pockets of golden light behind thick glass. Inside, the house was winding down: slippers on wood, cups clinking faintly in the kitchen. Somewhere, Violet was likely arranging books, and Leander...

The thought of him surfaced unbidden, unguarded. She pictured the slope of his shoulders as he bent over a page, the slight furrow between his brows when he was thinking. His hand steadying hers during their sketching earlier, his voice brushing against her ear like a secret. Her lips tingled at the memory of his nearness, and heat crept into her cheeks.

Leander Barrett was serious. Maddeningly so. But he was also kind in his own quiet way—always watching, always choosing his words with care. And she was beginning to see that beneath the ink and silence, there was a man who wanted to believe in something bigger than himself. A man who, for reasons she didn't fully understand, had started believing in her.

She shook her head, a rueful smile tugging at her mouth. Dangerous thoughts. Tempting ones. But there was too much to do, too much at stake, to let herself tumble too far into them.

Still, her feet didn't carry her toward bed. They led her toward the library.

The Hall was hushed, most of the women tucked into their rooms or murmuring behind closed doors. But a faint candlelight flickered beneath the library's door, and Gatty paused there for a breath before easing it open.

Leander sat at one of the long oak tables, half-turned toward the hearth. A book lay open before him, its spine curved with age, and a cluster of loose pages fluttered at his elbow. He didn't notice her at first. His pen scratched steadily, his brow faintly creased in thought.

She stepped inside, the creak of the floorboard catching his attention.

"Miss Carter," he said, setting his pen down. His voice was soft, a little tired, but not unwelcoming. And his eyes—those green, unreadable eyes—held a flicker of something warmer than curiosity.

"I thought you might still be here," Gatty said, lifting the tin slightly. "I wanted to thank you. For earlier—for the sketch, the book... everything."

Leander's gaze dropped to the tin. "You've brought me something?" His tone was teasing, but only just.

Gatty crossed the room and set the small tin beside his notes. "It's for your hands. I noticed the ink stains—and it's cold in here."

He looked at the tin like it was something rare, something more than it was. "That's very..." He paused, almost sheepish. "That's thoughtful of you."

"It's nothing," she said, though her cheeks warmed at the way he touched it—gently, like it mattered.

Leander opened the lid and inhaled the faint scent of lavender. His thumb brushed the balm's smooth surface. "You've a talent for this," he said, his voice quieter now. "And not just for plants. For reading people. For knowing what they need, even before they do."

The compliment settled between them like a hush. Gatty's throat tightened, but she forced herself to hold his gaze. "I'm trying," she said. "To make something of this place. To make something of myself."

Leander studied her for a long moment. Then he leaned forward slightly, folding his hands. "You already have."

She wasn't sure who moved first—him or her—but the space between them shrank until she could feel the warmth of the hearth, and his nearness again, like earlier. Just the promise of it.

Gatty's breath caught.

But then Leander sat back, the spell breaking, his expression as composed as ever—except for the faintest tug of a smile at the corner of his mouth. "If you ever need help with the compendium," he said, tapping the book beneath his hand, "you know where to find me."

She nodded, swallowing the words she couldn't quite speak. As she left the library, tinless and uncertain, she felt lighter somehow. Not safe, not entirely. But something close.

That night, tucked into her narrow bed, Gatty stared at the ceiling, her thoughts drifting like smoke: the curve of Leander's smile, the weight of Helena's expectations, the scent of lavender lingering on her fingertips.

She would learn. She would lead. She would keep the promise the Hall asked of her—and maybe, if she dared, the promise she was beginning to make to herself.

This is only the beginning.

Chapter Sixteen

THE MOCKERY

The wooden benches creaked under the weight of the gathered women, their chatter a low hum of speculation and complaint. Gatty sat quietly at the edge of the room, her hands folded neatly in her lap, observing the jostling and muttered protests as Helena's latest list of tasks was passed around. Each woman craned her neck to see what work awaited her—laundry, cooking, sewing, or tending to the poison garden.

Violet stood apart near the doorway, clutching a ledger against her chest. Her slight frame seemed even smaller against the weight of the room's noisy energy. Honoria, a tall, sharp-tongued woman with a proud stance and a mouth that rarely stayed shut, spotted her and elbowed a companion, nodding toward Violet.

"Look at her," Honoria said, her voice pitched just loud enough to cut through the murmur. "Hiding in the library all day while the rest of us break our backs. Don't know why Helena bothers keeping her around."

A ripple of murmurs passed through the nearest group of women. Encouraged, Honoria turned toward Violet, her sneer broadening. "Think you're better than us, do you?" she goaded. "Sitting on your little chair with your little books. Must be nice, not getting your hands dirty."

Violet shrank under the scrutiny, her cheeks flushing scarlet. She opened her mouth as if to respond, but no words came. The ledger trembled in her hands.

Gatty saw red, and her hands curled into fists. "How dare you..." Before she could rise, a familiar voice cut clean through the room like a knife through taut thread.

"Miss Fairlow." Leander's voice—low, clipped, and unmistakably stern—sliced through the tension with startling force. Every head turned as he stepped into the doorway, tall and straight-backed in his dark coat, his expression unreadable but razor-sharp.

Honoria blinked, caught mid-sneer. "Sir?"

"Your remarks are neither accurate nor welcome," he said, his tone icy. "Miss Bell's work in the library is essential to the operation of this Hall. If you'd care to review the inventory she maintains—by hand, I might add—you'd see it also includes every piece of linen you wash, every ounce of soap you scrub with, and every log of firewood you depend on to keep your hands from freezing in winter."

A stunned hush fell over the room.

"I would advise," he continued, taking a step closer, "that you spend less time counting the calluses on others' palms and more time minding your own tasks. Unless, of course, you'd like to try keeping the library's ledgers yourself."

Honoria sputtered. "I didn't mean—"

"I imagine you didn't," Leander said coolly. "But next time, keep it to yourself."

He turned his gaze to Violet, and it softened almost imperceptibly. "Miss Bell, if you're finished here, I believe I left a catalogue half-sorted. Your help would be appreciated."

Violet nodded, speechless, and Gatty, still half-standing, felt something shift in her chest. Leander wasn't just defending Violet—he had positioned himself between her and the cruelty of the room with a precision and calm that disarmed even the sharpest tongues. He hadn't raised his voice. He hadn't needed to.

As Violet stepped forward, clutching her ledger with new steadiness, Leander's gaze flicked to Gatty—just for a moment—and held. There was no smile, no nod, but an understanding passed between them.

Alice cleared her throat, her voice light but pointed. "You know, Honoria, he's right. Violet's usually elbows-deep in ink, paper, and records—things I'm not sure many of us would make sense of without her."

Honoria, face burning, opened her mouth again—then thought better of it. She turned sharply and muttered something under her breath, retreating to the back of the room.

The silence left in her wake slowly gave way to murmured assent and the creak of benches shifting. Gatty and Alice turned to Violet, who had paused on her way out of the room, her eyes wide with surprise.

"Thank you," Violet whispered.

"Don't thank me," Alice said softly, leaning in so only she could hear. "I wager you've got more power in that little ledger than most people realize." She gave Violet and encouraging grin and a squeeze on the arm as she left the room.

A flicker of warmth crossed Violet's face. Her grip on the book loosened. She stood a little taller.

Gatty turned to her, her voice low. "Come on. Let's get out of here before someone else starts bleating."

Violet nodded, casting one last glance over her shoulder before following Gatty out of the workroom—her steps quicker now, but more certain than they had been when she'd arrived.

As the heavy door creaked shut behind them, Violet's composure began to crumble. Her voice, thin and wavering, slipped into the hush between them. "Why did he do that?" she groaned. "I didn't ask him to. I'm not even the one he's sweet on."

Gatty paused by the hearth, then turned. "Because you shouldn't let them talk to you like that," she said, crossing to a nearby table. She pulled out a chair with a soft scrape and sat, nodding for Violet to join her.

Violet hesitated at the edge of the table, her eyes flitting to the door as though half-expecting Honoria to burst through it again. "It's easier to stay quiet," she murmured, finally lowering herself into the seat across from Gatty. "If I argue back, it just makes it worse."

Gatty studied her face—still flushed, still tightly drawn—and softened. "And staying quiet makes it better, does it?" she asked, leaning forward slightly. "You think Honoria's going to stop just because you didn't speak up today?"

Violet looked down, her fingers running along the spine of the ledger. The movement was automatic, nervous. "I'm not like you," she said, barely above a whisper. "You speak and people listen. I open my mouth and sound like a fool."

Gatty leaned back, her brow rising. "You think I wasn't scared the first time I said something?" she said. "I was shaking. Still am, sometimes. But if you never speak up, if you let them think you're easy to ignore, they'll keep doing it. That's how women like Honoria thrive—by betting you won't fight back."

Violet glanced up, her eyes round. "You don't seem scared."

"I am," Gatty said with a faint, wry smile. "I just don't give them the satisfaction of seeing it."

The fire crackled behind them, casting slow-moving shadows along the floor. Violet traced the worn edge of the ledger again. "You didn't have to stand up for me," she said quietly. "But... thank you."

Gatty reached across the table, resting her hand gently atop Violet's. "You're worth standing up for," she said, with a certainty that made Violet blink. "And you're stronger than you think."

Violet's eyes shimmered. She blinked once, then again, as if forcing the tears back down. "Do you really think I belong here?" she asked. "In the library, I mean. Honoria thinks it's ridiculous. She says it's useless."

Gatty tilted her head. "Do you think it's useless?"

Violet hesitated, then shook her head slowly. "No. I love it here," she whispered, as though afraid someone might hear. "The quiet, the order. The way everything has a place. It's the only space where I can breathe."

"Then it's not ridiculous," Gatty said. "Not one bit."

Violet's fingers curled protectively around the ledger. "But they don't see the point in the work. Records, old laws, dried ink. They think it's... irrelevant."

Gatty leaned in again, her voice low and sure. "And they're wrong. This work matters. These books matter. You've already seen what happens when the right passage turns up at the right time. It's power—not loud, not flashy—but real."

Violet's mouth twitched into a soft smile. "Leander says that too," she murmured. "That knowledge is a kind of power."

"He's right," Gatty replied. "And you have it, Violet. Whether Honoria sees it or not."

A small breath escaped Violet, almost a laugh. She straightened slightly, no longer curling in on herself. "Maybe you should spend more time here," she said, a flicker of teasing returning to her voice. "You speak like you've lived in the library all along."

Gatty chuckled. "Maybe I will," she said. "But only if you promise to stand a little taller next time Honoria opens her mouth."

"I'll try," Violet said, her voice still quiet—but this time, it held steel beneath it.

The fire snapped behind them, its glow wrapping around the high-backed chairs and tall shelves like an embrace. Outside, the wind pressed softly against the leaded windows, but within, the library felt like a fortress—quiet, unassuming, but full of secrets waiting to be weaponized.

Violet rested her chin on her hand, her gaze drifting toward the shelves that lined the library like silent sentinels. "I used to think if I just stayed quiet and did my work, people would leave me alone," she said softly, her voice tinged with something brittle and wistful. "But it doesn't matter, does it? They'll always find something to pick at."

Gatty tapped her fingers against the table, the wood cool beneath her skin. "No," she said after a beat, her voice careful. "It doesn't matter how quiet you are. If they've decided you're different, they'll find a reason to tear you down."

Violet winced slightly, her shoulders curling inward. "And I am," she murmured. "I've always been. Even before Blythewood. I'd rather read than sew. I never knew what to say when they talked about dances or boys or... what shoes the rector's daughter wore to chapel. I didn't fit." She shrugged one shoulder, as if trying to make light of it, but the words carried too much old ache.

Gatty's expression softened. "There's nothing wrong with being strange," she said gently. "Strange makes you sharper. Stranger girls survive when others break. And people like us"—she gestured between them—"we have to be sharp. Because the world isn't soft with girls it doesn't understand."

Violet tilted her head slightly. "People like us?"

"Women who don't fit," Gatty clarified, her voice low. "Women who won't bend and smile when told to. It frightens them. So they call us difficult, or odd, or unnatural. And if that doesn't work, they call us witches."

Violet let that settle in the silence. Then she leaned back, fingers still tracing the worn leather of her ledger. "I suppose," she said softly. "But I don't feel very sharp most of the time."

"That's because you don't need to fight like they do," Gatty said. "With noise and cruelty and gossip. That's not your strength. Yours is quieter—but that doesn't mean it's weaker."

Violet blinked at her. "You really believe that?"

"I do," Gatty said, steady and sure. "Let them think you're quiet. Let them call the library dusty and useless. But let them see what you build in here. What you keep alive."

Violet frowned faintly. "But what can I build? Honoria says no one cares what I'm writing down."

"Then Honoria's an idiot," Gatty said flatly, drawing a startled laugh from Violet. "And you're not. You've got all of this—" she swept a hand toward the endless shelves "—at your fingertips. You're the one keeping it in order. You're the one who knows what's here."

"But what do I do with it?" Violet asked, her voice tightening. "How do I make them see it matters?"

"You don't make them," Gatty replied. "You show the ones who matter. Helena. Leander. Me." Her tone softened. "This place is built on knowledge, isn't it? Everything Helena's doing... everything Leander's been working on—it's all tied to what's in these books. And you're the one keeping it alive."

Violet stared at her, eyes wide. "I hadn't thought of it like that."

"Well, think of it now," Gatty said. "You keep this heart beating."

Violet's lips parted in surprise, then pressed together as if to hold in a smile. "You make it sound like it's important."

"It is important," Gatty said simply. "And if you stop believing that, you let them win."

Violet nodded slowly, her shoulders no longer hunched. There was still uncertainty there, but it had shifted—no longer the shrinking kind, but the sort that preceded courage.

The fire in the hearth had burned down to its deepest coals, casting a steady warmth into the room. The tall shadows of the shelves stretched behind them, hushed witnesses to a truth that was just beginning to settle into place.

Gatty watched Violet sit straighter in her chair, something new and quiet lighting her eyes. A sense of decision. "You're right," her friend said at last, her voice quiet but sure. "I've been treating the library like it was something to hide inside. But it's not. It's... more than that."

"It is," Gatty said. "And so are you."

Before Violet could answer, the library door creaked open, and Leander entered. His dark hair was tousled from the wind, his coat dusted faintly with snowmelt. His gaze swept the room until it found them—two figures seated close at the long worktable, framed by fire-light and shadows. His brows lifted, not with disapproval, but with quiet interest.

"Hard at work, I see," he said, his voice steady, though there was a trace of something gentler in it now—an awareness, perhaps, of what he'd just walked in on.

He moved closer, hands behind his back in that bookish way of his, gaze flicking between Violet and Gatty. He paused longer on Violet, noting the flush in her cheeks and the slight lift in her chin.

"Discussing how Violet's work holds this place together," Gatty said, her voice firm, laced with a subtle defiance—daring him, just a little, to contradict her.

But Leander didn't flinch. Instead, he studied Violet for a beat longer before giving a slow, deliberate nod. "It does," he said. "With-out her, these shelves would descend into chaos. And I doubt anyone else here would know the difference between a lost ledger and a mis-placed confession from 1692."

Violet ducked her head, unable to fully hide the smile tugging at the corners of her mouth. "I've just been doing what you asked me to do," she murmured.

"You've done more than that," Leander replied, voice low but cer-tain. "And we've taken notice."

His words hung in the air like a protective charm, more powerful for their simplicity. Gatty glanced at him, surprised by the rare, open-handed praise—and the quiet authority with which he'd said we. He hadn't just offered Violet encouragement. He'd backed her, publicly and completely, without pomp or pretense. And that, somehow, was more stirring than any speech could've been.

"Actually," Leander added, shifting slightly, "I came to find a particular volume." He turned toward Violet, a hint of sheepishness softening his usually solemn expression. "The botanical index from France—Volume III. I can't seem to locate it."

Violet perked up immediately, rising from her chair. "I moved it to the southern wall," she said, already walking toward the shelves. "I thought it made more sense near the herbal manuals."

"Good thinking," Leander said, his tone warm with approval. "Would you mind fetching it? I've made enough mess for one evening."

Violet nodded quickly and disappeared between the rows of shelves, her footsteps light and sure.

Silence settled in her absence, punctuated only by the low crackle of the hearth. Gatty watched her go, then turned toward Leander, catching the faint gleam of pride still lingering in his eyes.

"She's brighter than people give her credit for," Gatty said.

"She is," he agreed, without hesitation.

Then she looked at him—really looked—and added, "You were right to defend her."

The weight of his gaze made her throat tighten. "I only said what needed saying," he managed. But something about the way he stood there—shoulders slightly slouched, voice low and genuine—unnerved her in a way she wasn't used to. She felt oddly seen.

Before Gatty could think of what to say next, Violet returned with the book cradled carefully in her arms. She placed it on the table with the reverence of someone returning a holy text. Leander accepted it with a nod of thanks.

"This is exactly what I needed," he said, with rare warmth. "You've saved me a great deal of time, Violet."

Violet's grin broke free this time, no longer small or shy. "If there's anything else—"

"Keep doing what you're doing," Leander interrupted gently. "It's more than enough."

Violet, beaming now, returned to her seat with renewed confidence, her shoulders looser, her eyes brighter.

Leander's gaze drifted once more to Gatty, his presence quiet but palpable.

"If you need resources for the garden," he said, his voice dropping just slightly, "let me know. The library is yours."

Gatty raised an eyebrow. "Are you offering to help me navigate it, then?"

"Perhaps," he said, and this time, the smile made it to his mouth—soft, real, and barely there. "If you're willing to learn."

Something in her chest gave an unexpected flutter. She didn't look away. "I might be," she said.

They stood like that for a moment longer, the firelight flickering between them. Then Leander nodded once, tucked the volume under his arm, and turned toward the door.

"You're definitely having an effect on him." Violet watched him leave, wide-eyed. "He's not usually so... kind."

"No," Gatty murmured, heart still thrumming, "he's not."

But tonight, he had been. And she wasn't sure what to make of that.

The long room in the women's dormitory was dimly lit by the flickering glow of a single candle set on the central table. The beds, narrow and austere, were made more bearable by small personal touches—a worn ribbon, a folded shawl, a charm tucked beneath a pillow. Outside, the wind stirred the skeletal branches of the oaks, their creaking limbs whispering against the windowpanes.

Gatty sat upright on her cot, the coarse blanket drawn over her knees. The hush of the room was broken only by the soft, even breath of sleeping women, some murmuring in their dreams—echoes of memories or fears that refused to stay buried. Gatty stared at the foot of her bed, her thoughts too loud for slumber.

Violet's voice, talking in her sleep, drifted back to her. Gatty smiled faintly, remembering the way Violet had glowed beneath Leander's praise, the way her eyes had lit when she realized someone truly believed in her. It had felt good and right to see another woman uplifted like that—to see strength begin to replace fear.

But the memory of Honoria's mocking voice still pressed at the edges of Gatty's mind, as persistent as a bruise. Blythewood might be a sanctuary, but it was no paradise. There were still dangers here. Dangers born not only of the world outside, but of women who had learned too well how to survive by turning on each other.

Her thoughts drifted again, unbidden, to Leander.

The steady cadence of his voice. The warmth of his shoulder when they'd sat too close by the fire. The way his fingers had guided hers—not commanding, but careful—over the fine strokes of a foxglove sketch.

She could still feel it—that moment he'd stood tall, defending Violet without hesitation. Not for show. Not to be seen. Simply because it was right. That, somehow, had undone her more than anything.

Gatty exhaled, sharp and shaky, and pressed the heels of her hands into her eyes. She couldn't afford to get lost in ideas of kindness and soft-spoken heroes. Not here. Not now. And yet, the memory of his gaze—steady, quiet, searching—refused to fade.

Her eyes drifted to the window, where the frost clung in starbursts around the glass. Beyond the thin pane, the poison garden lay hushed beneath the dark, its bare branches glinting silver in the moonlight. It looked almost beautiful from here—untamed and waiting.

She'd once seen it as a test. Now she saw it for what it truly was: a challenge. A calling. Helena had trusted her with it. No, not just trusted—tasked her. And for once, Gatty felt like she had a place. A place to make something grow again, not just from soil and seed, but from silence and survival.

She tightened her fingers on the blanket. If she could make something flourish here, if she could teach the other women what she was learning—what she was becoming—then maybe Blythewood could be more than a hiding place. Maybe it could be a beginning.

For Alice and Margery. For Violet. For all of them.

For herself.

The wind rattled faintly against the dormitory walls, and Gatty leaned back, letting the chill edge of it settle her thoughts. She watched the candle's flame dance in the dark until her eyes grew heavy.

"When women can't cast," she murmured, almost to the air itself, "they find another way."

And in that final breath before sleep claimed her, she saw Leander's eyes again—thoughtful, unreadable, and somehow waiting.

Sleep took her gently this time. Not like a fall, but a promise. One that hummed with roots and ink and firelight. One that asked her to keep going.

And she would. For all the women who had ever been told they were too strange, too dangerous, too much.

This was only the beginning.

Chapter Seventeen

TURNING POINT

The Blythewood Hall courtyard bustled with muted activity, the pale morning sun casting soft shadows across the cobblestones. Gatty adjusted the heavy basket balanced on her hip, her breath curling in the crisp air as she walked toward the storeroom. She'd been tasked with organizing the latest deliveries—sacks of dried herbs, bolts of linen, and a handful of oddments the hall seemed to endlessly require.

She welcomed the quietness of the chore. The storeroom, with its cool, earthy scent and dim light, offered a kind of solace. Gatty pushed the creaking wooden door open, placing her basket on the large worktable inside. As she began sorting the herbs into their proper jars, the faint sound of voices drifted in through the open window. Her fingers paused mid-motion, the rustling leaves outside carrying the familiar cadence of Lydia's voice.

Curious, Gatty stepped closer to the window, peering through the curtain of ivy that framed it. Below, in the courtyard near the old oak tree, Lydia stood with James Hartford. Their figures were partially obscured by the tree's sprawling branches, but Gatty could see the tension in their postures—Lydia's arms crossed, James clutching his hat in both hands.

She couldn't make out every word, but their tone was unmistakably serious. Lydia's voice, usually firm and commanding, was softer now, tinged with something Gatty couldn't quite place. James, normally so composed, seemed hesitant, his shoulders drawn tight.

Gatty felt a flicker of guilt for eavesdropping, but something about the scene held her in place. She leaned forward slightly, her cheek brushing the cool stone of the window frame as she strained to catch their conversation.

"You've done more for this place than anyone could ask," James said, his voice low but clear enough to carry. "But Lydia... you don't have to do it all alone."

Lydia tilted her head, her expression unreadable. "This place is my purpose, James. My responsibility. These women depend on me."

"And who do you depend on?" he asked, stepping closer.

The question hung in the air, not dismissed, but held—tender and unresolved. Gatty's chest tightened, a strange ache settling there as she watched Lydia look away, her lips pressed into a thin line.

But she didn't step back. She didn't shut him out.

"I do trust you," Lydia said, barely audible above the whisper of wind. "That hasn't changed."

James nodded, his gaze steady. "Then let me be here for you—even if it's from a distance. For now."

Something in Lydia's stance shifted—not a surrender, but a softening. A space carved out where there hadn't been one before.

Gatty took a step back from the window, the intimacy of the moment making her feel like an intruder. But she couldn't shake the weight of James' question. It lingered in her mind as she returned to her work, the rustling of herbs and the soft thud of jars filling the silence.

As she reached for another bundle of lavender, her thoughts turned to Leander. She'd come to rely on his quiet presence in ways she hadn't expected. His steady guidance in the library, his dry humor, the rare softness in his gaze—it all pulled at her, a quiet but insistent tug she couldn't ignore.

Could she depend on him, she wondered? And more importantly, could she let herself?

The courtyard had grown quieter now, the bustle of the morning fading as the women went about their assigned tasks. Gatty, still half-hidden by the storeroom window, caught her breath as Lydia and James moved closer to the oak tree. The way they stood, just a few feet apart but seeming to lean toward each other, drew her attention as much as their words. She was fascinated, and perhaps morbidly hopeful by their intimacy, and strained her ears to hear more.

James turned his hat in his hands, his usual composed demeanor giving way to a restless energy. "I've always respected your work here," he began, his voice low and steady, though there was an edge of vulnerability beneath it. "But seeing the care you give—how deeply you believe in what you're doing—has changed the way I see everything. The way I see you."

Lydia's hands tightened on the folds of her skirt, her gaze fixed on the ground. "You think too much of me," she said quietly, almost to herself.

"No," James said, stepping closer. "I don't. I see you exactly as you are—strong, brilliant, compassionate. And I've come to admire you more than I thought possible." He hesitated, his voice faltering. "But admiration doesn't quite cover it, does it?"

Lydia's head snapped up, her eyes meeting his, and for a moment, Gatty thought she might walk away. But Lydia stood firm, her expression softening as she said, "It doesn't."

Her voice carried an honesty Gatty hadn't heard before. Lydia seemed almost unguarded, her usual steel tempered by something warmer, more fragile. She turned slightly, gazing past James toward the sprawling garden beyond.

"Do you know why I stayed at Blythewood?" she asked, her voice barely above a whisper, and again, Gatty strained to hear. "It wasn't just duty. It was necessity. This place saved me as much as it saves these women. If I were to leave… if I were to give even a piece of myself to someone else, I don't know what would become of it."

James took a step closer, and this time, he did reach—his hand brushing just briefly against hers. "And if you gave nothing of yourself—if you kept all of this weight on your shoulders alone—what would become of you?"

Lydia smiled faintly, the kind of smile that carried more weariness than joy. "You ask the question I've been too afraid to answer."

Gatty's fingers stilled on the linen she was folding, her heart tightening at the rawness of their exchange. She couldn't help but compare their confessions to her own tangled thoughts about Leander. While Lydia and James stood in the open, their truths bared, she had spent weeks hiding behind excuses and fear.

"I'm not asking you to give everything at once," James said, his voice gentler now. "Only what you're willing. When you're ready."

Lydia looked up at him, and something in her face changed—just slightly, but unmistakably. A quiet thaw. She gave a small nod, not a promise, but an acknowledgment.

"I don't know what comes next," she said. "But I want to keep the door open."

James exhaled, some of the tension easing from his shoulders. "That's all I hoped for."

They didn't part, not exactly. They didn't kiss, didn't embrace—but they hesitated, standing close beneath the bare oak branches as if neither quite wanted the moment to end. The air between them was still full of weight, but it no longer felt like the kind of weight that crushes—it felt like something that might be carried together.

From her place at the window, Gatty folded the last of the linens with a new kind of determination. Perhaps she wasn't as trapped as she thought. Perhaps, if she let herself, she could choose a different path—one that didn't mean walking alone.

The sound of small, quick footsteps broke the silence. Ivy came skipping into the courtyard, clutching a bundle of wildflowers in her small hands. Her curls bounced with each step, and her bright, innocent laughter cut through the lingering tension like sunlight breaking through a fog.

"There you are!" Ivy exclaimed, beaming at James. Without hesitation, she slipped her hand into his, tugging slightly to make him stoop to her height. "You're always so serious, sir. You should laugh more."

James crouched beside her, the lines of worry at his brow easing just a little. "I laugh more than you think, Miss Ivy," he said, his voice warm, the edge of a smile tugging at his mouth. "Perhaps you've just not been watching closely enough."

Ivy giggled, then turned to her mother with unabashed joy. "Mama," she said, holding up the flowers as though they were a crown, "you always say to bring beauty where there's none. But there's already beauty here—because he makes you smile more than anyone else."

Lydia's composure flickered. Her eyes darted to James, who looked back at her with quiet, unguarded affection. Gatty, watching from the shadows of the window, felt her heart squeeze. There was something unbearably tender in that pause, that moment when neither knew quite how to respond to such a pure truth.

"Thank you, my love," Lydia said at last, bending to kiss Ivy's forehead and accept the flowers. "Why don't you go and see if Violet's telling stories by the greenhouse? I believe the brave fox might make an appearance."

Ivy's eyes lit up. "I'll make sure of it!" she declared, releasing James' hand and skipping away, her curls bouncing as she disappeared around the corner.

As her footsteps faded, the courtyard slipped into quiet again. James rose, brushing his hand along the front of his coat as though to collect himself. "Children see things clearly," he said, his voice softer now. "Sometimes painfully so."

Lydia looked down at the flowers, then back up at him. Her face was unreadable, but her grip on the stems was tight. "Simple truths aren't always easy ones," she murmured. "But they matter."

James stepped closer, just enough to close the space without crowding it. "You don't have to answer anything today," he said gently. "But I meant what I said. I admire you, Lydia. And when the time is right—when this place is fully yours—I'll be here. If you'll have me."

She looked at him for a long moment, her eyes brimming not with tears, but with clarity. "I'm not ready yet," she said honestly. "But I want to be."

His smile was small, but real. "Then I'll wait."

There was no farewell this time. No tipping of hats or turning away. James gave her one final look, full of understanding, before slowly walking back toward the hall. Lydia remained where she was, the bouquet of wildflowers pressed gently to her chest.

From her place beside the linens, Gatty watched it all unfold with a lump in her throat. Their love hadn't ended. It had been spoken aloud, at last. Not in grand declarations, but in something steadier—commitment, offered freely and without pressure.

And for the first time, Gatty wondered if love didn't always have to be a sacrifice. Maybe, just maybe, it could be something chosen. Something returned.

The courtyard settled around her once more, its quiet no longer heavy with loss, but with hope.

Lifting the basket, Gatty moved back toward the hall, her steps slow and deliberate as her thoughts churned. Lydia's strength and James' quiet devotion had been so clear—not a love lost, but one waiting, like a candle shielded from the wind. Their feelings hadn't been buried beneath duty and circumstance; they had simply been tucked safely away, waiting for the right time to burn brighter.

It wasn't just sacrifice—it was trust. Trust in something worth returning to.

Gatty let the weight of that settle into her bones. She wasn't Lydia, not yet. But she could learn from her. There was bravery in waiting, yes—but there was also bravery in beginning.

Her thoughts shifted to Leander. The way his eyes had softened in the firelight, how his fingers had stopped over hers—not possessive, not hesitant, but deliberate. As though he knew what it meant to touch gently. She remembered the dry timbre of his voice as he guided her through the herbals, and the rare warmth threaded through his praise. He wasn't a man weighed down by duty to somewhere else. He had chosen to be here. Chosen to stay.

Her stomach fluttered. That small, infuriatingly gentle moment over the foxglove drawing lingered in her memory like the scent of crushed lavender. It had been quiet, careful—but it had also been deliberate. A beginning, she now realized. An opening.

Gatty paused by the kitchen door, her fingers tightening on the basket's handle. What if she'd imagined it? What if the spark she felt had only ever burned in her? But even as doubt whispered, something else stirred louder—sturdier. A voice that sounded more and more like her own.

What if you're not wrong?

She breathed in sharply, then set the basket down on the table, her hands trembling just slightly with the force of her decision. She didn't need to declare anything. Not yet. She wasn't foolish enough to expect that kind of certainty. But she could take the first step. A kind word. A question asked with care. A thank-you said like it meant something more. It was enough.

Gatty glanced toward the narrow window. The garden beyond was bathed in the gold-drenched hush of late afternoon, every leaf tinged with light. There was still so much she didn't know. So much that could hurt. But for the first time, the fear didn't win.

She picked up the basket up again and walked toward the laundry room, her pace steady now. Her thoughts raced, but not with panic. With hope. With ideas. Small ways to meet Leander where he already was—by the stacks, in the quiet, in the shared care for this strange, secretive place.

And in that moment, in the stillness between tasks and expectations, Gatty made a quiet promise to herself: she would try.

Not with certainty. Not all at once. But with her whole heart. Because bravery didn't always look like firelight and declarations. Sometimes, it came in the form of small, trembling steps.

Steps toward something worth trusting in.

Something worth fighting for.

Chapter Eighteen

DISRUPTIVE EMOTIONS

The library glowed with the soft light of a dozen candles, their flames casting flickering shadows across the towering shelves. The scent of parchment, beeswax, and burning oak hung in the air. Gatty paused in the doorway, her hand resting on the frame, the hush of the room brushing against her like a breath held too long.

Leander sat in his usual place by the tall window, hunched slightly over a heavy tome. The firelight gilded the edge of his cheekbone, casting a golden glow along the sharp line of his jaw. His dark hair fell loose over his brow, and beside him, a glass of claret caught the light like garnet—untouched.

For a moment, she hesitated. The room always felt like something sacred—something that might close itself off if she entered too loudly. But she stepped forward anyway, her boots hushed by the thick rug, her resolve steadier than it had been the day before.

Leander's head lifted at her approach. His green eyes caught the light and narrowed with fleeting surprise before softening. "Miss Carter," he said quietly, setting a slip of paper between the pages of his book. "I take it the garden doesn't demand your full attention tonight?"

Gatty smoothed her skirts with more care than necessary. "I've been wondering about something," she said, steering past his question. "The plants out there... to Helena they're more than just ingredients for poultices and teas, aren't they?"

His brows lifted, just slightly. "Some of them," he replied. "Though the distinction depends greatly on who's holding the mortar and what they mean to make of it."

She stepped closer, drawn in by the flicker of interest behind his steady expression. "Do you have anything here that explains how they were used? Not just remedies, but... meanings. Folklore. Anything that might help me understand what they would have believed—what they feared."

His mouth curved—just barely. "You're expanding your studies."

"I want to do it properly," she said. "I didn't ask for the garden, but I have it now. I'd like to learn everything I can."

He studied her in silence for a beat too long, as if trying to read the shape of her intent. Then he stood, the motion smooth and quiet. The firelight stretched his shadow across the rug as he moved toward the shelves, fingers brushing familiar spines with the ease of a man who knew every volume by heart.

He plucked one from the middle of the collection and returned. "Dense," he said, offering it to her, "but thorough. Herbal lore, medicinal use, and enough half-believed superstition to keep you entertained for weeks."

She took it with both hands, surprised by the weight. "Thank you."

His gaze lingered on her face for a moment before shifting to the table. "You'll find foxglove and lavender both," he said, adjusting a candle. "Just don't confuse the former with something safe. It's beautiful. And deadly."

She stepped forward and placed the book on the table, then glanced up. "Would you show me where to start?"

He paused, fingers hovering over the back of the chair opposite his. "If you're quite sure," he said, a faint smile pulling at his mouth, "I can be rather merciless with beginners."

Gatty met his gaze evenly. "I've survived worse."

He gestured for her to sit, and as she did, something inside her eased. The room no longer felt like someone else's sanctuary. The quiet, the flickering light, the rustle of pages—they welcomed her now. And though her pulse still fluttered, it was no longer fear.

It was anticipation.

Leander remained quiet for a moment, his fingers brushing over the open page before him, thoughtful. The hearth crackled steadily, filling the space between them with warmth and possibility.

"I don't often speak of this," Leander began, his voice rougher than usual, like it had been scraped against something jagged and still hadn't healed. He didn't look at her—his eyes stayed fixed on the page in front of him, though he wasn't reading. "But you asked about women who used plants. Women accused of witchcraft. There was one."

Gatty leaned in slightly, her curiosity threaded with something gentler. "Someone you knew?"

He gave a small nod, his jaw tight. "Not well. She was a farmer's wife. Quiet, capable. A healer. She used what she knew—lavender for sleep, comfrey for wounds, willow bark for fever. Nothing elaborate, nothing sinister. But when a child in her village died suddenly... it didn't matter what she had or hadn't done." His fingers tensed against the table's edge. "The whispers came quickly. Her knowledge—the very thing that had helped people—became the reason they turned on her."

He paused, and Gatty didn't breathe.

"They came for her at dawn. Her husband pleaded with them, begged the magistrate to listen. But the court never really came into it. The village had already made its judgment."

Gatty's hand found the tabletop, her fingers curling into the wood grain like it might anchor her. "What happened to her?" she asked, though her heart already knew.

"She was hanged." The words dropped heavy and final. "Her husband left the village soon after. I found his account years later, folded into the back of a ledger from the next town over. He blamed himself. Said he should have taken her away when he had the chance."

The candlelight danced across Leander's face, catching in the hard lines of his brow. He looked up at her at last, something raw and unfinished in his eyes.

"It haunts me," he said, quietly. "Not just her. All of them. I've read too many stories like hers—buried in letters, in trial transcripts, in margins. Women whose names no one says anymore. And sometimes I wonder..." His voice dropped. "What's the point of all this? What good is preserving knowledge if it couldn't save them? What use are books full of ghosts?"

Gatty's chest tightened. The ache in his voice wasn't just for the woman—it was for the silence that followed her, the forgetting. "You didn't let her vanish," she said. Her voice came out steadier than she expected. "You remembered. You told me her story. That matters, Leander. It matters to me."

He stared at her, and in the stillness that followed, the space between them felt impossibly charged. The air itself seemed to listen. "I know what it feels like to be powerless," she said. "To be chased, hunted, punished for what you are—or what they think you are. To survive it... and not know what to do with the survival." Her voice caught, but she pressed on. "The garden helps. It's small, and quiet, but when I'm there, I feel... not helpless. I feel like I can make something grow."

His expression softened, something unspoken shifting behind his eyes. Slowly, Leander reached across the table, his hand brushing against hers. His touch was warm—real—and there was a tremble in it, just enough to make her feel less alone. "You're stronger than you know, Gatty," he murmured. "And more courageous than most would ever understand."

A soft, surprised smile touched her lips. "You're not so bad your-self," she replied. "For a man who spends most of his life buried under parchment."

That brought a small smile to his face. "They're not a hiding place," he said, gently. "They're a refuge."

"Maybe they're both," she countered, tilting her head. "Maybe that's why they matter."

He held her gaze this time, and she didn't look away. The hearth crackled on, a steady warmth against the quiet pull between them.

Leander closed the heavy tome in front of him with a quiet finality and rose from his seat. Without a word, he crossed to a tall cabinet set against the far wall—its surface gleaming in the firelight like a secret waiting to be opened. He retrieved a small brass key from his waistcoat pocket and slid it into the lock. The mechanism clicked softly.

Gatty watched, still and expectant, as he opened the doors to reveal rows of meticulously stored manuscripts and rare volumes, each one resting in its place like a relic in a cathedral.

"This," he said, selecting a slim, leather-bound manual with a reverent touch, "is something I think you'll find fascinating."

He brought it back to the table and set it gently before her. When he opened the cover, the worn pages released the scent of old parchment and pressed herbs. He turned to a page near the center, revealing a delicate botanical illustration—a flowering stalk rendered in fine strokes of ink and faded pigment.

Gatty leaned closer, her breath catching. The detail was exquisite—each leaf veined with precision, each petal unfurling like it had just been plucked from the soil.

"What is it?" she asked, her voice softened to match the hush of the moment.

"Angelica," Leander said. His tone was low, almost reverent. "A plant known for its medicinal and symbolic uses. The root was said to protect against illness, even plague. And the stalks... they sweeten bitter things." His finger traced the edge of the illustration, stopping just short of hers. "It's a plant of balance."

Her eyes flicked to his face, catching the faint smile tugging at the corner of his mouth—thoughtful, almost wistful. When her fingers reached for the page, they brushed his, a light touch that sent a bloom of warmth up her arm.

Leander didn't pull away. Instead, after a small pause, he placed his hand lightly over hers and guided her along the text, his voice a murmur. "Here—it describes the preparation of a tincture. The grinding motion must be careful. Too rough, and the potency is lost."

Their hands moved in tandem across the page. His was firm and sure; hers tentative but quick to learn. Gatty felt the heat of his skin through the brush of his fingers, and suddenly the world felt narrowed to this moment—his steady presence, the closeness, the subtle rhythm of their breath and touch.

"Like this?" she asked, her voice barely a breath.

Leander nodded, and their eyes met. "Perfect," he said, and the word settled between them like an ember.

Silence rose around them again, but it wasn't empty. It hummed with something neither had named, something ancient and tender and charged. Gatty's eyes dropped to his lips, and before she could talk herself out of it—before fear could steal the courage she'd built—she leaned forward.

The kiss was soft. Gentle. Like a question that didn't need answering. Leander stilled for a heartbeat, then kissed her back, his hand rising instinctively to steady her at the waist. The fire flickered in the hearth, but she barely noticed. There was only the warmth of his mouth against hers, and the quiet certainty of being seen.

When they broke apart, their foreheads nearly touched. Gatty's breath came quick, her cheeks flushed, but her voice was steady. "I think I've finally found something that makes me feel stronger."

"Plants?" A slow grin spread across Leander's face, catching her off guard. It was lopsided, boyish, and utterly disarming. "And here I thought I was the one giving you strength," he said, the tease undercut with something tender.

She let out a soft laugh, the tension in her chest easing. "You do surprise me," she said. "For a man who swears he prefers silence."

He tilted his head, the smile deepening. "And you," he murmured, "have an extraordinary gift for disrupting it."

Their mouths met again—this time with more certainty, less hesitation. Gatty felt his hand at the small of her back, drawing her closer, grounding her. She melted into the kiss, not minding the softness of it or the fact that it came without promises. It didn't need them.

When they finally parted, both of them slightly breathless, Gatty raised an eyebrow, mischief returning to her voice. "Does this mean I can expect you in the garden with a spade and apron?"

Leander chuckled, low and warm. "Hardly. I wouldn't dare trespass on your domain," he said, though his eyes sparkled with challenge. "But I could be convinced... under the right circumstances."

The door creaked open just as Gatty and Leander leaned into another kiss—this one softer, slower, like a page turning between them.

The sudden sound in the quiet library startled them both. Gatty jerked back, her hand flying to her chest as Violet stepped inside, a precarious stack of ledgers in her arms and a look of wide-eyed horror blooming across her face.

"Oh," Violet breathed, freezing in the doorway. Her voice was barely more than a squeak. "I... I didn't mean to—I'll come back later."

"No need," Leander said quickly, though his voice betrayed the faintest hitch. He adjusted his waistcoat with deliberate precision, but the pink climbing his neck suggested he wasn't quite as composed as usual. "You're not interrupting."

Violet blinked rapidly, her gaze bouncing between them like a startled rabbit. "I was just—just dropping these off for tomorrow," she muttered, edging toward a nearby table and setting the ledgers down with exaggerated care, as though afraid any sudden movement might provoke a second kiss.

Gatty, cheeks ablaze, pressed her lips together to stop a nervous laugh from escaping. Her heart thudded against her ribs, and she kept her eyes trained on the floor, acutely aware of the warm place on her arm where Leander's hand had rested.

"I'll... see myself out," Violet added, already halfway to the door. She nearly tripped over the rug in her haste but caught herself just in time. The door clicked shut behind her a heartbeat later, leaving behind a silence that felt louder than any words.

For a long moment, neither of them moved. Then Leander let out a long sigh and ran a hand through his hair, ruffling the neat waves into disarray. "Of all the times…" he muttered, casting a withering glance toward the now-closed door.

That was all it took. Gatty's laugh bubbled up before she could stop it—quick, breathless, and entirely unladylike. She pressed a hand over her mouth, but the way Leander's brow twitched in mild exasperation only made her laugh harder.

"What's so funny?" he asked, crossing his arms, though the reluctant curl of his mouth betrayed him.

"You," Gatty said, still giggling. "Trying to pretend as if nothing just happened."

Leander raised an eyebrow. "And you're handling it so elegantly, I suppose?"

She grinned, a spark of boldness still alight behind her fluster. "I've never once claimed I was elegant."

He shook his head slowly, but there was no scolding in his expression—only warmth. "Terrible timing," he murmured again, though with a trace of fond disbelief now.

Their eyes met, and the laughter faded, replaced by something softer. Deeper. A quiet understanding passed between them, made stronger for its simplicity. Whatever had just started—whatever was unfolding between them—it was real.

"Well," Gatty said, her voice gentler now, "at least Violet won't gossip."

Leander's mouth quirked into a wry smile. "Let's hope not."

Later that night, when the rest of the house was asleep, Gatty lay on her back, staring up at the darkened beams overhead. The dormitory was hushed, save for the whisper of wind rattling gently at the windowpanes, but her mind was wide awake—alive with memory.

She could still feel the weight of his hand over hers. The exact softness of his mouth. The quiet in his voice when he'd told her she was stronger than she knew.

Gatty had kissed him. And he had kissed her back. More than once! This was no chance encounter.

The thought made her heart flutter wildly in her chest. There had been no plan, no careful timing. Just a moment of instinct and courage and something close to hope. She hadn't expected anything tender to grow in a place like Blythewood—but there it was. Delicate, flickering, alive.

She touched her lips as if she could press the memory deeper into herself. He had looked at her like she mattered. Like she wasn't a burden or a scandal or a mistake—but something good. Something he saw.

The danger hadn't disappeared. But when she thought of Leander's steady hands, his quiet care, his stubborn belief in the power of knowledge—it didn't feel like a risk. It felt like trust. Earned. Shared. Beginning.

"I can't let fear hold me back," she whispered into the dark, her voice barely stirring the air.

It wasn't a vow. It didn't need to be. Just a quiet truth she was finally ready to believe.

With that, she closed her eyes and let the memory of his warmth pull her gently toward sleep—restless but full of light. Whatever tomorrow brought, she would face it. Not just for herself.

But for what they were building, together.

Chapter Nineteen

THE GARDEN'S SECRETS

The morning air was crisp—the kind of cold that hinted at the thaw to come, though the ground still carried winter's weight. Gatty drew her shawl tighter around her shoulders as she stepped into the poison garden, the dew on the leaves glinting like glass in the pale light. The earthy scent of damp soil and crushed herbs met her like an old companion. She knelt near the foxglove, fingers gently separating the strong shoots from the ones that had given up, her hands sure now, her movements practiced.

She let her breath rise in soft plumes as she worked, her mind drifting to the women who had once tended these same beds. Helena had spoken of them rarely, but always with a reverent kind of distance—wise women, careful ones, their knowledge feared as often as it was sought. Gatty imagined their hands—steady, roughened by work, confident in their power—and wondered if, in some distant echo, they would recognize her as kin.

The crunch of footsteps pulled her from her thoughts, and she looked up to find Alice and Margery approaching, baskets hooked over their arms. They were no longer timid in this space. Curiosity had replaced caution, and their presence now felt like an extension of the garden itself. Alice, always quick with a jest, moved as though the earth answered to her. Margery, quiet and steady, handled even the deadliest plants as if listening for their secrets.

"Morning, Miss Gatty," Alice called, her voice bright despite the cold. "What's on the docket?"

Gatty stood, brushing her hands against her skirts. "Chamomile and lavender for teas, comfrey for salves. We'll start simple—but getting it right's more difficult than it looks."

Margery nodded, surveying the rows. "Seems a strange thing, calling it a poison garden when half of it's meant to heal."

Gatty smiled. "It depends on the hand that wields it. Most of these plants can cure—or kill. It's all in the preparation."

Alice gave a mock shudder. "Well then, I'll be watching my measurements."

They fell into work, the rhythm almost companionable. Gatty demonstrated the crush and steep of chamomile, the fine slicing of comfrey root. Each instruction felt like more than a lesson—it was a gift, a quiet passing on of knowledge she had once hoarded for survival. Now she gave it freely.

The gate creaked open, and all three women looked up. Leander stepped into the garden, his coat buttoned high against the cold, his dark hair slightly tousled by the breeze. His eyes scanned the herbs before resting, as they always seemed to, on Gatty.

"Mr. Hawthorne," she greeted, rising again. "Looking for mint or mischief?"

"Not quite," he said, his voice low and smooth. "Though I suppose I've found a bit of both."

Alice elbowed Margery, who rolled her eyes with a small grin, and the two of them made a strategic retreat down the path, their laughter barely concealed.

Gatty felt the heat rise to her cheeks but kept her expression cool. "And what brings you to my corner of the world?"

Leander pulled the satchel from his shoulder and removed a leather-bound book, its cover creased from age and use. "This," he said, handing it to her. "A rather unusual apothecary's manual. Its author favored... flair. I thought it might suit your style."

Gatty accepted the volume carefully. Its heft was reassuring. Inside, the script was fine, the drawings exquisite. A page near the center showed belladonna—elegant, deceptive, deadly. She traced the curve of the inked stem with one finger.

"This is remarkable," she murmured. "Where did you find it?"

"In a box misfiled as parish accounts," he replied. "I nearly overlooked it, but something about the binding made me look closer. I suppose I've learned to trust instinct."

She looked up, heart catching at the softness in his expression. "Thank you," she said, voice low. The words felt too small for what she meant, but she hoped he understood.

Leander tilted his head slightly. "Use it well, Miss Carter," he said, his tone quiet but steady. "There's more to this garden than poison. And more to you than even you see."

He turned before she could find her reply, his coat brushing the rosemary as he passed through the gate and disappeared into the path beyond.

Gatty stood there a moment longer, the book still pressed against her chest, the warmth of it sinking through her shawl. The laughter of Alice and Margery floated back to her, and the scent of lavender lifted on the breeze. Her pulse was still fluttering.

The mid-afternoon sun spilled through the high windows of Blythewood Hall, casting long beams across the stone corridor in a warm, honeyed light. Gatty's boots clicked softly against the flagstones as she walked, Charlotte's short, efficient note still folded in her apron pocket. Clutched in her hands was the herbal manual Leander had given her.

Helena's private study was a room that commanded silence. The velvet curtains, the color of plums left too long on the branch, muffled the sounds of the hall. Tall windows reached up like cathedral arches, and every surface gleamed with order: neatly stacked ledgers, polished wood, and a row of precisely aligned quills. The air smelled of ink and lavender and something else older, like dried sage in a sealed drawer. It was the scent of authority.

Helena sat behind a massive oak desk, her quill poised in one elegant hand. She did not look up immediately, but the stillness in the room shifted the moment Gatty entered—acknowledgement without gesture. Gatty's spine straightened instinctively.

"You asked for me, ma'am?" she said, voice even, though she held the manual a little too tightly.

Helena lifted her gaze. Her sharp eyes softened—just slightly—at the sight of her. She gestured toward the chair opposite her. "Sit, Miss Carter. Let us speak plainly."

Gatty hesitated only a moment before crossing the room and perching on the edge of the seat. The manual rested in her lap like a shield.

"I've been observing your work in the garden," Helena said, setting her quill down with quiet precision. "It's impressive. You move through that space as if you were born to it."

Gatty blinked. Praise from Helena was rare, and it landed with unexpected weight. "Thank you, ma'am," she said, softly but sincerely.

Helena studied her with a gaze that seemed to see past skin and sinew. "The garden has always been a place for women like us. Not merely a patch of soil, but a place of survival... of study, of quiet rebellion. And now, perhaps, it can be more than even that."

Gatty tilted her head slightly, curiosity stirring. "What would you have it be?"

A flicker of something unreadable passed over Helena's face before she gave a rare smile—small, almost reluctant, but real. "That is not for me to decide," she said. "It belongs to those who tend it. To you. To Alice. To Margery. You are shaping it already."

She nodded toward the book in Gatty's lap. "Even that—knowledge handed from one hand to the next. It is not enough to preserve it. You must use it, adapt it. You must give it breath."

The words settled over Gatty like warm water. She had spent so long surviving, measuring each breath, each choice. But this... this felt different. This felt like trust.

"I'll do my best," she said, and this time, the words didn't feel small at all.

Helena inclined her head. "I suspect your best will be more than enough."

Gatty stood, unsure whether to bow or simply thank her again, but Helena's voice stopped her at the threshold.

"Miss Carter," she said, her tone softened but firm, "the garden is a legacy. Guard it well. Grow it wisely."

Gatty paused, her hand brushing the rough edge of the manual. "I will, ma'am."

She stepped out into the corridor, the heavy door closing with a soft click behind her, and the air in her lungs felt lighter than it had in weeks. The weight of fear hadn't vanished, but it no longer stood at the front of her thoughts. Instead, it was something gentler—curiosity, responsibility, a kind of pride that frightened her in a way nothing else h ad.

By the time she reached the garden gate, the wind had picked up slightly, stirring the rosemary and yarrow. Gatty flipped open the manual, her fingers already marking sections she might copy for Alice and Margery, new ideas blooming faster than she could catch them.

Helena's words still echoed within her, not like a warning—but like a blessing. The garden was a legacy. And now, it was hers to shape.

The library had become a haven for Gatty—quieter than the still-room, warmer than the garden after dusk. Tonight, the scent of parchment and old paper mingled with the soft crackle of the hearth, the firelight dancing across rows of worn leather spines. She sat at a corner table scattered with her notes on tinctures, the herbal manual Leander had gifted her open to a precise diagram of lavender roots. Her quill scratched steadily, a rhythm that soothed her until the creak of a floorboard broke her focus.

Leander stepped into view, his dark hair slightly disheveled as though he'd run a hand through it one too many times. In one hand, he carried a small bundle of dried herbs. A smile played at his lips, though his eyes, as always, held something unreadable beneath the c alm.

"Miss Carter," he said gently. "Burning the midnight oil?"

She arched a brow. "I could ask the same of you. Come to reorganize the entire taxonomy of wormwood again?"

He smirked, setting the bundle down beside her notes. "Valerian root," he said. "For your teas. I thought you might be running low."

Gatty blinked, surprised. Her fingers hovered over the dried stems. "You remembered," she murmured.

"You're not easy to forget," he said lightly, but his voice carried more weight than the words alone.

The moment stretched, quiet and full. Gatty dropped her gaze, busying herself with the valerian as if she could smooth the flutter in her chest. "Thank you," she said, her voice soft, the gratitude genuine.

Leander lingered at the edge of the table, his fingers resting lightly on the carved back of a nearby chair. "I've been watching your work," he said after a beat. "Not just with the herbs. With Alice. With Margery. They follow your lead."

Gatty looked up, narrowing her eyes in mock suspicion. "Is that praise, Mr. Hawthorne? Should I write the date down in my journal?"

His mouth twitched. "I suppose it is. Mark it if you must." He hesitated then, the humor slipping from his face. "There's something I've been meaning to say."

Her teasing faded. The shift in his tone tugged at something low in her stomach. "What is it?"

He drew a slow breath. "I'd like to court you, Gatty. Properly."

The words rang in the quiet space between them like a bell. Her breath caught, suspended in the moment. She stared at him, the sheer plainness of the request—no flowers, no rehearsed poetry—making it all the more disarming.

"Court me?" she echoed.

He nodded. "I apologize if it's unexpected. But I so admire you. Your strength, your mind, the way you've carved something meaningful out of chaos." His voice softened. "You've brought light into this place, more than you know."

Gatty's hands fidgeted in her lap, the emotion behind his words overwhelming in its simplicity. "Leander, I..."

"You don't have to answer now," he said quickly. "And I'd never move forward without Helena's consent. I'll speak with her."

"Of course, my answer is yes. I feel the same way." Gatty huffed out a breath that was almost a laugh, the pressure easing just a fraction. "You're very formal."

He chuckled, though he looked faintly sheepish. "Librarian's habit. I like things labeled and orderly."

She glanced at him then, and for the first time, didn't look away. "I admire you as well," she said softly.

"That thought brings me great strength." He straightened, a quiet satisfaction in the lift of his chin. "I'll leave you to your notes." He had turned halfway when she said his name.

"Leander."

He paused.

She met his eyes again. "Thank you. Not for asking...for really seeing, me and liking what you saw."

Something unspoken flickered in his expression. "It's impossible not to."

As the door clicked gently shut behind him, Gatty sat frozen in place, the valerian still resting in her hands. A slow warmth bloomed in her chest—not just affection, but possibility. A future, perhaps, where the bruises of her past didn't define her. Where someone could care for her without needing to fix her.

But still, the question lingered: Would Helena allow it? Could love exist here, under the watchful eyes of a woman who guarded her secrets as fiercely as her legacy?

Gatty didn't know yet. But she had trusted her instincts this far. She would trust them a little farther.

The late morning sun shone through the tall windows of Helena's study, casting long beams of gold across the polished oak desk. Leander stood before it, hands clasped behind his back, posture straight but not rigid. For once, his calm gave way to something taut and earnest, as if the gravity of what he was about to say had rooted him to the floor.

Across from him, Helena sat with the cool composure of someone who had seen and heard everything before—and was rarely impressed. Her quill rested beside a half-finished letter, and her gaze, sharp and steady, pinned him like an insect beneath glass.

"You've been pacing, Mr. Hawthorne," she said, tone dry but not unkind. "Either you've misplaced a manuscript or you've worked yourself into the rare state of giving a damn."

Leander offered a brief smile. "I've come to ask your permission to court Miss Carter."

"Miss Carter," Helena repeated, her voice smooth as silk drawn tight. "And why, pray, would I allow that?"

Leander's brows rose, but he didn't retreat. "Because not only does she make my heart sing, but I greatly admire and respect her," he said simply. "I've come to know her as someone remarkably strong. Brilliant, determined. She's built something of value here."

"She's built something because she was given the space," Helena replied coolly. "And now you would like to... what? Compliment her into leaving it all behind?"

Leander's jaw tightened. "No, Madam. I would never take her from her purpose."

"Then what is it you offer her?" Helena asked, steepling her fingers. "You have no property. No inheritance. Only the money you've earned in your stay here, a library and opinions."

A pause stretched between them like a drawn bowstring. Leander's spine straightened further.

"I offer her my respect," he said. "My regard. My partnership."

Helena stood, crossing to the hearth. "Miss Carter is not some shopkeeper's daughter. She is under my protection. And this house was built for women with magic in their bones. What makes you think someone like you belongs in her story?"

"I thought you might say that," Leander said, and—unexpectedly—reached into his coat pocket.

From within, he drew a coin and passed it from knuckle to knuckle with surprising deftness. He flicked it into the air, caught it, then made it vanish with a subtle flourish. From his other hand, he produced a folded card, flicked it open to reveal a sprig of dried yarrow tucked inside.

Behind Helena, two of the women seated quietly at the ledgers—Violet among them—giggled.

Helena did not smile. "Palming," she said, flatly. "And the coin trick is older than I am. Shall I name them all, Mr. Hawthorne? Do you think parlor sleight is true magic?"

"No," Leander said calmly, slipping the card away. "But I thought perhaps it would amuse you."

She gave him a long look. "It doesn't."

"Then allow me to be plain," he said, cheeks reddening. "I know I have no magic. But I believe in it. I've read every account in that library—every tragedy and every triumph. I've preserved the stories no one else will touch. I've seen the danger and the power and the need for places like Blythewood. And I will not take her from it—I will defend it with her, if you'll let me."

Helena remained silent. One of the ledger women coughed lightly to hide a laugh.

Then came another voice from the doorway.

"You don't need magic to protect magic," Gatty said. She stepped into the room, eyes steady, voice clear. "You need people like Leander. People who make space for it. Who don't turn away from it, even when it frightens them. That's just as important as anyone who can call the wind or make the tea leaves dance."

Helena turned to her, and the room held its breath.

For a moment, Helena said nothing. Then her lips curved into the faintest hint of a smile. "Well said," she murmured. "Though I'll expect you both to remember how rare it is to find such balance." She returned to her desk and picked up her quill again. "Very well. I will permit a courtship—on three conditions."

Leander let out a breath, slowly. "I'm listening."

"One: Gatty's work comes first. You will not interfere with her independence. Two: discretion. No public dalliances, no hallway whispers. And three..." Helena looked between them. "I admire your courage to come to me. I shall give you gift. Yes, one for each of you, and one to share."

Gatty blinked. "A gift?"

Helena inclined her head, her pen already moving across parchment. "For you, Miss Carter—full stewardship of the still room and its remedies. You may appoint apprentices if you wish, but more than that, you will own the work of your hands. Sell your tinctures in the market, build your trade as you see fit. We'll discuss rates. Let none say you are dependent on any man."

Gatty's breath caught, a flicker of pride stirring deep in her chest. Her work. Her name. Her future.

"For Mr. Hawthorne," Helena continued, "the key to the northern records wing. There are documents I believe only someone with your eye will handle properly. They are quite old, and should not leave that room until they have been recorded and restored."

"Of course." Leander's brows lifted, and he said with quiet reverence, "Thank you."

"And the shared gift?" Gatty asked curiously.

Helena's smile broadened. "The founding of a new herbalist apprenticeship program," she said. "Choose those who need not just shelter, but a future. Teach them, guide them, shape what Blythewood might yet become."

A hush settled over the room. Gatty felt her throat tighten, not with fear, but with wonder. It felt like freedom. She nodded, not trusting her voice.

Leander's voice was steady as he replied, "We'll see it done."

"Don't thank me yet," Helena said, waving them both toward the door. "You haven't earned the ending."

As they left, the ledger women tittered again. Gatty's cheeks were flushed, but her expression was radiant.

And Leander? He smiled all the way back to the library—coin tucked back in his pocket, hands ink-stained and his face hopeful.

The sun hung low over the horizon, painting the garden in hues of gold and deep green. Gatty knelt near a patch of lavender, her fingers brushing the soft tips of the fragrant leaves. The cool air was touched with the warmth of the day's last light, and the garden, for all its tangled wildness, felt like it was holding its breath.

Footsteps approached along the gravel path, careful but unhurried. "Miss Carter. Gatty..."

She looked up. Leander stood at the garden's edge, his coat still buttoned, a satchel slung over his shoulder. His hair was mussed from the wind, and his expression was—unusually—hopeful.

Gatty rose to her feet, brushing her apron with one hand. "You're not here for more foxglove notes, are you?" she teased, but her voice was softer than usual.

He smiled. "I can't believe I tried that coin trick," he admitted, sheepish. "It did not impress her."

She laughed quietly. "No, I suppose it wouldn't."

"But then you spoke," Leander added, more seriously. "And everything changed."

Their eyes met, and something unspoken passed between them—recognition, perhaps, or gratitude. Gatty's heart fluttered like a wing caught in her ribs.

"She's given her permission," he continued. "Your independence remains yours. Your garden remains yours. And apparently, I've been given access to the north wing." He shook his head. "I can't quite believe it."

She looked away for a moment, her eyes scanning the rows of green and violet, the leaves glistening faintly with the last of the day's light. Her fingers, still stained from the soil, curled at her sides. "I never imagined someone would ask to court me who I truly liked, to tell you the truth," she said softly.

"Then I'll ask again," Leander said. "Not to change you. Not to claim you. Just to walk beside you, if you'll let me."

Gatty turned back to him, the knot in her chest loosening with the steadiness in his gaze. "I'm not easy," she warned. "I still get angry. I still flinch at shadows. I don't always know how to be soft."

"I don't need soft," Leander said. "I just need real."

She studied him for a long moment. Then, quietly, she stepped closer. "I don't know if I believe in fate," she said, "but I do believe in this place. And I believe you're part of it."

His smile was small, but genuine. "Then that's enough for me."

She offered her hand—earthy, honest, worn. Leander took it gently, his fingers wrapping around hers like a promise.

The wind rustled through the lavender. In the hush between heartbeats, Gatty felt something shift—not just around her, but within her.

She wasn't just surviving anymore. She was beginning.

Chapter Twenty

COURTSHIP

G atty stood at a narrow window, her fingertips pressed white against the sill as sunlight spilled across the distant orchard. The high stone walls framed a tangle of gnarled fruit trees, their bare limbs reaching skyward in quiet defiance of winter. They looked stark and proud against the pale sky, like old souls unbothered by the cold. Her breath misted the glass, the cloud fading as quickly as her confidence.

Courtship.

The word lodged awkwardly in her mind, unfamiliar and fine as one of the brocade gowns she'd once dusted while scrubbing someone else's floors. Was that what this was now—her life being measured in terms she'd only ever heard from behind a tavern curtain or whispered in the village square?

She thought of the women at Blythewood, their whispers sharpening in recent days. Violet, wide-eyed and blushing, had giggled over breakfast, "Oh, he's a serious one, but you've gone and made him quite undone, haven't you?" Honoria, always the cynic, had muttered into her tea, "Careful with that one. Men who read too much think they're cleverer than they are."

Gatty had only smiled, unwilling to say too much. *What did they know?* What did *she* know?

She had no fine family name, no linen-lined hope chest or lace-trimmed letters from home. No dowry. Land left behind when she ran from the mob. No rules to guide her in the game of glances and gestures that seemed to shape a proper courtship.

Her fingers brushed the homespun fabric of her skirts. They were clean and sturdy, not delicate. But neither was she. "I've stood before worse," she whispered, the words fogging the glass again. "I'll not quake now."

———

In the library below, Leander Hawthorne stared down a far more intimidating opponent than any historical text: *The Gentleman's Guide to Proper Courtship.*

He frowned, the corners of his mouth twitching in displeasure as he read aloud under his breath. "'Speak plainly yet with grace. Do not overwhelm her with compliments, but neither should you appear indifferent...'" He glanced toward the hearth. The fire there seemed to crackle in solidarity with his nerves.

"I've read *Cicero* with less strain," he muttered, and slammed the book shut with an unceremonious thud.

He leaned back in his chair, one hand tugging at his cravat, the other drumming thoughtfully against the edge of the desk. He had faced sermons in Latin, catalogued letters soaked with grief and ink, endured the scrutiny of scholars twice his age. And yet, the prospect of walking arm in arm with a woman like Gatty Carter had left him utterly unmoored.

Still, for her—for her steady gaze, her nimble mind, her silence when silence was needed and fire when it was not—he would face the unknown.

Helena had made today's arrangement with all the subtlety of a stage director, though she feigned innocence when questioned. Over breakfast, she'd stirred her tea with lazy precision and said, "A walk in the orchard, dear. Fresh air will do you both good." Her tone was maddeningly casual. Her eyes were not.

And so, just before noon, Gatty stepped through the arched gate into the orchard, her boots crunching softly against the gravel path. She had spent the better part of an hour agonizing over whether to wear her bonnet or leave her hair uncovered. Practicality had won out—but not without rebellion. A few unruly strands had already wriggled free.

Leander was already waiting, tall and composed against the pale stone wall, though his hands—she noticed—fidgeted at his sides before he caught himself. He turned at the sound of her approach, and for a moment, something in his expression flickered—something soft and unguarded that made her breath catch in her throat. "Miss Carter," he said, inclining his head.

"Mr. Hawthorne," she replied, attempting a matching composure. Her voice betrayed her, just slightly, with a tremor at the edges.

He offered his arm, a gesture somewhere between invitation and reverence. She hesitated—just long enough for her heart to stutter—then placed her gloved fingers gently atop his sleeve.

The contact was light, yet the warmth of him bled through the wool. She felt the flush rising up her throat and cursed it silently.

"Shall we?" he asked.

She nodded. And together, they walked into the garden.

The orchard was quiet but not still—there was a living hush to it, the rustle of dry leaves clinging to bare branches and the occasional creak of wood settling in the wind. Gatty's thoughts darted like startled birds, her gaze flitting between the gravel path and the profile of the man beside her. Leander walked with a kind of quiet confidence, his posture upright, his steps measured. He was handsome, certainly—but it wasn't the cut of his coat or the angle of his jaw that stirred her. It was the steadiness. The thoughtful silences. The fact that he seemed to listen even when no one was speaking.

"Do you often walk here?" she asked, the question bursting out just to fill the quiet.

"Not as often as I should," he said, glancing down at her with a faint smile. "Though I suppose I have you to thank for reminding me there's more to life than parchment and ink."

She looked up at him, startled by the trace of humor in his voice. "You jest."

"Not entirely," he said. "You've a way of pulling people out of their hiding places, Miss Carter."

There was something in the way he said it—quietly, without ceremony—that made her throat tighten. She turned her face back toward the path, her fingers flexing against his arm, uncertain whether to deflect or accept the compliment.

"And what about you, Mr. Hawthorne?" she asked, her voice softer now. "Where do you hide?"

He was quiet for a moment, their steps slowing beneath a crooked archway of branches. "In my books, mostly," he said finally. "It's safer there. No one turns on you for knowing too much between covers."

Gatty tilted her head toward him, her curiosity overcoming her caution. "And yet you're here now."

He stopped walking. Turned toward her fully. "I am," he said.

That one quiet sentence unraveled something in her. He looked at her without pretense, without judgment, as though her presence—her questions, her scars—were welcome here.

He reached gently for her hand, not with bravado but reverence, and paused just before touching her glove. "May I?"

Her heart thudded, her breath caught. She nodded.

He lifted her hand to his lips, brushing a feather-light kiss against the fabric. The contact was fleeting, but she felt it like a match struck to skin. Her breath hitched. When he lowered her hand, his fingers met hers—warm, tentative.

"Shall we continue?" he asked, his voice calm, though his eyes betrayed the same nervous current rushing through her veins.

"Yes," she said, barely more than a whisper.

They resumed their walk, and the orchard felt changed—quieter somehow, not in sound, but in spirit. As if the trees themselves had leaned in. Gatty's mind tumbled ahead of her, struggling for something safe to say. She had never been courted before, not truly—and certainly not by a man who seemed carved from quiet steadiness and old pages.

"I never imagined you to be the outdoorsy type," she said at last, the teasing note soft but hopeful.

"Nor did I," he replied with mock solemnity. "But it seems you've inspired me to expand my horizons."

The playful tone eased the tension between them, and she felt her shoulders loosen. They passed under a knotted canopy of branches, the last dry leaves rustling like parchment. Leander gestured toward a cluster of apple trees, their bark mottled with age.

"These are Pippins," he said, "favored for their tartness. Good for cider and excellent for baking. I imagine you'd make quick work of them."

Gatty tilted her head, amused. "You know a surprising amount about apples, Mr. Hawthorne."

He gave a modest shrug. "A result of too much reading and very little pruning. Did you know the Romans introduced many varieties to Britain? The Pippin likely descends from those early cultivars."

She smiled at his unexpected fervor. "You speak of them as though they're old friends."

"Perhaps they are," he said, half-smiling. "Rooted, yet reaching."

That phrase—so quietly offered—settled in her like warmth in her chest. She looked at him, caught off guard by how easily he straddled the line between scholar and poet, as though language itself bent slightly in his presence.

They came to a wooden bench beneath the largest tree, its limbs spread wide like a watchful elder. Leander paused, his eyes flicking from the bench to her. "Shall we?"

Gatty hesitated, her stomach a knot of nerves and excitement. "Only if you've brought provisions," she said, aiming for lightness.

His answering smile was almost smug as he reached into a satchel slung over one shoulder. "Helena insisted," he said, drawing out a cloth-wrapped bundle.

They sat, the bench creaking beneath their weight like it remembered other such meetings. Leander unwrapped the bundle to reveal a small but thoughtful meal—two crusty loaves, a wedge of cheese, and a flask of cider.

He poured the amber liquid into a pewter cup and handed it to her with a small, deliberate bow. "To Blythewood's finest gardener."

Gatty raised the cup, the corners of her mouth curling upward. "And to Blythewood's most reluctant outdoorsman."

She took a sip. The cider was sharp and bright, with just enough sweetness to make her eyes water. She broke off a piece of bread and let its texture anchor her as the moment expanded around them. As they ate, the conversation flowed more easily than she'd expected—interspersed with small laughter, long glances, and the occasional shared silence that didn't feel like silence at all.

At one point, their hands brushed as they both reached for the same piece of cheese. The contact was fleeting but sharp, like the spark of flint against stone. Gatty froze, startled by the sudden warmth blooming up her arm. Leander, too, seemed caught off guard—his fingers hovered for a breath longer than necessary before retreating. "Apologies," he said, his voice lower than before.

"No need," Gatty murmured, though her own voice came out thinner than she'd meant. Each stolen glance, each accidental touch, built something between them—slow, quiet, but undeniable. As they packed away the remains of their meal, Gatty found herself wishing, absurdly, that the orchard might stretch on forever.

They resumed walking, slower now, more in step. The path meandered through tangled rows of trees, and the light through their bare branches dappled the ground in pale silver and gold.

"Did you know," Leander said after a pause, a glint of mischief threading his tone, "that even botany has theories about why people grow close?"

Gatty raised an eyebrow, her lips quirking. "Does it? Go on, Mr. Hawthorne. Enlighten me—what wisdom have the roots and leaves to offer on the subject of courtship?"

He gave a small, theatrical shrug, adjusting the book tucked beneath his arm. "Take the climbing rose, for instance. It flourishes best when paired with a trellis. Each one supporting the other, the plant winding upward, higher than it could ever grow alone."

"Ah," Gatty said, her smile widening. "So you're the trellis, then? Strong, dependable, and mostly stationary?"

Leander affected a thoughtful air. "That was one interpretation. But perhaps I meant the opposite—that I am the rose, and you are the support guiding me upward."

She laughed, the sound bright and unguarded. "Flattering, but not quite convincing. A rose is delicate and adorned with thorns. You, sir, are far too even-tempered for such dramatics."

He tilted his head, amused. "Then tell me—what would you compare yourself to, Miss Carter?"

Gatty pretended to consider, tucking a wind-blown curl behind her ear. "Perhaps a foxglove," she said, her tone light but laced with meaning. "Lovely to look at, but dangerous if handled improperly."

Leander chuckled, genuine and warm. "A fitting choice. I'll remember that. Tread carefully."

Their conversation moved like a dance—lively, teasing, with a rhythm that seemed to build between their footsteps. Gatty felt her confidence bloom with each exchange. For the first time in a long while, she wasn't just defending herself or dodging danger. She was holding her own—and being seen for it. Not pitied. Not rescued. But liked. Truly liked. A flicker of pride stirred in her chest as she met Leander's wit step for step.

"Tell me," she said, tilting her head toward him with mock seriousness, "is there a scientific explanation for your sudden fondness for fresh air and gardens? Or shall I attribute it to your growing admiration for Blythewood's poisoner-in-residence?"

Leander's mouth twitched, a flush rising faintly to his cheekbones. "Perhaps both," he said, voice quiet now. Earnest.

The answer made her heart jump. She fumbled with her shawl to cover it, adjusting the folds as the breeze picked up—but in doing so, her hand brushed his arm. The contact was brief, almost nothing at all, but it startled her with how warm it felt.

"Apologies," she murmured, her hand darting back as if burned.

"Not at all," he replied quickly, though the slight catch in his voice gave him away.

They walked on a few more steps in silence before the book he carried slipped from beneath his arm, tumbling to the path with a soft thud. They both bent to retrieve it, and their heads nearly collided.

"Oh!" Gatty gasped, pulling back too fast, her cheeks already burning.

"Forgive me," Leander said, straightening with equal haste. His ears were pink now as he stepped aside, giving her space.

She lifted the book and handed it back, their fingers brushing. This time, neither of them moved away quite so fast.

"Clumsy of me," he said, offering a sheepish half-smile.

"Hardly," she returned, unable to stop her own smile. "Even the most composed trellises have their moments."

He gave a quiet laugh at that, and they resumed their walk, the air between them still threaded with something unspoken, but no longer fragile.

As they passed the edge of the orchard, the wind eased and the gravel beneath their feet gave way to softer ground. Gatty glanced at Leander's profile, the sunlight catching the thoughtful crease between his brows. The sight of him now—calm, steady, undone just a little—struck her with a pang so unexpected it stole her breath.

"I've been wondering," he said suddenly, his voice low, thoughtful. "What do you hope to build here, Miss Carter? Beyond the garden, I mean."

She blinked, caught off guard by the question. No one had asked her that before. She tucked a curl behind her ear and slowed her steps. "I don't know," she admitted. "For so long, surviving was enough. But now..."

She hesitated, then looked at him. "Now, I think I'd like to help other women—women like me, who've been chased or bruised or silenced. I want them to know they're not alone. That they aren't ruined."

Leander's expression was unreadable for a beat, and then it softened. "A noble goal," he said quietly. "Not an easy one, but I suspect that's never deterred you."

She gave a small, almost shy smile. "It hasn't yet."

He glanced out toward the orchard trees, their bare limbs silhouetted against the sky. "I have a dream too," he said. "I'd like to build a library—open to all. A place where anyone can read, learn, ask questions. Not just scholars or gentlemen, but farm boys and kitchen maids and girls who've never been allowed to read anything but a Bible."

Gatty slowed again, struck. "A library for everyone?" she echoed.

He nodded. "Books have always been my shelter," he said. "But they shouldn't be locked away like treasures. They're tools. They're freedom. And I want to make that freedom available to those beyond this house."

Her breath caught at the fierceness in his voice. "I think you will," she said.

"And you?" he asked. "Do you believe you'll help them—those women?"

She paused. "I believe I must," she said simply.

They walked on, and they neared the gates, Leander stopped and turned to face her fully. "I look forward to our next lesson, Miss Carter," he said, voice soft but certain. "Whatever it may be."

She smiled, warmth blooming in her chest. "As do I, Mr. Hawthorne."

He bowed his head slightly, then turned toward the Hall. She watched him go, her shawl fluttering in the breeze, her hands still tingling with the memory of his touch.

As the last of the light spilled gold across the orchard path, Gatty stood still for a moment longer, the taste of cider on her tongue and hope humming quietly in her blood.

Chapter Twenty-One

BETRAYAL

Gatty knelt near the stone path, the sharp, clean scent of crushed herbs rising around her. She was bundling a handful of lavender—its scent familiar and anchoring—when the low murmur of voices pricked her ears. She stilled, head tilting. The voices weren't from within the garden.

They came from beyond the eastern wall, just past the holly bushes near the outer gate—where deliveries came and where trouble, if it ever knocked, might begin.

"...told you there's something unnatural about the place," a man said, his voice rough, laced with contempt and something colder.

"That doesn't mean I'll risk everything without proof," came another voice—one Gatty knew at once. Honoria.

Gatty's stomach clenched. She moved on instinct, slipping into the shadows of the trellised arbor where ivy grew thick. She crouched low, careful not to snap a twig or rustle a leaf. The scent of wormwood clung to her sleeves as she pressed closer, peering through a narrow gap in the vines.

Honoria stood with her arms crossed, rigid and tight-lipped beside a short, broad man with thinning hair and a merchant's worn boots. He held a rolled parchment in one hand, its seal already broken.

"Proof?" the man scoffed. "You think the magistrate needs proof? He only needs fear. That place is full of women who've been whispered about already. All it takes is one spark."

Honoria's jaw clenched. "Fear alone won't get me what I want. Helena needs to see she's backed the wrong women. That little gardener's pet, and the girl with ink on her fingers—they've done nothing to deserve her favor."

Gatty's pulse thudded in her ears. The insult stung—but it was the bitterness in Honoria's voice that cut deeper. This wasn't just ambition. This was something older and more personal. Jealousy. Insecurity. Spite.

The merchant unfurled the parchment and held it up between them. "This'll do it. Plant it in the garden, or somewhere they'll find it on her. Nothing too obvious—just enough to make it look like she's been hiding something. Dried herbs, symbols, maybe a bone or two. Let the imagination do the rest."

Honoria hesitated, her eyes scanning the symbols inked onto the parchment. "And if it turns back on us?"

"Then don't let it," the man said, voice flattening. "You wanted a way in. This is it. Just be clever. Make them afraid."

After a moment's pause, Honoria nodded. She took the parchment.

Gatty didn't wait to hear more. She ducked back into the garden, moving quickly and silently, heart hammering against her ribs. Her thoughts tumbled—symbols, planted evidence, the magistrate being summoned. The weight of it pressed down hard. If Honoria succeeded, everything could collapse. Not just for Gatty, but for all of them.

She cut through the orchard, her boots skimming over mossy stones, until she found Violet beneath the gnarled apple trees, bent over a ledger in the fading light. The girl looked up as Gatty approached, her brow creased in quiet concentration.

"Gatty?" Violet asked, rising to her feet. "What's wrong?"

Gatty didn't waste time. She knelt beside her, voice low but fierce. "Honoria's working with a merchant. He means to plant something—evidence—to frame me. To frame us. Witchcraft."

Violet blanched. "Are you sure?"

"I saw them. I heard everything. They plan to bring it to the magistrate."

Violet's lips parted, but no words came. Then, slowly, she nodded. Her hands tightened around the ledger. "We can't let them do it."

"We won't," Gatty said. "But we need to act fast."

Violet hesitated only a second before closing the ledger with a sharp snap. "Tell me what you're thinking."

Gatty exhaled, her shoulders squaring. "We outsmart them," she said. "If they want a performance, we'll give them one. And when they try to use it, we'll make them look like fools."

Violet's brow furrowed in cautious intrigue. "You mean... trick them back? How?"

Gatty leaned against the table, her hands braced on either side, eyes narrowing. "The merchant's not trying to prove the truth. He's trying to create a spectacle—something unsettling enough to shift public opinion. So... what if we give him exactly that?"

Violet frowned. "You mean... feed into it?"

"Sort of." Gatty pushed off the table and crossed to the shelf where bundles of dried herbs hung in shadow. "We give them a scene so absurd, so theatrical, that anyone with sense will see it for what it is—a sham. Something too obvious, too ridiculous to be real. If we control the performance, we control the narrative."

Violet tilted her head, unease giving way to dawning interest. "A trick?"

"A distraction," Gatty said, pulling down a bundle of dried mugwort. The scent—sharp and resinous—rose instantly. "This burns with thick smoke. Add just a little valerian, and it'll stink enough to make people cover their faces."

Violet edged closer. "And no one will get hurt?"

"No one," Gatty assured her. "That's the point. It has to look sinister without being dangerous. Something you and I can explain in two sentences if needed—something Honoria can't."

Violet's shoulders eased. "What else?"

Gatty grabbed a jar from the high shelf and turned it toward the lantern's glow. "Blue borage," she said. "If we steep it long enough and stir it just so, it'll tint the water faintly purple. That, with some tansy or even elder bark, could make it shimmer a bit. Like an old charm from a market-stall witch."

Violet let out a breath that sounded suspiciously like a laugh. "I think I'm starting to understand."

Gatty returned to the worktable, her fingers already moving to tie the first pouch. "We plant the smoke near something important—maybe the candelabrum. Somewhere it will catch attention but not cause damage."

"And the timing?" Violet asked. "How do we know when they'll spring it?"

"That's where you come in." Gatty glanced up. "You're the one no one notices. You've a knack for disappearing into corners. If you keep near Honoria, we'll hear when the moment comes—and we make sure it happens exactly when we want."

Violet's eyes lit with cautious determination. "And the merchant?"

Gatty's smile thinned. "We let him stumble over his own arrogance. Once this looks like a stunt, anything he presents will look like more of the same."

The room fell quiet for a moment, thick with purpose.

Then Violet nodded slowly. "This will work," she said under her breath, as if reassuring herself.

"It has to," Gatty replied, her voice steady. "We don't just need to stop them. We need to make them afraid to try again."

———

Morning in the poison garden arrived damp and still, the mist lying low between the rows of rosemary and hyssop. Gatty crouched near the bench, grinding dried mugwort and valerian root into a pungent powder. Beside her, Violet sat on a low stool, her brow furrowed in concentration as she stitched small cloth pouches, fingers moving quickly despite the tremble that hadn't quite left them.

"Is this enough?" Violet asked, holding one up. The stitches were uneven but sturdy.

"It's more than enough," Gatty said without looking up. "We're not trying to smoke them out, just startle them. Confuse the moment."

Violet tied the string with a confident tug, then turned to the next item on the list. She bundled blue borage and tansy with careful hands and passed the mix to Gatty. "For the water, right?"

"Right," Gatty confirmed, placing it into the basket beside her. "If we steep this just before the guests arrive, it'll look like something has brewed itself into a charm. Add a little heat, and the color will bloom."

They fell into a rhythm—grind, tie, sort, bundle—their movements precise but quick. Time was not on their side.

Finally, Gatty sat back, her skirts damp at the hem but her heart calmer now. Before her, the supplies lay in neat rows: pouches of herb powder, packets of dried flowers, vials of steeping water. Not weapons. Signals. Warnings.

Illusions, to fight illusion.

She looked at Violet, who straightened under her gaze. "You've done well," Gatty said quietly. "No matter what happens next, we've done something clever."

Violet gave a small, fierce nod. "Let's see if it's enough."

"Now we just have to get everything in place," Gatty said, rising and brushing the dirt from her skirts. Her hands trembled slightly, but her voice held firm. She turned to Violet, her expression intent. "Are you ready?"

Violet glanced at the rows of herbs swaying faintly in the mist. For a moment, doubt clouded her eyes—but then she straightened, her chin lifting. "I am," she said clearly. "Honoria and that merchant won't get away with this."

———

The great hall buzzed with the low hum of conversation, the warm light of lanterns flickering across velvet gowns and polished shoes. A lute player strummed softly from a corner, weaving a lilting tune through the air. Guests sipped cider and traded gossip in polite, glittering tones—unaware that a storm was quietly brewing among them.

Near the entrance, Honoria lingered like a shadow at the edge of the crowd. Her gown was crisp, her hair painstakingly smoothed, and her smile a little too sharp. She leaned in close to the merchant beside her—a broad, balding man with a sheen of sweat at his brow and a wooden box clutched tightly in both hands.

"They're getting ready," Violet murmured, drifting up beside Gatty with a soft rustle of skirts. "I heard Honoria say she wants Helena to arrive before the big reveal. She wants an audience."

Gatty nodded, her pulse quickening. She adjusted the basket on her arm, the bundle of smoke-laced herbs hidden beneath a neat layer of fresh lavender. "Let's give her one."

The two women slipped through the crowd with the ease of those accustomed to not being noticed. Gatty paused beside a tall candelabrum near the center of the room, where the light was brightest and the air thick with murmured speculation. She crouched to adjust the hem of her gown—just long enough to slip a pouch of powdered valerian and mugwort beneath the iron base.

Violet disappeared into the murmuring group near the merchant, her presence as quiet as a shadow.

Then Helena entered.

She stepped into the hall like a thunderclap masked in satin, her dark gown sweeping behind her, eyes sharp and unreadable. Conversation faltered, all attention turning toward her.

Honoria stepped forward, her voice ringing through the hush. "Madam," she said, drawing herself up, "we have discovered something deeply troubling. Evidence that could endanger the reputation of Blythewood Hall."

The merchant followed close behind, raising the box like a priest presenting a relic. "We bring this forward only out of duty, madam," he intoned, his voice practiced and oily.

Gatty caught Violet's eye across the room and gave a small, imperceptible nod.

Violet moved smoothly. She bent as if to retrieve a fallen ribbon, fingers brushing the hidden pouch beneath the candelabrum. A faint plume of smoke began to rise—thin at first, then swirling into curling wisps, pale and bitter with the sharp tang of valerian.

A murmur ran through the crowd. The smoke curled up toward the lanternlight, catching gold and silver in the haze. Someone coughed. Another woman pressed a kerchief to her nose.

"What's that smell?" a voice whispered sharply. "Is something burning?"

Honoria turned, blinking in confusion. Her smug composure faltered.

The merchant hesitated, his grip tightening on the box. "It's—it must be part of—"

Gatty stepped forward quickly, eyes wide and tone just a touch theatrical. "The smoke..." she said, raising a hand. "Could it be an omen?"

The word hung in the air, and the hall rippled with unease. The merchant dropped the box.

The lid flew open. Dried flower petals spilled out, along with a tangle of black thread, a piece of broken mirror, and a crude bundle of twigs bound with red ribbon. The contents looked more like a failed child's game than forbidden magic.

A silence. Then a single, stifled laugh. "An omen indeed," someone said wryly.

And then the dam broke. Laughter burst like a tide. The women pressed closer, some craning for a better look, others turning away to hide their grins.

Helena stepped forward, her expression unreadable. "Honoria," she said, her tone cold and deliberate. "Would you care to explain this... display?"

Honoria's eyes widened, her face flushing deep crimson. "I—I was only trying to—"

"Enough," Helena snapped, her voice cutting like glass. She turned to the merchant, who had begun to edge toward the doorway. "And you. I suggest you depart before I summon the actual magistrate to inquire about your intentions."

The merchant, suddenly very pale, bowed awkwardly and made a clumsy retreat, bumping shoulders on his way through the crowd.

Violet slipped back to Gatty's side, her mouth twitching with suppressed laughter. "Well," she whispered, "I don't think he'll be back."

Gatty allowed herself a slow, triumphant smile. "No. And Honoria won't be finding many ears willing to listen, either."

The smoke lingered a little longer in the rafters, curling above the room like a ghost of mischief well-played.

The laughter swelled again, rippling through the hall in a wave that echoed off the stone walls like the aftermath of a storm. Honoria stood frozen at the center of it all, red-faced and trembling, the spilled contents of the merchant's box scattered at her feet like the wreckage of a broken spell. Her eyes darted between Helena and the retreating merchant, searching desperately for someone—anyone—to defend her.

"This—this was their doing!" she cried, her voice high and shrill. She thrust out an accusing finger toward Gatty and Violet. "They used their tricks to make me look a fool! They're witches—both of them!"

A hush fell, sudden and cold. Even the music in the corner faltered. The room inhaled all at once, the silence sharp with tension as every gaze turned to Honoria.

Helena stepped forward, her figure tall and unyielding, casting a long shadow across the floor. Her voice, when it came, was soft—but it cut through the silence like the snap of a frost-bitten branch.

"Honoria," she said, her tone glacial. "Do you truly believe that Blythewood—a sanctuary for the wrongfully accused—would harbor witches? Or is this simply your own bitterness showing its face?"

Honoria's jaw worked uselessly. "They—" she stammered, but the weight of the crowd's skepticism crushed the words in her throat. Her gaze flitted from face to face, but found no sympathy.

Helena's expression hardened. "Enough," she said, each word clipped and final. "Your accusations are reckless and unbecoming of someone under this roof. If I ever hear you speak so again—without proof, without sense—your time at Blythewood will come to an end. Do you understand me?"

Honoria nodded mutely, her arms wrapping around herself like a shield.

The merchant, now clearly regretting his involvement, took a step backward. "I had no part in her accusations," he said quickly, holding his palms up. "This was all a misunderstanding."

Helena turned her gaze on him, cold and silent.

The merchant flinched. "I'll just… be going," he muttered, bowing so low it was nearly a stumble. He backed out of the hall with none of the pomp he'd arrived with, nearly tripping over the doorframe in his haste to escape.

As the door swung shut behind him, the atmosphere in the hall shifted. Conversation resumed in cautious murmurs. A few more chuckles rippled through the crowd. A woman near the hearth made a joke that earned a round of laughter. The tension ebbed slowly away.

———

Later, the flickering warmth of candlelight cast soft shadows across the shelves of Helena's study. The fire had been banked low, its glow painting the walls in amber. Gatty and Violet stood near the door, the scent of lavender and ink curling faintly in the air.

"Close the door behind you," Helena said without looking up.

The quiet click of the latch closing seemed loud in the small room.

Helena studied them for a long moment, her fingers steepled beneath her chin. Then, with a small nod, she leaned back in her chair and said, "I saw all. Well played."

Violet blinked, her hands clasping tighter at her waist. "Thank you, madam."

"You were clever," Helena said. "Decisive. You understood the stakes and acted without hesitation. And you, Gatty..." Her gaze turned sharp and appraising. "You've shown me something I've suspected for a while now."

Gatty straightened, her heartbeat quickening.

"You're not just capable," Helena said. "You're trusted. And when the moment came, others looked to you—not just for survival, but for leadership."

"I only did what had to be done," Gatty murmured, though a quiet pride stirred within her.

Helena nodded slowly. "That's exactly why it matters."

A pause stretched between them, not heavy but meaningful. "There will always be Honorias," Helena said at last. "Women who believe they are owed power, and who despise those who earn it instead." Her expression darkened for a moment, then cleared. "But tonight, you proved something I needed to see."

Gatty exchanged a glance with Violet, who looked just as stunned—and just as moved.

Helena's voice softened, but the authority beneath it remained. "Go. Rest. You've done well. And tomorrow... the work begins again."

———

As they stepped into the dim corridor beyond the study, Violet grabbed Gatty's arm, her voice breathless with wonder. "She said we handled ourselves well."

Gatty couldn't stop the smile that bloomed across her face. "We did," she said, her voice lighter than it had been in weeks. "We really did."

The moonlight drifted softly through the tangled lattice of the poison garden, turning every leaf silver and every shadow long. Gatty knelt beside a patch of valerian, her fingers brushing gently over its narrow leaves as if to soothe her own frayed nerves. The night was quiet but not still—crickets chirped in the undergrowth, and the scent of crushed thyme lingered in the air. A lantern sat beside her on the path, casting a warm circle of light.

Violet perched nearby on the edge of a low stone wall, her legs swinging just slightly above the gravel. Her braid had come half undone, and there was a smudge of dried borage across the front of her apron. "Do you think she'll leave us alone now?" she asked, her voice tentative, barely louder than the wind moving through the herbs.

Gatty glanced up, her lips quirking. "Honoria? Not for good. But she's embarrassed. That buys us time. And time," she said, returning her gaze to the valerian, "is often all a woman needs to take root."

Violet hugged her knees to her chest. The light made her freckles glow, soft and dappled like moth wings. "I don't think I've ever stood up to anyone like that before," she murmured. "Not really."

"You did more than stand up," Gatty said. She pushed to her feet and brushed the dirt from her skirts, her tone gentle but resolute. "You stepped forward. In front of everyone. And you didn't blink."

Violet's eyes filled, though she blinked fast to keep the tears at bay. "I didn't think I had it in me. I always feel... like the quiet one. The one who gets passed over."

"You're not invisible, Violet," Gatty said, taking a step toward her. "Not to me. Not to Helena. And certainly not tonight."

Violet gave a wobbly smile, her fingers fiddling with the edge of her apron. "Thank you," she said. "Really."

The creak of the garden gate broke the hush, and both women turned.

Leander stepped inside, the iron latch falling closed behind him with a soft click. A slim leather-bound book was tucked under his arm. His dark hair looked a little windswept, as though he'd come from the library by way of a long walk. His eyes found Gatty first, and his smile was faint but unmistakable.

"Is this where the revolution's headquarters has moved?" he asked dryly. "I feared I'd missed the last meeting."

Gatty arched a brow and crossed her arms. "We've gone underground," she said. "Your timing's nearly treasonous."

Leander smirked as he approached. "Then allow me to make amends." He extended the book. "A gift—for excellent subterfuge."

Gatty reached for it, her fingers brushing his. The contact was brief, but enough to send a flicker of awareness between them. She opened the book slowly. Inside, fine botanical sketches bloomed across the pages—foxglove, belladonna, feverfew—each labeled in precise, elegant script. Margins brimmed with notes.

"It's beautiful," she whispered, her thumb grazing a sketch of monkshood in full bloom.

"It was once the working journal of a Norfolk midwife," Leander said, his voice softer now. "She kept it hidden until the day she was arrested. There were pages sewn into her skirts, folded into her stockings. I've been transcribing them, and I thought... well." He hesitated. "You might appreciate it."

Gatty looked up, her throat thick. "I do," she said. "I truly do."

For a moment, neither of them moved. Violet, ever tactful, stood and gave a quick curtsy. "I should—go check the tincture baskets," she said, gesturing vaguely to the other end of the garden before slipping away with a conspiratorial glance at Gatty.

Leander watched her go, then turned back to Gatty. "You are remarkable," he said. "I hope you know that."

Gatty let the weight of the book rest against her chest. "I'm starting to."

He nodded, his expression thoughtful. "Then I'll leave you to your schemes." A beat passed. "But I do expect a full account tomorrow of the gossip I've been overhearing."

She tilted her head, teasing. "Only if you bring a new volume for bribes."

Leander smiled. "Done." He turned to leave, his boots whispering against the gravel, but her voice caught him just before the gate.

"Leander?"

He looked back, one hand resting on the gate.

"Good day," she said, her voice softer now, carrying more than the word alone.

His smile returned—quieter this time, but warmer. "Good day, Gatty."

The gate creaked shut behind him. Gatty stood alone in the hush of the moonlit garden, the midwife's journal pressed to her chest. Above her, the branches of the poison garden swayed gently in the wind, as if listening.

Chapter Twenty-Two

STORIES AND STRENGTH

The late morning sun slanted through the tangled boughs above the poison garden, dappling the beds with golden light. A breeze stirred the scents of rosemary, mugwort, and damp earth, rich and sharp in Gatty's lungs as she crouched beside a clump of marigolds, working her fingers into the soil. A smear of dirt streaked her apron, and her sleeves were rolled to the elbow.

Footsteps crunched softly over the gravel path. Gatty looked up to see Alice and Margery approaching with cautious steps, their skirts brushing the tips of thyme and tansy. Both women carried bundles of herbs in their arms, their aprons creased and faintly stained. They looked like they belonged here—almost. But unease still lingered behind their eyes.

"Morning," Gatty said gently, not quite cheerful but steady. "We've a fair bit to manage today."

They nodded in greeting, but their expressions were tight, guarded. Gatty saw the tension, felt it thread the air between them, and set her trowel aside.

"Come," she said, gesturing toward a patch of grass near the low garden wall. "Let's rest a moment. There's no rule that says we must charge through like horses at harvest."

Alice hesitated, then lowered herself to the grass with a faint sigh. Margery followed, more stiffly, settling beside her with slow, deliberate movements. Gatty joined them, wiping her palms on her apron and letting the silence settle—not heavy, not demanding, but wide enough to breathe in.

After a beat, she turned to Alice. "You've a good touch with the feverfew," she said, keeping her tone light but sincere. "Where'd you learn it?"

Alice blinked at the question. "My grandmother," she said, voice soft. "She kept a garden in our back field. Made teas for neighbors when they were ill. Said it was better than paying a doctor who didn't know your name."

Gatty nodded, encouraging. "And she taught you all she knew?"

"Not all," Alice replied, eyes dropping to her lap. "She died before she could." Her fingers tightened around the edge of her apron. "But I watched. I remembered what she'd say. After she was gone, I started making the teas. For headaches, bad bellies. Just tried to help."

"And that's when the trouble began," Margery murmured, her voice low and tight.

Alice flushed, her lips trembling. "There was a little boy—burning with fever. I gave him willow bark and thyme, like she would have. But he didn't get better. When he died, they said it was my fault. That I'd cursed him."

The words hung in the garden like a chill.

"They don't need much, do they?" Margery muttered. She stared at the herbs in her lap. "Just a reason to look at you sideways."

Gatty let the silence stretch, then gently turned her gaze to Margery. "What happened to you?"

Margery gave a humorless laugh and brushed her palms off on her apron. "Friend of mine—I thought she was, anyway—told people I'd cast spells. Said I made charms to win favors, that I whispered things under my breath. I thought it was just foolish gossip. Until my father called me into the kitchen and asked if it was true." Her jaw tensed. "I told him it wasn't. Showed him my journals—every remedy I'd tried, every blend of herbs. I kept them all, thinking I could prove myself. He burned them. Said I'd already shamed the family. That I'd brought it on myself."

Gatty's throat tightened. She reached for something to say, but the truth of it was, she'd heard stories like theirs before. Too many. Still, she turned her eyes to the third woman sitting beside them—the quiet orphan with the wary gaze, hands knotted in her skirts.

"I don't think I've learned your name," Gatty said gently. "Would you like to tell us what brought you here?"

The woman hesitated, her eyes flicking between them, weighing something invisible. But at last she gave a small nod.

"Rose," she said. Her voice was barely above a whisper. "I worked for a merchant's wife. She had bad knees, and I made poultices for the pain. Nothing fancy—just mustard seed and marjoram."

She swallowed.

"Then she died. It was her heart, I think. But her husband said I'd poisoned her. Said I'd cursed her because she didn't pay me properly. He took it to the magistrate, but they were cousins. I didn't even get to speak for myself."

Alice reached out and laid a hand on Rose's arm. Rose flinched at the touch, then stilled, her chin trembling.

Gatty looked between them all, her chest aching—not with pity, but with fury. These women had been cast out, silenced, punished for their knowledge. And they were still here. Still learning. Still reaching for something more.

And that, Gatty thought, was power. Not magic. Not curses. Just survival. And defiance.

The sun climbed higher, casting a golden haze over the walled garden. The scent of crushed rosemary mingled with lavender on the air. The women had gone quiet, not out of discomfort, but the kind of silence that follows something important being said. Gatty wiped her hands on her apron and leaned back, taking them all in—Alice, Margery, Rose—each holding something fragile just beneath the surface.

"You've all been called witches," she said softly, the words carrying weight rather than fear. "Called dangerous, disobedient, unnatural. But what they really meant was uncontrollable. And they tried to break you for it."

No one spoke, but the way they shifted—chin lifting, shoulders squaring—told her they were listening.

"But you're still here," Gatty continued, her voice steadier now. "And that matters. They meant to silence you, and here you are—learning, growing, healing. That's something."

Alice twisted a bit of lavender between her fingers. "Sometimes it doesn't feel like enough," she murmured. "I still wake up with the same fear. That someone's coming with a rope or a warrant."

"We all do," Margery said, her tone roughened by memory. "That fear doesn't leave you. It just stops knocking quite so loud."

Rose hugged her knees to her chest. "I tried to be heard," she whispered. "Tried to explain, to defend myself. But men like the merchant—like the magistrate—they never listened. They already had their story." Her mouth tightened. "They never gave me a chance."

Gatty's throat tightened. She looked at the hands around her—hands that had been slapped, bound, forced to beg. Now they were learning to tend, to build, to choose. "They didn't give you a chance," she said. "But now we give one another a chance. That's the difference."

Margery huffed a quiet breath. "It doesn't feel like power."

"It is," Gatty said without hesitation. She reached into the bed beside her, pulled a stem of mugwort, and held it aloft. "This leaf won't change the world on its own. But dry it, steep it, crush it into oil—and it becomes something that eases pain, helps sleep, calms the heart. That's not nothing."

Alice's brow furrowed as she studied it. "So we're not just using the plants... we're shaping them. Turning them into something else."

Gatty nodded. "And that shaping? That choice? That's power."

The women exchanged looks—guarded, unsure, but not dismissive. There was a flicker of something taking root, just beneath the surface.

"We can't undo what was done to us," Gatty added, her voice quieter now. "But we can decide what we do next. For ourselves—and for others like us."

Just then, a voice called from the garden gate. "Gatty?"

She turned toward the archway to see Lydia standing just outside the stone wall, framed by ivy and light. Her hands were folded, her expression unreadable but not unkind.

Gatty rose, dusting her palms. "Keep going," she said to the women. "You're doing fine."

As she approached the gate, her heart was still steady, rooted by what had just passed.

"Ma'am," she said, dipping her head.

Lydia's gaze swept the garden behind her. "They're working with purpose," she said. "That's new."

"They've started to believe they're worth the effort," Gatty replied.

Lydia's eyes returned to her. "And you? What is it you've begun to believe?"

The question caught Gatty off guard. She glanced over her shoulder—Alice speaking softly to Rose, Margery examining the stalk of a nettle with surprising care.

"I believe," she said slowly, "that surviving isn't enough. I want to build something they can be proud of. Something they can own."

Lydia stepped forward, the corners of her mouth twitching slightly. "And how do you imagine we begin?"

"There's a market in town," Gatty said. "They sell all sorts of things—coarse teas, useless tonics. But we could sell real remedies. Teas that soothe, salves that mend. We'd help the people who buy them—and we'd help ourselves. Helena suggested it."

Lydia lifted one brow. "And you think people will buy from us?"

"They'll buy if the work is good," Gatty said. "And if we present it properly. We're not calling ourselves witches. We're calling ourselves healers."

Lydia's silence stretched long enough to make Gatty's heart quicken.

"And this garden?" she finally asked. "You think it's enough?"

"It could be," Gatty said. "If we train more women. If we gather more tools. I believe it's worth trying."

Lydia studied her a moment longer. Then, with a slight nod, she said, "You've earned the right to try. Just tell me what you need from me."

Later that evening, the scent of fresh bread and steeped thyme filled the kitchen, warm and grounding like a hearth fire in winter. Lydia stood at the head of the long oak table, her posture poised but not unyielding. Gatty stood beside her, hands folded in front of her apron, steadying her breath as the women filed in.

Alice, Margery, and Rose entered first, followed by three others—newer arrivals to Blythewood, their faces guarded, eyes sharp with the kind of wariness that only comes from betrayal. They each took a seat around the table, the wood scarred with years of use, but solid beneath their hands.

"These walls were meant to shelter you," Lydia began, her voice even and deliberate. "But safety alone is a poor substitute for dignity. We've been a haven—yes—but that is not enough anymore. We must become something more."

The room went still. Gatty could feel the breath-holding quiet of women who had learned to expect disappointment. Lydia glanced toward her, and with a single nod, handed her the floor.

Gatty stepped forward and placed her hands lightly on the edge of the table. "You've all seen what we've started in the garden," she said. "You've felt it in your hands, seen it take root. But there's more we can do. We can use that knowledge—those skills—to create something lasting. Something useful."

She met each woman's gaze in turn, letting her voice settle like a calm wind. "We could prepare teas, tinctures, salves. Remedies for coughs, fevers, aching joints. And sell them. Not as charity—not as pity—but as trade. Work for fair coin. Work that earns respect."

Margery shifted in her seat. "And when they ask where we learned?" she said, voice taut with old wounds. "When the whispering starts again?"

"We stay ahead of the whispers," Gatty replied. "We don't dress this up as mystery or magic. We show them the plants, the measurements, the care. We offer them healing. Nothing more."

Alice's voice was quieter. "And if they still don't believe?"

"Then we stand together," Gatty said simply. "No one here works alone. Not anymore."

Rose leaned forward, hands flat on the table. "If this means no more hiding," she said, "then I'll do it. And if it helps other women like us find something to hold onto—then all the better."

One of the newer women, the tall one with windburned cheeks and a deep line between her brows, gave a short nod. "You've got spirit, I'll give you that," she muttered. "But trust is hard-earned."

"They don't have to trust you at first," Lydia said, her tone crisp. "Let them trust the work. I'll see to the rest."

That silenced any further doubts, at least for now. The room softened—just slightly. Shoulders loosened. Elbows rested on the table's edge. The smallest beginnings of something real.

Gatty felt it—something shifting. The moment when a group of wary women starts to become a team.

Lydia turned to her with the barest smile. "You've earned this, Gatty," she said. "Now let's see what you build."

Gatty swallowed, her heart both steady and racing. "We won't waste the chance."

The next morning broke crisp and golden, the garden cloaked in a fine mist that glimmered as the sun rose higher. Gatty stood amid the dew-dusted rows of herbs, her skirts damp at the hem, her hands already stained with soil. Around her, the garden buzzed—not just with bees and birdsong, but with something rarer: purpose.

Alice crouched beside a bed of hyssop, clipping stems with practiced care. Margery and Rose sorted bundles of lavender and comfrey, laying them out on clean cloth. Nearby, one of the newer women—Winifred, quiet but precise—ground dried valerian root into powder with rhythmic, steady strokes. Their movements were unhurried, but confident. The hesitancy of yesterday had begun to give way to rhythm.

Gatty stepped back for a moment, letting her gaze drift over the scene. A week ago, none of them would've spoken to each other in more than whispers. Now they worked shoulder to shoulder, sleeves rolled up, murmuring soft instructions or sharing bits of remembered knowledge. It wasn't just a garden anymore. It was becoming something larger—an act of reclamation.

Lydia arrived mid-morning, her boots slick with dew and her skirts trailing softly behind her. She paused at the garden gate, watching the bustle with unreadable eyes. Gatty approached her with a basket of rosemary clutched to her chest, the sharp scent clinging to her fingers.

Lydia's expression softened. "You've done well," she said quietly. "It's one thing to gather women beneath a roof. It's another thing entirely to give them reason to stay."

Gatty's throat tightened, but she managed a smile. "I couldn't have done it without your support."

Lydia lifted a brow. "Support, perhaps. But I didn't teach them to laugh again. Or to trust the work of their hands."

She nodded toward the women. "They follow your lead, Gatty. That's something I could never have forced."

Gatty felt the truth of that settle deep in her chest. "Then I'll lead them somewhere worth following," she said. "We'll make something lasting. Not just for the hall—but for ourselves."

Lydia gave a satisfied nod. "You'll have what you need. And I've spoken to Violet about keeping proper records in the library—names, measures, ingredients, outcomes. It'll give your work weight in the eyes of outsiders. And a place in memory, should others need it."

By evening, their first batch was finished—rows of tiny jars lined up on the kitchen table like treasures: salves sealed with beeswax, dried bundles wrapped in twine, tinctures amber in the candlelight. The air was heavy with the scents of calendula, rosemary, and pride.

Margery held one jar aloft, the pale green ointment catching the light. "We did this," she whispered, as if daring herself to believe it.

Rose beamed. "And we'll do more."

They shared a simple supper, passing bread and steaming mugs of thyme tea between them, the kitchen lit with warmth and flickering shadows. Gatty sat back for a moment, watching the others laugh softly over the labeling of jars. She'd thought belonging might never come again—not after all she'd lost. But here it was, real and rising like bread in the oven.

Later, as dusk deepened and the others retired, Gatty returned to the garden. The moon cast silver across the earth, and the rows of plants looked ethereal in the half-light. She bent to tidy the bundles near the trellis, her hands moving instinctively now—like they'd always known this work.

Footsteps crunched on the gravel behind her. She straightened, brushing her palms on her apron, and turned.

Leander stood at the gate, a leather-bound book in his hand and a familiar, quiet look in his eyes. His coat hung open, hair a little untamed, as though he'd run a hand through it one too many times while reading.

"I thought of you when I found this," he said, crossing the threshold and holding out the book. "The remedies are old, but some are still clever. Thought you might find it useful."

Gatty took it, her fingers brushing his as she did. The leather was cool beneath her hand, the pages worn but lovingly kept. "It's beautiful," she said, her voice low. "Thank you."

Leander's gaze lingered on her, his tone gentle. "What you're doing here—it matters. You've built something more than a garden."

The compliment nestled deep, warm as firelight. Gatty looked down at the book, then back at him. "I hope so," she murmured.

"You don't need to hope," he said. "You just need to keep going."

And for once, Gatty didn't argue. She only nodded, holding the book to her chest as the garden rustled quietly around them.

Chapter Twenty-Three

CONFRONTATION

The market pulsed with life beneath a low, grey sky. Vendors called out over steaming crates of chestnuts, children darted through puddles, and carts clattered over slick cobblestones. Gatty moved through the tangle of stalls with practiced ease, her basket nestled in the crook of her arm. One happy hour passed in which she did what she'd come for without bother. A misting rain clung to her sleeves, mingling with the earthy scents of rosemary, damp wool, and crushed thyme.

She passed a basket of early apples and handed over a coin for a neat bundle of the herb she'd come for. But as the stallkeeper turned to wrap it, voices rose in sharp contrast to the ambient bustle. They came from a shaded corner beyond the tavern door—low and barbed, just loud enough to catch on the drizzle.

"...Alive, is she?" came a jeering male voice, hoarse with drink and disdain. "Well, that's a surprise. Thought the river took care of her."

Gatty's spine snapped taut. The second voice answered, too familiar to mistake.

"She didn't drown," William Harper replied, his tone brittle with annoyance. "Turns out she's tucked up at that Magdalene house within Blythewood Hall." He gave a short, humorless laugh. "Imagine that—maybe she's not a witch after all. Maybe it was just one of her episodes."

The other man chuckled darkly. "And now you want her back? Changed your tune, haven't you?"

"What's changed," William said, low and clipped, "is that she's keeping Fenton from what should be mine. Her land is still tied to her name. And if I marry her, it's mine too."

The knot in Gatty's stomach drew tight as a garrote. She edged closer, staying hidden behind a curtain of drying linens. *Can I never escape them?*

"You think she'll have you?" the man scoffed.

"Oh, she will," William said smoothly. "She'll have no other choice. Who else would take her? Marry me, and she keeps her place at that fine estate. Refuse, and she loses everything." He lowered his voice, conspiratorial. "Besides, with her settled in a place like Blythewood, people forget what was said. She's respectable now. I marry her, Fenton signs over the land, and it's all tied up tidy."

Gatty's breath caught, cold and furious. He wasn't just coming for her—he was coming for what she had built from the ashes. As if she were an asset to be leveraged, not a person who had survived him.

The first man gave a snort. "And if she doesn't roll over?"

William chuckled. "Then I'll make her."

Gatty's fingers tightened around her basket until the wicker creaked. She turned and slipped back into the market crowd, fury burning under her skin.

"Gatty?" came a familiar voice behind her. She turned to find Violet, her arms full of dried rosehips, her brow furrowed at the sight of Gatty's pale face. "You're shaking. What happened?"

"Not what—who," Gatty hissed. "William Harper. He's here. I heard him."

Violet stiffened. "What does he want?"

"He wants to own me," Gatty spat. "He thinks if he marries me, he gets the land. Thinks he can scare me into it. That I'd be desperate enough to say yes."

Violet's jaw clenched, her voice flat and hard. "Then he doesn't know you."

Gatty met her eyes, the strength between them steady as an oath. "No. But he's about to."

They stood for a beat in the mist, unmoving, their rage tempered not by fear but by resolve. Whatever William planned, they would be ready.

The clouds pressed low and leaden over Blythewood Hall as Gatty and Violet strode through the gates, their boots slick with rain. The wind had picked up by the time they crossed the threshold, pulling at their cloaks, but neither woman paused. Inside, the fire in the library snapped and hissed, casting golden light on the stone hearth—but the warmth there seemed distant, irrelevant.

Gatty's thoughts churned with urgency and fury, her pulse matching her steps.

"I'll gather the others," Violet said quietly as they reached the library. Her voice was calm, but her jaw was set. "If he's coming here, we won't let him come alone."

"No," Gatty said sharply, catching Violet's sleeve. "This isn't just about me. He's threatening our right to exist without fear." She met Violet's eyes. "We need a plan that speaks louder than his threats."

Violet studied her a moment, then gave a single nod. "What do you have in mind?"

Gatty stepped into the library and let the heavy door swing shut behind them. The scent of woodsmoke and dried paper lingered, grounding her. She crossed to the large oak table and placed both hands on it, her mind racing. "William believes I'm weak. That I'll cower. He still believes in witches—and in his ability to control them." Her voice sharpened. "So let's give him what he fears."

Violet blinked, then her lips curved in a slow, delighted grin. "You mean to frighten him?"

"No," Gatty said. "I mean to unmake him." Her voice dropped to a murmur. "We don't just scare him—we make a mockery of his claims. Humiliate him so thoroughly he wouldn't dare return."

"The garden," Violet said quickly, already thinking. "Mugwort, valerian… the smoke alone is enough to set nerves twitching. And the scent's strange enough to feel like something more."

"And Alice," Gatty added. "She's learned how to make teas that change color. Margery's got that mix that catches firelight and throws sparks. If we work together, we can create a scene so strange, so unsettling, it'll make him doubt his own eyes."

Violet's expression turned serious again. "But if it doesn't work—if he pushes back?"

Gatty's gaze hardened. "Then we don't flinch. He leaves empty-handed, either way."

Within the hour, they'd gathered in the library. Candles glowed along the mantle, throwing soft light on the circle of determined faces. Gatty stood at the head of the table, Violet beside her. Alice and Margery leaned forward over small parcels of herbs, their hands moving with practiced care. Leander lingered in the shadows, arms folded, brow furrowed.

"This plan," he said at last, breaking the silence. "It's bold. Are you sure it won't escalate things?"

"It might," Gatty admitted. "But silence hasn't kept us safe either. William wants to bully his way through that front door, thinking no one will stand in his way. I plan to prove him wrong."

Alice glanced between them, fidgeting with a pouch of dried marigold. "If we make it look too real... what if it stirs up talk? More accusations?"

"He won't dare make them," Leander said coolly. "Not after we expose him for what he is. If he tries to bring this to the magistrate, I'll be the first to speak—and I'll say he stormed into a house of women with threats and false claims. Which he will have."

Violet's brows drew together. "Then we'll need timing. And subtlety."

Gatty nodded. "When he enters, I'll greet him as if he's expected. As though nothing is wrong. That's when you begin. One by one. The smoke, the water, the strange lights. Enough to unnerve him. Enough to make him think twice."

Leander's voice was quiet now, but firm. "You're braver than most, Gatty."

She looked at him, her anger tempered by a flicker of gratitude. "Not brave," she said. "Just finished with being afraid."

The group fell into a hush, the crackle of the fire the only sound. Then Margery spoke, her voice dry but resolved. "Let's make him wish he'd stayed in the tavern."

The others smiled, grim and ready. When William Harper came to Blythewood, he would not be facing one frightened woman—he'd be facing a house of witches, and none of them alone.

The great hall of Blythewood stood quiet as a held breath. Firelight flickered against the stone walls, casting shifting shadows like watchful sentinels. Gatty stood near the hearth, her chin lifted, hands clasped tightly in front of her. The scent of mugwort and valerian clung faintly to the air—an invisible veil, ready to unsettle.

The echo of heavy boots shattered the silence.

Leander, beside her, tensed. His stance sharpened as William Harper strode into the hall, rain clinging to his boots, arrogance radiating off him like heat. He paused just inside the doorway, sneer already in place.

"Well," he drawled, his eyes sweeping over Gatty, "you've been hiding in style, haven't you?"

Gatty didn't flinch. Her heart thudded beneath her stays, but her voice was steady. "I've been surviving. You wouldn't know the difference."

William's smile curled. "I've come for what's mine."

Leander stepped forward, calm but unmistakably in command. "State your purpose plainly, Harper. This is not a tavern floor."

William bristled, but puffed his chest. "She was promised to me. Her land. Her name. All of it comes to me if she's living and wed. And she's clearly not dead."

"You filthy liar," hissed Gatty.

"She's clearly not yours," Leander replied, voice like ice. "And whatever claims you think you have, I suggest you tread carefully. This is a house of peace."

"The magistrate will see it my way," William snapped, thrusting a hand into his coat. He produced a crumpled parchment, brandishing it like a sword. "I've got proof. Witnesses saw her with strange herbs. Muttering nonsense. It's witchcraft."

Leander's mouth twitched in the barest ghost of a smile. "Herbs. What terror. Shall we arrest every apothecary in England while we're at it?"

William took a step forward, but the air changed.

A haze began to unfurl from the far corners of the hall—smoke, thin and silvery, coiling in ghostly spirals. Mugwort and wormwood, their scent thick and strange, slipped into the atmosphere like breath in winter.

William paused. "What... what is this?" He waved at the air, blinking rapidly.

Gatty took a slow step forward. Her tone was soft, but it carried. "Perhaps the house doesn't care for liars, William. Perhaps it remembers things."

His brow furrowed, and sweat beaded at his temple.

From the side corridor, Alice emerged, cradling a pitcher. She moved gracefully across the hall and poured a glass, then offered it with a mild smile.

"Thirsty?" she asked. "It's rosemary and mint. Calms the nerves."

William stared at her. Then, as though unable to resist the temptation of appearing unbothered, he took the cup and drank.

The water shimmered as it hit his tongue, its hue deepening, slowly darkening to a cloudy green.

He froze. The cup slipped in his grip.

"What... what devilry is this?" His voice rose an octave. "What did you do?"

The room gave him no answer—only the hiss of fire, the whisper of smoke. A log in the hearth popped with a sharp crack, and the sparks that leapt from it flared unnaturally—glinting gold, as if bewitched.

William stumbled back, eyes wide. His earlier swagger crumbled under the weight of illusion and implication. He turned toward the door—

—and Honoria stepped into view, her expression wild.

"There!" she cried, pointing at Gatty. "They've done it again! They're witches, all of them! Can't you see what they are?"

Her voice rang shrill through the thickened air, but no one moved.

From the back of the hall, Helena entered like a shadow given form. She walked slowly, each step deliberate, until she stood at Honoria's side.

"Is that truly the story you're going with?" Helena asked coldly. "You want to accuse the women of this house of witchcraft—again?"

Honoria's mouth worked, but no sound came. The other women—Violet, Margery, Ellen—had gathered quietly along the edges of the room, eyes trained on William.

"You'll all regret this," Honoria whispered, turning to William. "Tell them. Tell them what you saw."

But William no longer looked like a man prepared to fight. He looked like a man out of his depth. "I… I've seen enough," he said hoarsely. "This place—it's cursed."

He backed away, nearly tripping on the hem of a rug, and bolted for the doors. The parchment fluttered from his hand, forgotten.

The doors boomed shut behind him.

Honoria hesitated for one breath, then turned and fled after him, her skirts catching in the doorway as she vanished into the night.

For a long moment, no one spoke.

Then Leander turned to Gatty, his voice a soft murmur. "You are absolutely terrifying."

Gatty smiled, just a little. "Good."

The great hall settled into stillness, the threat expelled like smoke from a snuffed-out flame. The air was thick with the remnants of tension—smoke, silence, and something fiercer that buzzed beneath the women's skin. Gatty stood near the center, her fists still loosely clenched at her sides, the rush of it all still pounding in her veins.

From the shadows, Violet emerged first, her face pale but lifted with quiet pride. Margery and Alice followed, slipping from their hiding places like spirits returned to flesh. They didn't speak—not at first. They simply looked to Gatty.

Helena's gaze swept the room, sharp and discerning, weighing the air. Her eyes passed over each woman before settling on Gatty.

"That," she said, her tone as crisp as frost, "was bold."

Gatty tensed, bracing for reprimand.

But Helena's expression shifted, softening with the faintest curve of her mouth. "And, evidently, effective."

Violet let out a breath she hadn't realized she was holding, her shoulders dipping as the fear eased out of her frame. "I thought he'd call the bluff," she admitted, her voice shaky with adrenaline. "For a moment... I almost believed it myself."

"That was the point," Gatty replied gently, moving to stand beside her. "You did beautifully."

Alice grinned, rubbing soot from her fingers. "The way his face twisted when the water changed—I'll think of it every time I need a good laugh."

A ripple of laughter passed between them, not loud, but warm. The kind that mended something small and invisible.

Then Gatty turned toward Helena, whose keen eyes flickered with thought as she lowered herself into a chair beside the hearth. The firelight danced over her features, casting her in half-shadow.

"I suppose I owe you an explanation," Gatty began, her voice low but sure, the nerves tight in her chest but no longer in command. "William Harper is from my village. He stood with the mob that tried to drown me. And if he'd stayed…" Her jaw tightened. "He would've made good on it."

Helena said nothing, but her silence felt like an invitation. "And the land?" she prompted after a pause, her tone unreadable.

Gatty nodded once. "It was my family's. After they died, there was… confusion over the claim. William wants it—not because he needs it, but because he knows it should be mine. He doesn't want the land. He wants to erase the fact that I ever had a right to it." She lowered her head.

Helena's brow furrowed slightly. The flames snapped in the hearth as if on cue. "And you think this was enough to drive him off for good?" she asked.

Before Gatty could answer, Leander's voice cut through the quiet, low and certain. "He ran," he said. "Like a rat cornered in a room too clever for him. He won't come back."

Helena studied him for a beat, then turned her gaze back to Gatty. Her expression was unreadable—half-approval, half-concern—but her next words were steady. "For all our sakes," she said, "let's hope you're right."

Later that evening, the garden lay cloaked in silver-blue moonlight, cool and quiet beneath the lingering mist. The scent of disturbed earth and crushed valerian drifted on the breeze as Gatty knelt beside the rows of mugwort, her hands moving in practiced rhythm. Violet, Margery, and Alice worked alongside her, their sleeves rolled, their skirts damp with dew, but their movements calm—steady.

"That was terrifying," Violet said softly, breaking the hush. She sat back on her heels, brushing a strand of hair from her cheek. "But I don't think I've ever felt... stronger."

Alice gave a low hum of agreement, her voice quiet but firm. "We've been blamed for so much—things we never said, never did, never were. But tonight, we turned it. We used what they feared and made it ours."

Gatty paused, her hand resting on a basket's rim. She looked around at them—Violet's determined expression, Margery's jaw still set with the aftershock of fury, Alice's quiet fire. Her chest tightened with something fierce and bright.

"We did it together," she said, her voice low and full. "And we'll keep doing it. For Blythewood. For every woman who's been cast aside and called a curse just for knowing her own mind."

Margery gave a rare nod, her hand brushing the soil from a bundle of roots. "We made our own kind of justice."

The women exchanged glances, small nods and faint smiles passed between them like a vow. Beneath the moonlight, they didn't look like outcasts. They looked like the beginning of something new.

Gatty turned her gaze toward the house, where a soft glow flickered in the upper library window. Her breath caught, not with fear this time, but something steadier—warmer. Leander was up there, she knew, likely reading by lantern light or pretending not to worry about her. He had stood beside her when it mattered most. Quiet, unyielding.

The moon hung high over Blythewood Hall, cool and watchful. Gatty lingered at the lavender beds, her fingers brushing over the velvety buds. The night's events pressed heavy on her shoulders, but it was no longer the weight of dread. It was the weight of choice—of action—and for once, she carried it gladly.

The soft crunch of footsteps on the gravel path broke the hush of the garden. Gatty turned, the hem of her gown brushing the dewy lavender, and found Leander emerging from the mist. The lanterns hanging near the hall's entrance cast a golden glow behind him, limning his tall frame in shifting light. He looked less composed than usual—coat unfastened, brows drawn, as if the words he carried were heavy and uncooperative.

"Gatty," he said, stopping a few paces from her. His voice was quiet, threaded with something unfamiliar—uncertainty, perhaps. Or restraint.

"You're out late," she replied, folding her arms, though her voice softened as it reached him. "Come to check if the garden's hexed?"

He smiled faintly at the tease, but it didn't last. "I thought I'd find you here," he said. "I couldn't sleep. Not after... earlier."

Gatty's pulse quickened. The memory of William's sneering face, the cruel certainty in his words, flickered in her mind—and with it, Leander's fury, controlled but unmistakable. She took a step closer. "You've been thinking about him."

Leander nodded once. "About the way he spoke to you. About the way he looked at you." His jaw clenched. "Like you were something to own."

His voice broke slightly, and he looked down, shoulders tense. "I hated it. I hated how helpless it made me feel. Like all I could do was stand there while he tried to reduce you."

Gatty's brows knit together, startled by the rawness in his tone. "You weren't helpless, Leander. You stood beside me. That mattered."

He let out a breath, still not looking up. "I wanted to do more. To say something clever, cutting—something that would make him turn and run without you needing to lift a finger." He shook his head, voice thick. "But all I could think about was how much you mean to me. And how terrified I was that he might find some way to take you."

Her breath caught. She crossed the distance between them and laid a hand gently on his sleeve. "You didn't lose me," she said. "And you won't."

At that, Leander finally looked up. His green eyes met hers, vulnerable and fierce all at once. "I know I'm not the sort most women dream of," he said. "I've no titles, no fortune. Just ink-stained fingers and far too many books." His mouth twisted in a rueful smile. "But I've never wanted anything more than I want you."

A stunned silence hung between them, thick with the weight of unspoken things. Then Gatty stepped forward again, close enough to feel the warmth of his body, close enough that her voice barely needed sound.

"You're wrong about one thing," she said. "I dream of a man who sees me clearly—and stays anyway."

Leander's lips parted, and for a moment, neither of them moved. Then he leaned in, his hesitation falling away. Their lips met in a kiss that was gentle at first—tentative, reverent. But as her hand slid to his jaw and his fingers found the curve of her waist, it deepened into something richer.

When they parted, breathless, their foreheads rested together. "I'm probably terrible at this," he murmured.

Gatty gave a quiet laugh, brushing her thumb over the edge of his cheekbone. "You're not. Not even close."

He exhaled a small laugh of his own, the tension unspooling from his frame. "I don't want to rush you," he said. "But I don't want to waste time either. If there's a future for me, Gatty—it's with you."

She didn't answer right away. Instead, she let the moment settle, let her heart catch up to her words. And when she spoke, it was with quiet certainty.

"Then let's face it together."

CHAPTER TWENTY-FOUR

A TROUBLING DISCOVERY

The air in Blythewood Hall carried a peculiar weight that morning—thick with tension, with whispers that curled like smoke through the corridors. Gatty moved briskly between the library and garden, a basket of herbs cradled in one arm, her ears pricked to the soft hush of conversation that always stopped just as she neared.

She caught snatches of words—traitor, spy, mole—each one striking sharper than the chill rising from the flagstones. The trust they'd all worked so hard to build now felt as fragile as the frost-laced petals clinging to the garden's last blooms.

She found Violet in the library, hunched over the large oak table with the ledger open before her. The fire in the hearth cast a soft orange glow, but it did little to lift the shadow from Violet's features. Her shoulders were tense, her brow furrowed in concentration—or worry.

When Gatty entered, Violet looked up, her mouth pressed into a pale line. "There's been talk," she said without preamble, her voice low and tight. "Not just nerves or nonsense. Something real."

Gatty set the basket down and pulled out a chair, sitting without removing her cloak. "Tell me," she said, keeping her voice calm even as her stomach knotted.

Violet reached beneath the ledger and withdrew a folded piece of parchment. "I found this tucked in the back. It wasn't there yesterday."

Gatty unfolded the paper, smoothing it carefully. The handwriting was tidy and precise, unfamiliar. Her eyes scanned the content: notes on the magistrate's recent visits, predictions about Helena's movements, even references to specific herbal preparations and who had handled them. Her skin prickled.

"This shouldn't exist," she said flatly. "No one outside the Hall should know these things."

Violet nodded. "It's someone inside. Someone who knows exactly what to listen for—and who to tell."

Gatty's jaw tightened as she reread the note. Whoever wrote this wasn't careless. They were deliberate. "Does Helena know?"

"Not yet," Violet admitted. "I didn't want to take it to her without more. You know how she is. She'll act—and if we're wrong..."

Gatty folded the paper again, more carefully this time, and met Violet's eyes. "Then we find out who it is. Quietly."

That afternoon, Gatty stayed out in the garden longer than necessary, her eyes tracking the women as they moved about their tasks. Most worked in pairs or alone, their conversations subdued. But near the back wall, tucked just behind the tangled rosebushes and wormwood, she spotted Honoria speaking in low tones to Anne.

Anne, who was usually shy and sweet-faced, had her arms folded tightly and kept glancing toward the house. Honoria leaned in close, her voice tense but too far for Gatty to hear—until a gust of wind carried a scrap of it toward her hiding place behind the foxglove.

"...we've waited long enough," Honoria snapped.

Anne's voice was barely audible. "But if Helena—"

"She won't," Honoria cut in. "Not if you follow through."

Gatty felt her pulse quicken. She waited until the pair had moved on before slipping back inside, the note like a weight in her pocket. When she returned to the library, Violet was still there, pacing now.

"I think I know where to start," Gatty said.

She told Violet everything she'd seen and heard. With each word, Violet's face grew more serious, her nerves tightening into focus.

"We need more than hearsay," she said. "If we confront her too soon, she'll twist it back on us."

"Then we don't confront," Gatty replied. "We catch her."

Violet met her eyes—and nodded. "Let's begin."

Gatty and Violet spent the evening deep in the hush of the library, the shadows long and the fire low. Candlelight danced across rows of spines, casting wavering golden lines across the walls. The parchment lay open between them like a wound, its neat script far too calm for the danger it posed.

"We'll have to be smart," Gatty said quietly, running her fingers along the paper's edge. "Honoria's bold, but she's not foolish. If we confront her too soon, she'll spin it to make us look paranoid—or worse."

Violet tapped a knuckle lightly against the table, thinking. "Anne might know more than she's said. You saw how hesitant she was. But if Honoria's pressuring her, she won't talk easily."

"Then we need to give her a reason," Gatty agreed. "Not fear. Trust."

The fire crackled, filling the silence between them as they fell into their thoughts. Outside, the wind moaned against the leaded windows. At last, Violet leaned forward, her eyes alight with a cautious spark. "What if we stage something?" she said. "Something that forces Honoria to act before she's ready?"

Gatty looked up, intrigued. "You mean draw her out?"

Violet nodded. "She craves power—loves being the one who knows more than anyone else. If we dangle something tempting, something that makes her think her position is threatened, she might walk straight into it."

Gatty smiled. "We plant bait. Let her come to it."

"But carefully," Violet added, though her voice had grown steadier. "If it's too obvious, she'll suspect a trap."

"Then we make it subtle," Gatty said. "Just enough to stir her pride."

The next day, the two worked in quiet tandem. They selected a little-used storeroom at the back of the Hall, one with a single window and heavy door—private, shadowy, and perfect. Violet scrubbed the dust from the shelves while Gatty laid out the bait: a copied ledger of garden recipes, a folded sketch of the grounds with notations about "planned expansions," and a forged note mentioning a "new role" Helena was preparing for Gatty.

Individually, the items were nothing. But together, they painted the illusion of insider knowledge—of secrets being shuffled just out of sight.

"Now," Gatty murmured, stepping back to inspect their work, "we need to make sure Honoria sees it and thinks it's her chance to strike first."

Violet hesitated, worry flickering across her face. "And if she doesn't bite?"

"She will," Gatty said, more certain than she felt. "She's too proud not to."

That afternoon, Gatty spread quiet hints among the women—casual mentions of Helena's meetings, whispers of reorganization, murmurings about roles shifting and power redistributing. The effect was immediate. By supper, Honoria was watching Gatty with sharp, narrowed eyes.

By twilight, Gatty and Violet had taken their places in the storeroom's shadows, crouched behind a shelf stacked with old linens. They'd rigged the space with mild herbal tricks: dried mugwort and lavender packed into a tiny cloth bundle that would release smoke when tugged; powdered wormwood to tint the water in the jug; just enough to rattle the nerves.

The door creaked open.

Honoria stepped inside, pausing to let her eyes adjust. She moved toward the table, her gaze sweeping over the staged materials. A smug look settled over her features as she picked up the ledger and leafed through it, then set her sights on the map.

Violet met Gatty's eyes. Gatty gave the faintest nod.

A soft snap. The pouch released a fragrant burst of lavender smoke, curling around Honoria's shoulders like a whisper. She coughed, swatting at the air.

"What in the devil—?" she snapped, irritation pinched into her voice.

Then the powder hit the water.

It shimmered to green in the low light, and Honoria's hand froze mid-reach. Her brows drew together in confusion that quickly shifted toward suspicion. For the first time, she looked less certain. And that was exactly what Gatty and Violet had hoped for.

Honoria coughed again, waving away the thick lavender smoke now curling through the air in lazy spirals. The green-tinged water shimmered like something cursed, catching the flicker of candlelight in eerie hues. Her gaze jerked toward every shadow, uncertainty replacing her earlier confidence. "That's enough of your tricks!" she snapped, though her voice cracked on the last word. "Who's there?"

From the gloom, Gatty stepped forward first, arms folded across her chest. Her stance was calm, her eyes sharp. Violet followed a beat later, hands clenched tightly but her chin lifted with quiet resolve.

"Expecting someone else?" Gatty asked coolly, her voice like a knife sliding into silk. "Or were you hoping to have this room to yourself?"

Honoria's nostrils flared. "I've no idea what game you think you're playing. I was checking the storeroom, just as Helena asked."

"Helena didn't ask," Gatty said flatly. "And you know it."

Violet took a cautious step forward, her voice steadier than she felt. "We know about the note, Honoria. About the information you've been feeding to the merchant. We know you're the one working against us."

Honoria scoffed, but the edge of her smirk quivered. "Baseless accusations. You've got nothing but gossip."

"No?" Gatty's gaze drifted to the table. "Strange, then, that you're rifling through private ledgers, maps, and falsified notes. Or that the water just turned a rather alarming shade of green in your presence."

Honoria opened her mouth—perhaps to protest, perhaps to lie again—but the door groaned open before she could speak.

All three women froze.

Helena entered, every line of her figure carved in shadow and firelight. Her eyes swept over the scene—the thick smoke, the scattered documents, Honoria standing at the center of it all.

"What is happening here?" Helena's voice was low, but each syllable struck like flint.

Honoria straightened, slipping easily into false civility. "I was investigating, Helena. I heard whispers about strange activities in the storeroom and thought it best to look into it myself."

Helena's brow arched, unimpressed. "Investigating without my permission?"

She turned to Gatty and Violet, and though her voice softened, it held weight. "And the two of you?"

"We overheard her speaking with someone in the garden days ago," Gatty said, her voice calm but sure. "She's been working with a merchant from town. Sharing information about Blythewood. Suggesting we're not what we claim to be."

Violet nodded, her eyes fixed on Honoria. "We had to be sure before we brought it to you. So we staged this—to see if she'd take the bait."

Helena's gaze lingered on the smoke drifting through the room, on the green-tinted water, on Honoria's red face and clenched fists. Her silence stretched so long it became unbearable.

Then, finally, she spoke. "Honoria. If you truly suspected something dangerous at Blythewood, you should have come to me directly. You chose betrayal instead. Tell me—why should I keep someone under my roof who would sell us out for silver?"

Honoria's mouth opened and closed. Nothing came out.

Helena turned back to Gatty and Violet. Her voice was quieter now, but still edged with steel. "Theatrics aside, you were right to act."

And that was the end of it.

By evening, Honoria was gone. No hearing. No farewell. No redemption. Her cries for reconsideration were met only with Helena's unflinching silence and a slammed door.

Gatty and Violet watched from the archway as Honoria was escorted down the path and out into the dark.

Violet exhaled shakily. "I thought I'd feel... relieved. But all I feel is tired."

Gatty nodded, her gaze never leaving the gate. "She won't trouble us again. But someone always will. We need to be ready."

The corridors of Blythewood Hall were unusually quiet that evening, hushed as if the very walls were catching their breath. The fallout from Honoria's exposure hung in the air like smoke after a storm—sharp, acrid, and lingering. In the kitchen, Gatty and Violet sat side by side at the worn wooden table, hands wrapped around mugs of steeped valerian and mint. The fire crackled, casting golden light across their tired faces, but the warmth did little to ease the weight pressing down on them.

Violet broke the silence first. "Do you think she's truly gone?" Her voice was low, her fingers tightening around the mug. "That she won't come back with more trouble?"

Gatty leaned back, the steam from her tea curling around her chin. "She'll try something," she said quietly. "But Helena knows how to make a message stick. Honoria's name will be poison in every household that matters. No merchant or magistrate will want to be tied to her."

Violet nodded, but her brows knit with lingering disbelief. "Still… she risked everything. Her place here, her safety, all for what? A chance to be the one in charge?"

Gatty's expression softened. "That's the same reason many of us were nearly ruined. Power. Fear. The need to be seen." She glanced down at the mug in her hands. "It's not so different from what brought us all to Blythewood. People saw something in us they didn't understand—and they made it monstrous."

Violet reached across the table, her hand finding Gatty's. "But we didn't let her do the same to us," she said. "We stopped it before it grew any bigger. That has to count for something."

Gatty met her eyes and gave a small nod, their joined hands grounding her more than any tea could.

Later that night, Helena summoned them both to her study. The tall windows were shuttered against the wind, and the only light came from the flickering candles arranged in a brass candelabrum. Helena stood behind the desk, her silhouette drawn sharp by shadow, her hands clasped with the same precision she used when dealing with estate matters or magistrates.

"You acted wisely," she said without preamble. "Honoria's meddling could have unraveled everything we've built. But you caught it early—and you handled it cleanly."

Gatty dipped her head, humbled by the rare praise. "We didn't do it alone. The others helped, in their way."

Helena's expression softened, if only slightly. "That's what I hoped to hear. Blythewood was never meant to be a shelter alone. It must be a web—a strong one. And you've begun to weave it."

She looked at Violet. "Your instincts were good. Your courage better. And you'll both need more of both before the year is out."

A chill ran down Gatty's spine, but she said nothing. Helena's words were always layered, threaded with foresight.

When they were dismissed, the two women slipped into the quiet dark of the corridor. But Gatty didn't return to her room. Instead, her feet carried her toward the one place where her thoughts always seemed to settle: the library.

The scent of old parchment and beeswax greeted her like an embrace. Here, the world felt slower. Wiser. She closed the door behind her, letting the hush of the shelves and the low crackle of the fire ease the tension in her shoulders.

And there—at his usual spot near the hearth—was Leander. He looked up as she entered, a flicker of recognition and quiet relief softening his features. "Come to check my footnotes?" he teased gently, his voice low in the hush of the library.

Gatty gave a faint smile as she moved toward him. "Not this time," she said, settling into the chair opposite. "I just needed a place to breathe."

Leander closed the book before him and folded his hands atop it. "I heard about Honoria," he said after a pause. "You handled it with more grace than most would've managed."

Gatty shifted in her seat. "I didn't do it alone. Violet—"

"Violet's a marvel," Leander said warmly, "but so are you. And you're always the last one to admit it."

She let out a soft laugh, caught between embarrassment and gratitude. "It wasn't bravery. Not really. It was fear. Of what she might do. Of what we might lose if she succeeded."

Leander's expression grew thoughtful. "Fear doesn't cancel out courage," he said gently. "Sometimes it's what drives it. You still stood your ground."

Their eyes met across the table, the fire casting gold into the quiet space between them. Leander reached out, his fingers brushing hers—a small, grounding touch that sent a spark straight through her.

"I thought about what it would've meant," he said, voice barely above a whisper. "If she'd succeeded. If we'd lost all this... if I'd lost you."

Gatty's breath caught, and for a moment, she couldn't speak. She turned her hand under his, their fingers lacing together with the ease of something long awaited.

"I'm not going anywhere," she said softly. "Not after everything we've built here."

A slow smile spread across Leander's face, his shoulders easing as though some great tension had been lifted. "Good," he murmured. "Because I don't want to face any of this without you."

Their foreheads touched, and in that small, sacred stillness, they kissed—quiet and unhurried, the kind of kiss that needed no declaration to make itself understood. When they finally pulled apart, Gatty's cheeks were warm, and the weight of the day had softened to something lighter, steadier.

The next morning, the Hall stirred with new energy. Gone was the shadow of mistrust that Honoria had left behind. In its place, laughter echoed from the kitchen, and voices in the garden rose not in suspicion, but in conversation.

Alice found Gatty near the stillroom, gathering bundles of dried marjoram. "Funny, isn't it?" she said, holding out a fresh sprig of rosemary. "We all came here expecting to keep to ourselves. And now it feels like we're part of something bigger."

Gatty smiled as she took the herb from her. "It's what happens when you stop surviving and start building. When you find people who believe in you."

Violet joined them, a basket of elderflower slung over one arm. "It's what happens," she said, "when someone gives us the chance."

Gatty shook her head, affection crinkling the corners of her eyes. "We gave it to each other."

Later that afternoon, Helena called a small gathering in the study. Those who had stood together through the week's storm sat around the long table, quiet but proud.

"You've proven something important," Helena said, her gaze sweeping the room. "That loyalty and trust are still possible, even in a house full of secrets."

She looked to Gatty last. "You've become something of a compass here. Not just because you speak with conviction—but because others follow when you do."

Gatty glanced at Violet, who gave her a quiet nod. She looked around at Alice, Anne, the others who had helped them see the truth through the smoke. And then back to Helena.

"We've all been called names," Gatty said, her voice even. "Witch. Thief. Liar. But none of those things matter as much as what we do with each other now."

A beat of silence passed—and then, as if on cue, the room softened.

That evening, Gatty returned to the library one last time. Leander was already there, quill in hand, surrounded by a growing stack of labeled journals and sketches of herbs.

He looked up when she entered, his face lighting without hesitation. "Back again?"

"I'm beginning to suspect it's your company I like," she said, grinning.

He reached for her hand, and she took it without pause.

Whatever came next, they would face it—side by side.

CHAPTER TWENTY-FIVE

CURSES

Weeks passed, and Gatty began to think her old village might leave her be.

The knock at the front door was not loud—but it carried. A precise, insistent rapping that broke the late morning quiet like a dropped plate. Gatty, mid-reach for a jar of beeswax in the kitchen, stilled. Violet glanced up from her slicing board, a frown already knitting between her brows.

Before either could move, footsteps echoed down the corridor, and the door creaked open. A voice followed—measured, but unmistakably biting.

"Gatty Carter. We have unfinished business."

Gatty's spine stiffened. *I should have known he'd come right after William.* She set the jar down with deliberate care, wiped her hands on her apron, and gave Violet a look that was all grit. "Stay here," she murmured, though Violet was already trailing her to the door.

By the time they reached the entrance hall, Edward Fenton had made himself comfortably unwelcome. He stood just inside the threshold, his boots damp with morning dew, his coat dusted with travel grime. Though not shouting, his voice held the weight of a man used to being listened to.

"There you are," he said, the faintest curve of a smile on his mouth—one that never reached his eyes. "You've made quite the home for yourself, haven't you?"

Gatty didn't bother returning the courtesy. "You've come a long way for a grievance, Edward."

"A grievance?" He took a step forward, and Violet's breath hitched. Gatty didn't flinch. "Try a blight. The land you abandoned, which I bought when you were declared dead, has turned against me. Crops wilt. Animals won't stay. The last farmhand fled swearing the place was cursed."

"Then perhaps it is," Gatty said flatly, folding her arms. "Or perhaps your land senses the rot in its master."

His expression soured. "You think this is a joke?"

"I think it's convenient," she shot back, her voice level. "When things go wrong, blame the woman. Especially one who got away."

Edward's face darkened. "You left your stain on that place, girl. Whatever trick you played—whatever unholy thing you did to it—I want it undone. Now."

Gatty's fingers curled around the edge of her sleeve. "I didn't curse the land, Edward. But if it's turning its back on you, maybe it's because you stole it."

He stepped closer. "Undo it, or I'll see to it that you're dragged before a real court this time. Let's see if the high and mighty ladies of Blythewood still think you're worth protecting when they hear what you've done."

Gatty stood her ground. "Try it. Witchcraft trials are outlawed, and your reputation's thin as old linen. You want to play at threats? Be my guest."

A beat of silence stretched—and then another voice cut clean through it.

"That's quite enough."

Leander appeared in the doorway to the drawing room, sleeves rolled, a thin ink stain on one wrist and something unreadable in his eyes. He didn't raise his voice, but every syllable landed like a weight dropped on a table.

Edward turned with a sneer. "This your protector now?"

Leander didn't blink. "This is her home. And if you've come to shout in doorways like a traveling lunatic, you can take your business elsewhere."

"I've come for justice," Edward snapped.

"No," Leander replied, stepping forward with quiet force. "You've come for land. You want her frightened enough to sign something away. But you've misjudged her. And you've very much misjudged me."

A strange stillness settled. The shadows stretched long from the stained-glass window, casting odd shapes across the floor. Edward's jaw worked, searching for a retort.

"I suggest you leave now," Leander said softly, "before you say something you can't unsay."

For a moment, Edward looked as if he might lunge—but then something in Leander's gaze stopped him cold. With a muttered curse, he turned and stalked out, the door thudding shut behind him. Only then did Gatty allow her shoulders to drop.

In the library that afternoon, Leander paced between shelves, his fingertips grazing the spines of old books as he turned over Edward's words in his mind. He knew the type—men who lost more than they could admit and hunted for someone to blame. Superstition was just a convenient mask for resentment.

The door creaked open, and Helena entered without ceremony. She closed it quietly behind her, eyes sharp beneath her velvet-trimmed cap. "I take it the shouting I overheard wasn't another delivery of firewood," she said dryly.

Leander offered a tight smile. "Edward Fenton. He thinks Gatty cursed his land and wants it reversed."

Helena exhaled through her nose, not quite a sigh. "Charming. They always return when their luck runs out, don't they?"

"He's not after an apology," Leander said, resting both hands on the edge of the reading table. "He's after her land. He's losing control of it—so he's come to punish the woman who once owned it."

Helena's brow lifted. "And your plan?"

"To let him believe he's no longer squaring off with a girl from his village—but with the Hartford family." Leander's voice was cool, but his eyes glinted with intent. "If he wants a feud, we'll give him one he can't afford."

Helena tilted her head, considering him. "A bluff?"

"A reputation," Leander corrected. "Our history is real. My uncle once sank a rival over nothing more than a poorly timed rumor. Fenton doesn't need to know how many of our contacts still take our letters seriously. He just needs to believe I'm still one of them."

Her lips curved—faintly, but unmistakably. "Very well. But mind your footing. You'll be playing his game now, and he might not be not as dumb as he looks."

Leander gave a slight bow. "I won't let him touch her. Or this house."

Helena left with a nod, her skirts whispering against the wood floor. Alone again, Leander reached for a familiar ledger from the upper shelf. He flipped through entries and letters—family histories filled with cunning partnerships, forced debts, veiled threats cloaked in polite correspondence. He marked the most damning tales with ribbon slips, preparing a legend that Edward Fenton could not ignore.

By dusk, he found Gatty alone in the garden, sleeves rolled and fingers stained from sorting calendula blossoms. The sky above them blushed gold and lavender.

She looked up, her brows knitting. "Is it over?"

"Not yet," he said, kneeling beside the drying rack. "But I have a plan."

Gatty's hands stilled. "What kind of plan?"

"One that involves reminding Edward what happens when a man crosses the wrong name. He can either sell your land to me or be buried under the weight of his own panic."

Gatty stared at him, wariness flickering behind her eyes. "You'd buy it? Just like that?"

Leander shrugged, brushing a sprig of rosemary aside. "Not because I want a farm, Gatty. Because he's using it to control you. And I won't let him."

She studied him, the breeze tugging strands of her hair loose. "You don't owe me this."

"No," he agreed softly. "But I can. And I've made a habit lately of standing beside things that matter."

The silence that followed was thick, not with fear, but with understanding.

"Thank you," she said, her voice steadier now.

Leander gave a wry smile. "Wait to thank me when it works. For now, just know he won't come at you again without facing all of us."

Gatty nodded, eyes following him as he rose and made his way back toward the hall. For the first time in days, she felt the tension around her ribs begin to loosen—not because the danger had passed, but because she no longer stood alone to meet it.

The courtyard of Blythewood lay hushed under the weight of waiting. Even the wind seemed to pause as Edward Fenton's boots scraped across the gravel, his figure a blot of rough gray and scuffed leather against the clipped hedgerows and orderly calm. He came alone, clutching a folded document in one gloved hand like a talisman. His mouth held the shape of a sneer, but it didn't quite reach his eyes.

Leander was already waiting on the stone steps, arms loose at his sides, his coat buttoned neat against the autumn breeze. The chill tousled his dark hair, but his posture held steady—neither defiant nor deferential, simply immovable. Behind him, Helena stood just inside the doorway, arms crossed and gaze unreadable, her presence subtle but undeniable.

"Mr. Hartford," Edward called, giving a stiff tilt of the head. "I thought we might speak like men of reason."

"You've come uninvited to the estate," Leander said evenly, his voice carrying without needing to rise. "Let's not pretend you're here in good faith."

Edward's jaw twitched, but he pressed on. "It's about Miss Carter. Her land, specifically. I've reconsidered the situation and thought we might settle this... peaceably."

Leander descended a single step, hands clasped behind his back, every inch the composed negotiator. "Peaceably would have meant not accusing her of witchcraft in the first place."

Edward's lips thinned. "A moment of frustration, nothing more. But the fact remains—the land's gone wrong. Sick animals. Spoiled soil. The villagers are talking, and talk spreads fast. If there's a way to fix this, I'd rather do it quietly."

Leander descended another step, calm as ever. "You're not here for a cure, Mr. Fenton. You're here to offload a bad investment and blame a woman for your misfortune."

Edward stiffened. "I'm offering to sell."

"No," Leander said mildly. "You're begging for a buyer."

A flush crept up Edward's neck. "Don't be smug. I know who you are, but I'm not scared of shadows and stories."

"You should be," Leander replied, voice still pleasant but iron-hard. "Because they're not stories. The Hartfords have ended careers over less than this. Men who overreached, who threatened people under our protection. They tend to vanish from polite society. Sometimes from trade entirely."

Edward's bravado faltered. "So you're here to intimidate me?"

"I'm here to give you a choice," Leander said, stepping down to the final stair, now level with him. "Sell me the land for a fraction of what you paid, walk away, and your pride will be the only thing bruised. Or refuse—and learn what it's like to find your name unwelcome in every merchant's book and every town magistrate's favor."

Silence stretched between them, taut as wire.

Helena shifted behind the door, and Edward's eyes flicked to her silhouette. He swallowed hard.

"I'll draw up the papers," he muttered.

"See that you do," Leander said, not unkindly.

Edward gave a curt nod, turned on his heel, and strode out of the courtyard without another word.

When he was gone, Leander let out a slow breath and ran a hand through his hair.

Helena emerged fully now, stepping down onto the first stair. "You play the role well," she said, voice low.

Leander gave a humorless smile. "I only borrowed it."

"But it fit." She gave his arm a brief, approving squeeze before turning to reenter the Hall.

From beneath the trellised arch of the garden gate, hidden just beyond the row of bay laurels, Gatty had watched the entire exchange unfold. Her heart beat hard—not from fear, but from awe. Leander hadn't raised his voice. He hadn't made threats or caused a scene. He'd simply stood firm, steady and unshakable, like a man who believed in her more than she had ever dared believe in herself.

Leander stepped into the library, the door clicking softly behind him as he exhaled the last of his tension. The air inside was warm, quiet, steeped in the familiar scent of vellum and dried lavender. His shoulders dropped slightly, though a lingering tautness clung to his frame.

Near the far shelf, Gatty turned from a row of books, her fingertips still trailing the leather spines as if drawing courage from their order and weight.

"You didn't have to do that," she said, her voice quiet but steady, somewhere between gratitude and guilt.

Leander didn't answer right away. He watched her a moment, the way the firelight touched her hair, the stubborn lift of her chin still shadowed by worry. "Yes, I did," he said at last. "That man has taken too much from you already. I wasn't about to let him take your peace as well."

Gatty crossed the room toward him, her skirts whispering over the carpet. She studied his face, noting the faint lines of restraint still etched at the corners of his mouth. "You were remarkable," she said, her voice softening. "You didn't flinch. I think he believed every word."

Leander gave a short, quiet laugh. "Good. I was bluffing through most of it."

"You didn't look like it," she said, tilting her head. "You looked like someone who could ruin a man's life with a signature."

He arched a brow. "I've read enough ledgers to know where the pressure points are."

"You didn't look scared."

"I was," he said, and his honesty caught her breath. "Not of him. Of what he might say. Of what it might bring back for you."

That admission settled between them like a shared secret. Gatty reached out, brushing her hand against the edge of his sleeve. "You're always standing between me and something awful," she murmured.

Leander's expression softened, the faintest smile tugging at his lips. "I'm not trying to be a shield," he said. "Only a companion."

Gatty's heart kicked against her ribs. For a moment, the library—the whole world—held still.

"When he accused me," she said quietly, "when he said those words... I thought I was back there again. In the marsh. The mob. The water." Her voice caught, but she pushed on. "But I wasn't. Because you were there."

Leander looked at her then, fully and without hesitation. "You're not alone anymore."

Their eyes held. His hand twitched slightly at his side, then rose, brushing gently against hers. She didn't pull away.

"I've never wanted to hurt anyone," he said. "But today, I did. Not because of what he said about you, but because of how easily he said it. As if you weren't real. As if you weren't..." He broke off, searching for words.

"Mine?" she offered, half-teasing, half-hoping.

He gave a soft, surprised laugh. "Yes," he said. "If you'll have me."

She stepped closer. "I think I already do."

Without fanfare, she reached up and pressed a kiss to his cheek—light and deliberate, yet with a heat that curled through her like smoke. He turned to her as she pulled back, eyes searching, lips parted.

"That's a dangerous promise," he said.

Gatty's smile deepened. "So is trying to frighten a witch."

Before he could answer, the sound of measured footsteps reached them. They sprang apart just as Helena entered, sharp-eyed as always, though a spark of amusement glinted beneath her usual composure.

"I trust Mr. Fenton has been handled," she said.

"He has," Leander replied, smoothing his coat with unnecessary precision.

Helena nodded once, turned on her heel, and vanished again, her approval left unspoken but understood.

Gatty glanced at Leander. "You should go before she decides we need another assignment."

He gave her a look that was equal parts fond and reluctant. "To-morrow, then?"

She nodded. "Tomorrow."

As he stepped from the room, Gatty remained behind, her fingers drifting once more across the spines of the books. But this time, she didn't need their steadiness. She had her own.

And she had him.

Chapter Twenty-Six

ACCUSATIONS

The morning broke in a hush, the sky a low, sullen gray and the earth slick with the memory of rain. Blythewood Hall stood motionless beneath the looming clouds, its weathered brick walls soaked in secrets, its windows watching like old sentinels. In the garden, Gatty's hands were stained lavender, the stems crushed into a ceramic bowl as she prepared a tonic for Helena's aching joints. The sharp, clean scent curled into the air—but it couldn't mask the tension carried on the wind.

She straightened, instinct prickling. From beyond the hedges, voices rose—too loud, too pointed, their urgency riding the breeze like an omen.

Squinting toward the courtyard, Gatty caught sight of Honoria, her skirts splashed with mud and her voice raised in theatrical outrage. She stood at the center of a loose cluster of townspeople, gesturing with the fervor of a street preacher. Beside her, a man in a travel-worn coat and a wide-brimmed hat cradled a leather satchel like a holy relic.

Gatty's stomach tightened at the sight. That man was no villager. He was here with purpose.

Helena stepped into view from the front doors, her figure framed by the Hall's columns like a portrait come to life. She moved down the steps with deliberate calm, the very image of a woman who refused to be hurried, even as the crowd rippled with anticipation. Honoria faltered at the sight of her, but quickly recovered, lifting her chin and raising her voice to the gathered ears.

"They harbor witches here, my lord!" she declared, pointing toward the Hall as though it burned her to look upon it. "This house is not what it claims. I have proof!"

A murmur passed through the onlookers, and the man beside her stepped forward. Gatty recognized him at once: a local magistrate, known for his fondness for spectacle and his habit of listening more to scandal than sense. He raised the satchel, the gesture theatrical, and turned his gaze over the crowd with quiet self-importance.

"I am here," he announced, "to investigate claims that Blythewood Hall harbors unnatural practices under the guise of charity and re-form."

The hush that followed was sharp-edged. Gatty's nails dug into her palm. At the edge of the garden, several of the women stood frozen, their expressions pale and taut. She caught one glancing toward the stables, another toward the gate—as though weighing the risk of flight.

But Helena didn't flinch. She stood as steady as carved stone, her eyes locked on the magistrate.

"Claims require evidence," she said, her voice smooth as polished silver. "And you are welcome to present what little you have before tarnishing the name of my household."

Honoria surged forward, emboldened. "I have testimonies from town, my lord. And items—objects used in their craft, hidden within the Hall itself!"

Helena's gaze dropped briefly to the satchel, then returned to Honoria, unamused. "You bring me bundles and hearsay. I suggest you take care before confusing healing with heresy."

She paused, then raised her voice just enough to carry. "Or perhaps the miller's wife misplaced her charms again. A harmless mishap—but an easy confusion for someone so eager to impress."

A quiet ripple of laughter broke through the crowd, but Honoria flushed deep red, her jaw clenching. "You mock us," she snapped, "but the magistrate won't be so easily swayed."

Helena inclined her head, expression unbothered. "I invite the magistrate to inspect every inch of my home," she said. "Let us leave theatrics behind and deal in facts."

The magistrate blinked, clearly unused to being addressed with such composed command. He glanced between Helena and Honoria, seeming briefly unsure of whom he should answer to.

At the garden's edge, Gatty wiped her hands clean and slipped through the hedgerow, catching Violet's eye near the greenhouse. A single tilt of her head was all it took—Violet nodded and vanished toward the house. Whatever Honoria had planted—or planned to present—they needed to find it first.

The magistrate followed Honoria through the entryway with deliberate steps, each echo off the flagstones as sharp as a gavel. Helena moved just behind them, serene as ever, though her eyes flicked to every corner, missing nothing. From the shadows near the garden doors, Gatty exchanged a taut glance with Violet as the great door swung shut behind the procession.

"Think she planted something?" Violet whispered, her voice tight with dread.

Gatty didn't answer right away. Her lips pressed into a grim line, her mind already racing. "If she did," she said at last, "we need to find it before he does."

They slipped inside, skirts brushing the stone as they hugged the margins of the corridor. The sound of Honoria's voice reached them—raised, indignant, already swelling with false righteousness as she guided the magistrate toward the library.

"Here, my lord," she called, as though unveiling a stage set. "This is where they keep it. The books. The items they don't want you to see."

Gatty's stomach turned at the sanctimony in her tone. As if she were unearthing cursed relics rather than medical texts and dried herbs. But in a world where fear spoke louder than truth, Gatty knew absurdity could still sentence a woman.

Inside the library, Leander stood with his back straight, his fingers braced against the desk. His usual calm looked more like a mask now, drawn tight over a storm.

"This is a library, my lord," he said evenly, as the magistrate stepped inside. "Not a coven."

The magistrate didn't respond right away. He surveyed the room with narrowed eyes, his gaze landing on Leander with cautious scrutiny. "We'll see what it is," he said at last. "Step aside."

Leander moved stiffly. His jaw worked as Honoria swept past him, her movements theatrical, as though she were playing the heroine in a badly written play. She yanked books from shelves with little regard for their order or value.

"Here!" she cried, seizing a worn leather volume and holding it aloft. "Look at this—recipes for tinctures and potions. Poisons, likely. What sort of respectable woman needs a book like this?"

Leander took a step forward, his tone clipped but controlled. "That book is a botanical manual, compiled by Nicholas Culpeper. It's been used by physicians, herbalists, and apothecaries for over a century. If you wish to accuse every home in Norfolk that owns a copy of witchcraft, I suggest you clear your calendar."

The magistrate flipped through the pages, his brow furrowed as he paused on an illustration of belladonna. Honoria's performance, however, was far from finished. She turned sharply, plucking a small glass bottle from a side table with a flourish.

"And this?" she said, lifting it toward the light. "What's in here?"

Leander's gaze barely flicked to it. "Lavender oil. Good for headaches. Bad for witch hunts."

The magistrate made no comment, but his expression remained guarded. Undeterred, Honoria crossed the room to a drawer and began rifling through it like a thief in search of stolen gold. At last, she held something up—a bundle of dried herbs tied with black twine, her expression triumphant.

"This," she announced, turning to the magistrate with a gleam in her eye. "This I found in the garden shed. Hidden beneath a stack of old crates. A charm. Cursed, no doubt. Do you deny it now?"

Just outside the door, Gatty's hands clenched into fists.

"She's playing her last card," she muttered. "And if we don't move now, it might work."

Without another word, she and Violet darted down the corridor and out into the wet garden, skirts catching on brambles and boots sinking into the soft earth. The sky threatened rain, the air thick with tension and the scent of cut rosemary.

The shed loomed ahead like a warning. Gatty flung open the door, and the familiar scent of damp earth and drying herbs enveloped them. Her eyes scanned the space quickly, seeking anything out of place.

"There," Violet breathed, pointing to a patch of overturned soil near the lowest shelf.

Gatty dropped to her knees and dug her hands into the earth. Her fingers closed around something cold and hard. She pulled it free—a crude pewter disc, etched with jagged lines meant to mimic runes. Her stomach turned at the sight.

"Honoria planted it," she said, her voice tight with fury. "Probably buried it herself last night."

Violet knelt beside her, eyes wide. "If the magistrate sees this—"

"He won't," Gatty said.

She didn't wait for Violet's answer. Together, they crossed to the compost heap and buried the charm deep, beneath wet peels and crushed stems.

As the soil settled, so did their resolve.

Inside the shed, the air was thick with the scent of damp wood and bruised mint. Gatty's eyes swept the cramped space, locking on a patch of disturbed soil beneath a shelf. Something about the pattern—too neat, too recent—made her gut twist.

She dropped to her knees and began to dig, her fingers cold and quick. Within moments, she uncovered a small pewter charm, smeared with earth. Its surface was etched with crude, jagged runes—a mockery of something ancient and sacred.

Violet inhaled sharply beside her. "Oh no," she whispered. "She actually did it."

"Honoria planted it," Gatty said grimly. "Probably last night while we were sleeping."

"If the magistrate sees that..." Violet's voice wavered.

"He'll believe her," Gatty finished. She stood, her hands tight around the charm. "But he won't get the chance."

Violet's brows lifted in alarm, but she didn't question. She just nodded. They crossed the garden in silence, slipping behind the hedgerow to the compost heap. Gatty buried the charm deep beneath the steaming pile of scraps and roots, tamping the soil down with her heel until the earth looked untouched.

By the time they returned to the hall, Honoria's show was in full swing.

The magistrate held the herb bundle Honoria had produced, brow furrowed, fingers tracing the black twine. "And where exactly was this found?" he asked, his voice crisp and suspicious.

Honoria stood a bit too tall, her chin high. "In the garden shed," she declared. "Hidden. Tucked behind crates like they knew it shouldn't be found."

Leander, who had been standing silently beside a shelf, finally spoke. "And how did you happen upon it so easily, Honoria?" he asked smoothly. "If it was so well-hidden?"

Honoria blinked, thrown. "I—I was investigating," she stammered. "Someone had to do something. Helena's too trusting. She always has been."

"Indeed," came Helena's voice, cool and clear from the doorway. She entered the room with slow, measured steps, Gatty and Violet just behind her. "And yet you never came to me with your concerns. Curious, isn't it, for someone who claims loyalty to this house."

Honoria's flush deepened, but she pressed on. "I only wanted to protect you, madam."

"By accusing the women under my roof of witchcraft?" Helena's voice sharpened like steel drawn from a sheath. "And inviting a magistrate onto my grounds without my knowledge?"

The room fell into taut silence. Even the magistrate shifted uncomfortably, glancing between the two women.

"Madam Hartford," he began, his tone bordering on placating, "if this has all been a misunderstanding, I will take my leave. But I must consider the gravity of the claims—"

"Of course," Helena said, her voice as smooth as poured ink. "But as the one whose household is under investigation, I expect the same right—to examine any evidence myself, especially when it appears to have been so conveniently discovered."

As the magistrate turned back to Honoria, distracted, Gatty gave Violet the smallest nod. They moved in tandem toward the discarded items Honoria had so theatrically revealed. With casual grace, Gatty reached for the lavender oil while Violet bent to adjust the herbal bundle, her movements slow and deliberate.

"Careful," Violet said quietly, but with just enough volume to carry. "Some herbs can react if mishandled."

Honoria stiffened. "React?" she repeated, voice cracking.

Gatty straightened, turning toward her with the calm certainty of someone holding a match above dry kindling. "Some combinations can cause strange effects. Especially when tied with black twine." She let the words settle. "But of course, you'd already know that."

The magistrate's head snapped toward Honoria. She flinched, backing a half-step toward the hearth. "They're trying to confuse you!" she snapped. "Don't let them fool you. They've been weaving tricks in that garden for months—conjuring, whispering—I've seen it!"

"Tricks?" Helena cut in, stepping forward. "You mean planting vegetables? Drying rosemary? Writing in journals? That is what frightens you, Honoria?"

She gestured toward the bundle still in Violet's hand. "Do you deny placing it there yourself?"

Honoria's mouth opened. No words came. "I..." she tried. "I only meant to—"

"Enough," the magistrate barked, the last threads of his patience fraying. "This is absurd. You brought me here to parade accusations without proof. I will not be made a fool."

He turned sharply to Helena. "Madam Hartford, I find no credible evidence here. I trust your judgment will suffice in addressing this... disruption."

Helena inclined her head, the barest of smiles playing at her lips. "You may be assured of it, my lord."

The magistrate swept from the room, his boots echoing down the corridor. The moment he disappeared, the breath seemed to return to the room—but the air remained thick with what had nearly been.

Honoria, pale now, stood frozen in the center of it all. Gatty watched the flicker of calculation behind her eyes turn slowly to dread.

The library settled into silence as the magistrate's retreating steps faded down the corridor. Honoria remained in the center of the room, her shoulders stiff, her fists clenched so tightly the blood had fled from her knuckles. But it wasn't fear that clung to her face now—it was fury, thin and cracking.

Helena turned toward her with the precision of a blade unsheathed. "You have brought shame to my hall, Honoria," she said, her voice low but thrumming with authority. "You will explain yourself."

Honoria's head snapped up. "Explain myself? To you?" Her voice was shrill, laced with spite. "You, who fills this place with outcasts and calls it grace? Who shelters witches under the guise of charity and claims the work we do is decent?"

Gatty tensed, but Helena merely lifted a hand, a quiet command that quelled the room. Her eyes never left Honoria. "You've mistaken mercy for weakness," she said, each word polished to ice. "But make no mistake—you have betrayed the women who welcomed you. Our Lydia had to send little Ivy away to her aunt in the midst of all this chaos. You are shrinking our joy and our number. That will not go unanswered."

Honoria's resolve faltered, just for a beat. Then she stepped forward, her voice rising. "You act so righteous," she spat. "But you're no better than the people you pretend to pity. This place—this whole charade—it's built on lies. And one day, people will see through it. You're not untouchable, Helena."

Before Helena could reply, Gatty stepped forward, her voice steady. "The truth's already out, Honoria. It's in the work we do every day. In the women who've found peace here. We grow herbs, not curses. We heal what's been broken. What have you done, except feed fear and watch it bloom?"

Honoria turned on her, sneering. "You think you've fooled them all. But I know what you are. A liar. A stray. A girl with dirt on her hands and blood on her roots. You're cursed, Gatty Carter—just like your land."

The words hit with the force of a slap, but Gatty didn't flinch. "Maybe," she said quietly. "Maybe I am cursed. Maybe I've done things I regret. But I've never tried to tear anyone else down to feel taller. And I've never been afraid to start over."

A soft murmur rippled through the women gathered near the shelves and windows. Heads nodded. Shoulders squared.

"You're running, Honoria," Gatty added, her voice low but firm. "You just don't have anywhere left to go."

Honoria's mouth opened, but nothing came out.

Helena allowed the silence to stretch before she spoke again. "You are no longer welcome at Blythewood Hall," she said with quiet finality. "You will pack your things and leave by morning."

Honoria's eyes widened. "You can't—"

"I can," Helena said, her tone like a closing door. "And I will. This house is not perfect, but it will never be ruled by fear. You've made your choice."

Honoria looked around as if searching for support, but found only stillness. No one stepped forward. Slowly, she turned and stalked from the room, her footsteps echoing one last time across the stone floor.

As the door closed behind her, the library seemed to exhale. The air, thick with tension moments before, began to clear.

Gatty let her breath out slowly. She didn't realize she was trembling until she felt Violet's hand on her arm.

"You didn't have to do that," Violet said softly, eyes shining. "Stand up for me. For all of us."

"I wasn't just standing up for you," Gatty replied. "I was standing up for the garden. For the still room. For every woman here who's ever been called a curse."

Violet's grinned. "You were right," she said. "Honoria was running in circles. But we're moving forward."

Helena stepped toward them, her presence still formidable, though something in her face had gentled. "You both handled yourselves with integrity," she said. "Honoria's venom was sharp, but you made it powerless."

Gatty blinked at the unexpected praise, and Helena placed a hand on her arm—a brief touch, but it carried a weight of recognition.

"This house survives because of women who know what they are and choose to be more," Helena added. Her gaze flicked to Violet. "That includes you. Don't forget that again."

Violet nodded, pride softening the flush in her cheeks.

As the room emptied, Leander lingered near the tall windows, one arm resting along the stone sill. Gatty caught his eye and crossed toward him, her boots whispering over the floor.

"Well?" she asked, tipping her head. "Did I give you enough drama for one afternoon?"

Leander's mouth curled into a smile. "More than enough. I half-expected you to conjure lightning."

Gatty huffed a laugh, though her cheeks warmed. "I wasn't sure I had it in me."

"I was," he said simply. He reached out, letting his fingers brush hers—just enough to say what words couldn't.

Gatty met his gaze, and for a moment, they stood in a silence full of promise. Whatever storms lay ahead, she wouldn't be facing them alone.

Chapter Twenty-Seven

A Shared Triumph

Despite the fire crackling in the hearth, the air held a weight today—thick with expectation, the kind that made breath shallow and silence louder than speech.

The women had gathered in clusters throughout the great hall, their voices low and murmuring like wind in tall grass. Aprons were straightened, trays were polished, ledgers reviewed one last time. Everyone moved with the nervous precision of people who knew they were about to be judged.

Gatty stood at the head of the room, hands clasped tight, her chin high despite the thunder beneath her ribs. Her confidence wasn't effortless—but it was earned, shaped from fear and fury and something harder to break than either. She caught the eyes of Alice and Margery, who stood near the doorway with tightly laced fingers. Violet clutched her ledgers like a shield.

"This is our moment," Gatty said, her voice cutting through the hush. "He may come looking for cracks, but we'll show him strength. Blythewood isn't just a roof and rules—it's a place for mending. For learning. For becoming. And today, he'll see that."

The words steadied them. Violet's shoulders loosened; Margery gave a brisk, determined nod. Alice whispered something to herself—perhaps a prayer, or a promise—and adjusted the tray she held with more purpose than before.

Then Helena entered, the tap of her heels as even and assured as a metronome. Her presence shifted the air—calm, controlled, unmistakably commanding. She moved through the room like a woman surveying her battlements, pausing before Gatty. "You're ready," she said simply.

Gatty nodded. "We'll make this a demonstration—not a defense."

Helena's eyes glinted with approval. "Good. Blythewood has survived worse storms. It will weather this one too."

As the women scattered to their roles—rearranging herbs, brushing dust from the bannisters, double-checking lists—Gatty remained near the hearth. She was flipping through the order of the day in her mind when the faint turn of pages caught her attention. Leander stood just beyond the fringe of movement, a book in hand.

He stepped closer. "I thought this might help," he said, offering it with care. "Legal precedents. Herbal remedies and their protections under English common law. A few of the cases are older, but they make your argument clearer."

Gatty took the book, her fingers grazing his. "You've been up reading late again."

A half-smile tugged at his mouth. "Some causes are worth the sleepless hours."

Something in her steadied at his words. She didn't need to ask who he meant. "Thank you."

He nodded once, quiet and sincere. "I'm with you."

Across the hall, Honoria lounged against the far wall, arms folded, a smug little smile resting on her lips like it belonged there. Her eyes flicked from Gatty to the book and back again, full of sharpness and calculation. But Gatty didn't look away. She let the silence stretch until Honoria's smirk wavered.

"When we stand together," Gatty said clearly—her voice just loud enough to carry—"there's nothing they can do to break us."

A soft murmur rippled through the women, like a low wind rising. Honoria's smugness frayed, her lips tightening, but she turned away.

The rest of the morning passed in a current of quiet movement. Blythewood's grand hall became something like a stage—one lined not with velvet curtains, but with poultices, clean ledgers, and women who knew the stakes. Gatty moved among them with a calm she wasn't sure she owned, her fingers brushing over the cover of the law book, her thoughts sharpened by Leander's voice, Helena's trust, and Violet's quiet determination.

Then came the sound they'd all been waiting for. The crisp clatter of hooves beyond the gate.

Gatty's head rose, her spine straightening as the room collectively stilled. Her heart beat a steady drum behind her ribs. Let him come, she thought. Let him see.

They were ready.

Gatty stood at the center of the great hall, the morning sun slanting through the high windows to catch in her hair and glint off the polished floor. Around her, the women of Blythewood gathered—close, quiet, alert.

Alice held a tray of poultices with both hands, her knuckles pale beneath the weight of nerves. Margery stood beside her, smoothing her apron compulsively until she caught Gatty's eye and stilled. At the rear, Violet hovered near a side table, her ledgers stacked with exacting care, her face pale but composed.

Gatty drew a breath and let it settle in her lungs. Then, with calm clarity, she said, "We know what we're doing."

Her voice reached into the corners of the room, firm without force. She looked each of them in the eye—Margery, Alice, Violet, and a dozen others just behind them—and saw their tension shift like wind in tall grass.

"This isn't just an inquest," she continued. "It's a moment to show the truth. Blythewood isn't a hiding place—it's a place of becoming. We'll show them what that looks like."

Alice straightened. "They'll see. They have to."

Margery nodded, her smile uncertain but blooming. "I'll do my best."

Gatty stepped forward, hands lightly clasped in front of her. She had no title, no estate, no station—but in that moment, she held the room like a baroness.

"We'll begin with what they understand," she said. "Alice and Margery—you'll demonstrate the salves and remedies. Violet, explain the ledgers and how we record every treatment, every success and failure. Show them our method. Our order. Our care."

Violet raised a tentative hand. "And the presentation? The, um... 'theatrical touches' you mentioned?"

A ghost of a smile curved Gatty's mouth. "We'll use them. The magistrate isn't here just to decide if we're guilty—he's here to decide whether we're worth backing. Let him see women who are capable and compelling. Let him see something worth preserving."

From behind her, Leander appeared without announcement, his voice a steady undertone beside her ear. "And if he tries to twist your words—" He held out the leather-bound volume again, a ribbon marking a well-worn page. "—you'll have this. Cited and ready."

Their fingers touched briefly as Gatty took it. She nodded once, her voice quiet. "Thank you."

The room began to move with renewed purpose. Margery and Alice rehearsed the names and uses of each herb in turn, their nerves hardening into certainty. Violet opened her ledgers and spread them out in tidy rows, smoothing each page like she was laying a table for judgment. Helena moved among them like a watchful flame, her commands brief, her tone measured.

Gatty walked the perimeter slowly, offering a hand on a shoulder here, a quiet word there—stitching their focus back together, thread by thread.

Across the hall, Honoria hovered just beyond the glow of the hearth, her arms crossed, lips curled in a smirk that didn't quite reach her eyes. She leaned toward a young scullery maid and muttered, "Doesn't matter how they dress it up. The magistrate will see the truth."

The girl didn't respond, shifting uncomfortably under the weight of Honoria's whisper. Gatty didn't react, but she caught the glance. She didn't need to speak to silence it—her calm radiated louder than rebuttal.

She turned back to the women and spoke with quiet authority. "We're not just proving we belong. We're reminding them we already do."

And then came the sound of footsteps—boots on stone, voices at the entry, and a gust of cold air as the great door opened.

The magistrate entered.

He was tall, iron-gray and thin-lipped, flanked by two constables and trailed by a small group of onlookers from the village—curious, cautious, hungry for spectacle. His eyes swept the room like a blade.

Helena stepped forward with measured grace. "Welcome to Blythewood Hall, Your Honor. We're grateful for the opportunity to show you what we do."

The magistrate inclined his head. "I've heard many things. Some admirable. Some... concerning." His gaze moved to Gatty, assessing, waiting. "And you are?"

Gatty met his stare with calm conviction. "Agatha Carter, sir. And I stand before you with the other women who live and work here." Her voice was clear, her posture unflinching. Behind her, the women stood straighter. Margery's hands were still. Violet gripped her ledger with quiet purpose.

The magistrate gave no nod of approval, but neither did he dismiss her. "Very well," he said. "Let's begin." His boots rang hollow on the stone floor as he strode into the center of the hall, each step measured, each glance calculated. His presence cast a long shadow, and the townsfolk who had followed—curious, uncertain—lined the perimeter, murmuring softly among themselves.

Honoria remained apart, leaning against a column with her arms crossed, her expression smug beneath a veil of feigned civility. Gatty caught her watching like a hawk, as though waiting for something—anything—to crumble.

"Let us begin," the magistrate said, his voice crisp as frost. He looked not at Helena, but at the assembled women. "I am here to observe, not to accuse. But I expect clarity. Convince me."

Helena stepped forward, her posture poised, her tone composed. "Blythewood Hall was founded to provide shelter, healing, and purpose to women who had none. Some come to escape violence, some to learn trade or science, some to recover from grief. What we offer is order, care, and dignity."

The magistrate's brow arched, his expression neutral but questioning. "I've heard both praise and suspicion surrounding this hall. Today will determine which it deserves."

Before Helena could speak again, Gatty stepped up beside her.

"If I may, Your Honor," she said, voice clear but unflinching. "You've heard whispers. We'd like to show you substance."

The magistrate turned his gaze to her, studying her face with professional detachment. "You seem young to speak for such a place."

Gatty didn't flinch. "I am. But youth doesn't disqualify truth. And truth is what you'll see, if you let us proceed."

Something shifted subtly in the room. Even the townsfolk, half-expecting fear, straightened at the steadiness in her tone. The magistrate gave a single, brisk nod. "Proceed."

Alice and Margery stepped forward, each carrying trays lined with small jars and bundles wrapped in linen. Gatty turned toward the gathered assembly, her voice measured and warm.

"Alice and Margery are among our herbalists. They've prepared remedies we've used for fevers, wounds, and pain. We don't make claims of magic—only of skill, learned through time and labor."

Alice lifted a small jar. "Calendula and comfrey," she explained softly. "Infused in beeswax and olive oil. For cuts, bruises. It prevents infection."

Margery held out a pale green poultice, neatly wrapped in cloth. "Willow bark and feverfew. For headaches, inflammation, and fever. We've used this in three nearby households this winter."

The magistrate stepped forward, inspecting the trays with a furrowed brow. "And these methods? Where were they learned?"

Helena responded smoothly, "Some are centuries old—passed down through midwives and apothecaries. Others come from published studies by physicians like Dr. Culpeper and Boerhaave. We don't guess, sir. We study."

Gatty added, "We also test every treatment, track it carefully. We don't risk what we cannot explain."

She turned toward Violet, who approached with her arms full of ledgers. Her hands trembled faintly, but her jaw was set.

"These books," she said, placing them on a table with care, "contain patient names, ailments, remedies, dates, and follow-up results. We keep exact records of every treatment given."

The magistrate opened one and scanned a page. His eyes narrowed slightly—at the detail, not the contents. "You've documented all of this?"

"Every salve, every dosage," Violet confirmed. "So we know what works. And so there is never confusion."

He closed the ledger slowly. "Meticulous." Then, more sharply, "Though others might say such documentation suggests conceal-ment—an attempt to appear legitimate while practicing something darker."

Gatty stepped forward again. "Or perhaps it's a sign of responsibil-ity. A man with a medical degree wouldn't be questioned for keeping such records."

The magistrate regarded her for a long moment. Then, with a slight nod: "Continue."

But before anyone could move, Honoria stepped from her post, her voice slicing through the stillness. "And what of the whispers, Your Honor?" she called, arms folded, tone sharp. "Healing is what they claim, but there are rumors. Strange lights in the gardens. Women speaking in tongues. Illnesses vanishing without cause. If that isn't witchcraft—what is?"

The magistrate turned, his expression sharpening. "Do you have evidence of any of this, madam?"

Honoria blinked. She hadn't expected the turn. "Only what I've heard. From women. From town."

He frowned. "Rumors are not evidence."

Honoria flushed. "But don't they warrant suspicion?"

Before he could answer, Gatty stepped in, voice firm but not mocking. "Your Honor, fear is a powerful thing—but so is ignorance. Our work may look unfamiliar to some. That doesn't make it unholy."

The magistrate's gaze flicked to her—sharp, considering. "An interesting point, Miss Carter. One I'll take under advisement." He the turned, his gaze hardening as it landed on Honoria. "If you intend to accuse, madam, then I suggest you present evidence. Tangible, credible evidence. Otherwise, you traffic in rumors—and I have no patience for rumo r."

Honoria stiffened, but a flicker of doubt passed over her features. Still, she pressed forward, her voice raised slightly, sharpened by desperation. "Rumors are born from truth, Your Honor. These women—what they do here—it isn't natural. Strange herbs, strange results. You saw their ledger—why would they need to keep such records unless they had something to hide?"

A low rustle passed through the crowd—some unconvinced, others curious.

But before the magistrate could reply, Violet stepped forward. Her shoulders were square, her stack of papers gripped tightly in her arms. Her voice, though quiet, carried like a bell in the hush.

"May I speak, Your Honor?"

The magistrate gave a small nod, intrigued.

Violet stepped into the center, the sunlight catching her as if to spotlight her resolve. "We have evidence as well—of Honoria's history of deceit." She set the papers gently on a nearby table. "These are signed statements from townsfolk. People she's hurt."

She opened the top page and continued. "One woman lost her seamstress work after Honoria spread lies about her dealings with a married client. Another nearly lost her home when Honoria convinced the land agent she'd forged her lease."

Gatty joined her, adding, "And here—these are notes from her dealings with the merchant who tried to sabotage Blythewood. She passed him information. She gave him names."

The magistrate moved to the table, rifling through the documents. His expression darkened as he read, and when he turned back to Honoria, his voice had lost all pretense of courtesy. "Well?" he asked coldly. "You have accused others. What do you say in your own defense?"

Honoria's mouth opened, but no words came. Her poise cracked, the veneer of superiority slipping. "They—they twist the truth," she stammered. "This is a coordinated attack. They've turned everyone against me—!"

Before he could answer, a woman's voice rang out from the back of the hall. "No one had to turn us. We know what we've seen."

The crowd parted, revealing two women stepping forward. One was a farmer's wife, her cheeks ruddy from sun and work. The other, quieter, wore the plain apron of a housemaid. Their expressions were grave.

"She told my neighbors I was a thief," the maid said, voice trembling but clear. "Because I wouldn't lie for her. She said if I stayed quiet, she'd ruin me."

The farmer's wife nodded. "And she tried to ruin my husband's contract with the miller when we refused to lend her more than she was owed. Said we were cheating her. We weren't."

Their words hit like stones. The air grew thick with the weight of Honoria's unraveling.

The magistrate folded his arms, his voice cold and clipped. "It seems you've made a habit of manipulation, madam. And your accusations today appear to serve no greater cause than your own bitterness."

Honoria's face flushed a deep, splotchy red. "You can't believe them over me—!"

He raised a hand to silence her. "I've heard enough. Blythewood Hall has presented order, skill, and community benefit. You have offered nothing but venom and hearsay." The magistrate turned to the room at large. "Let this be a lesson to all: False accusations are not only dangerous—they are punishable. Blythewood Hall will continue its work. Without interference." He gestured to his constables. "Escort Miss Honoria from the premises. And I trust she will find it... wise not to return."

Honoria sputtered something unintelligible, but her protests were swallowed by the heavy silence. The crowd parted again, but this time to let her pass. No one looked at her with sympathy. Not anymore.

As her footsteps faded down the corridor, a collective breath was released.

The room felt lighter.

The magistrate turned back, his expression once more measured. "Blythewood Hall," he said clearly, "is a place of healing and education. Let it be known: its work serves the good of this town."

Helena stepped forward, her voice steady and proud. "Your words carry weight, Your Honor. And they will not be wasted."

The townsfolk murmured, a few even clapping softly. Gatty turned to Alice, to Margery, to Violet—and the quiet pride on their faces mirrored her own.

As the crowd dispersed, Helena stepped closer, her voice low but warm. "You held your ground, Gatty. I've always known you were strong. But today..." Her eyes softened. "Today reminded me why I built this place in the first place."

Gatty's breath caught slightly, pride rising in her throat. "You taught me how."

Helena gave a small nod. "Perhaps. But courage like that can't be taught. It's chosen."

Later that evening, the library was hushed, its high windows catching the last amber threads of twilight. Gatty moved through the space slowly, shelving a few displaced volumes, her fingertips brushing the worn leather spines like familiar friends. The scent of ink and old paper wrapped around her like a shawl—steady, grounding, safe.

The door opened with a soft creak.

Leander stepped in, a modest stack of books tucked under one arm. He crossed the room in silence and set them down gently on the long table. When he turned to her, his expression was unguarded—warm, quiet, deeply sincere.

"You were remarkable today," he said, voice low, as though raising it might disturb the peace. "Not just for what you said, but for what you made them feel. You reminded them they're not alone."

Gatty gave a small shrug, still standing with one hand resting lightly on a shelf. "I only did what needed to be done."

"No," Leander said, stepping closer, his tone both firm and tender. "You did more than that. You gave them something to stand behind. And you reminded me that this hall isn't just a shelter—it's hope. It's proof that a better world can be made."

Their eyes met across the quiet space. The rest of the world—the chaos of the day, the voices downstairs—seemed to fall away. For a heartbeat, there was only this stillness between them.

Leander hesitated, then added, "I hope you know how much I admire you. Not just for today. For all of it. You've made me see the world—my place in it—differently."

A flush rose to Gatty's cheeks, but she didn't look away. "That's what you've done for me, too."

They stood like that for a moment, the silence not awkward but companionable—rich with unspoken things.

———

That night, the main hall glowed with firelight and soft laughter. The women gathered in clusters around mismatched chairs and hastily set tables, the remains of a celebratory meal scattered among cups and candles.

Helena stood at the front of the room, a glass raised in her hand. Her voice, when she spoke, was strong and proud.

"To Blythewood," she said. "To its resilience. To its courage. To the women who make it what it is—and what it will become."

A cheer rose up. The sound was not loud, but it was certain. Gatty felt it in her bones.

She turned slowly, letting her eyes pass over Alice and Margery laughing softly together, Violet deep in conversation with one of the newer girls, and Helena seated again now, a rare and genuine smile on her face. The fire cracked. Somewhere, someone began humming a song.

Gatty had never felt more at home.

As the evening waned, Violet found her, her cheeks pink with warmth and wine and something more lasting. "Thank you," she said simply. "For believing in us. In me."

Gatty placed a hand on her shoulder. "You've always had it in you, Violet. You just needed someone to remind you."

Violet nodded, eyes shining. "Then I'll do the same for someone else. Just like you did for me."

———

Later, in the hush of her chamber, Gatty sat beside the window with her legs curled beneath her. The moonlight spilled silver across the floor, and the garden below rustled gently in the breeze.

She thought of where she had started—mud and fear and running—and where she had ended up. Not safe, perhaps. Not certain. But rooted. Seen. Needed.

Her thoughts drifted to Leander's voice in the library, to the steadiness in his gaze when he said she'd changed the way he saw the world.

She smiled, just a little. The path ahead was unknown, but it no longer frightened her. It beckoned. And she would walk it—with soil beneath her nails, fire in her chest, and the strength of many women behind her.

Chapter Twenty-Eight

THE NIGHT WE STOOD

The sun broke gently over Blythewood Hall, its light spilling gold across the dew-slick garden paths. For the first time in weeks, the estate felt almost still—alive not with tension, but with purpose. Women moved through the herb beds with quiet intention, baskets on their hips and laughter on their lips. The sweet tang of crushed thyme lingered in the air.

Gatty knelt beside the foxglove, her fingertips brushing its velvet petals. She checked for pests, pulled back overgrowth, and breathed in the scent of damp soil. Beside her, Violet crouched with a small ledger in her lap, furiously scribbling notes.

"It almost feels normal," Violet said softly, glancing up from her page.

Gatty didn't answer. She wanted to believe it might last. Above them, Helena stood on the eastern balcony, her arms folded. The morning light sharpened her profile, but her gaze—sweeping the grounds like a general—was unreadable. Still, there was something softer in her posture. A rare kind of stillness.

Then came the clatter of hooves.

A boy darted into the courtyard, his breath catching in his throat as he waved a sealed letter high in the air. "Message for Mistress Helena!" he called, voice cracking with urgency.

Helena was down the stairs before anyone else could move, her black skirts catching on the wind like wings. She took the letter and broke the seal without ceremony. As her eyes scanned the page, Gatty saw the line of her jaw harden, saw the faint narrowing of her brow.

The laughter in the garden faded.

"They're coming," Helena said, loud enough for all to hear. "A group of men from town. Fools emboldened by Honoria's stories. They plan to attack Blythewood by nightfall."

A gasp escaped someone near the lavender beds. Another woman dropped her basket, dried rosehips scattering across the stones. Violet stood frozen, her ledger clutched to her chest like a shield.

"They're calling it a cleansing," Helena continued. "They'll bring torches. Perhaps more."

The women murmured among themselves—some frantic, others silent. Gatty rose, wiping her hands on her apron. Her heart was pounding, but she steadied her voice.

"When?" she asked.

"Tonight."

Gatty looked around. Alice had gone pale. Margery looked ready to cry. Violet's lips had parted but no sound came.

One of the younger women stepped forward. "We can't fight them. We're not—"

"Soldiers?" Helena finished for her. "No. But we are not without defense."

The hush that followed was thick as fog.

Gatty took a breath. "Then we stay. We stay, and we defend what we've built."

Helena studied her a long moment. Then she nodded. "Anyone who wishes to leave may do so," she said, her voice quieter now but no less commanding. "I will provide safe passage. But those who remain must be prepared. Not with violence—but with every ounce of knowledge, skill, and cleverness we possess."

A beat of silence. Then Violet stepped forward. "I'm staying."

So did Margery. Alice. One by one, hands lifted, shoulders squared. A quiet, steady wave of resolve. Gatty looked around at them—women who had been cast aside, beaten down, accused, and underestimated—and felt her chest rise with something unfamiliar but certain: pride.

"We've faced worse," she said. "And we're still here." She turned to the others, lifting her voice so it would carry. "Let them come. Let them see what a garden full of so-called witches can do."

By midday, the serenity of the garden had vanished. In its place, Blythewood hummed with movement—swift, purposeful, and hushed with tension. Smoke pots, dye buckets, and bundles of dried herbs were laid out across the courtyard like the makings of a war not fought with swords, but with scent, color, and illusion.

Gatty stood in the center of it all, sleeves rolled, voice calm and clear as she directed the women like a seasoned commander.

"Violet, you're with me in the still room first. We'll mix the smoke bundles and prep the dyes for the garden paths. Alice, Margery—get the calamus root soaking. We'll use it to cloud the stream. And make sure we have enough mugwort and wormwood for the fire pits. It has to smell like something out of hell."

Alice gave a tight nod, wiping her brow with the back of her hand. "They'll think twice once the smoke hits their lungs."

Helena swept through the courtyard like wind at their backs. "Every entrance must be secured. Use furniture, barrels, whatever you must. We may not keep them out forever, but we will make them question every step they take."

"I've already asked Anne and Ellen to watch the rear windows," Gatty said. "And we'll signal by candlelight once the smoke starts."

Leander appeared beside her, a stack of parchment under one arm and a satchel slung over his shoulder. His ink-stained fingers brushed her wrist as he passed her a page. "Legal statements. Signed testimonies from townsfolk in case the magistrate needs them. But more importantly—"

He reached into his satchel and pulled out a glass bottle filled with thick crimson dye. "—this will light up the garden paths when it hits the torchlight. Made it with crushed cochineal and iron salts. It should glow."

Gatty looked up at him, momentarily caught off guard by the warmth in his eyes. "You stayed up all night making this, didn't you?"

He offered a crooked smile. "For what it's worth, I prefer defending witches to cataloguing them."

She didn't answer—just nodded, taking the bottle and tucking it carefully into her basket.

All around them, the women moved like the spokes of a wheel—tightening, locking, preparing. They reinforced doors with broom handles, tucked jars of slippery salve into hallway corners, and measured long ropes of cloth steeped in acrid oils, ready to ignite.

"Violet," Gatty called, "the dyes. You said you knew a way to pour them into the stream?"

Violet nodded quickly. "We can run it from the east spout—just past the rose hedge. If we time it with the smoke, it'll look like the water's bleeding."

A beat of silence followed her words. Then Helena murmured, "Good."

Gatty placed a hand on Violet's shoulder. "Make it happen."

As Violet hurried off, Leander leaned closer to Gatty, lowering his voice. "Do you think it'll work? That this... theatre of herbs and shadows will really frighten them?"

Gatty's reply was quiet but sure. "I think fear is their greatest weakness. And we know how to feed it without lifting a weapon."

He nodded, then hesitated. "You're not just protecting Blythewood, you know. You're leading it."

Gatty blinked. "I'm just doing what needs to be done."

Leander smiled. "That's what makes you a leader."

She didn't let herself linger in the moment. There wasn't time. Instead, she turned toward the southern wall, where the younger girls were carefully laying herb bundles beneath the overgrown archway.

"Just enough to make the air hum," she called. "We want mystery, not madness."

As the sun slipped lower on the horizon, the shadows stretched long and uncertain over the garden. The women gathered for one final check, their hands stained with dye and smoke, their hair windswept and pinned back tight.

Gatty met their eyes. "We don't run," she said. "We don't cower. We stand in the garden we built and let them see who we really are."

"And what's that?" someone called softly.

Helena answered, her voice steady from the top of the stair. "We are women who survived. That alone is enough to terrify them."

A murmur of agreement rippled through the group.

And then the first torch appeared on the road.

The first torch flared at the edge of the wood like a false sun rising, its glow jagged and angry in the dusk. One by one, more lights emerged behind it—dozens of them—bobbing like fireflies fueled by hatred.

Gatty stood at the head of the garden, her posture still but coiled, eyes fixed on the tree line. The herbal bundles were set. The dyes were in place. Smoke pots lay hidden beneath lavender bushes and the roots of yew trees. Every woman was in position.

"Steady," she whispered.

Beside her, Alice gripped a jar of dye so tightly her knuckles had gone white. Margery adjusted a smoke bundle, her hands trembling as she nodded silently. From across the garden, Violet gave the smallest of signals—a flick of her candlelight from behind the hedge.

The first torch passed the stone path.

"Now," Gatty breathed.

A sharp hiss, then a pop—and smoke poured from beneath the rose beds, thick and grey-green, swirling with the bitter scent of mugwort and wormwood. Another hiss. Another plume. The air turned strange and heavy, the torches casting fractured shadows that seemed to shiver on their own.

From the undergrowth, came a low, uncanny whistling—crafted from hollow reeds strung between the trees. The sound warbled and wailed, like the garden itself had found its voice.

The attackers froze.

"What in God's name—" one man shouted, coughing as the smoke curled around him.

Then the dyes began to flow.

A stream of crimson snaked across the pebbled path, catching the firelight with an oily sheen. Violet, hidden near the fountain, tipped a second jar into the garden's trickle stream. It turned green-black, phosphorescent in the torchlight—like bile spilling through the earth.

"They're summoning spirits!" someone cried.

"They've cursed the water!"

Gatty ducked behind the sundial, her fingers curled around a smoke pot wick. She lit it quickly, then rolled it into the grass. It burst to life with a sulfuric hiss, joining the growing veil of smoke that now masked half the garden.

"Witchcraft!" another voice howled.

"No," Helena's voice cut through the air, clear as a bell from the top of the stone steps. She stepped into the smoke, her figure tall and still, cloaked in darkness and torchlight. "You call it witchcraft because you don't understand it. You call it evil because you fear what you cannot control."

The men faltered, their shouts crumbling into mutters. A few turned, trying to retreat—but the smoke clung to them, the garden confusing in the shifting light, each shadow stretched long and unfamiliar.

Alice tossed another smoke bundle into a hedge, and it erupted with a low boom. The men shouted, scattering, tripping over one another in their panic.

"It's the devil's work!"

"It's theatre," Gatty muttered under her breath, wiping soot from her face. "And it's working."

A whistle cracked overhead again, rising like a shriek through the garden canopy. One man dropped his torch entirely. Another backed into a bed of catmint and nearly screamed when the stems crackled beneath his boots.

From her hidden perch near the orchard wall, Violet poured the last of her dye into a narrow runnel that fed the basin. The water bloomed a ghostly purple, reflecting the flickering flames and painting the faces of the men with a ghoulish hue.

The leader tried to rally. "Stand your ground!" he bellowed. "They're women—just women!"

But the garden said otherwise.

Smoke twisted like breath from the earth. Light danced in unnatural hues. The air tasted of iron and incense, old magic that wasn't magic at all. Just knowledge paired with intention.

Helena raised her hand. "Leave this place before your ignorance brands you worse than any superstition ever could."

The men looked to one another, saw their fear mirrored back—and ran. One by one, they dropped their torches and bolted—through the hedges, across the paths, toward the woods. The garden swallowed their shouts. The smoke claimed their bravado.

The only sound was the hissing of the last smoke pot as it died in a curl of grey.

Gatty remained still, her shoulders tight, her fingers curled into her palms. She hardly dared to breathe. Then came the sound of slow, firm footsteps on gravel—boots not belonging to a mob, but to someone in command.

"Let us through!" a voice barked. "By order of the magistrate!"

Gatty's head snapped up. From the gates, a lantern cut through the haze, and a cluster of villagers emerged behind it—not with weapons, but with faces set in hard resolve. There was Mrs. Tyndale with a basket on her hip, Mr. Archer with his son by the hand, and half a dozen more: the baker, the smith's widow, the teacher from the village school. All had come.

"We heard shouting," the baker said, voice tight with fury. "And we came to stand with Blythewood."

Behind them came the magistrate, his black cloak billowing like a judgment passed down from the very sky. He took one look at the torches, the smoke, the crumpled dye-soaked ground—and then at the women.

Gatty stepped forward to meet him, her heart still racing. "Sir," she said, her voice steady. "You warned us they might come. We did what we had to do."

The magistrate's gaze swept the garden, the hidden bundles, the stunned villagers. He nodded once, curt. "I'd say you did more than that. You showed them what they are." Stepping forward, his gaze sweeping the scorched and smoke-laced garden. Behind him, the villagers fanned out, their lanterns casting a warm, flickering light over the shaken women of Blythewood.

Gatty turned slightly to glance at the others—Violet's soot-smudged cheeks, Alice's trembling hands, Helena's chin held high and still as stone.

Mrs. Tyndale planted herself beside the magistrate. "We saw them storm this place like wolves," she said, voice sharp with fury. "And for what? Because these women can heal a burn faster than a doctor? Because they teach girls to read?"

"We came to stop the madness," said Mr. Archer, nodding at his boy who clung tight to his side. "Blythewood saved my son's life. That's no witch's work—that's compassion. Knowledge. Care."

More villagers stepped forward. A seamstress. A young apprentice. The schoolmistress. One by one, their voices joined the swelling current of defense.

"They helped me walk again after the winter fever."

"They gave me tinctures when the apothecary turned me away."

"They taught my sister to write her own name."

It was not a shout, but a tide—each word lifting Blythewood higher, louder, prouder.

The magistrate raised a hand, and the garden hushed. He turned to the smoldering torches and the trampled path, his tone grim. "Let it be known: any further attacks on this hall will be considered an offense against the law. Those who incite violence—through superstition, greed, or cowardice—will answer for it."

A shift in the crowd rippled like wind through wheat.

And then, as if on cue, Honoria stepped forward from the shadows. Her gown was immaculate, but her face pinched with something brittle and faltering beneath its polish.

"Well," she said, with an air of wounded civility. "Perhaps now, in the light of such strong feeling, Blythewood might consider being more transparent about its methods. That's all I ever asked for—clarity, order, decency."

Silence.

Then Mrs. Tyndale snorted. "From you?"

"Honoria, you've done nothing but stir up fear," the schoolmistress said, eyes flashing. "You told me last week Gatty was poisoning the wells!"

"That's a lie," Honoria snapped.

"You told my husband they were cursing the rye fields," said another villager.

"She tried to bribe the herbalists to leave," Violet added quietly, stepping forward. "She promised me money if I slipped something suspicious into the ledger."

Honoria's smile faltered. "That's—ridiculous. I was misquoted—"

"You accused me of stealing bread," said one of the younger girls from Blythewood. "Just because I didn't give you mine."

Helena's voice, calm and cold, cut clean through the clamor. "Enough." She stepped forward and handed the magistrate a folded sheaf of letters, bound in string. "These are testimonies from villagers, staff, and women under Honoria's supervision—each one documenting a pattern of manipulation, false accusations, and threats."

The magistrate unfolded one page, then another. His brow furrowed deeper with each line he read.

"I've warned you once, Miss Honoria," he said, his tone colder than before. "But this—this is a pattern. This is intent. You've not only endangered this community; you've tried to unravel the very work that holds it together."

Honoria's composure cracked.

"You're taking their word over mine?" she hissed. "A pack of girls and castoffs?"

"No," Helena said, her voice like iron, "he's taking the truth."

For a long moment, Honoria stood still, lips pressed tight, eyes darting. Then, without another word, she turned sharply on her heel, her skirts snapping like a whip as she strode toward the gate.

The silence behind her was louder than a mob. The magistrate let her go, then turned back to the women. "Blythewood Hall is not a haven for witches," he said, his voice steady now, firm. "It is a place of learning. Of healing. And it has earned its place in this village through grace, skill, and perseverance. Let tonight mark the end of this foolishness."

He paused, then looked toward Gatty.

"You stood with courage tonight, Miss Carter. Not just in defense of this place—but of what it stands for."

Gatty nodded, words caught in her throat.

The magistrate looked to Helena. "You have the law on your side, and the people, too. And if anyone dares question that again, they will answer to me."

He gave a final nod, then turned and began the slow walk back through the gate, the crowd parting silently to let him pass.

One by one, the villagers followed.

Smoke still clung to the low hedges, curling like fog around the roots of the lavender and yarrow. The last of the villagers had gone. The torches were extinguished. And Blythewood Hall, battered but unbroken, stood in silence beneath the moon.

Gatty wandered near the center of the garden. Her shoulders ached. Her hands were stained with smoke and dye and soil. But she was still standing.

The poison garden loomed quietly nearby, the sharp scents of wormwood and belladonna mingling with the softer perfume of thyme and chamomile. Every leaf seemed to shimmer with breathless stillness, as if even the plants were catching their breath.

"Gatty."

She turned.

Leander stood at the edge of the path, his coat dusty, his hair disheveled. He looked tired—and utterly, unmistakably relieved.

"I thought you'd gone inside," she said, her voice low.

"I did. Then I couldn't sit still." He crossed the garden slowly, each step deliberate, his gaze never leaving hers. When he reached her, he didn't speak right away. He simply looked at her—really looked—and something in Gatty's chest loosened.

"You were brilliant tonight," he said finally. "You didn't just outsmart them. You steadied everyone else while doing it."

Gatty let out a breath, unsure whether it was laughter or something closer to tears. "I didn't feel steady. I still don't."

"But you were," he said. "For them. For us. For me." His voice softened on that last word, and Gatty felt something shift between them—an invisible thread drawn tighter. Leander stepped closer, his hand brushing hers. "I was afraid," he said, his words almost a whisper. "Not of them. Of losing you."

She turned toward him fully, the night air cool on her cheeks, her heart hammering in a rhythm she no longer tried to ignore. "I was afraid too," she said. "But not anymore."

There was no grand declaration. No speech. Just a moment of silence, thick with everything they hadn't said—and then, gently, she rose onto her toes and kissed him.

It wasn't a kiss of fireworks. It was quiet, steady, certain—like the first note of a song you knew by heart. His hand came to rest at the small of her back, pulling her a little closer. Her fingers curled into the fabric of his coat.

When they parted, neither spoke. They didn't need to.

Gatty leaned her forehead against his, her eyes closed. "You're not going to try and run from this, are you?"

"Never," he murmured.

A laugh bubbled out of her. The tension of the night melted into the soft hush of midnight, into the warmth of his hand in hers.

Behind them, the tall windows of Blythewood glowed with candlelight. Somewhere inside, Lydia was likely locking the doors. Violet was probably retelling the battle with dramatic flair. Alice and Margery were likely asleep, their fingers stained with dye and courage. Here, in the garden where the worst had almost happened, something else had taken root. Something better.

In the morning, the air smelled of damp soil, lavender smoke, and something sweeter: relief.

Inside Blythewood Hall, the dining room buzzed with gentle conversation. The women moved like a tide—tired, but no longer fearful. There were bruises to tend, rooms to air out, and dye splashes to scrub from the stone. But no one complained. They smiled as they worked. They had won.

At the head of the long table, Helena stood with her usual poise, though there was something softer in her bearing—an ease, like tightly drawn strings finally loosened. She tapped the edge of her spoon to a glass, and the room quieted. "We did more than protect a house last night," she said. "We protected what it means to live without fear. To study. To heal. To teach. To be."

Murmurs of agreement stirred through the crowd.

Helena's gaze swept the room, pausing on each face with quiet reverence. "Some of you came here broken. Accused. Disbelieved. But you stayed. You learned. You made this place more than stone and wood—you made it powerful. Let no one ever again say that you are weak."

A wave of pride moved through the women. Violet stood a little taller. Margery clutched Alice's hand under the table. Even Mrs. Havering dabbed her eye with the edge of a linen napkin, muttering something about smoke irritation.

Helena's expression warmed. "Now comes the real work. We have more women to help. More lives to reach. And this time, we will not wait quietly to be tested. We will grow."

Applause rose—not thunderous, but sure. Steady. Like roots taking hold.

At the far end of the room, Gatty sat between Violet and Leander. Her fingers were ink-stained, her dress still flecked with garden soot, but she looked more herself than she had in weeks. Her hand found Leander's under the table and held it, firm and certain.

"We should plan," Violet whispered, leaning close. "I have ideas for recruiting volunteers from the village. Women who are independent and clever, and wish for more options than they have. You could do it."

Gatty laughed softly. "Only if you're beside me."

"Always," Violet said, grinning.

Across the room, Helena raised her glass one final time. "To Blythewood," she said. "To what we've been—and what we're becoming."

"To Blythewood," the women echoed, their voices ringing like a vow.

Later, when the sun reached its highest point, Gatty wandered the edge of the garden alone. The beds bore signs of the night before—trampled thyme, scorched wormwood—but the plants were resilient. Already, green tips pushed up toward the light.

Footsteps crunched behind her. She turned to find Leander approaching, a thick book in his hands and a smile tugging at his mouth. "I brought you something," he said, holding it out.

She took it carefully. A leather-bound volume, its spine hand-labeled in his script: *Herbal Studies and Remedies, Vol. I.* Gatty opened it to find blank pages—and a single line written at the top: *For Gatty Carter, whose fire made the garden grow.*

Her throat tightened.

"I thought," Leander said, stepping beside her, "if we're to build a future here, we might start by recording it."

Gatty closed the book gently. "Let's do it together."

His smile deepened. "That's all I've wanted."

They stood side by side as the breeze stirred the garden. In the distance, bells rang faintly from the village steeple. A new day had begun—not without scars, but with purpose. With roots that ran deep.

And for the first time, Gatty didn't just believe they could build something lasting.

She knew they already had.

Chapter Twenty-Nine

A New Era

The first rays of dawn stretched thin and golden across the gardens of Blythewood Hall, casting long shadows over the labyrinth of herbs and blooms that made up the poison garden. Gatty Carter moved through the paths with deliberate steps, the cool earth beneath her boots grounding her as the soft rustle of leaves filled the morning air. Her fingers brushed against the plants—wormwood, belladonna, her favorite foxglove—symbols of both destruction and renewal.

She paused at a small patch of lavender, inhaling its calming scent. This garden had been her salvation, a place of learning, healing, and quiet rebellion. What had once been a symbol of her fear now stood as proof of her resilience. Gatty had transformed alongside these plants, each season of growth mirroring her own.

Her thoughts wandered back to the trembling girl who had arrived at Blythewood, battered by the accusations of a mob and a life devoid of hope. She hardly recognized that version of herself now. The journey had been hard-fought, but she had found her strength among the roots and soil, in the whispered guidance of Helena, in the trust of Lydia, and in the steady hands of the women who now called Blythewood home.

The hall was alive with the clinking of dishes and low murmurs of conversation when Gatty entered the dining room. The women looked up, their chatter quieting as she crossed the room. Gatty hesitated for a moment, then cleared her throat.

"I just wanted to say something before the day begins," she started, her voice steady but warm. "This hall has become more than a home to me. It's a place of courage, of learning, and of second chances. And that's because of all of you. Each of you has shown strength, not just for yourselves but for one another, and for that, I am endlessly grateful."

Her gaze swept the room, pausing briefly on Helena, who offered her a small, approving smile, and then on Lydia, seated near the hearth with her daughter now returned, Ivy, nestled beside her. Lydia's expression was unreadable at first—her arms gently around Ivy, her mouth pressed into a thoughtful line—but her eyes were warm.

"To Helena," Gatty continued, her voice softening, "for trusting me, and for giving us this place. And to Lydia, for being the quiet compass we all follow. You've shown me what steady, thoughtful leadership looks like."

There was a beat of silence—surprised, touched—and then Lydia gave a small, modest nod, her hand tightening protectively around Ivy's shoulder.

Gatty stepped toward her, the next words meant just for her. "You never asked for thanks, but I owe you mine. For seeing me clearly when I didn't even know who I was yet. For standing between me and fear, even when I didn't realize it. I'm honored to serve under your care, and to keep growing what we've planted together."

Lydia's reply was quiet, but firm. "You're all the reason this place is blooming."

A few women blinked away tears. Others smiled and whispered their agreement. Then Gatty turned to the rest of the room, lifting her chin.

"To all of you, thank you for making this hall what it is. You've taught me more than I could have imagined when I first arrived, and I hope I can do the same for the women who come after us. I'll make sure no girl walks through those doors without knowing her strength."

A wave of smiles and quiet applause rippled through the room, and Gatty felt a rare but welcome sense of belonging settle deep within her chest. For the first time in years, she felt truly at home.

The day began to wind down, the golden glow of the setting sun spilling over the walls of Blythewood Hall and into the poison garden. Gatty strolled the winding paths, her skirts brushing against the herbs she now knew by touch and scent alone. Her mind still buzzed with the morning's emotion—the women's laughter, Helena's quiet pride,

Lydia's steady hand at the helm. The thought of what they'd built together felt too big to hold all at once.

She paused near an especially tall patch of foxglove, its purple blooms nodding gently in the breeze. She reached out to steady one of the stalks, her fingers grazing the soft petals—beautiful, dangerous, healing if used wisely. She understood it now in a way she never had before.

"Careful," came Leander's familiar voice behind her, low and warm. "Those flowers are beautiful but deadly. Much like someone else I know."

Gatty turned with a grin. He stood a few steps away, his jacket a bit rumpled, a thin bundle wrapped in cloth under one arm. He looked utterly at ease here—ink-stained, bookish, and gently watchful—like he belonged."Flattery doesn't suit you, Leander," she said, teasing gently. "But I suppose you've earned it."

"I'd like to think so," he replied. "And patience. You'll need that too. For what I'm about to ask." He stepped beside her and placed the bundle on the stone edge of the garden bed. Unwrapping the cloth slowly, he revealed a small wooden box. Gatty tilted her head, watching him with curiosity as his usually unflappable expression shifted into something uncertain.

"I thought I'd be braver about this," he said, rubbing the back of his neck. "But it turns out, when something matters this much, I forget every speech I practiced."

Her heart caught in her chest as he opened the box. Inside lay a delicate silver ring, its band shaped like a winding vine, tiny leaves etched in exquisite detail. It looked as if it had grown right from the soil of the garden itself.

"I had it made," Leander said softly. "It reminded me of this place—of the things we've nurtured, and how far we've come."

"It's perfect," Gatty whispered, her voice trembling.

He knelt, his green eyes steady and serious beneath the slanting light. "Gatty Carter... I have loved you from the moment you walked into the library like a storm I didn't know I needed. Fierce, relentless, curious. You challenged every way I thought the world worked, and made me want to rebuild it—if only to see what it might look like with you in it."

She swallowed hard, tears rising despite the smile breaking across her face.

"I want to spend my life with you," he went on. "Building something that matters. Teaching, growing, making space for others the way we were once given space. I want to be the man who walks beside you—quietly, maybe, and not always perfectly. But always beside you. Will you marry me?"

For a moment, she couldn't speak. The weight of everything—the girl she had been, the women who had lifted her, the garden that had given her purpose—all pressed against her chest. And yet, none of it felt heavy. Not now. Not with him. "Yes," she said at last, her voice sure and bright. "Yes, Leander. I will."

He slipped the ring onto her finger with hands both steady and reverent. When he stood, she rose with him, and their kiss was slow, certain—more promise than passion, more home than heat. The garden seemed to hush around them, the foxglove swaying gently in approval.

When they parted, Leander's mouth quirked into a familiar, dry smile. "I should warn you—I'm not entirely sure how to be a proper husband."

Gatty laughed, full and easy. "Good. I've never wanted a proper one."

Hand in hand, they turned back toward the hall, their steps unhurried, the garden blooming behind them in soft defiance of every storm that had once tried to snuff them out.

The evening at Blythewood Hall was quieter than usual. Gatty found Helena in her study, the room aglow with the soft amber light of a single oil lamp. The desk, usually neat and commanding, was scattered with ledgers, letters, and open journals—as if Helena had spent the afternoon sorting not just papers, but memories.

Helena looked up as Gatty entered. A rare softness touched her sharp features. "Come in, Gatty. Close the door."

Gatty obeyed and took a seat across from her. Her heart, still full from the events of the day and the promise of what lay ahead, quieted into a steady rhythm.

"I wanted a moment with you," Helena said, leaning back in her chair. "To say what ought to be said plainly."

Gatty gave a cautious smile. "That sounds ominous."

Helena's lips twitched. "Not ominous. Just overdue." She folded her hands atop the desk. "You've done something remarkable here. Not just in surviving, or learning, or standing your ground—but in transforming. Yourself. This place. The people around you. That takes more than skill. It takes a kind of courage few people ever find."

Gatty felt heat rush to her cheeks. "I've had good teachers."

"And we've had a most unexpected student," Helena replied. "And now... it's time to begin the next season of Blythewood."

She reached into a side drawer and withdrew two small objects: a ring of keys, and a green ribbon-wrapped letter. She placed them gently on the desk.

"These," Helena said, "belong to Lydia."

Gatty blinked. "Lydia?"

Helena nodded. "She's been at my side for nearly a decade. She's raised a daughter in these halls, kept the books, balanced the house, soothed tempers, and never once asked for recognition. She is steady. She is loyal. And now, she is ready."

Gatty felt a wave of something she couldn't name—surprise, relief, something close to pride. "She'll be brilliant."

"She already is," Helena said. "And I will still be here for a time. But Lydia will handle the affairs of the house—its protection, its secrecy, its future."

Helena leaned forward slightly. "And you, Gatty Carter, are not being handed this hall—but you are being given something just as precious."

From a velvet pouch beside the lamp, Helena withdrew a small brooch shaped like a blooming sprig of lavender. The silver was worn in places, the pin slightly bent. She passed it across the desk.

"This was my mother's," she said quietly. "She wore it when she first took on the role of head herbalist. I've kept it close but never worn it—not until I found someone I believed in enough to pass it on."

Gatty stared at the brooch, the breath catching in her throat. "You mean—?"

"I want you to lead the gardens. The stillroom. And more than that—I want you and Violet to welcome the new ones who come here, the way you once were welcomed. Teach them. Steady them. Help them become more than what the world tried to make of them."

Gatty reached for the brooch, her fingers closing around it slowly. It was cool in her palm, but heavy with meaning.

"I don't know what to say," she whispered.

"Say you'll accept," Helena said, her voice low but certain. "Say you'll trust yourself, as I trust you."

"I do," Gatty said at last. "I will."

They sat in silence for a beat, the moment settling around them like dusk. Then Helena's voice softened even further.

"And one more thing," she said. "About love."

Gatty glanced up.

"It's never tidy," Helena said, the corner of her mouth twitching. "But I let pride keep me from things I might have cherished. Don't let fear do the same to you. You have something rare in Leander. He sees your strength, and he isn't afraid of it. That kind of love? That kind can last."

Gatty smiled, her fingers brushing the edge of the brooch. "I think I'm starting to believe that."

"Good," Helena said, rising. "Then we're all exactly where we should be."

Gatty stood too, her heart full to the brim. She reached for Helena and pulled her into a quiet, brief hug. When they stepped back, Helena looked a little startled—but not displeased.

"Go on," she said, flicking her hand toward the door. "There's work to be done."

Gatty left the study with the brooch clasped in her hand, the door closing softly behind her. She didn't need the keys to feel the weight of what she'd been entrusted with. This place had given her a future—and now, she would help others find theirs.

CHAPTER THIRTY

REFLECTION

The sun had barely begun its ascent, painting the horizon in soft pinks and oranges. Gatty sat on a low stone bench in the poison garden, the early light catching on the dew-slicked leaves of belladonna and monkshood. A thin veil of mist clung to the ground, softening the edges of the world and turning the garden into something suspended between dream and memory.

She pulled her shawl tighter, the familiar weave rough beneath her fingers. Her thoughts drifted, as they often did now, to the girl she'd been when she first arrived at Blythewood. Desperate. Mistrusted. One breath away from being lost forever. She hadn't known how to fight for herself then—not with anything but her teeth and fury. But here, she had learned different kinds of power.

The hush of the garden wrapped around her, the rustling leaves and distant buzz of waking bees a quiet chorus of belonging. Her fingers curled around the small bundle of herbs in her lap—valerian, mugwort, lavender. She had gathered them on instinct, the way one might gather old letters or relics from a journey's end.

They were proof. Not of magic—not the sort men feared—but of intention. Of healing. Of what a woman could build when no one expected her to.

Even when witches can't cast, she thought, we still make magic. With grit and memory. With skill. With each other.

Helena had taught her that. Violet had reminded her of it. Lydia had reinforced it, not just with her words, but with action—quiet leadership, steady loyalty, a mother's courage tucked beneath layers of grace. Gatty would never forget the look on Lydia's face when she returned, her little girl Ivy clutching her skirts, safe again under Blythewood's roof. The sight had pierced something deep and aching inside Gatty, and filled it instead with warmth.

They were all still healing, all still learning. But they were here. And they were not afraid.

For the first time in her life, Gatty understood what it meant not just to survive, but to belong. Not just to be safe, but to make something safer for those who came next.

She let out a long, slow breath, her eyes drifting toward the path leading up from the orchard. Somewhere behind the mist, footsteps approached. But for now, she sat still, and breathed, and waited. The garden—her garden—was listening.

The crunch of boots on gravel pulled Gatty from her thoughts. She looked up to see Leander approaching, his frame framed in gold by the rising sun. He carried a leather-bound book under one arm and wore a faint, thoughtful smile that deepened the lines at the corners of his eyes. "Up before the sun again," he remarked, settling beside her on the bench. "A habit I suspect you'll never break."

"And what of you, librarian?" Gatty teased. "Out of the library and into the garden twice in one week? Scandalous."

Leander chuckled softly, brushing a bit of dew from the edge of the book. "Even a librarian can be lured by rare and curious sights," he replied, casting her a sideways glance that warmed her straight through.

Gatty rolled her eyes but couldn't suppress the smile rising to her lips. Their rhythm—the ease between them—had become its own comfort, as familiar as rosemary and as steadying as tea.

Leander opened the book in his lap, revealing intricate sketches of herbs and notations in his tidy hand. "I've been thinking," he said, voice casual but purposeful. "About expanding the library's collection. There's room enough in the north wing to get started. A full section dedicated to herbal knowledge—remedies, histories, even stories from the women here. Things that could be passed down."

Gatty's breath caught. "You think people would come here just to learn?"

"They already do," he said, looking not at the book, but at her. "But we could make it more formal. Herbal classes. Apprenticeships.

Maybe even an herbarium. If you're willing, I thought we could build it together."

Her gaze swept the garden—the lavender curling toward the sun, the long shadows of the mint and valerian beds, the faint footprints of women who had walked these paths with fear in their bones and found courage instead. She imagined young girls kneeling in the soil beside her, learning the difference between power and poison. She imagined shelves full of their notes and recipes. A place where their knowledge wasn't hidden but celebrated.

"I'd like that," she said softly. "Very much."

Leander tilted his head, smiling. "I also brought something else." He reached into his coat pocket and produced a folded parchment, worn at the edges. He held it out.

Gatty unfolded it slowly. Her eyes scanned the lines—and then widened. Her heart stuttered.

"This is..." she breathed.

"The deed," Leander confirmed. "To the land you were nearly robbed of. The land tied to your name. I purchased it. Legally. It's yours, Gatty. To use however you like."

She looked at him, stunned.

"I thought you might want to plant something there. Or build something. Or let it rest," he said gently. "Whatever you decide, it's yours. No one can take it from you again."

Emotion rose like a tide—grief, relief, awe. She could hardly speak. "Leander..."

He shook his head, his voice low. "You've built something beautiful here. You've made safety out of what was once danger. Whatever else you want to create—out there, or here—I just want to help you do it."

The morning air seemed to pause around them, still and reverent. Gatty smiled through the sting in her eyes. "We'll build it together," she said, her voice steadier than she felt.

"For all of us," he said again, his smile soft and true.

Their hands brushed as he closed the book, and though it was the barest of touches, it carried the promise of everything they hadn't said yet—and everything still to come.

Gatty walked with Leander along the path leading to the hall, her thoughts lighter now, buoyed by the shape of the future they had begun to draw together. The garden buzzed with life—bees dancing through the lavender, the rosemary releasing its scent into the warming air. Each step felt like a vow made not in fear, but in purpose.

As they rounded the corner, the faint sound of voices reached them. At first a hush, like birdsong in a distant hedgerow. But then—closer. Fuller. Laughter, uncertain and hopeful.

Gatty slowed as the sight came into view.

A small cluster of young women stood just beyond the front steps of the hall. Their eyes scanned the grounds, alert and weary, and their clothes bore the quiet testimony of hard journeys—dust on their hems, stitched-up sleeves, shawls wrapped tight against the unknown. One girl, barely more than fifteen, clutched a worn satchel to her chest like a lifeline.

From the open doorway, Helena appeared, her familiar figure silhouetted by the morning light. But it was Lydia who stepped forward beside her—Lydia, now standing just a little taller, her expression calm and assured, her arm wrapped loosely around the tiny form beside her.

Lydia crouched beside her daughter, whispering something only Charlotte could hear. The child gave a small nod before bounding ahead and slipping through the door into the warmth of the hall. Lydia straightened, eyes scanning the gathered girls.

She smiled, serene and sure. "Come in," she called gently. "There's room for you here."

The women hesitated—but only for a breath. Then one by one, they stepped forward. The youngest paused at the threshold, glancing back at Gatty. Her eyes were wide, her voice nearly lost in the breeze. "Is it true?" she asked. "That this place is for girls like us?"

Gatty stepped closer, her voice as certain as the dawn. "It is. And you won't just be safe here—you'll grow. You'll learn things no one ever thought to teach you. You'll learn to be powerful."

The girl held her gaze for a long moment, then nodded and passed through the door.

Leander's hand found Gatty's, his thumb brushing against hers. "They're here because of you," he said quietly. "Word traveled fast."

"They're here because of Blythewood," Gatty replied, emotion threading through her words. "Because Helena built it. Because Lydia's ready to lead it. Because we made something worth believing in."

The sunlight spilled across the threshold, catching the curve of the doorframe and the bloom of late summer roses. Inside, the new arrivals' footsteps echoed softly, blending with the faint, bright sounds of laughter from deeper within the hall.

Gatty turned to Leander. "Do you think they'll be all right?"

He looked at her as though she were the answer to that question. "They'll be better than all right. They'll thrive."

And Gatty believed him. She believed in Lydia's calm strength, in Helena's quiet watchfulness from the wings, in Violet's growing voice, and in her own steady hands—hands that could coax medicine from roots and courage from fear. Hands that would now help these girls start again.

Below them, the garden stirred in the breeze, and from somewhere in the east corridor came the sound of new footsteps—young women exploring, settling, discovering the rhythm of a place made not just for survival, but for beginning again.

A movement at the edge of the courtyard caught Gatty's eye—James Hartford, Helena's brother, leaning slightly against a column, his coat dusted with hay and his gaze fixed, soft and unguarded, on Lydia through the study window. Gatty followed his line of sight, and something in her chest hummed.

She nudged Leander gently. "Do you suppose he'll ever say something?"

Leander followed her gaze. "James? Eventually. But it'll be Lydia who makes the first move."

Gatty laughed, the sound low and warm. "Perhaps I'll plant something for them. Something slow-growing. But sure."

They stood together in silence as twilight deepened and the lamps inside began to glow. The air carried the scent of rosemary and damp earth, the hush of a place that had survived and bloomed again.

This wasn't the end. It was a turning of the season.

Blythewood would continue to open its doors to the accused, the cast out, the courageous. It would whisper to them through leaves and pages and laughter that they were not alone. That here, even when witches couldn't cast, they could still change the world.

With hands that healed. With hearts that stayed. With gardens that grew stronger, year after year.

AUTHOR'S NOTE

In crafting the world of this novel, I sought to intertwine historical authenticity with imaginative reinterpretation, drawing from real locations and institutions to ground the narrative in a tangible past.

Blythewood Hall and Blickling Hall

Blythewood Hall finds its architectural and historical muse in Blickling Hall, a stately Jacobean mansion nestled in Norfolk, England. Constructed between 1616 and 1626 for Sir Henry Hobart, Blickling Hall stands on the remnants of a medieval moated manor. The estate is steeped in history, notably associated with Anne Boleyn, the ill-fated second wife of King Henry VIII. While the original Tudor house no longer exists, it's widely believed that Anne Boleyn was born at Blickling in the early 1500s.

The grandeur of Blickling Hall, with its red-brick façade, intricate gables, and expansive gardens, provided a rich tapestry upon which to model Blythewood Hall. The sense of history permeating its walls, coupled with its evolution through centuries, mirrors the transformation and resilience embodied by the characters within Blythewood.

Reimagining the Magdalene Laundries

The Magdalene Laundries were institutions primarily run by religious orders from the 18th to the late 20th centuries, intended to house "fallen women"—a term encompassing those who had engaged in prostitution, became pregnant out of wedlock, or were otherwise deemed morally wayward. These asylums often subjected women to forced labor under harsh conditions.

In reimagining such an institution within this narrative, I posed the question: What if a Magdalene house served not as a place of penance for perceived sins, but as a sanctuary for women accused of witchcraft? This inversion seeks to challenge historical narratives, transforming a symbol of oppression into one of empowerment and refuge.

By intertwining the architectural inspiration of Blickling Hall with the concept of a Magdalene house repurposed as a haven, this story endeavors to explore themes of redemption, resilience, and the redefinition of identity against the backdrop of a society quick to marginalize.

This novel aims to honor the real struggles of women in history while offering an imagined vision of hope and transformation.

MANY THANKS

This book would not exist without the brilliant minds and generous hearts who helped guide it into being.

To my wonderful beta readers, Yeng Cee Writes and Tehniat Reads—thank you for your thoughtful insights, sharp instincts, and encouragement at every turn. Your feedback helped me see this story more clearly.

To the amazing women of my Moms Who Write critique group—Katherine, Arlyn, Gretchen, SarahAnn, and Carrie—thank you for your wisdom, support, and the kind of honesty every writer dreams of.

To my friend Nicola, artist and gardener extraordinaire—your love for the land and your deep-rooted creativity inspired so much of the garden in this story. Thank you for tending both your flowers and our friendship with such grace.

To my parents, who filled my childhood with books and curiosity, thank you for making reading a way of life.

To my husband, who inspires every romance I write and makes sure I have the time and space to tell my stories—this book carries your love in every scene.

To my six-year-old daughter, who has already written thirty books of her own: may your creativity always be wild and fearless. You inspire me every day.

To the Emerald City Romance Writers, thank you for your community, resources, and the steady encouragement to keep going.

To JSTOR and ITHAKA, for the invaluable blueprints, maps, and historical archives that helped me bring Blythewood to life—your digital libraries made this book better than it could have been without them.

And to the authors of Blickling Hall from the National Trust—thank you for preserving such a fascinating piece of history. Your work helped me imagine a different kind of house, one that might have protected witches instead of punishing them.

To everyone who reads this book and sees themselves in its pages—thank you for believing in stories that celebrate resilience, sisterhood, and love.

About the Author

Matilda Lockwood is a writer, artist, tea drinker, and passionate believer in the magic of humans. A graduate of culinary school and a lifelong history enthusiast, she creates richly imagined stories that celebrate resilience, creativity, friendship, love, and the power of reclaiming one's voice.

When not writing historical romance with a touch of rebellion, she can be found sketching her characters, paper crafting, swimming in the Puget Sound, or browsing a good bookstore. She is a proud member of *Emerald City Romance Writers* and *Moms Who Write*, as well as being an avid researcher who believes that every story is rooted in something true.

When Witches Can't Cast is her love letter to the women who were once called witches for being wise, angry, curious, or simply themselves-and to the people who choose to stand beside them.

She lives in the Pacific Northwest with her husband, daughter, chickens, dog, and far too many books.

Also by Matilda Lockwood